SHE HARDLY DARED TO BREATHE AT THE SIGHT

The man towered above her. His familiar face was ruggedly strong, his eyes a piercing electric blue. So overwhelming was his presence that she temporarily forgot the immediate danger confronting her.

"You," she whispered, hardly able to grasp his reality. Too often she had seen him in dreamlike situations. She couldn't credit that he was here now, near enough to touch. For a moment his compelling magnetism almost forced her to reach out to him. But something held her back.

"Yes, Camilla," he said in a quiet deep voice. "We've found each other again."

Her heart leaped as his gaze held hers, for she knew that here was the one man who had the power to unleash her darkest passions....

AND NOW...

SUPERROMANCES

Worldwide Library is proud to present a sensational new series of modern love stories — SUPERROMANCES

Written by masters of the genre, these longer, sensuous and dramatic novels are truly in keeping with today's changing life-styles. Full of intriguing conflicts, the heartaches and delights of true love, SUPERROMANCES are absorbing stories — satisfying and sophisticated reading that lovers of romance fiction have long been waiting for.

SUPERROMANCES
Contemporary love stories for the woman of today!

CALL OF THE HEART
WANDA DELLAMERE

A SUPERROMANCE FROM
WORLDWIDE

TORONTO · LONDON · NEW YORK · SYDNEY

Published, July 1982

First printing May 1982

ISBN 0-373-70024-5

CHAPTER ONE

As THE PLANE CIRCLED SLOWLY for its landing, Camilla looked down into the open spaces beneath her window and in her rising excitement gripped the arms of her seat. Sprawled along a curving silver river below her was Kabul, the capital city of this strange exotic land she had traveled so far to reach. Small mud huts crept up the hills that embraced the city, clinging there like lizards and blending with the color of the earth. She saw, too, the sparkling roofs of thc mosques and palaces—some smooth with azure tiles, others glittering and metallic.

"There's the Blue Mosque," said her seat companion, and she followed the line of his finger to a great dome-roofed building, made miniature by the height of the plane and shining like a blue glass marble.

"It's so beautiful!" she exclaimed, turning to the man who sat beside her. His name, she had learned at the beginning of the flight out from Rome, was Johnny Hagan. He was an American, a doctor, and she was grateful for the cheerful boyish enthusiasm he had shown and the friendly way he had helped her, a nervous first-flighter, answering all her questions with his lopsided grin. She was grateful, too, for the way he'd unconsciously made his position clear right from the start.

"I can hardly wait to get back to Janet. She's expecting a baby—our first—and it kills her when I go away, poor kid. Kills me, too. Still, I've brought her letters from her folks."

"Don't you miss being at home—America, I mean? There must be such a difference. Wouldn't your wife prefer to have the baby somewhere...well, more civilized?"

He had laughed like a boy. "I guess not. At least, she hasn't mentioned it. Our son's going to be a real little Afghan—will grow up speaking the language, which is an opportunity I only wish I'd had. If we stay long enough he'll be taught by Malcolm Armstrong—another one of my missed opportunities."

Camilla had been slightly intrigued. "You've mentioned this Malcolm Armstrong several times. Who is he?"

"A fixture of the country. English, like you, but to look at him, if he's dressed properly, you can easily be fooled into thinking he's a real Afghan. Grows more and more like them every day. We bet on the day he'll wake up with his blond hair turned black." He chuckled. "You ought to meet him. You'd admire him."

"Surely you mean *like*," said Camilla, puzzled.

"Not at all," answered Johnny, smiling. "Not a lot of people really like him, I guess, but everyone admires him. It's too difficult to get close enough to him to really know him and like him."

Camilla had understood. This Malcolm sounded like a standoffish expatriate who tried to impress other people by going native and playing at the silent Afghan, the man of mystery. Well, he could impress other people; he wouldn't find it so easy to fool her. She had turned the discussion then to different topics, feeling unwilling to linger on the subject of Malcolm Armstrong.

But her instant dislike of Johnny's strange acquaintance was offset by her growing liking for the American himself, young and redheaded with a nose just recovering from the peeling effects of sunburn, and a face liberally freckled. If his wife was as... as—she cast about her for a description and settled for that overworked one, "nice"—if his wife was as purely nice as he was, she could count on two friends at least in this unknown land the plane was fast approaching. And heaven knew she needed friendship and help—without any demanding ties.

Now Johnny leaned over her again, and with the excitement of a proud householder showing off his possessions to impressed guests, he pointed out the four points of the compass and what lay there.

"South," he began. "That's the desert. Ghazni and Kandahar are the two biggest cities. Kandahar is dominated by the strict mullahs—"

"Mullahs? What are they?" queried Camilla.

"Muslim priests. Kandahar is the black Islam area of the country. Nearly every month we get rumors of some stoning authorized by the mullahs—"

"Stoning!" Camilla exclaimed, her face blanched. "How horrific! It sounds positively B.C.—biblical."

Johnny laughed again. "As long as I've been here I've never found a stoning rumor to be true. But it shows what kind of a place Kandahar can be if even those ridiculous rumors can be believed and passed around. I've been to Kandahar, and the worst thing about it was the flies that settle on everything like a black blanket."

"Sounds just as bad," said Camilla. "I hate insects."

"Well, it was worth it to see Kandahar. But I'll admit it's no place for a woman."

Camilla's lips curled. They were all the same, these men. Tall, short, fat, thin, sandy, blond, dark, handsome or ugly, clever or charming or selfish or... mysterious—in the end they all believed that the primary need of a woman was protection. And she, Camilla Simpson, had had enough of that in any form. Freedom was a new drink to her, a strange and heady draft, and she was prepared to drain its joys to the fullest. Who was to say what was and what was not the place for her to go? No one would restrict her activities. She knew now she was not the kind of woman to act merely on the sufferance of some dominating male.

"I wouldn't be put off by a few rumors," she stated, holding her head proudly. "I shall see Kandahar if I want to. After all, I've come this far alone."

Johnny looked sheepish. "I didn't mean to imply that you couldn't handle anything in the normal run of things. It's just that...oh, you don't know the Afghans. Their way of life and their basic philosophies are so totally different. It's very difficult to explain. Freedom for women is growing a bit in Kabul with the Western influences that touch the capital city, but in most of the country women still dress in their *chadaris*—head-to-foot veils—and I wouldn't like to say what you'd be risking if you went to Kandahar dressed as you are now."

Camilla looked down at her outfit. On the advice of a well-traveled friend she had worn a creaseless apple-green cotton, leaving her arms and legs bare, with her feet shod in white espadrilles. The cool appearance of the dress was a foil to the flame of her auburn hair, and its color was reflected in the depths of her sea-emerald eyes. Such an outfit would be perfectly acceptable in England, but customs were very different here. She'd just have to be careful, that was all, she told herself.

"To the east," Johnny went on, "is the city of Jalalabad, near the Northwest Frontier Province of Pakistan. You probably know more than I about the political battles that have been fought at the borders, since you're from England, and the British have been involved in so many Afghan wars, so I won't display my ignorance. To the northeast is Nuristan—that is, Land of Light, so-called because the natives at the end of the last century were all converted to Islam; you know, 'seen the light.' Before that the place was called Kafiristan—"

"Land of the Kafirs?" smiled Camilla.

"Good guess. They were pagans before their conversion, and many Afghans still fear them and the whole of Nuristan. It's a restricted area; you need a special visa to go there. They have little compunction about murdering foreigners."

"What a place!" Camilla exclaimed.

"Armstrong visited it once, several years ago—only foreigner I know who's been and come back to tell the tale. And even he had to get out in one heck of a hurry. Apparently one of the chiefs took quite a shine to his looks and tried to sell Malcolm his daughter. He only went to collect some Mongol relics and nearly came back with a wife!''

"I'll bet the chief's daughter was relieved that the bargain fell through,'' Camilla commented dryly. "Imagine being sold off to the highest bidder! Like some farm animal.''

"Women do a fair bit of the heavy labor in this country, so somebody's got to make up to poor dad for the loss of an extra pair of hands.''

Camilla knew this was the custom in most Islamic countries, and so she said no more. But the story had repulsed her, and the fact that it had happened to a compatriot brought it strangely close.

Johnny continued, "Beyond Nuristan, which is mostly woods and mountains, is the Vakhan corridor, which leads into China.''

"I didn't know we were that near to China,'' said Camilla, startled.

Johnny nodded and continued. "To the north of Kabul are the high mountains, then the steppes and fertile foothills, and beyond that, Russia. The mountains are called the Hindu Kush, which means Killer of the Hindus. They're known by such a gory name because every time the Hindus tried to invade Afghanistan they were driven back by the harsh mountains. High plateaus and sandy deserts lie southward. And to the west is Bamian, where two giant ancient Buddhas are built into the cliffs; Bandi Amir, the lakes of the king, is near there, too. These five small lakes are famous for their rare hues, which vary from white to dark green and are apparently caused by underlying bedrock. They're the first place you must visit if you've got the time.''

"Safe, I suppose," muttered Camilla, but her thoughts were scarcely on her words. Through the window she could see nothing of these places he had mentioned, except for the outline of the dark purple mountains he had called Killer of the Hindus. But in her mind's eye she could see beyond them, to east, west, north and south, and the picture he had given her was a vast expanse of loneliness—desert or steppes or mountains, a hostile landscape with violent men. The strangeness of the place assailed her, and with it a painful sense of her own isolation and ignorance. Her hands twisted, and beneath her tightened seat belt her stomach lurched in fear. She was gripped by the thought, *my sister, the only family I have left, is lost in that place.*

Her hand felt in her pocket for the two scraps of paper, little lightweight things that had brought her halfway around the world. They were her only reassurance that she had a purpose in that alien landscape.

The first was a postcard. She had no need to look at it—its gaudy retouched colors were engraved on her memory. It was of a street whose dirt surface was the same color as the mud-and-timber houses that lined it. The road was shaded by thickly foliaged bright green trees. Beneath them sat men dressed in what resembled dirty pajamas, behind stalls loaded with the most delicious-looking fruit she had ever seen: melons, grapes, mulberries, pomegranates. It was the fruit that had first struck her when the postcard arrived in her London flat three months ago. On the reverse was a scrawl in her sister's handwriting:

We have been a week in Kabul, and it is the most wonderful place you can imagine. I know it's unoriginal, but I really wish you were here. It's worth suffering the dens of the other countries just to get here; it's *clean*! The Kuchis—they're nomads—are just passing through the city. They're fascinating people, incredibly rich, and the women are the only ones in Afghanistan who don't wear veils. They look like they're from some movie epic with their camels and donkeys and dogs. I long for such a life. By the way, it's not a bit like the picture, but cold with a bit of snow still. A relief after India! Going to Kandahar tomorrow. I'll write soon.

Meghan

Meghan and her husband, Thomas, had been traveling through Asia by car on their way back to England from Singapore, where Tom had been stationed with his company for several years. When Camilla had received the postcard she had thought little of it; having scanned it, she'd merely pinned it up alongside the other cards from Thailand, Bhutan, India and Pakistan on the wall of the little kitchenette in her flat. She little thought that it would be the last communication she would receive from her sister, and that its battered well-fingered edges would contain within their borders one-half of the clues with which she must begin her search.

The second piece of paper was a letter, typed on thin official airmail paper with all the impersonal coldness of black ink and white paper. It, too, was grimy with nervous handling, as she had turned it over and over while trying to reach a decision. It read:

British Embassy
Kabul
April 30

Dear Miss Simpson:

It is with deep regret that we inform you that Thomas Cowley, who we understand was your brother-in-law, was found dead on the morning of March 28 at 9:35 A.M., ten miles off the road to Kandahar, southwest of the town of Ghazni. The local police report shows that the cause of death was a blow to the base of the skull. Mr. Cowley was found under his car, a Singapore N-registration Land Rover, from which every removable object had been taken. The official investigation has recorded a verdict of death by misadventure.

Since Mr. Cowley did not make himself known to us on his arrival in Afghanistan, and in the absence of any personal documents with the deceased, it has taken us considerable time to establish Mr. Cowley's identity. With the help of the border authorities we learned that he had entered the country from Pakistan through the Khyber Pass, accompanied by his wife, your sister. It is thus with deep regret that we must now also inform you that no trace has been found of Mrs. Cowley, and she has been declared by the authorities as missing, presumed dead. Naturally, we shall continue to make every effort to trace your sister, but must inform you that the difficulties we encounter in such endeavors are enormous. . . .

Here Camilla's thoughts trailed off. She could feel the aching loneliness of a death in those great and empty expanses beyond the city. She herself had never cared for Thomas, she admitted with a slightly guilty feeling, but his was not an end she would have wished upon anyone. She had always thought him a bit of a layabout and, although she disliked saying it, a snob, the sort who always walked about as though he had a bad smell under his nose. But she was willing to concede that there might be good points in him that she had never seen; there must have been if Meghan had chosen to marry him. At any rate, his death was not the sort she would have wished on her most bitter enemy.

Thomas was dead. She had to find Meghan. These two thoughts ran rings around each other as she stepped out of the plane. Descending from its air-conditioned fuselage, she felt the heat from the tarmac rise up and hit her like a great fist. She gave a gasp and staggered, but Johnny behind her quickly caught her elbow and prevented her from falling.

"It's hot," he smiled, "but you'll soon get used to it. It's not muggy or humid like your London summers. You'll be glad of the climate here when you have a deep golden tan."

"With my hair?" Camilla laughed. "I peel—like bananas." However, she knew the heat was affecting her, for the laughing made her dizzy. "Would you mind helping me get a taxi? I've got a room at the Kabul Hotel." She supposed the taxi drivers did not speak much English.

"I certainly would mind," replied Johnny, laughingly stern. "I'll take it as a personal insult if you don't allow me to escort you straight to your hotel. That way the drivers won't be able to rip you off for twice the proper fare, and I'll be sure you get there safely."

Still trying to protect me, thought Camilla as they went though customs. Perhaps he missed having his wife to shelter. But her jet lag made her too tired to refuse such an energy-saving offer, and the presence of Johnny would be far more cheering than the face of some turbaned stranger.

"Where is your car?" she asked, looking around her as they came out of the small stone-and-glass airport terminal. The parking lot was almost totally empty, which seemed odd for an airport.

"You're thinking how different it is from Heathrow, aren't you?" Johnny said, reading her thoughts. "Come along. I'll try to break you in gently."

She understood what he meant by that as he steered her toward a light blue Volkswagen van. New and fascinating sights were all around her: a string of camels silhouetted against the gleaming metal of the plane; little dark men sidesaddle on donkeys weaving in and out among the traffic; honking and rushing foreign-looking taxis and buses; and a billowing figure in a pleated robe who glided past on silent feet and regarded her through the lattice of a lacy veil.

Beside the blue van stood a smiling man in the ubiquitous white pajamas, with a cap of curly black karakul—the fur from a newborn lamb, she happened to know—upon his head.

"Camilla," said Johnny by way of introduction, "this is my driver, Rajab. Rajab, this is Miss Simpson. She's come to visit Afghanistan."

The driver's face broke into a broad grin, displaying a showcase of wide and irregular teeth. He held out a gnarled hand. *"Salaam aleikom."*

Camilla took the proffered hand and shook it. "Hello," she smiled back.

"How is the *memsahib*, Rajab?" asked Johnny as they climbed into the back seat.

"Khubnes," said the driver, shaking his head.

"Bessiar?" urged Johnny anxiously. "He says Janet is not too well," he explained, turning to Camilla. "I could never forgive myself if something happened to her while I was gone."

But Rajab's next words were reassuring. *"Ne,* not so bad; she no like Mr. Hagan go."

"But what's wrong with her?" asked Camilla, worried. She had heard so much of Janet that she already thought of her as a friend and hated to think of either she or Johnny coming to any sort of grief. She knew too well about the pain one felt when loved ones suffered.

"I haven't been here long enough to really know much Persian," admitted Johnny. "And Rajab speaks next to no English, so I'll have to wait till I get home to find out how things really are." She saw him hunch his shoulders forward, as though trying to will the car into a faster speed. "It's a shame—I really wanted to ask you for supper tonight, Camilla, to help you find your feet a bit more; I haven't told you half the things you ought to know, and there are some things only a woman can help you with. Still, I can ring you at the hotel when I know how matters stand at home. I know Janet will love to meet you."

"It's so kind of you to ask," smiled Camilla wearily in reply, "but I would have had to refuse anyway. I'm so tired I can hardly keep my eyes open."

"We've both covered quite a distance to get here," agreed Johnny. "It would have been pushing things a bit to have you over tonight." He settled back in his seat and looked at the wan fragile face of the English girl as she gazed out the window, caught in the hypnotic vision of an Asian city. A thought struck him.

"Would you object to my bringing in anyone else to help you?" he asked. "Or would you rather your search was kept between us?"

Camilla nodded tiredly. "You've been so helpful already, I know I can trust you. I hardly know how to thank you. Whoever you bring in will, I'm sure, be invaluable."

She turned back to the window, thanking her lucky stars that she had met someone as sincere and reliable as Johnny, for the enormity of the task ahead of her in this strange land was finally hitting her. If she hadn't had Johnny to talk to on the flight, she knew she would be in a near panic by now.

After some initial friendly chitchat about flying, he had been intrigued about her destination. "Why Afghanistan of all places?" he had politely asked.

And slowly the whole story had come spilling out—the disappearance of her sister, Camilla's grief, her growing belief that her sister was not dead, the sudden inspiration that slowly blossomed into a decision, the opposition she faced, the quitting of her secretarial job, and the need to pour her life savings into this journey. As Camilla had spoken, Johnny's admiration for her foolhardy courage was written clearly upon his face. She had also sensed that he was too kind to tell her what he really thought about her undertaking such a trek on her own. Instead he'd offered to help her and had assured her that as soon as Janet heard the story her enthusiasm would match his. And his own interest had grown as he listened to Camilla's tale: most uplifting of all, in the end he had started to share her conviction that her sister was alive, despite those cold damning words, "missing, presumed dead." In Johnny, Camilla knew she had found a friend.

The exhaustion that had so suddenly come over her now disinclined her to conversation, and she left Johnny to his own worried broodings on the nagging thought that all was not well with Janet. She watched the passing scenery with a strange sense of dislocation, as though she were floating through a dream— the donkeys, the turbaned men, the wooden stalls of the bazaars and the women dressed in ghostlike long gowns moving as if from another era among the high-rise apartments, buses and telephone wires of the modern age. Most unnerving of all was the fact that everywhere advertisements might be found in a city—billboards, buses, the walls of buildings—there were advertisements here, too, but all in the flowing backward script in which Persian is written, so deceptively similar to the shorthand Camilla knew but, when she tried to read it, so totally incomprehensible. Everything was both real and unreal somehow, as in a dream when familiar places are turned into scenes of frightening symbolism. But even in her deepest thoughts Camilla would not admit to herself the half-formed feeling, *I wish I had not come.*

They drew to a stop behind a red traffic light, the suddenness of the halt nearly jerking Camilla forward, startling her for a moment into full consciousness. She raised her head and looked in front of her.

Two men stood by the intersection, some twenty feet ahead. Both seemed Afghan, dressed in striped robes and wearing turbans, but one was of average height, slightly built with dusky skin, while the other was a head taller, and even his loose dress could not hide the lithe strength of his body. Camilla's eyes were drawn to him, and slowly, almost intently, his face turned toward her. His skin was slightly drawn and deeply tanned, not dark brown but warmly golden, fine skin that might, away from this climate of heat and sunlight, turn to rough ivory.

For a brief moment their gazes locked. Camilla had no more than a flash of blue, a glimpse of desert sky, a blue so electric it sent a shock thrilling down her spine. Then the light changed, the engine roared and with a whir of wheels they rounded the corner. The two men had vanished.

Eyes wide, she turned to Johnny. In such a large city would he possibly know who the blue-eyed Afghan was? But he leaned in his seat, eyes closed, sunk in thought, as tired as she was and anxious for his wife. She did not disturb him. Now she could hardly even be sure if the two men had been real at all, or anything more than figments of her tired mind, so miragelike did they seem. And yet...that blue!

CHAPTER TWO

THE VAN DREW UP beside a large impressive building, stately as a cliff and built of thick gray stone. A flag flew on a pole outside the main door, and Camilla registered its fluttering form as Johnny helped her out of the vehicle and guided her through the revolving door. Rajab followed behind with her luggage—two small cases only, because she had been told to travel light. They came to the reception desk.

"Would you like me to stay and see you to your room?" asked Johnny.

But Camilla, seeing the anxious look on his face that she knew was not for her, said with a smile, "You've done so much for me—I think I can manage well enough on my own now. I know you're dying to get home."

"Well, if you're sure you can manage..." said Johnny vaguely. He took her hand and shook it warmly. "We'll call you tomorrow to see how you're getting on." His voice dropped, and she leaned closer to hear his words. "If you'll take my advice, I wouldn't mention anything about...that business." His hands moved expressively. "Not that—I mean, there might not be anything fishy in it, no need to worry. Still...." He was obviously seeking for the right word.

"If you're trying to unnerve me, you're doing very well," said Camilla quietly.

"Don't worry. It's just—there's no reason to let the whole of Kabul know why you're here. Let's keep it just between you and me and people we can trust. To anyone else you're just another tourist. Okay?"

Camilla was too tired to question his advice. "Okay," she replied, smiling at the Americanism.

"See you soon then, kid. Good luck!"

Johnny was gone then, with Rajab, leaving her alone in a strange land. She looked around the lobby. It was open and spacious, with high stone walls and marble floors that were covered by Afghan carpets in rich gold and mellow red. The height, the lack of cluttering furniture and the fact that the air conditioning had brought the room temperature down to a tolerable level all gave an effect of restrained coolness and culture. It was a charming hotel, and she sighed, almost with relief, as she turned to the reception desk to ring the service bell.

Alone in her room, she closed the heavy curtains to shut out the bright hot light. The white linen of the bed was cool as she slid her tired limbs into it with a feeling of sheer luxury. She had expected to sleep as soon as her head touched the pillow, but she found that, as her body settled into immobility, her brain became more and more wide awake. Her eyes unblinking, she stared up at the pale shadowed ceiling while her thoughts traveled over all that led up to her being here in this bare hotel room. And especially, as her thoughts touched for a moment on Johnny, she remembered the last bitter encounter with Jeff.

Over the polished table of the London restaurant

where they'd had their last dinner together, he had gripped her arm so hard that it made a red mark and said angrily, "It seems you have really made up your foolish mind to go, then."

A hundred glib remarks had sprung to her mind, but at last she'd replied, rather inanely, "It seems a waste not to." He only looked at her with his stony glare, and she stumbled on, "What with the tickets bought, reservations made and all the vaccinations I've had—I think the only one they left out was foot-and-mouth disease." She laughed weakly, but Jeff did not respond, and, irritated, she tried to pull her arm away. His grip tightened.

"I don't believe you want to go at all," said Jeff lowly. "I think you just got the idea into your stubborn head for a moment, and now you're too proud to back out, even though you know I'm right."

"That isn't it at all," exclaimed Camilla desperately, hurt at his lack of understanding. "I've tried for weeks to make you understand, and your lack of any desire to understand, or cooperate even if you don't understand, is tearing our relationship apart. Why can't you see? It's not something I have any choice about—I *have* to go and try to find her. You're right that I don't want to—can't you see how frightening it is for me, especially after what happened to her?" She paused sadly for a moment. "But she's my sister."

"*Was* your sister," Jeff corrected her coldly. "Missing, presumed dead."

"She's not dead!" cried Camilla. Her voice rang above the silence of the restaurant and the low conversation of the diners, who looked up at the disturbance with patronizing disapproval. At any other time she would have been acutely aware of the embarrassment of causing such a scene, but now she was oblivious.

Jeff hissed through his clenched teeth, "How can you possibly say that? Do you have ESP or something?"

"If you like," replied Camilla proudly. "But that's a silly way of putting it. I just happen to know she is not dead. I would know if she died. I feel this so strongly that I have to believe it. She is my sister." To Camilla, those last four words seemed to explain everything she felt, but she pressed on, trying to express it more fully. "She's the only person I've got left." With a pang, she briefly recalled her parents' tragic death in a car accident two years earlier.

"You've got me," replied Jeff softly, taking her hand. "Or could if you wanted." He smiled. "Marry me, Camilla. Then I can come with you. You need me. You could never do it on your own. By your own admission you're scared. Let me come, just to help you."

For a brief moment she was tempted. How easy it would be to sit back and go as if on a holiday, with Jeff to make sure they got everywhere on time and that nothing got lost, to manage all the little details of travel that were so tedious and confusing. But that would be a life in which nothing was changed, where Jeff organized everything as easily as he now chose the restaurants and cinemas, the theaters and the galleries they visited; where he advised her on everything from dresses and perfume to diets and soap. She would see Afghanistan with as little effort as it now took for him to show her around one of those museums he was so fond of, where she had no need for a guidebook because he knew it all and would tell her everything he wanted her to know.

"Marry me, Camilla."

Suddenly she salt bolt upright in her seat. The realization came that if the affair of her sister's disappearance had not arisen, he would not have needed to ask that question, for she was drifting into marriage with him as surely as a sailboat goes with the wind that directs it. He had always been such a charming companion. She would never have doubted the rightness of one day floating up the aisle in a cloud of white to become attached to his arm, and he would guide her through life as confidently as he now drew her toward him. She pulled away.

He urged again, "We've been together for three years now, Camilla—and you're right, yes, our relationship is being soured. We've got to do something to get it together again. I've been good, I've been patient; three years I've waited for you because you're worth it. Let's save what we've got—marry me."

Camilla's stomach suddenly turned over at the thought of all that marriage implied. All the time she had known him she had kept him at arm's length and told herself she would remain true to the virtues her parents had brought her up to respect—but it hadn't really been that difficult for her to resist him, she saw that now. And she realized that she didn't want him. She never truly had. He was forcing the issue, and she knew that she could not have both Jeff and her sister. Of the two, her sister was infinitely preferable.

"I can't marry you," she said finally.

"You can do whatever you want."

"Then I don't want to marry you." Camilla saw the look of absolute amazement on his face, and that broke the last of the hold he had on her.

"You never thought I would refuse, did you?" she cried. "But I have a mind of my own, much as it may surprise you, and I'm going to do some things and see some places before I marry anyone. And I'm going to do them alone. I can be as free and independent as anyone. How blind I was not to see it all before! I needn't ask your permission or anyone's for the things I do, and I'm going to make sure it stays like that. I'll go where I like and see what I want without a single string attached. And," she concluded triumphantly, "I'll begin by going to Afghanistan, to look for my sister." Her eyes shone as they opened to limitless possibilities, the sort she had always dreamed about: France, Italy, America, Africa, Australia—and first of all, Asia. A free and untrammeled existence.

"And when you come back, what then?" asked Jeff.

She turned her eyes back to him. "I could never marry you. There was no spark between us, no passion, no—I never remember feeling any...desire. Surely there must be that."

"I felt it."

"No, Jeff, I lacked it. I never told you. I thought it was me, that I'd grow out of it, but...there's nothing there. At least, not enough for me. When I marry, it will have to be because I can't live without the man I love. And I don't think that would ever happen with us. Maybe I'm not really meant for marriage."

"You don't know what misery you're making for

yourself," hissed Jeff. "You probably think love is the be-all and end-all of life. Well, it isn't, and I know you're not the sort who can survive on casual relationships. You think you are because you're too proud to admit the truth and too proud to admit you'd be better off married to me."

"If marriage is what you seem to think it is, then I will never marry at all. I will never give any man legal permission to order me about this way and that. I have my pride."

"I see that now," said Jeff bitterly. "But if you think you'll be happy, you're mistaken."

"You seemed to have offered me the choice of being either a married slave or alone but my own master. I think I can look after my own life."

"I've yet to see evidence of that," he answered sarcastically. But she did not need to reply, knowing that he was taking refuge in sarcasm when he saw that all his arguments and threats had no effect on her new determination. Through her exaltation she heard a phone ring somewhere, and when the waiter came to say softly, "For you, Miss Simpson," she rose from her seat in a light-headed swirl of euphoria and seemed to walk on a cloud to the booth in the reception.

"Camilla?"

"Yes?" she answered lightly.

"It's me, Jennifer." Jennifer was Camilla's friend who worked at the travel agency where she had booked her tickets and received a lot of good advice. "I tried to reach you at home earlier, but you were out all day, so I took a chance you two would be at your favorite restaurant. Your plane time has been moved to the day after tomorrow. If you find it dreadfully inconvenient we can book you another next week."

"No, no, that's great. The sooner the better."

"Is anything wrong? You sound so strange."

"How do you mean?"

"Really happy. . . excited somehow."

"Yes, I am," replied Camilla. "I've just turned down an offer of marriage."

"Really!" Her friend let out a deep breath. "Well, I only hope Afghanistan's worth it."

"Anywhere would be," Camilla had laughed, and Jennifer joined her.

The memory of all that had passed that evening claimed her as she lay full length on the bed, and she knew that however difficult her task might be, she had made the right decision. Here in this foreign land she would make a new beginning with her freedom, she would make her own decisions, accept or reject advice freely, seek her own friends and find her own way.

I like the Hagans, she thought. *I want them to help me.* And in the end? Their reward would be boundless thanks—a gratitude she could not put into words, but nothing like the chains that Jeff had demanded in return. Her assurance came leaping back to her again. She would be in control. Johnny's words in the plane came back to her: "You'll find it a strange place at first, but you'll soon come to love it. We all do. Afghanistan grows on you."

She finally slipped into deep sleep, but it was not dreamless. She fell through blue sky, and a face with piercing eyes set in tawny skin kept turning and turning an inscrutable gaze toward her, as she tossed, between the white sheets of her bed.

CAMILLA SPENT THE NEXT DAY settling into the routine of the hotel. She had been advised to take it easy for the first while; finding oneself suddenly at an altitude of more than five thousand feet could do funny things to one's stomach and blood pressure. So she unpacked her cases, moved the pictures in her room, set up her toilet articles on the dresser, bathed, read and slept. She phoned the embassy, but they had no further news for her, no new clues. Discouraged, she bought some postcards and sent them off to various friends—Jennifer at the travel agency, a distant relative in Essex, some school acquaintances. She sent nothing to Jeff.

The following day Rajab dropped by with a note from Johnny.

Camilla:
   Janet isn't feeling too hot at the moment, although she says she's been feeling a lot better since I got back. Still, I'm sticking near her for a day or two—a bit of rest and relaxation for me. I hope you're okay on your own, though I'm sure you'll find plenty of willing helpers. Janet's dying to meet you and says she feels up to it; can you come to dinner tomorrow night? Till then Rajab is at your disposal, since I won't be going anywhere much. We'll see if we can get going on your business tomorrow—till then forget about it and enjoy yourself.

Camilla folded up the letter, written in Johnny's exuberant style, and smiled. She had heard Americans were friendly and she was only too thankful. *And they certainly waste no time when they get going on something,* she thought to herself. Tomorrow. That left her only one day to find something suitable to wear. Camilla mentally scanned her wardrobe and realized that her greatest need was for an evening dress, since she had not foreseen any such invitations for dinner. But where to begin looking?

"Where you like to go today, *memsahib*?" Rajab's voice broke into her thoughts.

"I need a dress, a long dress. Where can I buy one?" Rajab, holding his head quizzically to one side, obviously did not understand, so she thumbed quickly through her little English-Persian phrase book.

"*Peyran.*" Her tongue stumbled over the strange inflections. "A dress."

Rajab smiled at her efforts. "Miss Simpson try much. You like *peyran*, we go bazaar. Many, many *peyran*. Bazaar okay?"

"Bazaar okay," she replied, laughing.

As Camilla rode down the hot and shaded boulevards, she found herself enjoying the strange experience of being a passenger in a chauffeur-driven car. It gave her a heady feeling of importance—mock importance, she knew, laughing wryly at her own thoughts. She gazed with interest on either side of the van and saw something that had escaped her notice the day before: among the dark figures of the Afghans was a liberal sprinkling of pale European skins, probably resident foreigners in their hot, tight-fitting Western clothing. The dreamlike quality of her first twenty-four hours was totally dispelled by her long sleep, and what had unnerved her yesterday amused her now.

But she knew that she could not sightsee purely for her own amusement. She was no tourist. She had a real purpose here—the thought of the difficulties ahead made her pause for a moment, and a cold shiver ran down her back. Then she put the thought firmly aside. Every trip, every expedition she made would have some value to her task—even this short journey to the bazaar. It was necessary to get a good basic knowledge of the country if she ever expected to delve into the mysteries behind her sister's disappearance, and the best way to do that was to plunge right into the city life.

The van drew up at a corner, and Camilla, getting out, found herself at the end of a long narrow street. The buildings were made of wood and the road covered with dirt, but the dull earthy tones contrasted with the gay riot of color that hung from every eave, door and shop window at the bazaar. She saw silk veils and shirts of every hue, cotton blouses and pants, long dresses and bright floral prints, sandals, purses, bags, belts and hats of golden or dark leather, intricate embroideries and pressed-felt rugs. And gleaming in the sunlight were silver and gold jewelry and gems of all sorts: rubies, aquamarines, amethysts, emeralds, topaz and the deep blue lapis lazuli, winking expensively. Along the street, vendors pushed heavy timber carts loaded with woolen socks or bales of cloth. Bright fruits that seemed to burst with their ripeness made Camilla's mouth water. And there was the creak of carts and the bray of donkeys, a dog barking, a cock crowing, mingling with the cries of the shopkeepers. It was all so lively and so very exhilarating! Her spirits soared with her new sense of freedom.

"You like a bracelet? Very cheap!"

"For you, *memsahib*, I give away."

"Why you no like my shop?"

"Out of my way, camel!"

"You offer two hundred afghanis, you son of a dog? You insult my family. It is worth at least five hundred afghanis!"

Up and down the road the moving crowd churned and raised up a cloud of fine pale dust. Camilla could only stare, amazed by the colorfulness and the strangeness of the scene.

"What a wonderful place!" she exclaimed breathlessly.

Rajab beckoned. "Come, *memsahib*. Want *peyran*, know shop plenty good *peyran*. Good for *memsahib*."

He motioned for her to follow him, and they started down the crowded street, weaving in and out of the horde of people, animals and goods. Rajab moved with quick and flowing movements that carried him effortlessly through the uproar, and she struggled to keep up with him. The feeling was claustrophobic, and every now and then she could feel strange hands touching her or tugging the hair that streamed in a fiery fall down the back of her neck.

When she gave a little shriek and darted sideways Rajab merely grinned. Touching his own thick black hair and then pointing at her tresses, he said, "They think too much good."

Before she could reply he entered a doorway and she followed quickly, delighted to get out of the heat and dust and noise. Inside, the shop was cool and dark, and as soon as her eyes became accustomed to the light she could make out varieties of cloth, hung from the walls or stacked in shelves. They were all long dresses of every style, wide or narrow sleeved, patterned or plain, rainbow-hued, made of silk, cotton or heavier woolen cloth; they were dresses of the sort, she realized with a shock, that could be seen for sale every day in the select shops of London at exorbitant prices. The native Asian gowns were all the rage at home—and here she was, thousands of miles from London, in the very land where these dresses were sewn and printed.

"Peyran-i-Kuchi," said Rajab. "Nomad dresses. You like?"

The word "Kuchi" struck a familiar bell, and Camilla looked at the dresses with greater interest. These were the dresses of the people her sister Meghan had admired so much. In the brilliance of the colors, the flowing lines and the delicate yet flamboyant embroidery, Camilla could detect something of the beauty that had attracted her sister to the nomads. She decided immediately that she would have one of those dresses. One hanging in the window appealed especially to her. It was bright blue and white, patterned over with green and red flowery sprigs, and with fine multicolored embroidery at the bodice, cuffs and hem. Such a color scheme would perfectly complement her own very English complexion.

"You like?" repeated Rajab.

"This one," said Camilla, pointing to the blue-and-white creation in the window.

The shopkeeper was at her elbow in a moment. "Would *memsahib* like to try it on?" he asked briskly, whisking it from its place before the glass and hustling her with a single movement toward the back of the little shop. "The fitting room is through there."

She took the dress from his arm and groped through the gloom. She passed one door and was about to go in, but she saw through the corner of her eye a turbaned old man with a long beard sitting on a red mat and sipping something pale brown out of a glass cup, so she passed on. She came to the next room and found it empty, with only one long mirror on its bare walls. Assuming this to be the changing room, she went in and drew the curtain behind her.

Again the strange combination of familiar and unfamiliar; the long mirror and the ringed curtain were fixtures of any fitting room, but the pressed-felt carpet beneath her feet and even the dress in her hand were definitely foreign. Quickly she slipped the dress on and felt with delight the cool swirl of the swaths of silk about her ankles. It fit perfectly and, as she had thought, suited her down to the ground. She would have it.

She returned to the front of the shop, the dress over her sleeve. The shopkeeper was attending to another customer, and Rajab stood a little to one side, watching the proceedings with a tolerant eye. When he saw Camilla waiting, the shopkeeper immediately left the new customer and came over to her.

"It is pleasing?" he said.

"Yes," she replied. "How much?"

"For you, *memsahib*, because you are so charming, only eight hundred afghanis."

Camilla did some quick calculations in her head and worked out the cost. Remarkable, for a dress she would have expected to pay almost double for in the London shops. She was about to agree, but Rajab suddenly came to her elbow and whispered in her ear, "This greedy man. You go—I decide how much. He ask too much."

Camilla was amused. She had heard of the system of bargaining in the bazaars and was interested to find out how Rajab would handle it, even though she considered herself fortunate to get the dress for the original price. She handed him the dress and went out, slowly working her way back to the car and window-shopping along the way through the jostling crowds. She sat and waited for the return of her knowledgeable driver.

For long minutes she lay back in her seat, closing her eyes and letting the heat and noise wash over her, drinking in the exotic flavor of the bazaar. A tap on the window startled her and she opened her eyes and looked out. Several dark ragged children peered in at her, and when they saw she was awake, they stretched out their hands to the foreign lady and, grinning widely, asked for alms.

"Baksheesh, baksheesh, memsahib!"

She felt in her pocket for some loose change, found it and opened the car door, leaning forward to hand it to them. Then she saw something that tore her attention from them, fixing her eyes on a spot some way down the street.

A tall man stood there, tall even by the standards of the long-limbed Afghan. A slow recognition permeated her trembling body, a remembrance of a dreamlike stranger, vague yet haunting: sky-blue eyes. She hung suspended for a moment, a hand on the open window, one foot on the ledge of the van, watching him walk. He moved deliberately but with grace, easing his way along a fluctuating path, a head above the crowd. Several times he paused, as if looking at something that had completely absorbed his interest; only for a second, though, and then he moved on.

She remembered. The man—one of the two men by the traffic light! And she had thought her image of him was no more than a dream. She had a strange compulsion to follow him and had already gone a few paces into the street when she just as swiftly dismissed the idea. Why on earth would she want to do something like that? The bizarre atmosphere of the place must be affecting her in more ways than she realized.

"Memsahib!" Startled out of her reverie, she looked down into the smiling face of Johnny's Afghan driver. "I am here." He handed her a neatly wrapped parcel. *"Peyran,"* he said, smiling.

Half-dazed, she took it. She stood holding it yet not looking at it, feeling like an island in the tumult of the Chicken Street bazaar.

"Memsahib too much tired. We go hotel." The Afghan began to walk back to the waiting van. Camilla shook her head in the bright sunlight.

What had the moment of insanity been? She looked up again, to see where that hypnotic enigmatic figure had gone. He had disappeared from sight. Once more she shook her head, as if to clear it. Was it the heat, the sunlight? Or merely the altitude playing tricks on her mind? Standing in the middle of Chicken Street, clutching a brown parcel to her breast and staring after a man who had vanished, she felt supremely foolish. But that feeling could not totally drown the immense magnetism she had felt in those few moments when she had seen him.

I must be overtired, she decided, trying to be mundane. She turned and walked slowly back to the van where Rajab waited, climbed in through the open door and laid the parcel down beside her. Then she looked at it again and her enthusiasm returned.

"How much was it?" she inquired eagerly.

"He say eight hundred, I say four hundred, we have *chai*, he say five hundred afghanis, I say yes." He handed her back three hundred afghanis.

"Next time I'll try it," she commented as they drove back to the hotel, the strange incident forgotten. "If only we had this wonderful system of arguing with the shopkeepers in England."

But later, when she turned off the lights and went to bed, she found that her dreams were once again pleasantly disturbed.

CHAPTER THREE

THE NEXT DAY dawned the clearest and the hottest Camilla had yet seen in Kabul. After getting up late she ordered room service to bring her a glass of iced tea. She passed the day leisurely, looking forward to the pleasant evening she was sure she would spend with the Hagans. Toward five she took a long cooling bath, then did her hair. She slipped into the zipless buttonless dress of blue and white she had bought on Chicken Street, and once again experienced the sheer sensuous pleasure of the silk about her ankles. The bodice clung tightly, pleasantly molding the shape of her small firm breasts, and the material fell in soft swaths about her slender hips. With a little pale lipstick and a touch of eye shadow to heighten the tan her face was fast acquiring, she was ready to go.

The city was situated on a mountain plateau, and its high altitude kept the air very clear and dry; but it also meant that the temperature rarely cooled down. The air was as hot at six-thirty as it had been at noon. Moreover, Camilla had not taken the precaution of ordering a taxi beforehand, and consequently as she paced back and forth along the pavement outside the hotel, she had the extraordinary experience of not being able to hail a Kabul taxi. Every one that passed her seemed to be full, and her vigorous waving was in vain. She spent twenty angry minutes in the heat and noise of the rush-hour traffic, slowly walking in the direction of the Hagans' house. But it was right on the other side of the city, in the Karte Char suburb, and it would take her at least an hour to walk there.

"Oh, this is impossible!" she exclaimed. "It's incredible that I can't get a taxi."

She became more and more heated and more and more angry, with a red flush creeping up her face and her hair damp with perspiration. *Perhaps I left it too late,* she thought. *I should have had a cab come round.* There was little left of the cool collected creature who had left the Kabul Hotel, and when she finally got a cab that was jerking and puffing with a broken muffler, she was thoroughly disheveled.

"Karte Char, fifty afghanis," said the bearded driver. The fare was exorbitant, but Camilla was in no mood to argue. Agreeing gratefully, she sank into the town seat and listened to the strange sounds of Persian music on the radio for the fifteen minutes it took to drive to the Hagans' house.

The driver pulled up outside the high cement wall that, as with every other house belonging to a foreigner or a wealthy Kabuli, surrounded the Hagans' house. She paid him the fifty afghanis and he drove away happily. The wall was imposing, but she had already become accustomed to the military flavor of much of Kabul, so she approached the wide wooden door and rang the bell.

"Oh, Camilla," a voice cried, the door opening. "We'd nearly given up on you!"

She entered and was greeted by a pretty but anxious-faced woman, dressed in pants and a becoming maternity smock. Camilla suddenly felt she had overdressed. The woman shook her hand warmly and Camilla scarcely had a chance to get out her question, "You must be Mrs. Hagan...?"

"Janet, dear; do call me Janet. Oh, I am pleased to see you, but you've no idea of the hassles here. Brody from the Nebraska team has just had a stroke—" She shook her head. "Sorry, Camilla, I am an unwelcoming hostess. Do come in, please."

They crossed a cement pathway toward a screen door. Camilla watched Janet walk with a compelling grace, a swaying movement, sylphlike despite the burden she carried. She was very slender, almost too thin, and Camilla, comparing herself, felt positively curvaceous.

From around the corner of the house a streak of golden lightning suddenly came bounding, and Camilla found herself being embraced around the knees by a large woolly dog that resembled a honey-colored bear cub and was endeavoring in vain to lick her face.

"I hope you like dogs," said Janet anxiously, but Camilla laughed as she pushed the affectionate thing away.

"Who could help liking this one? She bowls you over," she replied. "What's her name?"

"Elsa." Janet returned her laugh. "Our cook, Kayyum, named her that because she looks like the lion cubs he saw once in *Born Free*."

"She's certainly beautiful," agreed Camilla. "What kind is she? I thought the only sort of dogs they had in Afghanistan were those aristocratic Afghan hounds."

"Yes, they *are* magnificent, aren't they?" said Janet. "They're incredibly swift with keen eyesight, so they are used for hunting. But Elsa is a fighting dog. In fact, we got her from some people who found her in a ditch, along with her two sisters and mother. The females of the breed are no good for fighting, you see, and expensive to raise, so often they are just thrown into the nearest *jui*—that's those open ditches you see along the roads."

"How awful!" exclaimed Camilla. "Poor Elsa. But at least she has a good home now. You must have had her for quite a while—she's some size!"

"No, only six months. I know she's enormous, but you ought to see the full-grown fighters. They're like bears. Anyway, come on in. No, Elsa," she added, pushing the dog away from the screen door. "You can't come in. She knocks everything off the tables with that tail of hers."

They went into the living room, spacious and cool with marble floors. Camilla again drank in the glory of air conditioning.

"Our organization provides air conditioning for all its people," chatted Janet. "I don't know if I could survive in my state without it. Have a drink." She handed Camilla a glass of cool refreshing liquid and lowered herself slowly into the seat next to her.

"You seemed very rushed when I got here," said Camilla. "I hope I didn't arrive at a bad time."

"Well," replied Janet, "I'm going to sound very rude in a minute, so I'm trying to soften the blow. Johnny's had to rush off and see Brody—you know, I told you, the one with the stroke. And in fact I'm going to have to leave in a minute to join him."

"Whatever for?" exclaimed Camilla. How could anyone expect a woman in Janet's condition to rush about tending to sick men?

Janet seemed to guess Camilla's thoughts. "Normally I wouldn't go, but you see I work as Johnny's nurse—we came out here as a team—and Brody is an exceptional case. He's had a stroke before. This really isn't the climate for him, but he's a stubborn old rascal and refuses to go. We could only hope that he wouldn't have another, and now...."

"Aren't there any other nurses on the program? Couldn't they take your place tonight? They must fill in for you usually."

"Yes, that's so, and if the patient were anyone else I'd leave them to it, but Brody's a special case. I've been on it ever since I arrived, and I know all the ins and outs. Besides, I have a personal interest. I'm fond of the old man. He's been out in this country for years. Still, I'm afraid it ruins our evening, which is a real disappointment."

"Never mind—there'll be other evenings," said Camilla philosophically. Then she exclaimed, "Oh!"

"What?"

"I forgot—I told the taxi to come for me at eleven. You have no idea what trouble I had getting one—it took me twenty minutes. Perhaps it won't be so bad now...."

"Nonsense, my dear, I couldn't think of your going if you've got no transportation. Unfortunately, we need Rajab, or he could have run you back to the hotel, but you are certainly most welcome to stay here until your taxi returns."

"Oh, I couldn't—"

"Of course you can! Look at the lovely supper I prepared, going to waste with no one to eat it, because Johnny certainly has no appreciation of gourmet cooking. It was a treat for me to make it and it will cheer my thoughts while I'm with Brody to think that you've enjoyed it."

"But I couldn't eat alone—"

"That's what you would have done at the hotel, isn't it?"

"Well, yes, but... I really do feel very tired and sticky. I think I'd like to go back and have another bath. I had one this afternoon, but the effects don't seem to last too long in this climate."

"We've got a tub. You can take your bath here. Lots of hot water—big fluffy towels!"

"You're very persuasive...."

Janet gave an enchanting smile. "How do you think I won my husband?" Camilla laughed. Janet wagged a finger at her. "Now, I'll have no more arguments—not another word. You'd be all alone at the hotel if you went back, and since I'm breaking all the rules of hospitality by running off like this, the least you can do is make yourself at home. We've got books and a radio and tapes and records—look on it as a bit of dog minding. Elsa gets very lonely when we go away." She looked so earnest that Camilla laughed again.

"You've won me over. I can't say I don't appreciate the prospect of a radio."

The doorbell rang. "That's Rajab," said Janet, snatching up her bag. "I've got to go. Don't worry about locking up. We never do. Love your dress—Chicken Street?"

"How did you guess?"

"I know the place. But if you paid any more than five hundred afghanis for it you were ripped off. Anything higher is tourist prices. See you." She was gone.

The house was quiet. Not silent, but with a sort of calm that was refreshing after the bustle of the past couple of days. Camilla luxuriated for a few moments in the atmosphere. Her welcome from Janet had been warm and kind, if rushed; she felt her fondness for the two Americans increasing every minute. To think she would never have met them if her sister had not— The thought was too disturbing to dwell upon.

The first order of the evening was to have a bath. The house was so welcoming that Camilla did not feel in the least bit out of place having a bath in a strange home. Like its owners, the house opened its arms in friendship. She wandered up the stairs, looking for the bathroom, and came upon a large room, again marble floored, with fixtures in white porcelain and blue-tiled walls. The bath was enormous, like a child's swimming pool, and she contemplated it with pleasure; the thought of a great hot bath to steam away all her worries was wonderful to her.

She turned the tap on as hot as she could stand it, and as the billows of steam rose in the tub, she stripped off the new dress and hung it carefully behind the door. She pinned up her hair, which gleamed like soft strands of copper, and lowered herself slowly into the inviting water. The heat stung her, but slowly she became accustomed to it, and the tensions in her muscles unwound. The water was never this beautifully hot at the hotel.

She had planned to meditate on the subject of her sister, but strangely her mind had become vacant, and she found it hard to focus on any thought. The warmth of the bath was enough, and sheer physical enjoyment had lulled her mental processes to slumber. Each long shapely limb was suspended in the steamy water; the heat was soporific; Meghan retreated to a nebulous memory in the back of her mind. For a moment Camilla was in heaven. She relaxed completely, sinking deeper into the embracing warmth of the water, half closing her eyes. . . .

Suddenly she leaped up, causing a great surge of water to splash over the edges of the tub, and shrank back, her eyes fixed in terror on the porcelain space between the taps—on the shiny, sinister dilating body of the great black scorpion, its globular eyes fixed upon her with an expression of mindless evil.

She was frozen. Only three feet separated her from the deadly insect. She dared not move. She hardly dared to breathe. There was no one in the house to call upon. The barking of Elsa outside the house broke against the muteness of her terror. She was paralyzed by the sight of the scorpion, slowly waving the poisonous stinger curved above its back.

Then she heard a sound of movement in the rooms below: Janet, perhaps, had returned. The thought gave her enough courage to jump from the bath, startling the trembling black insect. Quickly she wrapped a big blue towel around her streaming body and ran to the landing.

"Help, Janet, help!" Her voice conveyed the painful terror of her mind. There was silence pregnant with presence from below, and even in her fear she was angry that her cry had not been answered when she knew someone was there.

She ran down the stairs. "Janet! Please, oh, I had such a...."

She stopped, the words sticking in her throat, her lips suddenly dry, her heart beating at a pace that had nothing to do with her recent terror in the bath.

Her first impression was of height—at least six-foot-two, he towered head and shoulders over her. His face was ruggedly strong, deeply golden with the perpetual tan of years in the sun, out of which sky-blue eyes, as piercing as an eagle's, looked with a fierce gaze. He had a thick mane of sun-bleached hair, and he studied her with a slow lingering glance.

"Him!" she whispered, almost to herself; she was still hardly able to grasp his reality. Too often she had seen him in situations that verged on the trancelike: she could not credit that he was here, near enough to touch, electric beams of blue scanning her from a mere foot away. For a moment some compelling magnetism almost forced her to reach out her hands to him, to run her fingertips over each part of his body, to reinforce his sudden three-dimensionality. But something held her back, and folding her arms across her chest, she gasped louder, "You!"

He said nothing, only regarded her with that intimidating stare. Suddenly she was very conscious of the towel wrapped tightly around her wet body; of her heat-flushed limbs, which the towel molded intimately; and of her damp hair, one lock hanging brightly across her reddened cheek. She had to look away.

"I," he restated simply. "And you are—Miss Simpson, I believe?" he asked, surprising her with a voice deeply modulated and resonant. Perhaps an actor's voice. She gulped down some of the turmoil into which his unexpected presence had thrown her and suddenly remembered that he was not the only cause of her frantically beating heart.

"I was beginning to think you'd never show up," she blurted hurriedly to hide her confusion. "I was simply terrified! There's the most enormous—black and ugly—it just sat there—I was frightened out of my wits—I thought I was going to—I mean, to be confronted in a bath—I thought they lived under stones."

Her words seemed incapable of describing the fear that had gripped her. As he said nothing else, she fell silent, despairing.

"Miss Simpson," he said finally, startling her again with his deep voice, "you must not blush so easily." But his low drawl only heightened her redness. "It does not match your outfit." His voice was heavily sarcastic.

"Oh, I wish you'd kill it!" she blurted out.

He mimicked a startled expression, the very copy of her face when she had first caught sight of him. "Miss Simpson, what exactly are you going on about?"

"There's a scorpion up on the bath—big and black and hairy and ugly and—"

"Scorpions are never hairy." Having effectively silenced her, he went up the stairs. She sat down, drawn and unnerved.

"Do you mean this little beast?" he drawled from upstairs. "Dare I kill it?"

"Oh, please hurry!" she cried, but he only reappeared with something small struggling in his hand. Moving back, she could not stop herself from uttering a scream.

"There is little reason to fear a creature that could do you about as much harm as a fly. It's probably more terrified than you are."

"Put it down! Don't you know that its sting can be deadly?" she demanded in extreme agitation.

"Not this scorpion. This species is practically harmless. One flick of your towel and it would have disappeared into whatever hole it came from." He opened a window and let it drop out onto the ground. Then he shut it again and without another word to Camilla walked past her into the foyer, took his hat and coat and was about to walk out of the door. She stood there stunned for a moment, merely watching his movements, unable to think of anything to say that could possibly explain the situation. She was afraid, too, to be on the receiving end of another one of his sardonic remarks. There she stood, dripping water onto a marble floor, watching the stranger of her dream—now not a total stranger—watching him depart, this flesh-and-blood man who had a few minutes ago appeared when she was in desperate need.

"Wait!" He paused at the open doorway, hat in hand.

What strange ability did this man have to make her uncomfortable at every moment, wondered Camilla furiously. "I just didn't want you to think," she stated, "that I am in the custom of having strange men kill my scorpions for me."

One eyebrow arched. "I am sure you can always find strange men to do many strange things for you, Miss Simpson."

Camilla gasped, then reddened with rage. "I thought you were someone else," she explained, head held high.

"I didn't think you were expecting me, Miss Simpson," he retorted, casting his piercing eyes over her scantily clad trembling body. Anger made her flush more deeply, and she pulled the towel tighter around her body in one aggressive movement.

"I am a friend of the Hagans'. I came for dinner, but they were called away to a medical emergency. I haven't been long in this country and—"

"Oh, yes, I know all about you, Miss Simpson."

"How do you know my name?" Suddenly she looked at him more keenly, suspicion sharpening her thoughts. "And what are you doing in this house?"

"I, too, am a friend of the Hagans'. One who cares a great deal about their welfare—more, it might seem, than others do."

"What do you mean?"

"Johnny's told me all about you, Miss Simpson. He seemed quite taken with you. Have you met his wife?"

"I have," Camilla smiled. "She was charming to me. Very friendly."

"Kind to a fault, those two. Trusting, too. I'd hate to see anything come between them."

"What do you mean?"

He took a step toward her from the door and

seemed about to raise his fists to her shoulders. Then he paused for a minute and let his hands drop.

"Your story I know is true. I remember the incident about Mrs. Cowley's disappearance myself, quite well. Caused a minor stir in the little foreign community. Your identity I can believe in, but I wonder about your character. You are either an unprincipled thrill seeker or an innocent babe-in-the-woods; and your looks tonight, Miss Simpson, very much indicate the former. I know nothing of you—you may drag yourself into whatever dangers you choose, but for God's sake leave the Hagans out of it. You'll soon learn Afghanistan is no place to play amateur detective. Thrills cease to be so thrilling when you're face to face with a wolf, a deadly snake, murderous tribesmen and cutthroat highway robbers—or with dysentery, jaundice or malaria. And having seen the way you reacted to a harmless scorpion perched on the edge of that imported bathtub, I very much doubt, Miss Simpson, whether you'll ever be able to cope. Feminine charm counts for very little in the desert or on the steppes. It won't get you far."

He picked up his hat again and strode back to the door. Opening it, he turned back to her and nodded a quick farewell. His very politeness infuriated her—and yet the sight of him with one foot on the doorstep aroused in her an overwhelming impulse to call him back.

"*Baamane khoda,*" he said, unsmiling. Half angry, half urgent, she took a step forward.

"And what does that mean?" She was not sure whether she asked out of a real desire to know, anger at him for having used a word she was unfamiliar with or a strange urge to have him linger.

"Persian, Miss Simpson. It means God keep you safe."

"How very kind." Now it was her turn to be sarcastic.

"It's the traditional goodbye in the Afghan Dari dialect. You might do well to learn a little, Miss Simpson. And now, if you do not intend to keep me standing at the door all evening, I will wish you goodnight." He was gone before she could say another word.

She wandered back to the sitting room, trembling so much that she fell with relief into a chair. Yet she felt heady, exhilarated. It had been a sparring match that had set her blood pressure racing. Her eyes blazed; the anger still boiled within her.

The immense arrogance of the man, that smug self-satisfaction, that irritating air of superiority! How could she be expected to know which scorpions were dangerous and which were not? And surely it was far wiser to avoid all unless one was an expert. It was commendation she deserved, or at least comfort, and all she had got was mockery. Just like the men she had known in England, ready to help the "poor helpless female," but laughing at the very weaknesses that they assumed made them so indispensable. How dared they! How dared he! She would show the whole tribe of arrogant, selfish, smug, hypocritical, sarcastic—

And how dared he presume to offer her unasked-for advice or condemn her, unknown, on his own assumptions from hearsay? Johnny could not have presented

such an unflattering report of her. She presumed the
men were friends, or how else would he have known
of her purpose here? Regardless, how dared he presume to interfere in her arrangements, in her affairs,
in her decisions, her friendships; an interference unsought and unvalued. . . .

Her heart pounded, and it was not an unpleasant
feeling. Somehow the entire incident had excited her,
aroused every nerve in her body, a glowing reaction
far beyond what the mere gist of the argument had
warranted. She hardly liked to identify it; she only
wanted to enjoy it.

Her reflections were cut short by the sensation of
something cold and wet pressed into her hand.

"Elsa!" The dog wagged her whole tail and half
her body furiously, overjoyed at human company yet
afraid she might be sent out in disgrace. "However
did you get in?" Elsa barked lightly, almost a laugh.
"That man must have left the door open." Camilla
went to shut it, but Elsa hung back, her eyes pleading. "Don't worry, pup, I won't send you away. I'm
in need of a little undemanding company." Elsa
leaped in the air and landed, her great ungainly paws
spread out all splayed.

Camilla went up to the bathroom and dressed,
then, coming downstairs, put a tape of soft music on
the machine. She sat letting the deep notes wash over
her, stroking the silky golden ears of the big head
resting on her knee; a peaceful enough scene, but inwardly she could not remove the thought of the tall
stranger, and all her meditations were disturbed.

At eleven precisely, the taxi arrived to take her
back to the hotel. Strange, she thought as she was

driven along the vaguely familiar route, then let herself into her welcoming suite, she was already starting to feel more at...home here in this new and exotic land.

CHAPTER FOUR

ON HER FIFTH DAY IN KABUL, Camilla decided to venture out into the bazaars by herself. She donned a pale pink linen sundress, slipped low-heeled sandals on her feet and taking up her purse set forth. Emerging from the hotel and pausing as she always did to let the first shock of the unaccustomed heat expend itself, she looked around. Down the road from the hotel was a huge craggy building, built of a rugged gray stone, with a guard and cannon posted in front of its marble walls. It had the appearance of a medieval fortress and had once been a royal palace, the Arg. Behind the site were long swards of lush gardens.

Having gathered her thoughts about her, she set off down the street. She scarcely watched where she was going, her eyes hungry for every new experience. A grizzled man in a green turban passed her, his quilted robe sweeping the ground and his hands hidden inside the extra long sleeves. Camilla wondered how he could wear a costume so like a winter jacket on a day when the temperature must be more than one hundred degrees. To the left and right of her she could see the passing buses, black-and-white taxis, the horses and donkeys pulling carts and traps. On wide lawns in the center of traffic circles, tribesmen from outside the city sat in groups, talking and smoking.

With all her attention concentrated on these strange new sights, Camilla did not notice that many dark eyes were upon her. She slowly made her way toward the center of the bazaar, passing stall after stall. Her eyes never tired, drinking in the glorious display of color and goods. She lingered over the scarves, sighed over the jewelry, admired the pottery. In the shade of a spreading elm tree she stood cooling, and then thought of Jeff as she cast her eyes over the biblical scene. Poor Jeff, with his narrow round of restaurants, theaters and museums—he would never know what it was to open his mind to new experiences. Here were places she had never dreamed of, things she could never have seen herself doing—and it could happen to almost anyone. But never to Jeff. He was not a darer.

As she stood wrapped in her thoughts, she stared out at the bazaar without really seeing. Then a familiar movement, a reminiscent shape, caught her eye, and she looked harder. She was not really surprised—she had come to expect finding him in unexpected places—so that could not be the explanation for her rapidly beating heart. Again, as always, her first blind instinct was to push her way to him, but she dug her toes firmly into the ground and held back. She put a hand on her thumping chest and swallowed the anger rising in her throat.

Leave him alone, she admonished herself firmly. Or was she a glutton for punishment? He was a rude and arrogant man, and though she might feel she had come out the worst the previous evening—at this thought she blushed and wrapped her other arm protectively around her—there was no need to pursue it. He didn't deserve her attention.

Then another idea struck her. Was he, perhaps, following her? Spying? "Unprincipled thrill seeker," she remembered in indignation. She supposed he wanted to try to prove some point to Johnny about her—to warn him off, perhaps, as if there were any need for that! And his talk about her playing amateur detective—he was right, of course, but the *way* he'd said it irked her. She tossed her head so that her heavy hair swung in glossy lengths about her bare shoulders. She spun on one foot, about to stalk away.

Camilla was never sure what exactly happened next.

There was a sudden uproar in the crowd around her, and a seething movement—action—then a white-robed figure, shouting and gesturing, burst toward her, and she felt a wetness drip down her cheek, then the pain of being beaten on her bare arms. The noise and the heat and the harsh pain made her head spin, and but for the crowd milling about her, angrily shouting and pushing, she would surely have fallen. She sensed a darkness envelop her and heard loud hating vituperations in a foreign language: *"Khaarh! Sag!"*

Then—oh, relief!

"Get away! Stop, you fools, stop. *Bas, bas!*"

She felt a falling away of the masses around her. Strong hands gripped her arms and shook away her near fainting spell. A reassuring voice, in faintly accented English, shouted in her ear, "Quick, come with me!"

Half walking, half dragged, she let him take her,

for instinctively she trusted him, and they hurried to the road. Suddenly she found herself inside a moving car, taking her farther and farther away from those few short nightmarish minutes in the bazaar. It had all been over so quickly that it was like a blur of fear in her mind. All in an instant, she began to tremble uncontrollably, and she burst into loud shaking sobs, tears streaming down her flushed cheeks.

"Here, *mademoiselle*, take my handkerchief. You will be all right in a minute."

She took the proffered piece of snowy linen, hardly caring where it came from, and wept in the aftermath of shock. But soon the level motion of the car and the peaceful presence beside her calmed her nerves, and she looked up to see who her benefactor was.

Her lifted eyes met small bright brown ones in a smooth tanned face framed by dark hair. Each curl was neatly in its place, the nose was long and fine and the upper lip decorated with a fringe of trimmed mustache. His figure was slender, immaculately dressed in a three-piece suit and a white Panama, and the smile he wore was well polished. He extended a slim beautiful hand, which in her confusion she took.

"Patrice Desmarets," he said, shaking her hand. "And you, fair *mademoiselle* in distress?"

"Oh!" she cried. "You can't joke about it. It was horrible."

"You were attacked by a mullah," he said. "Here, let me wipe that." He took the handkerchief and delicately wiped the wetness off her left cheek. "It would seem he spat at you. Very vulgar."

"But why?" exclaimed Camilla. "He hit me on the

arms, too.'' She looked down at the bruises that were beginning to rise, black and blue on her battered arms. "He tried to beat me. I think he wanted to kill me. Why?"

"Why, indeed, would anyone want to strike so fair a flower? But then, perhaps this mullah has no artistic taste. I think he objected to your frock."

"What's wrong with it? It's not indecent."

"Indeed, *mademoiselle*, it is *très chic* and certainly becomes you, but not quite what they are used to. I refer to the sleeves."

"There aren't any."

"That is my point, *mademoiselle*, precisely. The sight of so fair a limb exposed can rouse some of the stricter Muslims to an ungovernable rage. You may have noticed that many of their women remain swathed in their top-to-toe veils."

"*Chadaris*, yes," replied Camilla. "But I thought the sort of thing I just went through only happened in Kandahar."

"It may well have been a Kandahari mullah who attacked you. Anyway, such things are not unknown in Kabul, though rare."

"I want to report it to the authorities immediately."

"*En, voyons, mademoiselle*, I think it would be best to leave it alone. They will not be able to punish the man, and you do not want to get yourself a name as a troublemaker."

"But I didn't—" Camilla began.

"If you are going to say, 'I didn't start it,' *eh, bien*, you are perfectly right in the immediate sense, but finally the fault lies with you for wearing such a provocative dress."

"I've seen much worse on Oxford Street."

"But that is in London. In Paris, too, your dress would cause no stir, though I cannot vouch for what is in it; however, here they are less civilized. It is an unwritten law—you will only get into further trouble if you wear that dress again in the bazaars. They will not consider it the man's fault. It is better to have as little to do with the Afghan authorities as possible."

Although Camilla did not want to surrender the point so easily, she could see that this man was a great deal better versed in the ways of this strange country than she was, and she bowed to his judgment. Besides, she owed him a deep debt of gratitude.

"I suppose I must take your word for it, since you seem to know," she admitted at last, grudgingly.

"Indeed you must. It would not be nice to see so *charmante* a young woman come to harm. You must take my word for it."

Camilla looked away, out of the window of the car, though her mind was not on the scenery. She noted the lines of the car, sleek and expensive, the metal a restrained dark chocolate color, and the upholstery cream leather. The driver was a powerful thickset Afghan with a red turban wrapped around his skull. The whole effect—driver, car and the man himself—was one of luxury.

"I—I'm afraid I didn't catch your name," she stammered.

"Nor I yours. Shall we recommence introductions?" He held out his neat hand again. "Patrice Desmarets."

"Camilla Simpson," she replied. He kissed her hand, and she withdrew it quickly.

"Your name is so charmingly English. How pleasant it is to meet a product of real civilization here in this godforsaken spot."

Camilla was flattered by his compliments. Here was a truly accomplished man. None of the false sophistication of Jeff about him, nor even the rather overwhelming eagerness of Johnny Hagan, nor the...the crushing self-assurance of one tall blond stranger. She was ready, at that moment, to agree with her rescuer's estimation of Aghanistan as a godforsaken spot. At least, after the last experience, it was not growing on her yet.

"But if you find it godforsaken, why are you here?" she asked shyly.

"Ah," he replied archly, "why does the sun shine and the tide turn? We do what we must. My business calls me here. Anyway, I might ask you the same question, for it seems to me you must be new here."

"I arrived four days ago."

"Four days!" sighed Patrice. "Four years—that is how long I have been in purgatory. How long are you here for, Mademoiselle Simpson?"

"Oh, I'm not sure..." she replied vaguely. There was a nagging reminder in the back of her conscience of Johnny's warning, "No reason to let the whole of Kabul know why you're here."

"What do you do, then, Monsieur Desmarets, to occupy yourself in...purgatory?"

"I? I'm a free-lance journalist waiting for something to happen. *J'attend les événements.*"

"Funny," said Camilla musingly. "I wouldn't think much really happened here. Still—" she thought of the car, the suit, the chauffeur—"—you seem to find enough to keep going."

"Well, enough, enough—or as they say here, *khaafi*."

Camilla noted that he was trying to dismiss the subject, and thinking he might interpret her questions as unwarranted prying, she decided to turn the conversation to another track.

"I hope you won't think I'm in the custom of letting myself be driven around in strange cars by strange men."

"Nor I of driving strange women, however beautiful," he replied lightly. "But the circumstances were rather extraordinary. However, since we have, by a series of fortuitous circumstances, made the acquaintance of each other, I hope you will do me the honor of taking a little drink with me."

But Camilla was doubtful. She felt she was being rushed off her feet and could not push away a nagging suspicion that it was all too sudden.

"I—I don't usually drink this early, Monsieur Desmarets," she answered him haltingly. Then above the purr of the car's engine was heard, from a distance, a loud and sonorous single boom of artillery.

"What was that?" she exclaimed.

"Nothing to be alarmed about, *mademoiselle*. It's the cannon on the Bala Hissar fortress—the Noon Gun, the Americans call it, because they shoot it off every day at noon. And since it is midday, I hope a change of invitation from drinks to lunch will be acceptable."

She *was* hungry, and his charm was irresistible. "Thank you very much," she smiled.

Soon the car pulled up in front of a large modern

building, all shining glass and chrome and concrete. It looked indestructible after the mud-and-timber houses of the bazaar. The sun glinting on its many windows and the cleanliness of driveway, lawn and metal appealed to her eyes, which were starved for traces of Western life.

"It reminds me of a restaurant I used to go to in London," she remarked.

"This is the Bagh-i-Bala Hotel."

They entered through a high-canopied doorway and were saluted smartly by the doorman, dressed in the uniform of a horseman of the steppes. He wore a thick leather-and-fur hat, a quilted jacket, brightly dyed cotton trousers and leather boots with multi-colored laces. A braided whip hung by his side.

"Good afternoon, Monsieur Desmarets."

The great tapestried foyer was slightly intimidating, with thick luxurious carpets absorbing every sound as they trod silently across. The very walls, hung with rich works by local master craftsmen, reflected the expensive air of exclusivity. Gold fittings reflected the light from dimmed chandeliers. All noise, all hurry, was left outside, and restraint and decorum took their place. At the bar were several little cliques of well-dressed men and chic women, conversing in undertones, who greeted Patrice with a wave or a quiet nod.

They quickly found a table, for the restaurant was nearly empty, and a waiter in a white jacket was suddenly at their chairs with a menu. "Good afternoon, Monsieur Desmarets."

"They certainly seem to know you here," said Camilla when the waiter had gone.

"The foreign community is rather small," replied Patrice. "Perhaps a thousand people, counting children. So one tends to see the same faces over and over again. That is why it is so refreshing to meet someone new. As for Hussein, he has been my special waiter ever since I arrived here four years ago. I always patronize this restaurant."

"I can see why," said Camilla appreciatively.

"Well, what would you like?" he asked, handing her a menu. "I can recommend the veal."

"If you say so. You're the expert," she replied. Oh, the joy of basking in real sophistication, real culture! How could Jeff ever compete in this world?

They made desultory conversation throughout the meal, while he told her of this and that of importance to be seen in Kabul, including the more out-of-the-way sights that most casual tourists never saw.

He mentioned the tomb and gardens of Babur at the other end of the city, off the road to Kandahar.

"I enjoy gardens," she said, "especially because they're alive, not objects stuffed in glass boxes, like in museums."

"If you like gardens, then I must lay claim to one of your days to show you around the best ones in the city."

So the conversation went. Camilla was enjoying herself, more perhaps than at any other time since she had arrived in Kabul. Then over the excellent Turkish coffee that finished their meal, Patrice suddenly became serious.

"*Eh, bien, mademoiselle*, we have talked about many light things, but you have still not told me what brings you to our little country."

"Really—well..." she stumbled, seeking a way around such direct questioning. She did not want to insult him by a straight refusal.

"You know," he added thoughtfully, "you very much remind me of someone I once met here. Not so long ago, in fact—a tragic end." He watched as her face went white.

"Meghan Cowley!" she cried, unable to restrain her emotion. "You know her?"

"Well, Thomas Cowley really, but I found his wife *très sympathique*. Did you know her?"

"She—" choked Camilla, "she is my sister."

"I did not know she had a sister," said Patrice matter-of-factly.

But Camilla's mind had leaped far away from Patrice's words and lingered on the thought of Meghan. Her sister. He had actually known her sister. She could see no reason now to avoid telling Patrice of her mission. He knew her sister—he knew her well, it seemed—which was more than Johnny and Janet, however kind, could offer. Here was a lead. Surely this was an incredible piece of luck!

"I have come to look for my sister," she said firmly. "I must find her."

"I thought she was dead." Patrice's tone was faintly quizzical. "We all heard that they had both been killed—truly very tragic. Perhaps you do not know the entire circumstances?"

"Yes, I do. I was kindly sent a full report from the embassy. But they have only done *so* much." She finished on a sarcastic note.

"Surely you cannot believe she is still alive?" he asked, a trifle incredulously.

"I *know* she's alive."

"Know?" His voice sounded skeptical, in direct contrast to her optimism. "How do you know? What evidence do you have?"

"No evidence. Just faith that she is alive. Of course, I don't believe Tom can still be alive, since it's pretty difficult to deny the evidence of a dead body, but they haven't yet found Meghan's body, and until they do— I am going to stay fixed in the determination that she is still alive." She spread her hands expressively across the table, unaware that she was arguing her case again, just as she had pleaded for it with Jeff. "She's all I have left. After father and mother were killed in that car accident—I can't lose her, too."

They sat in silence for a moment. Camilla's head hung, the feeling of grief pervading her. How could she explain the certitude she had come to live with, that had grown slowly but surely, denying the first bewilderment of bereavement, until the belief was so powerful she could no longer keep it silent. It had goaded her into action; it was the same feeling that had finally brought her to this very table—the unbreakable conviction that her sister was alive. Patrice watched her struggling with her emotions, looking concerned as he gently patted her arm.

"Never mind, *chère mademoiselle*, I believe that you are right. I will do whatever I can to help you. Now tell me from the start—what exactly do you propose to do?"

IT WAS LATE AFTERNOON when Camilla finally returned to the hotel, hot, exhausted, her battered arms aching. But she was filled with an enormous sense of relief. It felt as if the Frenchman had lifted a burden off her shoulders, listening, commenting and understanding with such a depth of kindness; with wit and charming urbanity he had made her feel attractive, flattered and feminine. He even knew the Hagans, which didn't surprise her, because Patrice seemed to know a *lot* of people. When his long car had rolled up to the very doors of her hotel and she stepped out, he had kissed her hand and smiled, *"A demain."*

Now she rang the bell on the reception desk with a weary hand, desirous of only two things—a bath and bed. She had a sudden urge to kick off her sandals and let her tired feet slide across the cool mottled marble of the hotel floor, and she was dreamily loosening one strap with her toe when she sensed something tall and warm standing by her side.

"Miss Simpson." The voice sent tremors rippling from the line of her brow to the insteps of her feet, and the blood rushed unbidden to her face. She remained where she was, not looking up at him, in an attempt to hide her sudden confusion.

"You have done well for yourself, haven't you? Two men in three days. Attractive you may be, but such a success is quite phenomenal. To what do you ascribe it?"

This was too much. Camilla spun around, her cheeks burning, now not from embarrassment but from anger. "For your information, the man who dropped me here was simply behaving as a gentleman ought. Having rescued me from a very dangerous situation, he then kindly took me to lunch to restore my nerves. So there!"

He smiled sardonically. "You certainly don't have

to explain yourself to me. I am merely a humble observer, and let me observe that I can envisage few things more fraught with danger than riding about town with that Frenchman Desmarets."

"That Frenchman Desmarets, as you call him, had the presence of mind to rescue me from an attacker, a mullah, who could very well have killed me had not Patrice been there."

"No more than you deserve, wearing a dress like that in the bazaar." His eyes blazed at her, and she read there the accusation "Thrill seeker, thrill seeker!" printed again and again. Then they blinked and became sea-calm. "You've hurt your arm," he said quietly, reaching a finger out to touch the bruises. Camilla shrank from his hand as if from a live wire and looked away from his face.

"Just leave me alone." Her voice was low. "Don't touch me." One might almost have detected a note of pleading in the request. "Leave me alone. Go and observe someone else."

For a brief moment his fingertips stroked her arm. Electrified, she jerked her head up and continued angrily, "Anyway, you were more than a humble observer last night, if I recall correctly. You made several unwarranted accusations, along with giving some quite unasked-for advice. And what are you doing here, anyway? You've been following me all day—first in the bazaar and now here. So take your observations and go away and leave me alone!" She noticed the desk clerk was waiting patiently, so she said, too loudly, her mind still on the argument, "My room key, please." She remained facing the office, away from the tanned stranger.

"I assure you your paranoia—or if I were conceited I would say your delusions of grandeur—is quite unfounded." He spoke to the nape of her neck, his lips so close that his breath ruffled the delicate hairs. "This meeting was just as unsought and undesired on my part as it evidently was on yours. And I certainly did not see you in the bazaar this morning—nor did I go there with the purpose of hunting you down. Although you evidently saw me."

Camilla clenched her jaw. The caress of his breath on her neck was quite disturbing, the more disturbing because it was pleasantly so, and she stepped forward a pace. "As if I would care. I don't even know who you are—and I'm not much interested." She lifted a hand to her forehead and noticed the fingers were trembling. "Whoever you are, I've seen too much of you and don't really want to see any more. Good day." But her move away from him was halted by a hand placed commandingly on her shoulder.

"And I," he drawled mockingly, "have seen a great deal of you, but as far as I'm concerned, not nearly enough." His gaze was a shockingly intimate caress. "Charming, quite—"

His words were cut off by a resounding slap that echoed in the high-walled lobby. "How dare you!"

He caught her wrist as it was still held in midair and crushed it till she bit her lip in pain. "You'll regret that," he whispered lowly, his eyes piercing into her own.

Her throat constricted, and for a moment she felt cold with fear. Mustering what bravery she could, she stammered, "Never! You deserved it."

She held her breath and could see nothing in front

of her but two angry eyes the color of hard blue steel. She stared into them, drawn to them, unable to look away. Then the lids, with their thick fringe of lashes, dropped like a curtain and rose again on blue skies. He smiled strangely, without any spirit of a smile, more frightening to Camilla than his cloudy anger. He let her hand go, and it dropped lifeless to her side.

"You may be right." His expression was inscrutable as he looked at her for a moment and then, all trace of anger gone, slowly raised his own hand to her cheek. He laid it there and stroked his thumb hypnotically along the line of her jaw. For a moment she pressed her chin into the broad palm of his hand in an unthinking, unconscious, natural action. She was so tired.

"But keep away from the Frenchman, English rosebud. Trust me."

Camilla jerked her head away, eyes open, and again her temper flared. "Just leave me alone. What business is it of yours who my friends are? Who are you to order me around and make accusations? Warning me off this one and warning me off the other! Go away. Just go away."

He had already broken from her and his long strides brought him quickly to the door, but she followed. "I'm just surprised no one's warned me off you yet, whoever you are."

He smiled again, but the smile was not for her. "They will, don't worry, they will." It was the voice of a cynic. "By the way, my name is Armstrong, Malcolm Armstrong."

He was out of the door, letting a burst of hot air into the room where Camilla stood. She shook with indignation as she watched his retreating form and then followed him outside. When she reached the pavement she shouted the last word after him: "I might have known!" Her first impression of the pompous teacher-playing-at-native whom Johnny had mentioned on the plane was now heartily confirmed.

She whirled about again to face the lobby, breathing heavily, fists clenched. Guests were buried in papers or travel brochures, pretending to have seen, heard and noticed nothing. Head held high, she stalked to the reception desk and picked up her key with a defiant gesture. She walked at a slow and stately pace out of the lobby up to the stairs, and not until she reached them did she run—all the way up to her room.

CHAPTER FIVE

CAMILLA WAS AWAKENED late the next morning by the ringing of the telephone beside her bed. Half-asleep, she groped for the receiver.

"Yes?" she yawned.

"Call for Miss Simpson from Mrs. Hagan. Will you take it?"

Camilla sat up quickly. "Yes, please."

There was a drawn-out whirring noise and then, through the static of the line, Janet's faint voice.

"Janet?" said Camilla. "You sound miles away."

"Dreadful connections," she replied. "You sound pretty dopey . . . did I just wake you up? . . . Gosh, I'm sorry."

"Sheer self-indulgence," said Camilla. "I don't usually sleep this late. How's Mr. Brody?"

"Not so good. They're flying him back to Nebraska today. What I really phoned for, dear, was to apologize for the fiasco of the night before last. Funny about the taxis; we don't usually have any difficulty."

"There's absolutely no need to apologize."

"Still, we're hoping to make it up to you by inviting you to come out with us tonight. Actually, not really out for you. We were wondering if you'd care for a visit to the Afghan Room—you know where it is?"

"On the top floor of the hotel, yes, but I've never been there myself."

"You'll love it." Janet's voice faded away. "See you at nine, then. *Baamane khoda.*"

"Janet, wait!" exclaimed Camilla, but the American had hung up before Camilla could stop her. Camilla had wanted to press her for information about the tall strange man who had so disturbed her evening, to find out more than his name and his teaching post in the country. Still, she could easily wait till the evening—it was hardly that important. What had Janet said? *Baamane khoda*—the very words of Malcolm Armstrong. "You might do well to learn a little, Miss Simpson," she recalled.

She dressed quickly and with more experience chose a white long-sleeved tunic dress. Then she set out to find a teach-yourself-Persian text, some notebooks and a pen. No one would be able to accuse her of not making every effort to find her sister, and she could scarcely begin if she did not know the language of the country in which Meghan was lost.

"I want to find a bookshop," she said to the receptionist. "One with English books. Where do you think I ought to go?"

"There is a good shop in Shar-i-nau," replied the male clerk. Camilla had yet to see a woman in any such public employment. "It's an Indian bookshop, across from the Hajji Yakob mosque, next to Marks & Spencer."

At that Camilla had to laugh. It was typical of the country that her directions would include an ancient blue-tiled monument and a modern department store; the old and the new. However, Camilla had her doubts about Shar-i-nau, the New City, for it had been in the park there, only down the road from the Hajji Yakob mosque, that she had been brutally attacked by the mullah. Her arms still ached at the memory.

"I don't think—is there anywhere else?"

"You can try any of the supermarkets—Azziz or Hamidi. Or you can look down Jad-i-maiwan. But the best place is the Indian shop. I always recommend it to tourists."

"Thank you," said Camilla. "I've got the whole day, so I may try them all. It's a way of getting to know the town."

"*Baamane khoda,*" said the receptionist.

"*Ba—baamane khoda,*" smiled Camilla.

The day was cooler than any she had yet experienced, although it was all relative, since every day was roasting by British standards. Still she decided to walk, as she needed the exercise and wanted to begin to settle a map of the city in her mind. However, she had hardly gone a few yards when a sleek chocolate-colored car drew up alongside the pavement and stopped just beyond her.

"So, *mademoiselle*, we meet again. I am pleased to see you took my advice on your costume."

"Good morning, Monsieur Desmarets. I heard it was a good idea to wear white in hot climates."

"And so it is, *mademoiselle*, especially with hair as remarkable as yours. I know an artist who would pay a great deal to paint you. I see you are walking somewhere in this formidable heat. It would surely not be *galant* to pass you by without the offer of a lift."

"I wouldn't like to take you out of your way."

"*Assurément*, every way is my way. I was just

driving aimlessly, waiting for something to happen. Do bring me a bit of relief from my boredom by allowing me to escort you."

Camilla found again that his charm was irresistible, and with a smile she opened the door of the passenger seat and slid onto the pale leather.

"One condition, Monsieur Desmarets: that we drive slowly. I'm trying to fix a mental map of Kabul."

"The condition is accepted with pleasure. Where shall we wend our weary way?"

"I'm looking for a bookshop to buy one of those teach-yourself-Persian books. I really feel I need to be able to hold a conversation with these people if I'm going to get anywhere in my search."

"Persian is a terribly difficult language to learn, as you will find. I would be willing to volunteer as interpreter and save you the trouble."

"Thank you, but no." Still, Camilla was touched by his offer. "It's as much personal satisfaction as anything, really. Besides, I'd like to know Persian."

He nodded and drove her to the Indian bookshop, the one the receptionist had recommended.

"You think this is the best, do you?" she said.

"I would go nowhere else," he replied.

They entered its large cool interior and were greeted by a large thickset Indian with a long beard and a steel bracelet on his arm.

"*Mademoiselle* would like a teach-yourself-Persian book."

"Certainly, Monsieur Desmarets."

They spent about half an hour inside the shop, examining and rejecting various texts. Their thickness and small print daunted Camilla, who was beginning to have second thoughts about this self-imposed task. She found Patrice an invaluable help, sparing in his advice, deferring to her opinion, yet politely pointing out the merits and the disadvantages of each text as it was brought out. After they had finally purchased a slim encouraging volume, he took her on a tour of the carpet shops to be found nearby, where she was fascinated by the richness of color, and the variety of design, and entranced by the deep soft texture. "I must take at least one home with me," she decided. All too soon the morning had been whiled away in leisurely window-shopping, and the Noon Gun again signaled the arrival of midday.

"Luncheon, *mademoiselle*?"

"I suppose I ought to be getting back to the hotel...."

"Unthinkable. The second luncheon is always most important. Today I will take you to a favorite little place of mine, full of—what is the phrase—local color."

They headed back toward the hotel and then turned right and drove along Chicken Street, finally parking at the corner, next to a leather shop. As they crossed the road a flower seller begged a few coins of Camilla, but the Frenchman hurried her along and soon she was following him up some narrow windowless stairs.

Suddenly they were in the light-filled entrance of what seemed to be a sort of café. Called the Green Lantern, it comprised an interior restaurant with more tables outside on a balcony overlooking the street.

"Can we sit outside?"

"Your wish is my command."

Soon they were seated at a charming little table for two with a red-checked tablecloth. The only ornament was an old wine bottle with a white candle in it, dripping wax down the side of the glass. They ate slowly, savoring the homemade excellence of the food.

"I do like this place," smiled Camilla as she sipped her coffee, hoping it would revive her. She felt strangely weak. "You can see everyone and everything."

Patrice put his elegant hands together. "I rang last night to your hotel, but there was no answer. I was... *désolé*." Camilla looked up at him, slightly guilty.

"I'm sorry," she said, "I was tired. I'd asked not to be disturbed."

"Oh, I thought you might be at the Hagans'. You talked so favorably of Mr. Hagan the other day, and you were so grateful for his assistance on the plane."

She hesitated, but then decided there could be no harm in telling him of a simple dinner invitation. "I did go to dinner there the other night."

"I hope you had a pleasant evening?" he asked with polite interest.

"Unfortunately, they were called away on an emergency. Not that I minded; my own father was a doctor, so I know how it is."

Some strange reticence prevented her from mentioning the incident with the tall stranger; it was as if her lips had put a ban on the subject.

"Obviously you find the Hagans friendly?"

Camilla wondered at the tone of his voice. "I do

quite like them. Maybe you don't share my opinion."

"I can't say that they have ever gone out of their way to be friendly to me. Not that I blame them. I must have done something to offend them—though what I am not sure."

"Well, they've certainly gone out of their way to be nice to me," Camilla retorted, a trifle defensively.

Patrice Desmarets sat silent for a minute, his eyes half-open. Camilla watched him, worried. He seemed to be struggling with a thought.

"Mademoiselle," he said at last, then stopped. "No, never mind."

"What, Monsieur Desmarets?"

"It doesn't matter."

"Yes, it does. I can see you're upset about something."

"I don't want to disturb you."

"Well, you've interested me now. Please...."

"It's just that—I must speak my mind, *mademoiselle*. I don't like it, not one bit. I'm very sorry, *mon Dieu*, but that's how it is. I have thought about you a great deal since we met, and strange as it may seem, during our brief acquaintance I have become quite fond of you. I am worried, worried and frightened." He paused to see what effect this had on Camilla. She was taken aback. "Yes," he continued, "worried and frightened. I thought of everything that could happen to you in this folly you have embarked upon. The men of this country are rough and violent, and any woman traveling alone is in danger. Murder, robbery—or other—getting lost in the wilds of the mountains or the steppes, dying in the desert, attacked by wolves, stung by scorpions or bitten by snakes." He took a deep breath and continued candidly, "You could be shot by a gun or wounded by a knife; stolen by white slavers or by the nomads; perhaps thrown into a filthy jail pit for pursuing an investigation that the authorities, for good private reasons, have declared closed."

Camilla's lips were white. "What good private reasons?"

"How should I know?" he snapped sharply. Then, seeing that perhaps he had been too impatient, he added more gently, "It's just that I'm concerned about you. I see all these things that could happen to you, and for what? To track down a body that is probably buried somewhere in the mountains?"

"You said you thought she was alive! You said—"

"*Mademoiselle*, my worries for you overcome every other consideration, even if I should alarm you; and believe me, it was only that fear that prevented me from saying it before. I must say what I think, and truly I do not believe your sister is alive. Since I last saw you I have explored my contacts and drawn a blank at the end of each. I say this not to hurt you but for your own good. No one thinks she is alive. No one even knows how her husband really died."

"The report said he died from a blow on the head while he was fixing the car."

"The report!" Patrice sneered. "I think he was more likely murdered. There is no trace of your sister, not one, and surely a living person would leave some track. You must understand what I am saying—I see no hope for you, and no success for your search. Your decision was the mad folly of a person who did not know what she was letting herself in for, the mad folly of a person who let herself be blinded by her love and her bereavement. I am telling you this because I sincerely want to help you. I think you ought to go home, Camilla."

Camilla, trapped in the hypnotism of his glowing eyes, like a rabbit before a hungry snake, could neither move nor protest.

"You must go home, Camilla, for you do no one any good here."

A car backfired in the street below, startling Camilla from her trance. She looked about her. *I feel so tired,* she thought.

"It is the heat, *mademoiselle*." Camilla did not realize she had spoken aloud. "I think I ought to take you back to the hotel," he added softly.

"I'll just go to the ladies' room," replied Camilla, rising stiffly.

Patrice directed her: "Over behind the green door."

In the washroom Camilla splashed cold water over her face, trying to wash away her drugged heavy feeling. What had Patrice been saying to her? Her head swam; she could not remember the exact words, but he was obviously convinced of the foolishness of her venture. She felt depressed and frightened, for he, who had once seemed so confident, was now disheartened. Perhaps she was wrong; perhaps she should give up and go home. She felt a need to see Janet and Johnny, to be reassured by their own lively good humor. Another good drench of water, and her head seemed clearer. She would talk to them tonight and find out their true opinion of her determined search. Perhaps they felt the same way as Patrice. Perhaps they all believed it was hopeless and were only humoring her until she saw how little chance of success she had and gave up of her own accord. Now she would go back to the hotel and rest.

When she returned from the ladies' room, Patrice immediately stood up and searched her face with gentle concern. "You look better, but I think it best that we go now." Camilla merely nodded.

They made their way down the dark staircase, Camilla clinging to the banister for support. When they came over to the car, Patrice felt in his pocket. "Will you excuse me for a moment? I think I left my keys in the café."

She watched him go, surprised at his forgetfulness when he usually had such presence of mind. He disappeared into the shadow of the stairwell. She felt a tap at her waist. She whirled around. A little grimy urchin stood there, dressed in tattered rags. He seemed to pause for a minute, then, seizing her limp hand, shoved a piece of paper into it and fled, his dusty feet tearing around the corner into the anonymity of the Chicken Street crowds. Camilla's first thought was to run after him, but he was gone before she could put thought into action. So she took the crumpled paper in her hand and was unfolding it when Patrice returned.

"What have you got there?" he asked casually.

"I...I don't really know. It was suddenly in my hand. Some little boy—he ran away." She began to read the note and blanched. "Oh!"

Patrice took the paper from her unresisting hand and read:

You want to find out what happened to your sister. If you do not want firsthand experience of it, leave now. Leave.

His hand dropped. "Let me take you back to the hotel quickly." He would have ripped the little piece of paper up, but she laid a restraining hand on his arm and took it from him.

She stepped duly into the car, and he got behind the wheel.

"The threat is unmistakable," he said, starting the engine. "Someone must be following you *mademoiselle*, or how else would he find you here? It is most perplexing. I can only say I hope you take his advice."

But she sat and said nothing, staring at her fist clenched tightly around the grimy note.

SHE SAID LITTLE TO PATRICE as he drove her back to the hotel. When he left, she went straight to bed. Not to sleep—her mind was racing too fast for that—but she had to lie down, for her shaking legs could hardly support her. She realized now, too late, that she had probably overextended herself in the heat this morning. Only the knowledge that she would be seeing the Hagans that evening helped her through the afternoon. The paper lay neatly folded on her night table, ready to show to her American friends.

They came for her at nine. She was waiting in the lobby, wearing the same blue-and-white dress she had worn two nights before. Her face was still pale beneath her tan, and her eyes were large. However, the Hagans breezed in and seemed to notice nothing as they greeted her. Janet appeared cool but tired, wearing a charming printed maternity smock. Johnny was casually dressed in jeans and a light jacket.

"You look great," said Johnny, kissing her lightly on the cheek.

"So do you both," said Camilla, returning the compliment. Janet kissed her other cheek.

"What's in your hand?" asked Janet as they made for the elevator.

"I'll tell you when we really get down to business."

"Any leads yet?" said Johnny and Janet nearly simultaneously.

Camilla was too strung up to laugh, and replied, "I'll tell you everything I've discovered when we've had our drink." The elevator went up. "But fill me in. What is this place we're going to?"

"You might call it a cabaret," answered Johnny, "only they don't serve drinks. All Muslims are teetotalers by law, so only tea or coffee is on order here."

"By the way," broke in Janet, "how did you get on puppy sitting the other night, Camilla?"

Camilla winced at the memory but tried to play it down. "All right, except I had a bit of a fright. I was threatened by a scorpion in the bath." She hoped that she would not be called on to elaborate the tale, but Janet made clear no explanations were necessary.

"Yes, we heard," she said, laughing. "Don't be embarrassed, Camilla; it's a very funny story!"

"It wasn't funny to me!" exclaimed Camilla indignantly as the elevator stopped. How dared Malcolm Armstrong make her a laughingstock? He might be able to make her experience with the scorpion sound funny, but how could she explain the tension the air had been charged with in the presence of that giant of a man, or the turmoil her emotions had been thrown into? And not only that night, but yesterday, in the hotel.

"You'll have to get over your embarrassment quickly," said Johnny, smiling, "since we invited Malcolm along tonight."

"You what!" Camilla gasped, but they had opened the door off the landing and she found herself in the most extraordinary room she had ever seen. For some reason she'd expected it to be big and felt a moment's disappointment at the smallness of it, but as they plunged into its warm smoky atmosphere she was entranced by its coziness and momentarily forgot everything else. Low tables, rising about a foot off the ground, ringed the wall and were draped with thick soft carpets of the sort she had been shown that morning; carpets hung on the walls and covered the floor. The lighting was dark, and people lounged around the low tables sipping tea from glasses or smoking long cigarettes. Most of the clients were Afghan men, dressed in their light loose cotton garments, excellent for this hot climate, in bright or pastel colors, with turbans or skullcaps; some were dressed in Western suits and looked very hot and uncomfortable. Around a distant table two German couples squatted self-consciously.

Two of the Afghans left their table and came over to Camilla and the Hagans. One was shorter than the other, clean-shaven and handsome, with sloe black eyes and a turban wound around his dark head.

Camilla sensed a vague recognition. The other was tall, deeply tanned, with a cap of thick golden hair. His blue eyes pierced through hers. Camilla wanted to turn away, but they were already shaking hands.

"Salaam aleikom," said Malcolm Armstrong. Camilla's stomach lurched. He kissed Janet. "You're looking more beautiful than ever."

"And you more wild!" she replied lightly. "Be careful you don't frighten Camilla. She's not used to madmen."

"I know our Miss Simpson doesn't frighten easily." Camilla bristled at the use of the possessive, but he turned to her and took her hands in his own, looking into her face. Despite her trembling, she glared back with what she hoped was an expression of insolence.

He looked for a long moment. "You're pale, Miss Simpson," he said in a low voice. "Our climate not agreeing with you?"

"You might say that," she answered quickly, tugging her hands from his grip.

He gave a shrug so slight as to be almost imperceptible, then added, "Nice to see you again."

If he thinks I can forgive his unpardonable behavior as easily as that, he's mistaken, thought Camilla furiously. "Good evening, Mr. Armstrong," she said coolly. He gave her an odd look and then turned away with another shrug.

"Come and sit down," he said, showing them to a quiet corner of the room. "It's more crowded than usual tonight. What will you have?"

There were calls for coffee and tea. "Nothing for me, thanks," said Camilla shortly. A bit of light conversation followed, but Camilla sat stonily silent. She was in a turmoil—of all the people to spend an evening with, to have his company forced upon her...! She could hardly bear to talk to him. To look at his face, to hear his voice, confused her and made her all the more angry with him and with herself. As for him, he seemed hardly aware of her presence. She might have thought he was avoiding her as carefully as she was avoiding him.

What was he doing anyway, dressing up as if he were some native, she wondered scornfully. His whole aspect was foreign, unfriendly; Janet had called him mad, and perhaps he was. Surely the Hagans weren't thinking of bringing him in on her case?

The door to the little room opened again, and in came three Afghans in flamboyantly colored costumes. One carried a drum, the second an Indian sitar and the third a reed flute. A space was opened for them in the middle of the floor, where they immediately sat down cross-legged and, to the sound of great applause from the audience, launched into some pleasant background music, nothing too loud. Hot coffee and scented tea were brought in, and Camilla's group got down to business.

"I've asked Malcolm in to help," began Johnny, "because I think he'll be extremely useful. Speaks Persian like a native, don't you, kid?" There seemed something extraordinarily unfitting in calling Malcolm Armstrong a kid. He nodded coolly. "Also, the school term has just ended, which leaves Malcolm free to investigate full-time. I've had my holiday for the year, and at the moment things are pretty hectic."

Camilla remembered the reason why both her friends had been called away on that fateful evening, and felt a pang of guilt. She had been so wrapped up in her own problems that she couldn't remember one old man.

"How is Mr. Brody?" she asked, turning to Janet.

"Oh, he'll pull through," she replied cheerfully. "It's stateside for him, though. We'll miss him."

"Plenty more patients where he came from," Johnny retorted lightly, but Camilla could see the look of concern that had briefly flashed through his eyes at the mention of the dear old man. "So you see, Camilla, I might find it pretty difficult to get free time to go with you when you need it. Not only that, but Malcolm knows the whole terrain of the country much better than I do, and he's got a car of his own and an international driver's license, so he can take you wherever you need to go."

"I thought it might be a good idea to bring Ali Shah along," Malcolm continued. He indicated his dark friend, who inclined his head graciously. "I don't believe you know Ali Shah, Miss Simpson." His voice was studiously polite. The handsome Afghan held out his hand and Camilla shook it gingerly. *No friend of yours,* she could not help but think, *is a friend of mine.*

"Ali Shah is a student of mine at the university, and he helps me with my work over the summer."

"What exactly is your work, Mr. Armstrong?"

"I teach history at the international school during the term, and lecture at the university. In the holidays I research into early Afghan history. At the moment I'm preparing a thesis on the effect of Genghis Khan and the Mongol invasion—but then, this can hardly be interesting to you."

Camilla sat tight-lipped and said nothing.

"Suppose we start by reviewing everything we know about the circumstances of Camilla's sister's disappearance," suggested Janet, breaking the silence.

"It was somewhere between Kabul and Kandahar," supplied Camilla quickly. "We know because the last postcard I received from her was mailed from Kabul, and she said they were setting off for Kandahar the next day. Not only that, but the car was found about ten miles off the road to Kandahar, beyond Ghazni."

"Now, why would they leave the road?" said Johnny. "It's pretty wild country there, difficult even for people who know the area."

"Perhaps they wanted to sightsee a bit?" suggested Janet.

"Hardly likely. There's nothing but sand and rock and a few poplar trees between Ghazni and Kandahar," said Malcolm.

"Perhaps they were taking a shortcut," said Camilla.

Malcolm shook his head. "There is only one road from here to Kandahar. They haven't got shortcuts in Afghanistan. The car was ten miles off the road, they say—that means it was ten miles lost in some field of boulders and dust."

"The car had broken down," added Johnny. "Could it be they pulled off the road?"

"They wouldn't have pulled ten miles off the road," his wife pointed out.

"But since it had broken down, it's conceivable that Meghan left Tom to fix it while she went for help," said Camilla.

"That's one possibility," agreed Johnny. "In which case one of three things may have happened to her: she was either kidnapped, murdered or she died of exposure and thirst."

"I hope the first, if it has to be a choice of those three." Camilla shivered. "It *must* be the first; I *know* she isn't dead."

"And we all agree, or we wouldn't be here," said Janet kindly, looking around the circle.

"It seems as if it must be kidnapping," said Johnny. "There's no other option."

The circle was quiet for a moment, sunk in contemplation of the various possibilities surrounding Meghan's disappearance. It was Malcolm who broke the silence.

"That is the only option," he drawled, "if we accept the story of the breakdown and her going for help. But there are other possible explanations for her disappearance."

"Such as?" queried Camilla curtly.

"Could I see the postcard, Miss Simpson?"

She drew it slowly out of her bag. She was always reluctant to pass it to anyone and loath to hand her last link with her sister into those large masculine hands.

Malcolm read it with care and handed it to the quiet Ali Shah. Then he sat back, legs folded, arms wrapped around his knees, and commanded Camilla's attention with his eyes.

"Tell me a little about your sister, Miss Simpson. Was she fond of adventure—excitement?"

Camilla felt herself bristling against his haughty manner, but deemed it best to keep her temper. "Yes," she replied. "She's always been the adventurous one in our family, the outgoing one. That's why the idea of living in Singapore and traveling across Asia appealed to her."

"She liked new experiences, I suppose?" How could he make it sound so nasty?

"Yes, she liked trying out new things, but basically she is a nature lover—camping and ecology, that sort of thing."

"Did she ever say she'd like to get back to nature, to live in the rough?"

"Yes." Camilla was intrigued despite herself. "How did you know? She used to talk all the time of how people were happier and healthier when they were living in the wild, living in what she called a natural state."

"And was your sister happily married, Miss Simpson?"

Camilla's eyes flamed, and she tossed her auburn mane. "How dare you insinuate such a thing!" she exclaimed. "The state of her marriage is none of your business."

His laugh was deeply sardonic. "Your reaction tells me everything I asked; it's obvious she wasn't."

Once again Camilla's temperature was dangerously near boiling point. What could she conceal from a man of such quick perception?

Johnny saw the look in her eyes. "What's all this leading to, Malcolm?" he cut in, as if anxious to avoid upsetting her. "What are you trying to prove?"

"In the best tradition of crime novelettes, I'm merely trying to establish her character. Now, we have a picture of a woman, young, idealistic, vibrant, loving nature and adventure, and unhappy in her marriage. An accurate sketch, would you say, Miss Simpson?" Camilla had to admit that it was so; he had drawn her sister's character perfectly. "What about her husband?"

"Tom?" She thought for a moment. "I suppose I never really knew him, but what I saw of him I found dull and temperamental, but not often emotional, and very lazy. That was really the worst thing about him. He had ambition and he was greedy, but he never really did anything about it, because he didn't have enough drive. He was always looking for the easy way to anything. That's how I saw him, anyway."

"A masterly sketch," drawled the tall man. "In other words, he shared neither her ideals nor her aspirations."

Camilla paused. "I must admit," she finally said half-unwillingly, "that I could never understand why they married. I think it was the job in Singapore that won Meghan over."

"It's quite possible, then, don't you think, Ali Shah?"

"I think it more than likely."

"What?" demanded Janet eagerly. "Tell us!"

"It was really the first thing I thought of," replied Malcolm. "She's run away with the Kuchis."

Johnny laughed. "You're crazy, Malcolm! Run off with the nomads?"

"It's happened before."

"You cannot call the possibility remote," added Ali Shah. His voice was so reasonable that he compelled attention. "It would fit in with what we know of her character, and explain the fact that no body has been found."

"Oh, but this is incredible—" Camilla began, then stopped, groping for words.

"Why do you find the suggestion that your sister has joined up with a romantic band of primitive wanderers less credible than a kidnapping, Miss Simpson? Do you know about the Kuchis?" Camilla turned her head to Malcolm and shook it slowly. She knew no more than the name, that it was given to a group of nomads, and that the dress she wore came from their tribe.

"They are a people as old as Afghanistan itself," he taught her. "No one is sure from whom they are descended, only that nomadism has always been their way of life and it is essential to them if they are to survive. The rise of modern nations and new borders has begun to curb their wanderings, but they would as soon die as settle down to a life of farming. They live from their livestock—camels, sheep, goats, horses—and they must follow the seasons in order to find them pasture. They spend the summer in the uplands of the Hindu Kush—" his hand gestured away to an imaginary north, toward those fierce mountains "—and in the winter—" here his hand swept to the corresponding south "—they gather everything together and journey down to the lower country. Each tribe, each family, has its own summer and winter grazing lands that it has held the rights to since time immemorial.

"Many of the chiefs are men of immense wealth, yet they live in drafty leather tents, walk barefooted, their riches draped around their women in the form of jewelry. You cannot imagine the splendor of a Kuchi caravan making its majestic way across the desert, camels swaying, laden with rich brocades, folded tents, clothes and carpets, the women in their flowing rainbow dresses, the men impassive, mounted on shining horses with great liquid eyes. They are, in my opinion, the most beautiful people in the world, with eyes dark as coals and thick black plaits of hair, tall and straight backed and long limbed, striding through the hills. To many people they symbolize a perfect existence, for their life seems, on the face of it, to be empty of materialism and the petty problems of civilized Western life. They represent a freedom that our farms and our factories, offices and cities have robbed us of."

His voice was golden. Camilla, all grievances forgotten, was enraptured by the vision this professor conjured up. In her mind's eye a line of people and animals moved gracefully in silhouette, heightened against the backdrop of a setting sun, framed by snowcapped mountains. She heard the jingling of silver bells, the bark of dogs and the quavering call of the flocks of sheep. Malcolm was lecturing now, as to an audience, and he had them in the palm of his hand. For a moment Camilla felt the same urge to travel wherever the seasons might take her. His very words were magic.

He continued weaving the same beauty. "Many are tempted to give up everything they have for a taste of this freedom, for a windblown tent in the desert at night, for snow-fed cascades in the high pastures. For them, in an imperfect world, they see a mirage of perfection." He paused, letting the word take effect. "I say mirage, for the Kuchis are plagued by their own pitfalls, their own problems and hazards. Their life is one of hardship and endless walking in heat and snow. Disease is rife. They wash clothes rarely and themselves less often. Death is no stranger to them. They had been born and bred to this life and in it they thrive. Not so the Westerners."

Camilla sensed the spell beginning to break, and she lowered her eyes almost regretfully. She startled herself. For several minutes now she had been listening openmouthed to him speak, almost hanging on his every word. But he was skillfully leading them right off the track. She hadn't come to Afghanistan to listen to a lecture on the history of nomad peoples, for heaven's sake! She struggled with herself to wipe his picture from her mind and get a proper perspective on the situation. But he was still speaking.

"Three or four years ago a girl, an American, a student of mine, ran away from her family and was found with the Kuchis three months later, living in the most appalling squalor."

"You're being ridiculous," Camilla broke in, her sharp voice cutting above his low one. "If it's so disgusting, then my sister could hardly have gone with them."

Slowly Malcolm's voice lost its magic, returning to the tone she remembered, light, arrogant, with a note of sarcasm.

"The Kuchis live their life the way they like it. It suits them. To some ignorant foreigners it appears superficially attractive. In her postcard your sister said that she admired them very much—'I long for such a life.' Her exact words. Anyway, different tribes are different tribes, some better, some worse. She may enjoy it. Some foreigners remain forever. Others beg to be taken away. For it's likely that when she joined up with the Kuchis she enjoyed herself at first and when she later found that life with them was not to her taste, they would not let her go."

"Is that possible?"

"Anything is possible. This is as likely a solution as any we've yet proposed."

Camilla sat cross-legged, tensely twisting the hem of her dress between her slender fingers. The two solutions they had so far discussed were, on the face of it, equally likely; yet somehow she now felt sure that Malcolm had come nearer to the truth. How she hated to give him that satisfaction.

"If, as you say, my sister is living with the Kuchis, I cannot understand why she hasn't contacted me— even a word to stop me from worrying."

"If, as I suggested, she is being held against her will, they have probably prevented her from having contact with anyone outside the tribe. Do you think this is possible? Does your sister have any special talents that would make her invaluable to the tribe?"

"Yes," admitted Camilla slowly. "She's a qualified nurse."

Malcolm grabbed her arms roughly, and she felt her flesh tremble with dislike beneath his grasp. "You obviously haven't grasped the implications of this at all," he said harshly. "It's imperative that you not keep any information back from us, however small. Things like your sister's unhappy marriage, or the fact that she is a nurse. Each further supports my theory that she is living with the Kuchis."

"I know. I know!" Camilla retorted.

"Now, what else are you keeping back that you haven't told us?"

"Malcolm, please!" Janet interrupted.

"It's all right," said Camilla, the warmth in her voice meant for Janet alone. She shook off the offending hand. "In fact there are two things I must tell you, although I hadn't meant to." There, it was out. Now she would have to tell.

"I've been talking to a friend of mine," she began, and noticed that the muscles in Malcolm's jaw had begun to tighten. "And he. . . he knew my sister and brother-in-law pretty well while they were here. He seems to think that it wasn't an accident at all— Tom's death, I mean."

"What are you saying?" demanded Malcolm.

"He thinks Tom was killed—I mean murdered." She was confused by the steady blue glare Malcolm had fixed on her. She glanced away, then looked up at him again.

His face was white. "You've been talking about this with other people!" His voice was level, but it was all the more terrifying for the repressed fury she could sense beneath it.

"He. . . he said he knew my sister."

"Who is he?"

Transfixed by the anger in his eyes, she could only whisper, "Patrice Desmarets."

"Oh, Camilla," sighed Janet, before Malcolm slammed his fist on the table with a ringing blow.

Then he leaped up and stood, facing away from her, his hands deep in his pockets.

"I knew it, I knew it," he muttered.

"And why shouldn't I? He's been just as much help as you have, Mr. Armstrong." Her voice was equally low and angry.

"Let's not quarrel," he said at last. Her anger subsided a little—it seemed this was all the apology she could expect to receive. He went on, "What's done is done. I only wish you hadn't. What did he have to say?"

So you are *interested in what Patrice has to say,* thought Camilla. "We were talking about the report the embassy sent me. He didn't seem too impressed by it, and to tell you the truth, neither was I. He said something like, 'They have no idea how Tom really died.'"

What a man of swift mood Malcolm was, thought Camilla, for after she said this he took her hands, almost tenderly, not roughly like before. He was more changeable than the weather; she couldn't keep up with him. Only the strange trembling of her skin was the same as at the first touch.

"Camilla," he said, "I've warned you before. Now you must promise me something. If I'm to help you, you must never see that Desmarets fellow again. Don't ever talk to him, never consult him, and above all never tell him anything we have found out."

Looking into his eyes Camilla instinctively wanted to trust him. It went against all logic—since her arrival he had scarcely spoken to her, but had insulted or patronized her; whereas Patrice really had been a help. Logically it was wrong to trust Malcolm Armstrong, but his clear blue eyes demanded it of her. She remembered the hypnotic power of Patrice's eyes, and shuddered. When she was trapped in the brown gaze of the Frenchman, it felt as if her will was being drained from her bones, and she could do nothing but acquiesce to him, feeling all the time confused, half-fluid. But this man Malcolm...he seemed to give her back all her energy in his electrically charged gaze, making her a fighter. Up till now she'd fought with him—she'd felt almost driven to fight with him—but if she could only choose to trust him, she could turn all this energy in a more productive direction. Instinct said to trust him, logic warned *don't*! But could she trust her instinct?

"Tell me why," she demanded, her keen gaze probing his. "Tell me why I should forget Patrice, and I'll trust you."

"Can't you believe me without proof?" he replied.

"It's just not logical," she said, spreading out her hands in a half-unconscious begging movement. "Patrice *has* helped me—and you know he has, too."

"He has ulterior motives," said Malcolm darkly.

Camilla's instinct nodded agreement to this. She had sensed something intangible but wrong about Patrice—or at least in the considerate, well-bred, altruistic character the Frenchman had presented to her as his own. It was, she thought in a flash of insight, like gold lettering on tin, badly applied and beginning to flake off. If only Malcolm could provide her with some real proof to corroborate what he was saying....

"How do you know?" she persisted. "What has he done?"

"It's better you shouldn't know. This is a case in which what you know can really hurt you," said Malcolm. "Please believe us; we're doing what's best for you and your sister."

"It just doesn't make sense," Camilla responded. "How can I make a promise based on such a flimsy reason? He really has been a help to me, and that must count for something."

"You're repeating that over and over," said Janet, "as if repetition could make it true."

"I just can't promise!" Seeing the concern on Janet's generally cheerful face, Camilla went on, almost agonized, "How can I promise not to see someone who might hold the clue to my sister's disappearance?"

"It wouldn't be any advantage to you if he did," said Malcolm urgently.

"Tell me why!" she repeated anxiously.

"Camilla, please!" exclaimed Janet. "Malcolm knows what he's doing."

"And I don't, I suppose," Camilla snapped without thinking. But then the real reason for this argument was suddenly obvious to her. She had broken away from England, from her sheltered life, and stepped willingly straight into a situation fraught with danger. Here she could make or break her faith in herself. Here she had to stand on her own two feet. If she followed Malcolm Armstrong blindly, doing what he said, going where he went, believing what he told her to believe without reason or proof, she would be no better off than she had been in London, and Malcolm would simply be another Jeff. She had to begin to have some faith in her own judgment; she had to be allowed to make her own mistakes. Otherwise what would she ever be but a child?

"If you don't end your acquaintance with Desmarets, there's little we can do to help you," said Johnny quietly.

"Very well, then," said Camilla, oddly calm. "I'm terribly sorry, but I hope you will understand. You've been more help to me than I can ever repay. But now it seems it has to be a choice between unquestioningly accepting Malcolm's word or believing in my own integrity—and you see that I must choose the second. Goodbye, and thank you."

She stood and walked from the room as evenly as if she had just concluded a convivial evening with close friends. Her mind was peaceful. Her decision was made. She had removed from her life the disturbing presence of the tall man.

By great good luck the elevator was waiting. Without breaking the flow of her movement she got in, and as the doors closed behind her she pressed the third button and began the slow descent. Her mind was strangely contented.

The elevator halted with a jerk at the next floor down. She leaned and watched the doors slide smoothly open.

Before she had a chance to gasp a tall man had darted in, the doors closing behind him. He pressed the four button, but between floors he pressed the stop, and the elevator ground to a halt. His tall frame almost touched the ceiling of the elevator, standing between Camilla and the control panel.

"What was the second thing you meant to tell us, Miss Simpson?" he asked in a drawl. "I think it slipped your mind."

"You and I have nothing more to say to each other." She tried to speak coldly, dispassionately, but how could mere mental effort control her fear, this trembling in her limbs?

"On the contrary, we have a great deal to say. Our relationship has hardly begun."

"I consider it terminated. Please let me go."

"Not until I've said what I have to say. You seem remarkably confused in your mind, and I hope—" his lips twisted sardonically "—that the caustic sarcasm and knife-edged accuracy of what I'm about to say will clear up your mental mess."

"*If* I needed that sort of treatment—which, let me assure you, I don't—you're hardly the person I'd go to for it. Anyway, I know my own mind, thank you."

"You are a pretentious little hypocrite, aren't you? Making grand speeches about personal integrity when you're still wet behind the ears. What would you know about it?"

Camilla looked at him with dignity. "Perhaps that's why I'm trying to find it."

"My God, woman, I really am trying to help you, despite what you think. Why you've taken such a ridiculously aggressive stance with me I don't know."

How long was he going to keep her trapped here, Camilla wondered. It was beginning to grow claustrophobic in the elevator, and she felt edgy. "This playacting is ludicrous," she snapped. "Let this lift go down at once—there may be people wanting to use it."

"I need to know the rest of what you meant to tell us upstairs."

"Take me down first, and then I'll show you," she bargained.

"I'm afraid not. The elevator's broken—it needs some information to fix it."

"All right!" she exclaimed. "You win!" She pulled the crumpled note out of her handbag. "If you read it maybe you'll leave me alone."

He took it and read it once, then twice.

"I think," she said cautiously, "it must be some kind of practical joke. It shook me up at first, but really it's so corny. . . ."

"Why didn't you tell me?" he demanded roughly.

"It isn't important, it's just a joke—"

"What do you think this is—a game?" His hands raked through his shock of flaxen hair, thick wavy strands of gold. Suddenly Camilla's fingers itched to do the same; the feel must be exquisite. . . . She pulled herself up sharply, alarmed, and missed his next words.

". . . a little game—oh, God! What am I going to do with you? You ought to be old enough to know this isn't some little round of hide-and-seek in the back garden. It's life and death—something you shouldn't be playing at your age. How old are you? Nineteen?"

"I'm twenty-one."

"Oh, yes, well, that makes all the difference. Two whole years."

"I'm tough enough." Camilla was surprised at her

own words, but felt compelled to follow them. "I'm capable of looking after myself. My sister has faced death, perhaps—I won't be any less brave, for her sake. She has had to undergo a great deal, and I am prepared to undergo as much."

"Regular little heroine, aren't you? Your words sound very impressive, but actions, as they say, speak louder. Quite frankly, I don't think you're capable of looking after yourself at a garden tea party."

"I don't see what I have done to deserve such remarks, nor why you feel called upon to deliver them." But Camilla, even as she spoke, could not draw her eyes away from his hair, his face, his eyes and lips. They towered over her in confusing proximity.

"You can't see what you've done? But the mere fact that you can say that illustrates what I've been trying to tell you. You're the girl who called on me in desperation to save her from a small and harmless insect." He was smiling, mocking now. "You're the girl who spends her time doing things she's been warned not to do, from walking around in sleeveless dresses to divulging secrets to any sympathetic Frenchman who happens along; who despite having been warned about him, jumps into bed—"

This time he was quicker than she, and caught her hand before it could reach its mark.

"You have no justification for saying that," she protested, struggling against his imprisoning grip. "I don't jump into bed with anyone!"

"Maybe so, maybe no. Your morals don't interest me. But I wanted to see your reaction."

"How dare—"

He stopped her words, a hand placed swiftly over her mouth, and with the other twisting her arm behind her back, drew her head and body nearer to him, until he whispered in her ear.

"How dare you!" He mimicked her expression precisely. "My dear Miss Simpson, you may be an attractive and exciting young woman, but that very proper admonition won't get you far in Afghanistan. I'll soon teach you that the proprieties one observes here are very, very different from Western ideas. He who dares, wins. That is the law."

He leaned even closer, until his warm lips almost touched her ear. "I, for instance, might dare this." He ran a wet tongue around her pulsing earlobe, until every hair on the nape of her neck tingled and quivered. At the same time he pressed back on her left arm, not painfully, but pulling her even tighter to him. With his other hand he stroked her lip until the sensitive skin responded, and then he lowered his head. "And I might dare this," he murmured, the hot tip of his tongue describing delicious circles of pleasure on her soft neck. He let her other arm drop, and one hand slowly traveled up her trembling back till it reached her shoulder, upon which he exerted a sensual kneading pressure.

Camilla felt totally enwrapped by his powerful body, folded into warmth. She was dizzy from the ceaseless motion of his tongue, not quite responding to his caresses, and yet unable, and glad she was unable because she was unwilling, to draw away. His hard arms encircled her waist, lying there for a moment, the fingers gently pressing, then moved upward with maddening slowness, the fingertips as light as a butterfly on the soft curve of her breast where they rested at last.

She uttered a tiny sigh and let her body move into his. She hardly remembered who or what he was, or indeed she was, and it no longer mattered where they were. All that mattered was that this was pleasure, sublime pleasure, and she could sense that what she was tasting now was no more than the first delicious drop from a jar of nectar that promised to be bottomless. She raised her mouth to his and he, so tall as he was, bent to reach her lips. She saw the thick inviting mane of golden hair and indulged, twining and retwining her fingers through each fine strand. Their open mouths met, and for one drunken moment she lapped the wine.

"Well," he drawled, pulling away abruptly, "perhaps you are a big girl after all." He smiled, his clear blue eyes looking beyond her. Then it was as if he gave himself a mental shake and his eyes became alert. He held up the note, which, after all this time, he still held in his hand. "May I take this home with me? I've a feeling there's more here than meets the eye."

Camilla could hardly believe that her bliss had been shattered so quickly. She still felt his hot tongue on her ear, his soft lips on hers. How could he drop it so suddenly, as if it were some common experience, and pick up the thread of a conversation his kisses had obliterated from her mind? Perhaps, she thought bitterly, such encounters were everyday to him. She touched her lips and folded her arms protectively across her vulnerable chest. "How can you? Why did you?" Her head spun and she could hardly focus.

"Why," he laughed, and this time there was no trace of sarcasm or derision, just a hearty laugh, as if they had enjoyed a good joke together. "Why, you asked me to show you how I dared, and so I did. After all, a young lady in your position ought to be taught a thing or two—about the law—if she's to look after herself."

Camilla knew that she must take her cue from him. There was no place here for tears and tantrums. She had already returned to cold sobriety. So she drew herself up to her full height, which brought her eyes level with his shoulder. She looked up at him angrily.

"I've told you before and I'll tell you again, Mr. Armstrong: I don't need your help or your advice. I never asked for it and I don't want it. It's obvious to me that you only volunteered out of some inflated egotistical idea you have that you and only you can solve the entire mystery, and not out of any real concern for me or my sister. Well, I can do without that sort of help, thank you."

"You're wrong," replied Malcolm. "I said I would help you because Johnny asked me to. I care for both the Hagans and I'd do a lot for them. More, it seems, than you are willing to do. Have you any idea how much you hurt their feelings tonight—after all they've done for you, when they had absolutely no need to help a total stranger?"

"I'm sorry. I was upset," replied Camilla automatically. But why should she apologize to him? He was the one who had upset her in the first place and continued to do so even now.

"So," she added, "it seems you don't even believe my sister is alive."

"Belief doesn't come into it. My job is to find out if she is alive, and if she is, where she is."

"Job!" Camilla was stunned. How strange the man was, who seemed to regard almost dispassionately events and situations that other people—herself, for instance—might find highly emotionally charged. "You look on it as a job? It's perfectly obvious to me that it's no more than a sort of obligatory burden to you. If you feel that way about me—I mean about Meghan—then you needn't bother."

"This may be difficult for you to understand," he said sardonically, "but I don't take up responsibilities only to put them down again as soon as I find them difficult, or tiresome, or boring. It's an attitude you might do well to try to emulate."

So he found her boring, unenjoyable! So she was a duty! She could no longer hold back her. . . what was it. . . disappointment, and in a choking voice cried out, "I want none of your attitudes. Leave me alone!"

"Oh, no, I've taken you on and I'm stuck with you."

"I'm also stuck with you," she retorted bitterly.

"Come now, my dear Miss Simpson, that wasn't your reaction a moment ago. I recall for a while there I almost thought I had won you over to appreciate my company."

His arm reached out to her, and instinctively she put out her own hand halfway to it, looking into his face, knowing her own eyes were already alight with anticipation, and hating herself for it. She had learned a great deal about herself in a very few minutes and this, she knew, she could not fight. She was too weak from the last encounter.

However, his own eyes had the power to make her draw back, for they gleamed narrowly, like the eyes of an eagle. Nothing could be further from the tenderness she had so recently embraced. She wanted now to turn away, but she was cornered in the elevator. There was nothing in his face of either the warmth that had overwhelmed her or the bantering mockery that followed it; only cold flintiness. She had the strangest feeling that he was putting on some sort of mask, but why, she couldn't fathom. Before she could think on it he'd grabbed her arms determinedly and pulled her to him, and though she struggled she could not escape his relentless grip. He held her around the waist with one tanned arm while the other hand grasped her chin firmly and pulled it up. She twisted violently. "Let me go!"

His face came toward hers, the deeply bronzed visage with the long straight nose and the eyes of cold flame that looked more than ever like those of a bird of prey. She was afraid, not of herself this time, but of him. She closed her eyes. She barely whispered the words, "Let me go," waiting for his mouth to seal her own.

Instead she felt the brush of his lips on her cheek, a sharp intake of his breath, then the loosening of his grip. Startled, she sprang back against the wall. The elevator gave a lurch and started downward.

His eyes were hooded, his gaze strangely unreadable; then he seemed to force himself to smile. "Miss Simpson, you do get worked up over a little peck on the cheek. All in the spirit of friendship. Anyone would think I wanted to impugn your honor; which, I assure you, is quite safe with me. I'll get to work on this note. Where did you get it?"

Camilla was bewildered by the instantaneous change of mood. Could she have been mistaken about the dangerous glitter in his eyes, so suddenly changed to that mysterious look and the effort at platonic camaraderie? She could only reply woodenly to his question, "From some little boy on Chicken Street. I was with Monsieur Desmarets."

The elevator halted at the ground floor, but the door did not open yet. Malcolm kept his finger firmly on the closed button.

"Please don't forget what I've said about Patrice," he told her gravely. "I think I know what you think of me, but believe me, take my advice on this or I may be too late to help you. He is a dangerous man." Still stunned, Camilla could only nod her head vaguely. Malcolm let the door slide open.

"We ought to be friends, Miss Simpson," he said, smiling, as he walked out. "You see, I don't bite."

Camilla stepped out into the lobby and waited a moment, unsure whether to go left or right, forward or backward, and feeling that no matter which decision she made, she would end up going in the wrong direction.

CHAPTER SIX

AFTER A FITFUL SLEEP Camilla woke to a clear, hot, bright, matter-of-fact day and found she was mistress of herself again. Her first realization was that her behavior the night before had been abominable, and she knew she had wronged the Hagans. The thought of losing their friendship distressed her. So she wrote a long note to them, apologizing, and gave it to a fellow guest who was traveling that way in the evening and promised to drop it in their mailbox. Somehow Camilla could not face the thought of phoning them.

Her next thoughts were cool, collected, rational ones on the subject of Malcolm Armstrong. A fevered night had forced one inescapable fact to her attention: physically she found him extremely attractive. The combination of shining hair and penetrating blue eyes set in a tanned masculine face was quite overwhelming, but since she could admit this to herself, half the battle was won; she could fight this attraction. It was impossible to think of any entanglements with him. In the first place, such a development could only complicate the real issue at hand—finding Meghan and finding out why she had disappeared. But, she acknowledged, Malcolm would be invaluable in her search; he knew the language, the land, the people, the ins and outs of the bureaucracy they might have to fight their way through, and he had qualities of character that made him an excellent choice for a commander.

Arrogance, for one, she thought as she tallied on her fingers. A ready wit. A sense of superiority. Self-assertiveness. Self-righteousness. Impatience with delays. Yes, they would do, she decided, for someone who had to hack through red tape and desert to find a missing Englishwoman. As a personality, of course, he was insufferable. She nodded her head at this thought, as if she could take strength from it. *So listen to me, Camilla, no foolishness. Close your eyes to his admittedly quite stunning good looks and remember he can turn that charm on and off whenever he feels like it. Concentrate on his bad qualities—that'll keep you from being swept off your feet.* She sighed resignedly, having reached the conclusion that, insufferable and attractive as he might be, she would bear with Malcolm Armstrong for her sister's sake.

It was Saturday, and she spent the rest of the morning in frustration at the British Embassy, trying to discover any scraps of additional information. The embassy itself was an imposing residence, massive and white, and the people were cooperative, but there was little they could tell her apart from what she already knew. The young man she spoke to was almost as recent an arrival as she was, and all he could do for her was to point out on a large-scale map of Kabul the site of the British cemetery where Thomas was buried.

For lunch she returned to the hotel and then spent the afternoon on a chore Janet had suggested: cataloging all the clues and leads they had in the mystery of her sister's disappearance, however unlikely they seemed. It was something she had not looked forward to doing, but actually found it interesting when she got down to it. Things began to come clearer in her mind. Most important of all was the question: why was the car found ten miles off the Kandahar road? She thought through several possible answers, but none seemed suitable. Perhaps the car had been driven off the road by someone else—but Tom's body was found under the car, the back of his head injured, so he must have been alive to crawl under the car in an attempt to fix it. The report said it had broken down, but they could not say whether on the road or in the desert. Tom must have been alive when the car broke down— unless he had been put under it. But then how could he have cracked his skull?

Her mind balked at the thought she had nearly voiced. Who could do such a thing to Tom? And if they had, where was Meghan? Unless Meghan. . . .

She was saved from her thoughts by the ring of the telephone.

"Hello, Mademoiselle Simpson?"

She cradled the phone in the hollow of her shoulder.

"Monsieur Desmarets! What can I do for you?"

"I am hoping you will do me the honor of dining with me this evening, since I have now missed that pleasure two nights running."

Malcolm's warnings and the humiliating experience that had accompanied them were still uppermost in her mind. But she did not pause.

"I would love to. What time?"

Patrice sounded mildly surprised at her quick acceptance. "I'll send the chauffeur around at eight."

"Where are we going?"

"Ah, it is a surprise, *mademoiselle*. I will see you. *Au revoir!*"

Although she supposed an early night would do her more good than all the Patrices in the world, Camilla looked forward to seeing him again, and being reassured by his charm that she was to him no boring obligation. The day's activity, combined with the altitude, had tired her.

But this is only the beginning, she reminded herself sternly. *We've got to toughen you up, my girl. Work up a resistance.* And to more than just long hours and mountain heights, she told herself. She would show Malcolm Armstrong that she was capable of holding her own in any situation, and above all that Patrice Desmarets was a man to be trusted. He certainly knew how to treat a woman as a lady, not roughly and rudely. Her judgment of people was as sound as Malcolm's, and she would show it.

The evening soon came. Camilla refused to wear that disastrous blue-and-white dress, for it reminded her too much of those occasions when *he* had been there. Instead she achieved a sophisticated effect with a clinging creation in beige jersey. As she reclined in the back of the car, she could almost feel herself a credit to the urbane refinement of Patrice.

The car took her into a part of the city she had never seen before. The roads and houses created an atmosphere of newness, as if they did not belong to the rest of the ancient city. All was laid out in ordered rows; the pavement was clean and the marble shiny. Tree leaves glimmered in the growing dusk.

"What part of the city is this?" she asked Patrice's driver, but he spoke only French, so she got no response.

They drew up at last before a gaudily lit building, replete with multicolored awnings over the door and windows. The Golden Calf blazed above the door in neon letters. From inside came snatches of raucous music as every now and then a person wandered in or out of the great double doors. She got out of the car and, looking about her suspiciously, went reluctantly in.

The lights were dim, the conversation low, but this was amply made up for by the flashing lights and wild electric screams of the rock group on stage. To her left was a round bar where boys and girls in jeans or shorts lounged, and above it a fish pond where goldfish swam round and round in tight little circles. It was obviously a nightclub patronized by the younger set in the expatriate community. She could not think why Patrice had brought her to such a place.

She was beginning to wonder if he was there when he was suddenly at her elbow, his advance having been camouflaged by the gloom and the blinding electricity from the stage.

"I have a table for us," he shouted. "You will find it quieter around here." He led her around behind the bar, and they sat at a little double table shadowed by a palm tree. Camilla looked at Patrice and was surprised to see how well he fitted in here among the noise and action. She had always thought him a man of tranquillity but now began to feel she had misjudged him. Groups of teenagers greeted him every so often as they passed by.

They ordered some sweet-and-sour Chinese dishes and some pancake rolls, which seemed to be the specialty of the place. The food was not especially good nor was Camilla hungry—the atmosphere put her off—but under Patrice's gaze she felt uneasy and toyed with her food, looking down at her plate to avoid meeting his eyes.

"Do you like it here?" asked Patrice conversationally over dinner.

"I...I don't know. It's certainly active," she replied truthfully.

"I brought you here because I thought we could talk without being overheard."

"Why, what have you got to tell me?"

"It's more what I've got to show you, *mademoiselle*," he replied, leaning over the table confidentially. "Now close your eyes."

Suspiciously she shut them, wondering what the mystery was about. She felt her heart beating; she was disturbed.

"Now you may open them."

At first she had a minute's difficulty focusing in the gloom. Then she saw a glimmering gold object. She looked closely: a watch—a familiar watch.

"May I hold it?" He gave it to her. Slowly Camilla turned it over, hoping and fearing. What would it prove if her supposition were right? Silently she read the inscription on the back:

To our dearest Meghan—Happy Sixteenth.
With love from Mother and Father.

"Meghan's birthday watch! But how did you get it?"

"I spotted it in the bazaar; I remembered seeing it on your sister's wrist—a very distinctive watch. Reporters have to have an eye for this sort of thing."

"But where—I mean, what does it mean? Is she alive or dead? What does it prove? Where did you find it?"

"I do not know whether you have been to the Kuchi bazaar or not. It is behind Jadi Maiwand street in the old city. They sell all sorts of nomad jewelry there—I found it in one of the shops."

"So!" Camilla was breathless. "She *is* with the nomads!"

"With the nomads, you say?" muttered Patrice to himself. "So you think she is traveling with the Kuchis. But what tribe?"

"I don't know. But this must prove she is with one of them." Camilla was nearly beside herself with excitement. "After all this time—definite proof! It seems like a miracle. Which shop was it?"

"Now, you mustn't get too optimistic," said Patrice slowly. "To the contrary: this is almost sure confirmation that she is dead."

Camilla started. "Dead—no, it can't be; I know it can't! How can you say that? I don't believe it!" Her breathing was agitated, her voice tremulous.

"It seems to me quite obvious," continued Patrice calmly. "Would your sister otherwise part with that watch?"

"No, she loved it; it was a present from my parents. She hardly ever wore it because she was afraid of losing it."

"I would say the shop owner must have got it from some robber, who either killed her and stole the watch or took it when he found her dead body."

The thought was too awful to contemplate, and Camilla put her hands unconsciously to her ears, as though not to think. Then, in a sudden jerky movement, she covered her mouth and looked at Patrice through eyes as wide as those of a startled fawn. A piece of the puzzle seemed to have just, frighteningly, fallen into place, though she wasn't yet sure what the total picture was.

"Why are you so vehement about my sister's death? The other day, at the Green Lantern, and now tonight—why do you want to persuade me that she is dead, when the fact of her being still alive is the one thing I must hold onto?"

"Your faith in the continuing existence of your sister is touching but naive—and dangerous," he replied. Then he added some glib excuse, but Camilla did not hear it. She only read the message in the hard glittering brown eyes. His words had been lying all along, luring and beguiling her, probing her for facts; his eyes had never lied, and she had a paralyzing moment when she knew that she could not trust him, should not have trusted him, and had said far too much already.

Some logical element in her mind told her that to shut up suddenly like a clam would be too suspicious. She stammered out some remark, hardly hearing what she said, for his word *dangerous* echoed in her ears and was mirrored in his eyes. She saw herself reflected in his narrow dark pupils, almost as if he had captured her and held her imprisoned there. Her hand tightened around the watch till the metal bit into her skin.

"Do you know...Malcolm Armstrong?" she asked jerkily to see what effect the name had on him. It was a risk, but she had to take it. At the same time she slung her handbag over her shoulder, for it contained too many valuables to leave lying unattended.

The Frenchman rolled his eyes and struck his forehead with a very histrionic gesture. "Ah! You certainly choose your friends for contrast."

Camilla's thoughts raced. *But which of you is my friend?* A pair of blond teenagers in Maple Leaf sweatshirts sat down at the table next to them.

"Hardly private anymore," whispered Patrice to her. "We shall dance."

"It's not really my style," Camilla tried to protest, but he already had her up and sweeping toward the stage. The number was a heavy rock song, loud and tuneless, and she moved rather desperately among the gyrating young bodies. Patrice, as might be expected, was excellent at this sort of dancing, and he tended to lurch near her, whisper something and then lurch away again.

"So you think she's with the Kuchis. What other proof do you have?"

Camilla cast desperately in her mind for some noncommittal reply that would not give away anything more to Patrice.

"Just that it...fits, I suppose, with everything she's said."

Suddenly he grabbed her and pulled her to the wall, not at all gently. "What did she say? Have you seen her? I must know everything if I'm to help you."

Camilla's flesh crawled at his touch. "No," she gasped, "I haven't seen her—don't be ridiculous." She struggled to get free from his grip.

"But you say she spoke to you?" His face was as grim and cold as a hatchet, and as murderous. Camilla was too frightened not to speak the truth.

"No, it was in a postcard I received from her before she disappeared." She gave a sharp twist and was free.

"I must see it," Patrice demanded, reaching out for her again. To forestall him, she rummaged the card out of her handbag and thrust it at him.

"Here, read it for yourself."

He seized it and read it avidly, and she could see his eyes grow calm as he reached the end. He returned it to her, visibly relieved. "That's all right, then. Kuchis, *crois-tu*?" And almost musingly, *"Mais la quelle? Quelle tribu, je me demande?"* He was thoughtful for a moment. "Will you excuse me? I want to make a phone call that might help you."

She was about to ask him what the call was about, but he had already hurried away. She shivered. It always unnerved her when he spoke in French, for he spoke to himself and at such times seemed almost to forget her presence.

She intended to make her way back to the table, but seeing it had been occupied in their absence, she returned to her space by the wall. She sensed someone come up to her and turned to look into the fresh face of a girl, surely no more than fifteen, with dull dark eyes and heavy lank black hair.

"Hi," said the teenager, giving a smile of straight strong teeth. "I'm Nina. My father's with the United Nations. I see you're Patrice's new bird."

A shiver went down Camilla's back at that. "I'm Camilla," she replied, giving an unsure smile. "But I'm not Patrice's 'bird'—or anyone's."

Was it her imagination, or did the girl's face fall? An angry hungry look came over it. "Well, you're his friend, anyway. Put in a good word for me and Angelo—ask him why he doesn't invite us to any more of his parties. And come round to our place next Saturday—tell him he can bring the door prize, if you know what I mean."

"No, I don't." Camilla backed away. "Anyway, I don't think I can come, thank you all the same."

The girl tossed her black hair angrily. "Man, you can't do that." Her hollow eyes were painful to look at. "Tell him we're desperate—he can't let us down. He's so cruel—look what he's done to me." Nina raised her arm at the same time as a loud shout down the other end of the club caught Camilla's attention, and she swerved away from the girl. It was a young man who shouted, at a tall Afghan who waved his arms violently. The argument grew louder—the Afghan swung, and the other stumbled back and fell—but Camilla would have sworn the blow hadn't connected. He fell against another table, and a young blond boy, Swedish perhaps, sprang up and hit him with a bottle.

It was the cue for general uproar. Camilla tried to struggle toward the rear of the restaurant, someplace to hide, but the flow of the crowd heaved her forward into the center of the scrum. A glass smashed at her feet, and she felt wine trickling down her dress. Over the fighting and the shouts she saw Patrice standing by the door, observing the battle but not participating, and she knew that he saw her. Why didn't he do something? Her heart was leaping wildly; she was dangerously close to that level of panic where she would no longer be able to think clearly or rationally.

She heard a movement by her shoulder, and because it sounded full of purpose in that unthinking mob, it was extraordinary. She turned and saw the same Afghan who had swung the first blow towering above her, a knife in his hand. It was so near it was unreal, and she neither screamed nor moved as the blade descended. *I am going to die,* she thought clearly, and it was too close to be afraid.

But as the silver blade flashed down, someone jostled her from behind, she slid sideways, down onto her knees, and the knife glanced off her, scoring a shallow cut in her right shoulder. She glanced at it—a little crimson blood bubbled up and stained her dress, but it did not hurt. . . yet. She merely felt faint, and as she tried to struggle to her feet, Patrice was there, supporting her in his arms.

Now she felt terror and with new strength pulled herself from him. "Don't touch me!" she screamed. She turned on her heel and fled, through the parting crowd, to the ladies' room.

Camilla crouched over the sink, her arms leaning on the basin and her forehead resting on the cool surface of the cracked mirror. She raised her head and looked at her face: huge brilliant eyes, skin as pale as milk, and the mouth drawn, jaw clenched. She slowly became aware of her wounded shoulder, throbbing with a mild burning sensation. Turning her right side to the mirror, she checked the cut—it was slight and had already stopped bleeding. Fortunately she had had a series of tetanus shots before she came out here, so that was one fear she would not have to face. But just in case, she tore off some tissue paper, soaked it in hot water and washed the cut clean of blood and dirt, then pressed a pad of dry paper over it as a sort of makeshift bandage.

The practicalities finished, Camilla's strength seemed to drain from her, and she slumped to the floor, her head resting on her uninjured arm. *He waited,* her brain cried accusingly. *He watched and waited.* Here was a proof more violent than any she had asked for. She wouldn't have been surprised, she realized, if the whole thing had been engineered for her benefit—but no, he couldn't. Yet if so, why? Surely he couldn't! But then why had he waited? Why? That one questioning word seemed to sum up everything about her predicament, and, her steely resolve snapping, she broke down and wept dry sobs.

A few minutes later a hand touched her shoulder. Shaking, Camilla looked up into the odd dulled eyes of the girl Nina. They seemed to have a new sparkle in their brown depths. The girl's friendship with Patrice seemed strange to Camilla, but she was too upset to dwell on it.

"Come, don't cry," she said soothingly. "You're not badly hurt—just a scratch, I see. You needn't worry; Patrice will look after you." She seemed to smile triumphantly. "He always does—as long as you never let him down. Now come with me."

"No!" pleaded Camilla. "Don't let him near me."

"Get up, get up." Nina drew Camilla to her feet and steadied her shaking frame. "He'll drive you home now. You're safe."

As safe as I'd be in a snake pit, thought Camilla, but the girl had already shepherded her out into the restaurant. The chaos had faded, the troublemakers had disappeared, and Patrice had taken firm hold of her uninjured arm.

Camilla maintained as calm a face as possible, but inside she felt sick and cold, and her legs were unsteady at the knees. Patrice put his arm around her to steady her, but this only increased her nausea, though she tried to hide it from him.

"Do you want to go to the hospital?" he asked, all unctuous concern.

"It's only a scratch," she muttered. "But I suppose I could go see Johnny at the U.S. A.I.D."

"You can't use it!" Camilla's heart sank at the note of triumph in his voice. "*Ma chère*, the A.I.D. is for Americans only—Johnny would lose his job if he let you in, and you know he couldn't refuse you because he's your friend."

Camilla realized this but felt that somehow, some way, Patrice was contriving to keep her from her friends. "Take me back to the hotel," she said wearily.

"Are you sure?" he said, touching her shoulder gently. She winced. "Are you sure you oughtn't see a doctor?"

"It's a surface cut; all it needs is a bit of iodine.

Please, take me back to the hotel.'' There was an un-compromising firmness in her voice.

They got into his car, and she leaned dizzily against the leather, inclining her body away from his. He started up the engine and as they rolled smoothly away he suddenly spoke.

''That *bagarre*—the brawl—it was no accident.''

Camilla tensed her shoulders, breathing sharply at the pain. What startling confession was he going to make?

''From where I was standing it looked decidedly choreographed to me. It appeared you were attacked on purpose. The Kuchis are very powerful in this country.''

She did not dare to look at him. ''What—what do you mean?''

His voice grew more strident. ''It proves what I've been saying all along. That and the note—it was no idle threat. Someone is warning you off, and a less brave person would have taken the hint before now.''

What was he playing at, Camilla wondered. Was this some sort of double blind? Would he be so open about it if he were involved—she had guessed it was planned, so it must have been obvious to him—or was he merely putting up an innocent front by expos-ing his plans as those of some unknown other? Was he the architect or merely the observer of her misfor-tunes? Her logic was tied in knots. *At least,* she thought, *I'll put him straight regarding my own posi-tion.*

''No one can put me off now that I have solid proof—''

''On the contrary,'' Patrice interjected. ''This incident only backs up my theory of your sister's death. Obviously the murderers of both her and Tom know you're on the trail. . . ."

Camilla felt uneasy. There were too many things that did not fit. "Why exactly do you say Tom was murdered?" she came back sharply. "The report claimed otherwise."

For a moment Patrice was put out. "*Eh, bien*, it seemed to me likely that what happened to the one must have happened to the other. But I hope you will take warning, *ma chère*! Meghan is dead, and you could be the next. *Dieu le défende!*"

Camilla kept her silence, teeth clenched in pain. Despite the concluding "God forbid," Patrice's last speech had only added to her uneasiness. It was more than simple concern; it was almost. . . threatening? But she did not want Patrice to know her suspicions—yet.

"Who did you phone?" she asked as nonchalantly as possible.

He seemed to measure his words carefully. "It was a long shot—is that how you say it in English? I know someone who had lived with the Kuchis and recently returned. I thought he might have heard of your sister, dead—" he put distressing emphasis on the word "—or alive; but alas, no such luck. *C'est dommage!*" He shrugged, twirling his dark mustache between long fingers.

Camilla studied him thoughtfully. His whole manner now struck her as too smooth, too well rehearsed. Funny, she had never noticed it before. She hadn't started off her search as thoroughly as she'd wanted to, but she was learning, and she was damn well going to use her new knowledge to the fullest. And right now her best course of action would be to play dumb around Patrice and find out what exactly he knew about Meghan's disappearance or in what way he was involved. Her relationship with Patrice had certainly changed and she no longer felt able to tell him her thoughts.

THE INSISTENT BUZZING OF THE TELEPHONE aroused her early the next morning. *What early risers these people are,* she thought ruefully. *I seem always to be awakened by phone calls.* Her right shoulder was painfully sore and stiff as she reached for the receiver.

"Yes?" she said unthinkingly, looking at the wound. It had already closed and would heal quickly if she did not put a strain on it. She shifted the receiver to her left.

"*Mademoiselle?* Camilla?"

She was immediately on guard. "Oh, Patrice, hello. I was looking at the cut. Healing well, you'll be glad to know. Just aching."

"I was wondering if you would care for me to make you the reservation to return to England," he said hurriedly. "I have friends at the airline who can get you in."

"That's very kind of you, Patrice, but I have a return ticket. Anyway, it's a little early to think of going home yet."

"I was thinking you might want to go home tomorrow."

"You're not thinking of my little adventure last night, are you?" she laughed, a shade too lightly. "I just happened to get in the way of some drunkard's knife. My fault, really. Anyway, I feel much better this morning.''

"You yourself said that it was done on purpose." She intensely disliked the aggressive tone of his voice, so unlike the suave Patrice she had known. "It was a warning, *mademoiselle*. You must leave."

"How can I leave when I've just found my first big lead? Be reasonable. And if she is. . . well, I want to find whoever did it.''

"You do not have a chance. It would be healthier for you to leave.''

Camilla took the receiver more firmly in her hand, as if trying to get this fact firmly in Patrice's mind. "I am not going, so that's the end of it." There was a long silence.

"You are a very silly woman if you neglect my warning." Patrice clicked down the receiver before she had a chance to reply.

Immediately the phone rang again. Hesitating, she picked it up.

"Miss Simpson?"

"Yes, speaking. Who is it?"

"Get packed quickly; bring a pair of lightweight pants and some pajamas.''

"Why?" she demanded, immediately recognizing the offhand dictatorial manner of Malcolm Armstrong.

"We're going to see the car in Ghazni. Be ready in an hour.''

"But. . . ." A second time she was cut off in mid-conversation as he hung up. She frowned. Of all the nerve! He had such a cryptic, rude manner of ordering her about, without question of whether she wanted to go or even if it was convenient for her. She had a good mind to refuse!

But she couldn't, really, she decided as she packed her case. She did want to go. After all, it was a good idea to examine what was left of the car, for any further clues it might offer. Besides, she didn't have anything else to do, so there was no question of real inconvenience. She wasn't looking forward to the drive with Malcolm but that, she supposed, would have to be put up with. Otherwise she found herself quite anticipating the trip.

The sight-seeing would be tremendous. It would be a shame if she went home having never seen the country. They must be staying in a hotel overnight, she realized as she packed the nightgown he had ordered.

The car arrived precisely in an hour. It was an old Land Rover with the name Sally painted over the hood in silver lettering.

"An old flame," explained Malcolm when he saw her scrutiny of the writing. "Sally's a good old girl— she looks like a rattletrap, but she's got a lot of life left in her."

Camilla saw, to her relief, that Ali Shah occupied the place to the right of the driver's seat. She liked the gentle Afghan, who seemed soft-spoken and strangely wise for his dearth of years; his being there also saved her from two hours' close proximity to Malcolm, whom she found, as always, a disturbing presence. Today, in tight faded jeans and a loose mustard-colored shirt open at the neck to reveal a smooth dark triangle of bronzed skin, he exuded masculinity. His hair was a mass of loose golden curls, and his eyes took on the scorching blue of the heavens as he looked her up and down, disapproving of the white dress and sandals she had donned.

"Unsuitable," he said shortly. "But we can't wait now; you can change when we get there. I hope you brought some heavy shoes, if you have them."

She looked down at the sturdy hiking boots he wore. "Yes, as a matter of fact I bought some before I came out here."

"Well done." His voice was still sarcastic.

"I'm afraid there's no back seat—you'll have to squeeze in next to Ali Shah."

"That's all right," she replied, thinking, *as long as I'm not next to you.*

She noticed the Afghan watching her arm as she got in and slammed the door, and she tried to camouflage its stiffness, but Ali Shah, too perceptive for her, touched her arm and asked, "What is wrong? Your arm is stiff."

"Oh, nothing," she replied, trying to shrug it off.

"Something hurting your arm?" said Malcolm absentmindedly, trying to start the engine.

"No, I just banged it on a dresser," she lied, but she could feel Ali Shah's eyes on her and knew that he sensed the deception. Because she had not sorted out the significance of the incident in her own mind she was reluctant to discuss it with them yet. Besides, it would mean she would have to admit she had been wrong about Patrice, and she didn't want to give Malcolm that satisfaction.

The drive was not nearly as unpleasant as she'd imagined it might be. At the beginning there was rather a strained silence between herself and the tall man, but Ali Shah tactfully led the conversation by telling Camilla all about his family life and customs, something he guessed she would be interested in.

"I am the eldest son of the eldest son of our tribe," he told her. "My father is dead and his other wives had no children. My mother was his third wife, and when I leave the university I will be the chief of my tribe."

He lived in a house outside Kabul, on the road to Mazar-e-Sharif.

"What's it like?" asked Camilla.

"It is very large; the inside is wood and the outside is all of mud. All my family sleep on the roof in summer." Camilla thought it sounded not unlike the communal arrangements at the dormitory in her old school.

From these beginnings they went on to discuss school in general, Camilla telling lively tales of her boarding school. Malcolm laughed heartily at her adventures, and for the first time Camilla felt they shared a good rapport without any clashing or restraints. And something else, something she dared not define, was between them, too. Several times their eyes met, and such a vital awareness sparked that Camilla was left almost breathless yet wholly alive. But, strangely, she did not try to cover up the feeling, this once, nor hide the dancing lights that she knew shone from her eyes, for she liked the answering warmth in his eyes too much.

So she smiled uninhibitedly as Malcolm told stories of the schools he had taught in. He kept them fascinated with anecdotes of his colleagues at the international school—people like the guidance counselor who was to be found more often at the golf, tennis or skiing clubs than in his little book-lined office, or the tall bald Spanish priest who taught modern languages.

"The staff is so small we have to double on a lot of subjects. The science teacher does everything—chemistry, biology, physics, geography, the lot."

"How highly qualified you must all be!" exclaimed Camilla. And how versatile, too, she thought. It began to come home to her just how intelligent and accomplished Malcolm Armstrong really was. One thing was certain: if he could hold the interest in the classroom as well as he held her interest on this trip, she envied the pupils he taught. She remembered the first time she had heard his well-modulated voice and thought he was an actor. But how much more noble the use it was put to!

Too soon, she thought, the journey was over. The mighty gorges and sheer rocks of the Hindu Kush that they had driven through had enthralled her, and now they were driving in the scrubland, which stretched away in pale sands that rose in the near distance to red and yellow cliffs. She could see a spiral of sand that rose a hundred feet into the air, whirling like a dervish as slowly it broadened and flattened, finally losing its shape and rushing off in a wind as the scattered sands fell to earth.

"Dust devils," explained Malcolm.

"This is, of course, not the real desert," said Ali Shah, noting Camilla's rapturous look. "It's merely dry. Some three hundred and fifty miles to the south the real desert starts. That is not just dry—that is hell. They call it the Dasht-e-Margow, the Desert of

Death. There is a mighty river that flows into it—the Helmand—and in the middle of the desert it suddenly disappears. Armstrong, what is *taft kardan*?"

"To evaporate."

"Yes, it evaporates."

"Just dream of a Thousand and One Nights and Scheherezade, Camilla," Malcolm added. "Many of those stories describe what a desert is like—great palaces....." His voice trailed off wistfully.

"My imagination is running wild," Camilla replied, bemused by the lovely sound of her name rolling off his tongue.

They drove into the city, past what looked to Camilla like a very good hotel. The place did not seem large enough to have two such hotels, and she wondered why they passed it.

"That looks like a good spot," she pointed out. "Why didn't you stop there?"

"I know a better place," answered Malcolm without looking, and they drove on. They passed groves of hot and bedraggled trees and a caravansary with a troop of dusty camels penned outside it, but otherwise Ghazni was little more than a collection of houses and wooden bazaars, and Camilla wondered where they would find another hotel.

"It does not look much like it was once one of Asia's most glorious cities," remarked Ali Shah.

They drove out of the city—rather, the town—and soon were back upon an almost deserted road. There were no cars, and only the occasional camel or donkey, and once they passed a herd of fat-tailed sheep, waddling ridiculously with their bulbous behinds swinging, driven by a wrinkled shepherd. It was the hottest hour of the day. The open windows let a rushing breeze into the car, which kept them cool but also allowed the wind-borne sand to enter, and Camilla could feel her hair becoming gritty.

"I thought we were going to Ghazni," she said, wondering as the town became smaller and smaller behind them. "Or are we going back after we see the car?"

"It's better to be nearer the car," replied Malcolm. "Ah, here we are...."

They entered a large village. The houses were composed of timber and mud bricks, some quite substantial, lining either side of the street behind straggling rows of thick shading trees and open ditches. A thin dog wandered in front of the car and Malcolm slowed, missing it. Children ran to the roadside to see the foreign car and the foreign people in it.

The Land Rover pulled up beside a large openfronted building, its patio furnished with the same table-cum-benches that had been used in the Afghan Room at the hotel. Men lounged along the benches under the shadow of striped awnings or sat at tables in the cooler darkness of the interior. There was not a single woman's face in sight. Camilla felt very selfconscious.

No sooner had they stopped then the car was surrounded by a gaggle of curious children. The girls hung back, modestly veiling themselves, but the more aggressive boys crowded forward.

"Hey, mister, *baksheesh!*" they cried with eager faces. Malcolm handed a ten-afghani piece to the loudest boy, saying in Persian, according to Ali Shah, "That's for all of you." The boy ran off, pursued by the others, and Malcolm led the way into the caravansary.

"I thought we should eat first," he explained, "and when it gets cooler we can set out to examine the car. It would be madness to try anything very energetic in this temperature—at least for Camilla, who isn't used to it."

"I can take anything I have to," she declared proudly, again touched by his use of her first name. Somehow, today, the haughty air of formality he had previously adopted had drifted away. "I assumed we were staying overnight," she added, and the thought sent a shocking sliver of delight racing through her.

"Yes, we won't be able to get back tonight if we stay out late to get the cool of the evening."

"Have you made reservations at the hotel?"

"No, we can stay here."

"What!" Camilla nearly jumped out of her skin. "Is that a joke? They haven't got any rooms or showers or—or...."

"They have got rooms at the back; you can have one to yourself, so set your mind at rest. As for showers—you can have one tomorrow when we return."

She swallowed uneasily. "Anyway, there's no one here but men."

"So?" She had the uncomfortable feeling that he was playing with her again, although his face betrayed not the barest hint of a smile. Because she had found him such pleasant company all day, this regression to his old ways put her temper right off.

"I can't stay in a hotel full of men—probably murderous cutthroats and thieves, half of them—without running water or proper beds and probably bedbugs and fleas in the rooms! You can't expect me to!''

"You are simply dramatizing the situation. Look at these men: one is the local grocer, another a shepherd, two more are perhaps nearby farmers. Several are probably on business from Kabul. I've stayed in this caravansary several times and never had my throat cut! As for the other... well, you're the one who said she could take whatever she had to. And you may have to face worse things than this before we're finished.''

Camilla was furious at being thus chided in front of Ali Shah, who was tactfully looking the other way, but at the same time—and how it annoyed her—she had to admit Malcolm was right. She had acted foolishly.

"I stand corrected," she said grudgingly.

"Good, then let's eat.'' They sat down at a table and were quickly met by a very obsequious host. Camilla expected a menu, but Malcolm said, *"Naane chaast, tashakor,"* which might have been Persian or Chinese to her, as she had not had much chance to learn her Persian.

"Don't we get a menu?'' she asked, half-afraid of another rebuff.

Malcolm only laughed. "You don't get a choice here.''

The host soon returned with three platefuls of steaming rice, which he set before them, and several loaves of long flat bread shaped like the sole of a sandal and slightly burned at the edges. Camilla was a bit suspicious, but the smell the food gave off was overwhelmingly appetizing, and she suddenly felt very hungry. There was no cutlery; she supposed it would be coming, but looking at Ali Shah and Malcolm she saw them eating with their fingers, and suppressing a lifetime of training she plunged her hand in.

"Use only the right hand," said Malcolm, stopping her. "To use the left is bad manners." She obediently switched, but found her arm still sore. It seemed the men had accepted her explanation, for they made no comment on her rather clumsy handling of the food. It was, as she had suspected, delicious, and to her surprise she found, hidden under the rice, a quantity of spiced mutton. The bread was equally satisfying—hot, fragrant, very chewy and mealy.

"This is wonderful!" she exclaimed. Malcolm and Ali Shah seemed surprised.

"Haven't you ever had this before?" said Malcolm.

"No, never. I wish I had. It's delicious."

"It is the traditional meal of our people," explained Ali Shah. "The rice is called *pilau*—mixed with raisins, pine nuts and chopped carrots."

"The fruity taste must be the raisins," decided Camilla.

"The bread is *naan*," continued Ali Shah. "Unleavened dough; we cook it over camel dung."

Camilla gulped, feeling slightly ill. Malcolm laughed again, not unkindly.

"It's perfectly safe," he reassured her. "Look at all these people—they're marvelously healthy. They practically live on *naan* and tea."

Camilla had to admit they all looked extremely

healthy, with their leathery brown skin, wiry bodies and bright black eyes.

"But they're all used to it," she said doubtfully. Her appetite for the rest of the bread was spoiled, but she devoured the *pilau*. Then they were served a splendid concoction of yogurt cooled by large chunks of ice floating in it and mixed with slices of cucumber and mint. It slid coolly down her throat and had a marvelous effect on her slightly hot body.

"I feel as though I could carry on now," Malcolm said some time later, standing and stretching his long legs. "How about you, Ali Shah?"

"I am ready when you are," replied the Afghan, rising gracefully.

"All right. Come on, Camilla, let's get your suitcase from the car, then you can go to your room and change into some slacks and we can set off." He threw her the keys, and she caught them, and again their eyes met playfully... and with that deeply sensual awareness. Her face as warm as her insides, she turned on her heel and walked out into the sunlight, over to the trunk of the car.

Again the children swarmed around her, but she ignored them, and having hauled her case from the car she carried it back to the caravansary, her heart racing, but not from the work. Malcolm would have taken the case from her, but she held tightly to it and pretended not to notice as she handed him back his keys. She was more than capable of carrying her own luggage, although she was careful to take the weight on her left arm. He led her out a back door and across a courtyard, and they came to a row of sturdy wooden doors. These at least, she felt, were encouraging. Within she found the room sparsely furnished, but did not take time to look around, for she could hear Malcolm restlessly moving about outside, eager to be gone. She pulled on a pair of jeans and a roomy cotton shirt, then donned her heavy flat-heeled shoes, and she was ready.

"That's much better," he said as she came out, giving her a long lingering glance of appraisal that made her stomach do a funny somersault. As they walked back together Camilla was acutely conscious of an electric energy that seemed to pulsate between them. Ali Shah was conversing with the host, and Malcolm went to pay him; lively greetings and compliments were exchanged in Persian.

Camilla went outside to try to restore a feeling of normalcy to herself. Why was she letting him affect her like this? She wasn't sure, and though in all honesty she wanted to bask in the new and wonderful sensations, she knew she couldn't. Malcolm Armstrong was not the kind of man to take seriously: he was too sure of himself, too attractive; no doubt women fell for him all the time. He was probably a master in the art of seducing a woman, Camilla sensed with profound accuracy, but he would also be aware of the power he had over her—and that could be fatal to the vulnerable heart of any woman who gave herself to him freely.

After a few more minutes of waiting by the car, the men came out. But she hadn't fully recovered from Malcolm's overwhelming presence, for the sight of his rugged face and strong lean body sent her right back to square one—almost trembling with the force of his masculinity.

"He wanted to know why we were stopping down here, miles from anywhere," said Malcolm conversationally to her as they drove off. "I said we wanted to look at some strange rock formations in the hills."

"That satisfied him?" Camilla was incredulous but glad for the neutral topic. Some of the tension she felt when alone with Malcolm left her.

"They think all *farangis*—foreigners—are crazy," answered Ali Shah, and both men laughed. "The only thing he could not figure out was why a nice young Afghan like myself was with you."

"So be sure you bring back a few rocks in your pocket when you return," advised Malcolm.

"But why shouldn't we tell them the truth?" she wondered.

"Just a feeling I have," replied Malcolm. "I still wonder about that note. It might have been a hoax— still, as Hagan says, no reason to advertise our purpose."

"But don't you think one of them might know something?"

Malcolm considered this. "It's quite possible. I don't like to let everyone know we're on the trail— but we'll never get anywhere if we don't ask. Perhaps tomorrow morning, before we leave."

Camilla felt a slight twinge of guilt that she had not told them of the incident in the restaurant. But more and more as the ache lessened, her memory of the event faded and blurred. She could not be sure whether it had been intentional. Most likely an accident, she finally convinced herself.

They turned off the road and headed through the scrub toward the cliffs. The red and yellow ridges seemed near, and Camilla was surprised to find that they did not come closer much more quickly.

"How do you know where to find it?" she suddenly asked, and wondered why the question had not struck her before. But Malcolm had seemed so assured; she had never doubted that he knew what he was doing.

"I got a map at the British Embassy."

"You never told me you went!" she cried accusingly. It seemed he'd had more luck there than she.

"As it happens, I have a friend at the embassy who kindly marked the map for me. He's a secretary to the consul and went with him to look at the site when it happened."

"Turn left here," said Ali Shah.

They drove around a clump of silvery gray boulders and drove on to the top of a pebbly knoll. From this knoll they could see the distant mountains fading into the haze of extreme heat. Nearer rose round low sandy hills—and in the gully beneath them, the shell of a car, half-filled and covered by the sand, and stripped of every removable article: tires, steering wheel, engine, even the seats.

"Too bad about the seats," said Malcolm. "I would have liked to look through them." He shrugged. "Still, the rest is worth a look over. Ali Shah, will you stay with the car?"

Malcolm and Camilla got out, but before they started down the little hillside to the car, he drew something out of his pocket. They were sunglasses and he handed her a pair.

"You'll need these; the sun's pretty strong."

She took them and put them on, wondering whether they were a gift or a loan. His manner seemed rather brusque. They were not the sort she would have chosen, for they had the mirror-type lens that allowed her to see out but hid her gaze from others. Camilla liked to see the eyes of the person she talked to. She noticed Malcolm had a similar pair and supposed they were the proper glasses for the climate.

"I'll examine the car," said Malcolm. "You look around and see what you can find." Wordlessly she obeyed the order. She could not see a single bit of evidence that any form of life had ever been here, apart from the thin grass. The car shell resembled an ancient ruin, and the sand was unmarked, as if no foot had ever trod upon it. She did not know what she was expected to find, but it seemed as if she would disappoint him at any rate—the whole scene was desolate and bare.

She walked around the back of another pile of boulders and suddenly felt herself cut off. The mere fact that the two men and the cars were no longer in sight filled her with an indescribable loneliness; not unpleasant, for she knew two steps would bring her back to company, but in the silence of rocks and dust she could pretend for a minute she was alone in the world.

Then she saw a glint out of the corner of her eye and swirling around could have sworn she caught a glimpse of glass reflecting the sunlight, but then either she or it moved, for it was gone. She thought she could hear a thudding. She quickly ran to the top of a nearby hill but could see nothing suspicious, only a horseman in the distance riding very swiftly in the direction of the village, with some small animal, probably a dog, running at his stirrup. It was that which had made the thudding in this land of carrying echoes. The glimmering had probably been a piece of mica on a hill.

Then she looked down and saw something she instantly knew would cheer Malcolm's heart—the rear seat from the shell of the car.

"Malcolm! Come quickly!"

He ran around the heap of rocks, down the gully and up the hill to her, breathing heavily with the heat and the exertion.

"What is it?" he exclaimed worriedly. "I thought you'd got yourself into some mess."

"No, but I've found one of the seats," she said proudly. "Look!" She saw his face light up.

"Great! This could be a break. Come on!" Seizing her hand to hurry her along, they scrambled down the scree of pebbly earth to the discarded seat, looking oddly surrealistic as it sat juxtaposed to the primitive scrub.

Her hand burned at the contact with his, in a strange way she had never felt before; not painfully, and for a moment she had no real desire to pull it away, for it felt amazingly natural there.

As they slid down the hillside in their haste he held her up. Once they reached the seat he released her just as naturally as he had first touched her, but then seemed totally occupied with the rusting piece of auto furniture. Camilla tried to look on this as the common reaction of anyone stumbling upon a potential piece of evidence, and was the more angry with herself because the true conviction would not come.

"Don't stand there mooning!" exclaimed Malcolm, and the curt words broke her out of her reverie. "Give me a hand."

She came over, and before he could get out his warning, "Don't touch it," she had touched the leather of the seat and quickly snatched her hand away in pain. The upholstery was nearly roasted in the heat and the steel hot enough to boil a pot of water on.

"I've got some gloves," he said, and pulling a thick leather pair out of his pocket, he donned them and examined the seat minutely. By his face Camilla could see the results were disappointing.

"Let's turn it over," he said as he wiped his brow. He stripped off his shirt, and she could not tear her eyes away from his brown hard torso, his muscles rippling, pulling and stretching with the action beneath his taut skin. Camilla was fascinated by the movement of his body and longed to press her hand against the firm sinewy flesh of his back, to feel it writhe and ripple. What pleasure it would be to twine her arms around him, feel him support her, wrapped like an ivy round an oak, yielding to his hardness, here in the desert, in the hot sand, her mouth locked to his as she had felt it before—

"Camilla!" His voice snapped her from her fantasy, and she opened her green eyes. "Is it too hot for you?"

She must have looked silly, she realized, with her eyes closed and her face rapturous in the heat of the sun, while he squatted by the upturned seat intent on serious matters. If he had turned to her then and seized her as he had in the elevator, she would have melted to him here in the dirt of the desert. How simple it had been to resolve that his attractiveness, once acknowledged, would no longer threaten her; she realized now that the danger was greater than she had anticipated—or perhaps her own resistance too weak. *Thank God,* she thought, coming over to him. *Thank God he startled me out of it.* The curtness of his tone had given her back her self-control, and she managed to squat beside him with only a slight betraying tremor of her hands, and as she kept these tightly clasped it was easily concealed.

"Look," he said again. "A little gash, only about an inch long, and sewn up."

Camilla squinted. It was almost impossible to see, but it was there.

He took out a knife and slit the upholstery, and then, carefully inserting his hand, he drew out a small plastic bag full of a fine white powder.

Camilla did not want to look too closely. It was almost like sugar—but too powdery, too refined.

"What... what is that?" she asked, although she was not too sure she wanted to know.

Malcolm looked incredulous. "You mean you really don't know what it is?"

"Of course I don't know. Would I pretend that I didn't if I did?"

Malcolm shrugged. "I don't think I ought to tell you. Quite apart from the fact that I don't believe you can keep a secret, I feel it would be better for you if you didn't know."

Camilla was so furious for a moment that she could hardly speak, and she raised her shaking fists above her head in frustration. "You make me so angry!" she sputtered. "I'm sick and tired of being treated like a little child. 'Camilla shouldn't know this—Camilla mustn't play with that—Camilla shouldn't mix with such and such people.' Who the hell do you think you are, Armstrong—my father? Look at me. Look at me! I'm a grown woman. Treat me like one.''

He stopped dead in his tracks, face away, broad muscular back toward her, the taut muscles moving beneath the smooth bronze skin. "I know you're a woman," he said thickly, his shoulders hunched forward. "Don't think I've forgotten what happened in the elevator—I'd never behaved that way before, but—but...." She saw the outline of his jaw, clamping down on the unspoken words, biting them off, the sinews of his neck prominent and corded. Then he straightened slowly and turning to face Camilla presented her with an almost smiling face.

"But, Camilla," he continued, "you are innocent in so many ways. It makes your defiance almost... provocative." He reached out and placed a caressing hand on the smooth peachy skin of her cheek. "That's what I always try to remember, Camilla— you're so young, so...fragile. But I keep forgetting...."

The strange depthless azure look he gave her was too poignant to be endured. She turned her head sharply to the right, into the shadow, so that he would not see the flushing redness that betrayed her. Away from her stretched the hot loneliness of the desert.

"This is terrible," she half whispered at last. "You're...you're almost making me like you."

"That's okay," he replied, and she could see in her

mind's eye his expression, drawn from the forced lightness of his voice. "Let's like each other by all means—it's sensible and adult and...maybe it will keep us sane." She turned to him to try to catch some corroboration of his tone from his face, and for a fleeting moment she saw the smile that did not quite reach his sober blue eyes. But Malcolm then swerved as quickly from her; it was as if each in turn was unwilling to reveal the truth behind their words.

Malcolm started up the hill, the little plastic bag cupped in his broad palm. She watched him walk, supple, loose limbed, graceful as a panther, and then his voice made her jump.

"Come on, my little redhead. Let's get back to Ali Shah."

She scrambled after him, panting, "My hair is not red, and you know it." Reaching him, she laid a restraining hand almost deferentially on his forearm. "It's auburn," she stated firmly. He let her hand rest lightly for a moment, and then, with a visible effort, shrugged it off.

"Malcolm, what's in the bag?" She tried to look into his face, but tall as he was he held it far away from her. "Please," she urged. "You must see that I need to know."

He took a few steps away from her and tossed his head as if he were arguing with himself. Then she watched him deftly undo the tie that bound the bag, and he came back to her, holding it out, open, on the palm of his hand.

"Here," he offered, "take it." She did so gingerly. "Be careful; don't drop it. Look at it. Smell it." But the white powder was so light and fine Camilla was afraid she would inhale it. Inside her she fought the recognition that told her what it was.

"It's heroin, Camilla."

"No." She thrust the bag so roughly from her that Malcolm had to leap forward and catch it before it spilled its pale precious powder all over the dusty desert.

"You know it is," he replied firmly. "What else could it be, that color, that powder, done up in a tight little bag and hidden where even the vandals who ransacked the car couldn't find it."

To hear it out loud was shocking, too shocking to let her speak for a moment. The objections that tangled in her mind were too nebulous to distinguish, but she still felt it could not be possible. Her sister—and Tom—drug traffickers? Surely not! Not Meghan. . . .

"I don't believe it—I won't accept that they could have had anything to do with that sort of thing."

"Why both of them?" asked Malcolm as he tied the bag up and thrust it, with one violent gesture, deep into his pocket. "How about Tom on his own? Could you buy that?"

Camilla's tongue was tied. Much as she wanted to, it was not a theory she could reject out of hand. She ran up to Malcolm again, trying to protest and question at the same time, but he would say nothing. They stalked silently back to where the Land Rover was parked, and it was only as they approached the car that he turned to her and said, "Remember, not a word to anyone. We could be imprisoned forever for carrying this, thrown into some Afghan jail where no one would ever hear from you again. The fewer people who know, the fewer who are in danger."

"Danger!"

"Knowing a person is in possession and doing nothing about it is almost as criminal as actually possessing."

"Will you tell Ali Shah?"

"Yes, because he knows why we're here. But it is imperative that you keep the secret."

She stood up straight. "Of course I shall."

"I hope so." He seemed disparagingly doubtful.

"Can't you tell me why—I mean, how you knew it was there? You did know, you were sure, and you didn't tell me." Her words were reproachful.

"Wait till we get back to Kabul."

"How can I wait?"

"Who's the person who can take whatever she has to?"

Were those fatal words to be thrown back at her forever? They came to the Land Rover and climbed in silently. Ali Shah merely looked questioning, and one pat by Malcolm on his bulging pocket seemed to satisfy him. They drove back to the caravansary without speaking.

A damper had fallen on the whole evening. Their supper was eaten in a strange contemplative quiet, each wrapped in private thoughts that forbade conversation. Camilla would have found it difficult to make small talk with Malcolm anyway, since he was plunged into his serious mood. A little later on, after the dinner of *pilau*, with *naan*, chicken and mealy fried biscuits completed by tea, an old Afghan came in and told stories, incomprehensible to Camilla with her few words of Persian.

After a while she went out onto the patio to watch

the sun set behind the mountains, lighting up the scrub to gold and shadowed red. As she sat there, the muezzin in the village mosque began to cry, calling the faithful to prayer: *"I allah illah Allah."* The words soared up the scale. "There is no god but Allah." Choruses rang out of *"Muhammad rasul Allah,"* and "Muhammad is His prophet." Men hurried to the mosque, or to their home for evening prayer, and one old man laid his rush carpet on the dirt edge of the street and knelt there, rocking backward and forward, forehead touching the earth.

From within the caravansary came the same sounds of evening prayer, and for a few moments, as the long shadows of evening darkness from the mountains stretched across the plains, swallowing the colors of the day, Camilla could feel the power of this desert religion. But soon the prayer was over, the feeling gone, and she shivered in the spreading chill of evening.

CHAPTER SEVEN

CAMILLA ROSE, brushing off her pants, and returned to the inside of the caravansary. Here she found that the conversation, the story telling and the laughing would probably be going on far into the night. But she was tired, and the language barrier made it of no interest to her, so she said good-night to Ali Shah and Malcolm and made her way to her room. The wooden door was heavy as she leaned against it to push it open.

"Remember," Malcolm had said to her as she went off, "we've got to be up early tomorrow—no sleeping in. If you want anything, Ali Shah and I are right next door."

As if I could forget, she thought ruefully, shutting the door. He probably snored, she giggled irrationally—but the walls looked thick and the rugs absorbent. There were few furnishings in the room: a woven carpet on the floor and pressed-felt rugs covering the bare mud-brick walls, a window with garish curtains, and one article of furniture—a bed. She drew the curtains and looked at the bed dubiously. Its framework was of poplar wood, pale and strong, obviously rounded on a lathe, with brilliant multicolored paintwork ringing the legs and posts. But there weren't any springs! The thin mattress rested on a latticework of rope, sagging in the middle, which boded ill for any person with a bad back. Still, it was all the bed she was going to get that night, and she decided to make the best of it. She hung her clothes carefully over the edge of the bed, for fear of spiders and other insects, then slipped on her wispy nightgown, after switching out the light—one modern convenience at least—she slid between the sheets, pulled up the woolly blankets and felt coverlet and soon, despite the continual scrabbling on the ceiling above her head, was fast asleep.

She must have slept for about three hours, for when she awoke a glance at her watch told her it was midnight. She had been awakened by the sound of the two men in the next room, and was strangely comforted by the thought of their near presence. Then, in the dim light, she noticed a small movement at the foot of her bed.

Perhaps it was her foot. *Keep still and see,* she told herself. There, it moved again! What was it? A spider? A pretty big one if it was, to make such a noticeable stirring.

Camilla had no love of large and probably hairy spiders, and she wasn't waiting to make the acquaintance of one on the bare skin of her leg. She leaped out of bed and scrambled for the light. Shivering, she flipped the switch. It was a little less frightening now, and gingerly she approached the bed; reaching out for the covers, half-fearful of what hideous insects she might find there, and yet needing to know, she flung back the top coverlet.

There, quivering and glistening, was another scorpion, pale and white this time, but fully as terrifying as the black one that had begun that unpleasant encounter at the Hagans'. Her first instinct was to cry for help—but before she opened her mouth she reconsidered. She did not know which was worse—that little yet hugely frightening scorpion, or the stinging scorn of Malcolm Armstrong. She had already experienced the latter and had no desire to be indebted to his mocking help a second time. He had said that scorpions were practically harmless. If she were stung it would be no worse than a bee sting. She would show Malcolm Armstrong she had as much courage as the next person and was certainly not frightened by a harmless little insect.

It cost her a great deal in courage to approach the scorpion, and she felt her forehead pricking. She seized it in the way she had seen Malcolm hold it, and was surprised to find it was not slimy, as she had supposed. She anticipated a slight difficulty in opening the door, but it was a drop handle and she managed to maneuver it with her free hand and her feet. The scorpion was furious and waved the end of its tail about in a challenging way. She felt like laughing triumphantly—it couldn't harm her. She stepped into the cool of the dark, and rapped on the men's door.

"*Chi as?* Who is it?"

Camilla whispered, "Camilla! Open up, I've a surprise for you!"

"What fool thing are you on about?" Malcolm grumbled as he opened the heavy door. She held the scorpion up, smiling victoriously, and saw the expression on his face change from annoyance to horror.

"Drop it!" he cried, and Camilla was so astonished that she did so. He pulled her away and kicked at the scorpion, which lay threatening on the floor, and before it could move into the room he had kicked it out of the doorway. He picked up a thick piece of wood that lay nearby and threw it at the insect. Its body was completely crushed by the blow.

Malcolm turned back to Camilla, whose face was as white as the flimsy nightgown she wore. "My God!" he exclaimed as he sat her down on the bed. "Why did you do that? Do you want to be laid up in the hospital for a month?"

"What's wrong with it?"

"Nothing, if you're in the custom of picking up deadly scorpions."

"Deadly! But at the Hagans' you said—"

"That was a different breed," he replied ruefully as his blue eyes looked keenly into her face, then swept boldly down the length of her, making Camilla achingly aware of every curve. She sorely wished she had thought to pack some sort of wrap.

"What's the difference?" she asked quickly to hide the confusion that his lingering appraisal was arousing.

Malcolm forced his eyes upward. "There are different types of scorpions, and while the black one you saw earlier was harmless, this white one can kill. Take my word for it: the first wasn't dangerous, the second—pretty frightful. I don't play with deadly scorpions, you know. I leave them strictly alone."

Camilla's complexion had changed from white to green, and her body sagged as the first realization of the danger she'd just experienced came home to her. Malcolm, too, looked terribly shaken, without his usual composure; not surprising, she thought, since she had nearly thrust the scorpion into his face. She felt her lip tremble, and a hot rush behind her eyes; then, to her horror, she burst into sobs.

"I didn't mean to hurt you!" she exclaimed, gulping her tears. "I just thought I would show you I wasn't afraid—after you laughed at me—I could do it, too!"

"Shh," he said gently. "I didn't think you meant to hurt me."

This wave of sympathy was too much, and Camilla, sobbing afresh, leaned against the pillow and cried until its material was wet. Malcolm touched her shoulder awkwardly, but she continued to cry. There was no sound in the room but her crying. She had not cried like that since the death of her parents, not even when she received the news of Meghan's tragedy. The strain of her visit to a completely foreign place and the seriousness of her mission had finally decided to take their toll on her, once sparked by her encounter with the deadly scorpion. Ali Shah, true Muslim, tactfully turned away from the spectacle of a weeping woman.

At last Malcolm, hearing her sobs slowly calming, said, not unkindly, "Poor Camilla, always brave at the wrong moment."

This last insult was more than she could bear, and with a toss of her fiery-colored head she wrenched herself away from his near presence.

"I don't need your sympathy," she began proudly, but the movement had been too much, and she gasped in pain as the newly healing wound on her shoulder suddenly opened.

"What is it?" asked Malcolm. "Were you stung?"

She shook her head dumbly and tried to mumble, "Nothing," but a trickle of blood had soaked through to her nightgown and made a dark stain on it.

"Just where I banged my shoulder on the door," she tried hastily to explain, but Malcolm brushed her excuse aside.

"Don't lie to me. It was a dresser last time. No bump would bleed like that." With a deft tug he bared her shoulder, despite her protests, and winced at the long slash. "Very sharp wood your hotel has. Ali Shah," he went on, his eyes not moving from the wound, "come over here and tell me what you think of this."

This! As if she were a piece of meat! Once again she tried to struggle away. "It's really all right. Nearly healed." But he would not let her go. Ali Shah came over, modestly, as it involved the baring of female flesh, but he looked at the wound with interest.

"Knife cut," he decided after a brief examination. "On the surface, not so very bad; it will heal quickly, but you will be left with a scar like this." He rolled up his sleeve to show her a short pale mark below his elbow.

"How did you get it, Ali Shah?" Malcolm queried, and Camilla was glad to be off the hook, however briefly.

"My cousin and I had a quarrel."

Some quarrel, thought Camilla. *Just what I feel coming up now.*

"More to the point," said Malcolm stonily, "is where you got this, Camilla. And please don't say you bumped into a carving knife, because I won't believe you."

"There's no need to be facetious. And I wasn't going to say that," she added, feeling she had scored. "In fact I caught a glancing blow in a scuffle at a restaurant last night."

Malcolm's lips were grimly closed, and he turned a taut expression toward Ali Shah. "Could you leave us?" In his voice there was no request, only command. The Afghan instantly went out of the room with a silent tread, closing the door behind him.

"Now," said Malcolm slowly, moving toward Camilla. "I have told you not to lie."

"I haven't lied!" Her protest was nervously high, for his own voice was so calm it breathed danger.

"No, but you haven't yet told me the truth. You needn't be ashamed, because Ali Shah's gone now. So out with it to me."

"Ashamed! What have I to be ashamed of?"

"You tell me."

"What is this, the Spanish Inquisition?" Her emerald eyes were shot with green flames of rage and she sprang up to face him, her body tense. "No, I will not answer you! You're not my keeper! You're brutal and selfish and arrogant and cruel. I'm not answerable to you!"

At the list of insults Malcolm had raised his hand in an involuntary gesture, but she mistook it and cried out, "Go on, hit me then. I'm just a helpless woman, aren't I? Don't you like to play the big strong man! Well, this is one woman who won't give in to your pressure tactics. I won't bow and sway to your whims. I won't come and go at your beck and call like Ali Shah, like some trained servant—"

His hands had seized her upper arms like twin vises, clamping tighter and tighter as the pain shot like needles. She would not give him the benefit of crying out, but it hurt too much to speak.

"I would never strike a woman," he said, his breath coming in short rasps, "but by God I'll not stand by and see myself and my friend insulted by lies. Have I silenced you now?"

Taking her pain-induced quiet for intransigence, he gripped tighter than he intended, and then she could not prevent herself from begging in a choked voice, "Stop, please—you're hurting me."

He lessened the grip but did not release her. "Physical violence is not my preferred weapon." He left it at that, his words hanging like a threat, greater than the threat of physical violence. She managed, by looking away from his blazing eyes, to summon the strength to break from his grasp. But he had loosened his hands, intending perhaps to pursue her, stalk her and capture her. She was against the wall, for she could go no farther backward. Her legs were jelly beneath her and she could not run. Suddenly she was afraid of him as he came menacingly toward her, but her fear whipped up her anger, and her rage set her nerves alight, till even the hairs on her arms were tingling.

He lifted his hands to her throat, but instead of tightening, they lay on either side in a gentle caress, while a thumb ran down each side of her neck, back and forth, rubbing as if trying to get her to purr. The pleasure was as inescapable as iron bars—she could not have escaped if she had wanted to; but so ecstatic was the feeling his moving hands gave that she closed her eyes, blind and deaf to all sensations but this. Then one of his hands moved up to play with the tender lobe of her ear, and the other moved with delicious slowness to the nape of her neck. Eager to taste more of the unbearable delight his hands gave her, she leaned her head back, and as each finger teased pleasure from her nerves, stroking with masterful skill her silky hair, her anger and fear escaped her in a long half sigh, half moan. He was caressing only her head and neck, and sometimes an exploring finger reached her face and teased her open lips, but so expert was his touch that all the skin of her body was tingling with delight, moving as if seeking more. She was alive with sensation, and she could hear, beating a rhythm to the delight, the eager pounding of her heart. A stirring warmth spread throughout her pliant body, and as she melted, she curved toward him instinctively, raising her parted lips and flushed cheeks toward his face.

One of his arms dropped with a smooth suddenness to her waist, encircling her firmly while the other knotted itself into her hair and forced her head upward. Their eyes met briefly before his hard lips were pressed on her soft ones like burning coals, the sensation so hot that she opened her mouth to cry out. His mouth was invincible and iron-hard, and the kiss he locked her in as demanding as it was possessive. His arms bound her like steel; together with the deep thrust of his kiss they forced her breath from her, but his lips did not give her enough respite even to gasp. She could feel the gentle swell of her stomach, the ripe roundness of her breasts, crushed against his hard masculine body. The pain throbbed.

Then it was no longer the pain that filled her, but the onrush of the ecstatic warmth that coursed through her veins and muscles, turning her limbs and her will to water. Her legs went weak, and to support herself she flung her arms around his neck, drawing herself still deeper into his kiss. His arms no longer held her relentlessly tight and immobile, but roved across her curves, caressing her with sensual purpose. Then with one finger he traced a light line of ecstasy down the length of her spine, and so thrilling was it that Camilla drew away in a spasm of pleasure and uttered a little moan. The last threads of her resistance were snapped—he could do whatever he pleased with her. Camilla no longer remembered what had begun all this; she was no longer aware of her will, only of the hot ache in her body.

It was the moan that brought Malcolm back to his senses. With her body limp in his arms, he picked her up and flung her onto the bed. He strode to the other end of the small room, his back to her so that she would not see the extent of his arousal; she was too concerned with her own, ebbing now like the outgoing tide. All the power she had felt awakened in her body now concentrated itself in tears, but she refused to let them fall. For a few minutes neither of them spoke.

"So," Camilla said at last, when she had managed to get a tenuous grip on her senses. "That's your weapon. That is your punishment for me."

"Camilla, I...I'm sorry. I lost my temper." He still did not turn to face her.

She could not prevent herself from going on, "I'll bet it amuses you, doesn't it, to know you can play with a woman's body like a bit of putty. I've never been treated like that in my life before—a beating would have been less humiliating."

He turned around in one fluid motion. "That's a time-honored feminine trick to play, isn't it? I've yet to know a woman who would refuse to be humiliated in that fashion, and then afterward recriminations—"

"You forced me!"

"I might have felt guilty, but I can't stand hypocrisy. You enjoyed it as much as I did. You wanted me as much as—"

"I want you! You must be joking. If you were the last man alive I'd move halfway around the world from you!"

He shrugged wearily. "I'm tired of fighting with you. Say what you like about it. But perhaps now I'll have the truth about that—the cut."

He seemed prepared to drop the issue as long as he got the truth, which he would wrench from her one way or another. Camilla, too, was tired of fighting.

"You win. I'll tell you. But ask Ali Shah back in here. I don't want to be alone with you anymore."

Malcolm went to the door and called Ali Shah back from across the courtyard, where he had been quietly smoking. For some reason his presence, quiet, composed and uninvolved, irritated Camilla, for it was so opposite to the havoc of her own emotions; she could see Malcolm was irritated, too. *We're tired and angry and hot,* she thought, and she was already regretting the impulse that had prompted her to confess. She folded her arms across her chest, still tender from his fierce embrace.

"Come on, Camilla," prompted Malcolm quietly. "Ali Shah's here now. Out with it."

She drew in her breath. "I went to The Golden Calf last night with Patrice, and we talked and danced, and then he had to go and make a telephone call, and while he was gone a fight started at the end of the restaurant and—I was sort of carried into it by the crowd and then—well, this man almost stabbed me, but I was jostled and his knife only nicked me."

"Almost stabbed you. For no reason?" His gaze was eaglelike again, and intense.

"Y—yes. It was just a general brawl. Everyone was involved."

"Camilla, why the hell should I put myself to all this trouble for you if you still won't tell the truth?" He paused and collected himself. "Was this man foreign?"

"No, I think he was an Afghan."

"Afghans do not stab women for no reason," cut in Ali Shah, who appeared hurt. "Women are meant to be cherished."

"Maybe he wasn't Afghan—he had such horrid little gleaming eyes."

"You saw his eyes?" Malcolm spoke again. She felt trapped.

"Yes."

"Looking at you?"

"Yes! Yes! Yes!"

"Look, there's no reason to get bad tempered; there'd be no need for this if you'd tell us the truth. So this man, who stabbed you by accident, a glancing blow, did in fact look straight at you, long enough to give you a very graphic description: horrid little glea—"

"All right, all right, I'll tell you what I think. I think he did it on purpose. I saw him leer down at me as he struck. His aim was very accurate—he could have killed me. He meant to miss."

Malcolm got up and paced around the room, trying to contain the anger and annoyance he felt; but it did little good, for he burst out at her with a far more lashing tone than he had intended. "I think I told you before about the stupidity of keeping information from us. How on earth do you expect us to help you if you persist in indulging in adventures with shady characters whom you have been repeatedly warned against? I don't know why I bother with you, for God's sake!"

He paused, drew breath and continued on a more sardonic note, "Where was your good friend Patrice Desmarets in all of this?"

Completely demoralized, Camilla had nothing to offer but the truth. "He watched."

"Watched you being stabbed!"

"The dog!" exclaimed Ali Shah with emotion, his hand instinctively flying to his waist for a knife that was not there.

"Now that was hardly gallant, was it?" drawled Malcolm.

Camilla could not bear to hear his deep modulated voice, so pleasant when cheerful, turned to such cutting and bitter effect.

"Well, when I was stabbed, he was right there and prevented me from falling," she protested, more in self-defense than to vindicate Patrice. She didn't need to hear from Malcolm how foolish she had been to trust the Frenchman. Then she added, "In fact, it was lucky I went out with him yesterday, despite the...trouble, because I learned he's found my sister's birthday watch, which I recognized from the inscription. He discovered it in the Kuchi bazaar."

"Did he say which shop he found it in?"

"Well, no," admitted Camilla. Then, seeing Malcolm's knowing shake of the head, she continued defiantly, "There wasn't time."

Looking at Malcolm, sitting tired on the edge of the bed, his face creased with worry, shoulders hunched, golden hair ruffled and tangled, she might have felt a twinge of guilt at the sight of the drawn harried man if she had thought his concern was in any measure for her. But she knew her confession had been a blow only to his pride, which would admit no rival in any enterprise.

"I think you'd better go back to bed," said Malcolm, "while I think this over."

"You can't just send me off! We ought to discuss this together—whatever you think there is to discuss."

"But not at twelve-thirty at night," Malcolm pointed out. "The brain is hardly clear at that hour."

"But I'm not in the least bit sleepy!" she retorted. How could she be, after such an unnerving half hour?

"Some of us are, though." Malcolm's face was tired, as was Ali Shah's. She could not think of a reply that would not seem selfish. Malcolm took her elbow and steered her toward the door, their closeness reviving Camilla's memories of their earlier passion. An uncontrollable tremor shot through her.

Malcolm's hand on her arm stilled, as if he were aware of her reaction to his mere touch. But instead of pulling away abruptly, as she'd expected, he gave her a gentle squeeze, his strong warm fingers lingering in a maddening caress.

"Bed's the best place for you, too," he said in a low voice, and there was a mysterious quality there that she could not define. "Have a little think about dear Patrice and the whole incident—maybe you'll come to the conclusion that I'm not such a selfish ogre as I appear. Good night." And the door was shut on her.

As she stumbled back to her room in the dark, Camilla's mind was not on the deadly scorpion and her near escape. She was not even considering Malcolm's remark about Patrice and everything that had happened at The Golden Calf, for she had already formed her own doubts about the Frenchman. As she switched out the light and crawled into bed, she was filled with impressions of Malcolm himself—his touch, his voice, his strength and self-assurance. Somehow he was starting to affect her profoundly, deep within, to the very heart and soul of her womanhood. This knowledge disturbed her greatly, for she had no idea how he felt about her other than that he found her sexually attractive at times. But she didn't put too much significance in that, for she knew that he had probably reacted to her tonight as any hot-blooded male would have done in the same situation— alone in a bedroom late at night with a provocatively dressed female.

The words of a popular song suddenly came to her—"Love the one you're with..."—and she realized how apt they were in this case. But she knew that the "love" in the song referred to a passing sexual feeling rather than deep and lasting emotional commitment. Yes, convenience and availability, plus Malcolm's anger at her, had triggered his fiery lovemaking, Camilla was certain. It would be naive to believe otherwise.

And then, as if to drive the truth deeper into her troubled consciousness, she heard Malcolm's voice next door.

"You may be right, Ali Shah, but if I hadn't pushed her out the door at that moment I'd have been tempted to do something we'd both regret."

CHAPTER EIGHT

"COME ON, CAMILLA, rise and shine! It's time we got ready—breakfast and then we're off."

The heavy banging on the door battered through Camilla's sleep, and she registered Malcolm's voice. Wearily she pried her eyes open and squinted at her watch. Seven o'clock! Sunlight glowed behind the cloth of her curtains, and a cock crowed raucously from some distant farm. She dragged herself from the bed and with tired eyelids half-shut dressed slowly. Her deep dreamless sleep made her feel as if she had returned from some drugged state.

The sunlight outside hurt her eyes, and quickly she put on the dark sunglasses. Malcolm had gone on, no doubt to order the breakfast, but Ali Shah was waiting to escort her.

"I hope you slept well?" he asked politely.

"Oh, yes," she yawned, rubbing her hand along her hair. "Like a log." She had always found sleep the greatest escape from problems, and last night she had needed to forget a lot.

Ali Shah looked puzzled. "Logs cannot sleep."

Camilla smiled at this as they crossed the courtyard and entered the restaurant. Malcolm was sitting on one of the carpeted benches out on the patio, with their breakfast spread before him: more hot crunchy *naan*, black coffee and boiled colored eggs. She cast him a quick uncertain glance, then suddenly finding that she was famished, she ate with fervor.

By seven-thirty they were on the road. Already at that hour the sun was hot, the bush hazy. They drove along in almost absolute silence, and Camilla for one welcomed it, as she was too exhausted to make any but the most monosyllabic conversation. She had firmly decided to put all the events of the previous night right out of her mind and not allow herself to be embarrassed by the memory of them; she was thankful that no mention was made of the incident.

Nevertheless, Camilla could feel a nameless sort of disquiet fill her, the sort one gets after a sleep full of realistic nightmares, still half believing the dreams to be true. It was a restless discontent, a nagging worry, and a fear that, because she could not identify it, she could not talk about.

They had not driven very far when Camilla looked up with a jerk and saw that they were on the outskirts of Kabul. The car had stopped.

"What's happening?"

"You went to sleep," replied Malcolm, but he was looking out of the window. Two Afghan policemen in thick gray uniforms and black boots, one much taller than the other, were approaching. They did not look very formidable.

"Come on, out we get," ordered Malcolm cheerily, but then he leaned down and hissed in her ear, "For God's sake don't give us away!"

Camilla felt weak behind the knees. Never having had much to do with the police before, she had no idea of their tactics—surely they were clever and could get what they wanted. They must be used to dealing with criminals. The prospect of years and years incarcerated in an Asian prison rose before her. She imagined it—concrete walls, barbed wire, mud walls rising beyond—and the vision terrified her, till she felt giddy. She was, after all, technically guilty. Watching Ali Shah and Malcolm, from whose calm easy manner one might have supposed they had done no more than go on an innocent picnic, she decided she must take her cue from them. Fighting down a gripping desire to run, she tried to compose herself, but she could not alter the white color of her face.

"Salaam aleikom," said the taller officer. Malcolm and Ali Shah greeted him amicably, but Camilla could say nothing. The officer looked oddly at her for a minute, then turned back to what he was doing.

"We have a warrant to search your car," he said, waving a piece of paper.

"Go right ahead," replied Malcolm. This show of cooperation disarmed the officer.

"Do you not wish to know why?" he asked quizzically.

"If you feel like telling us."

The nonchalance seemed to upset the policeman, who exclaimed rather defiantly, "We have reason to believe you are carrying heroin, which, as you know, is a serious offense."

To his annoyance Malcolm did not show the slightest sign of guilt or nervousness at this charge, but only laughed, a great laugh of amusement.

"Search all you like, then. Search our suitcases, too, if you feel like it. They're in the trunk. All you'll find is a few rock specimens."

Camilla gulped. This was it—her guilt was to be revealed. She felt goose pimples all down her arms and thought she would not be able to stand up much longer. The policeman, meanwhile, defeated by the good humor of his victim, turned with a grunt to the examination of the Land Rover.

"Careful," warned Malcolm, smoothly smiling. "You'll be held accountable for any damages to the car when you find no heroin." The policeman made no reply, but he must have heard, for his movements immediately became much less forceful. Malcolm turned to Camilla and whispered harshly, "Don't look so much like a scared rabbit. He won't find anything."

She tried to keep the surprise out of her voice. "But didn't you. . . ?"

"Shh."

A crowd had gathered to watch the scene, keeping a respectful distance from the two policemen. Among themselves they laughed and chattered—it did not seem in the least serious to them. Camilla felt as if she had been put up as a show. Ali Shah was deep in an incomprehensible conversation with the other officer.

Camilla and Malcolm waited in silence, watching the Afghan conduct his search. Perhaps the presence of so many pairs of keen eyes watching his back unnerved him, or maybe he felt that, considering Mr. Armstrong's attitude, there was little likelihood of anything incriminating being found; in any case, he decided to give up his search.

"There you are. It seems we were misinformed."

"But you've only examined half," Malcolm pointed out, trying to restrain his smile.

"We are finished. I am satisfied as regards this vehicle."

"But don't you want to ask us to accompany you to the station?"

Camilla caught the twinkle in his eye and grinned.

"Please?" said the policeman, obviously not understanding.

"Any questions?"

The policeman paused for a minute, then, evidently deciding he must consult his colleague, went over for a whispered exchange. The second officer drew out a piece of paper and jabbed it with his finger, as if proving a point. The officer came back.

"What were you doing in Ghazni?"

"Sightseeing." The policeman looked doubtful. "Miss Simpson, my cousin, is here on holiday and wanted to see the famous city. She is also an amateur geologist and so we went for a bit of rock hounding—the area is especially rich in some very rare minerals. Show him your rock, Camilla."

Obediently she pulled a piece of mica out of her pocket.

"A wonderful example of fool-them-every-time-ite, wouldn't you say, officer?"

It was all beyond the policeman, but unwilling to display his ignorance, he nodded enthusiastically. "But did you not see a car?" he pursued.

"Yes, come to mention it, we did—at least, the shell of a car. Strange thing, there in the middle of the scrub. We had a little look at it. It was stripped bare."

Faced with this half-truth, the officer had no line of attack left. There seemed no way to oppose their story, so he shrugged rather grudgingly and said, "You are free to go."

"Why, thank you, officer," said Malcolm pleasantly. "Ali Shah, the officer is kindly letting us go now."

They drove off, leaving the two policemen arguing furiously, and the crowd of spectators dispersed.

"Did you leave it in the caravansary, then?" asked Camilla when she had recovered from her relief.

"No," replied Malcolm. "I sewed it up inside Ali Shah's hat."

At that the two men burst into laughter. Ali Shah took off his hat and showed Camilla the little lump in the lining.

"You seem to think it's vastly amusing!" cried Camilla, overcome with fear and anger. "We could all have been arrested!"

"Ah, but we were not," pointed out the young Afghan. Camilla couldn't argue with that. Her anger didn't have to do only with the danger they had faced; it stemmed, she realized, from the fact that they had planned for this possibility between them and left her in ignorance: they had hidden the heroin and formed their alibi for the police, and now they were laughing together. She felt an emotion almost like envy. To laugh with him like that, to share secrets and easygoing jokes. . . . But he thought so little of her he did not even trust her with his plans.

Tears, perhaps of tiredness, were beginning to prick her eyes, and she saw with relief that they were on the street that led to the hotel. As they drew up, she gabbled a quick thanks to Malcolm almost under her breath, because her voice trembled, and was out of the car as soon as it stopped. She longed for the cool of the air-conditioned interior.

Hurrying up the steps, she was at the door when she felt Malcolm's hand on her arm and turned to hear his voice say, "Must your haste be so obvious?"

Wrenching away from him, she went through the doors the porter held open, a step into the lounge—and realized she had completely misunderstood his remark. He had assumed she was eagerly on her way to meet someone who meant a great deal to her. But this time he was wrong.

For there, reclining on a settee, his citron suit pale against the dark leather, was Patrice. Seeing her, he rose and came toward her, his elegantly shod feet treading lightly across the carpeted floor. He held out one slender hand with a perfect glittering smile on his face. Instinctively she took a step backward. Her shoulders came to rest against Malcolm's chest, and absorbing his strength, she felt better prepared to handle the Frenchman.

"Miss Simpson." Patrice's suave tone made her shudder. Malcolm seemed to sense it, for he laid a protective hand on her shoulder. Patrice saw the action and came a step nearer. "I am so glad I managed to catch you."

"Have you waited long?" Camilla asked coolly.

"No, no—though it would be worth it if you would do me the honor of lunching with me."

"Sorry, Desmarets, she's booked." Camilla's blood froze at the undisguised antagonism in Malcolm's voice, and knew it was directed at Patrice. What could the Frenchman have done to deserve that kind of hatred? She felt Malcolm's hand tighten on her shoulder. "Aren't you, darling?"

She started at the endearment but knew what it meant—warning and urgency. For a moment she stared into Patrice's dark shadowed eyes, which blinked and showed no feeling; at the same time she felt the gaze of Malcolm's burning blue ones. Then Patrice seemed about to take another step nearer, as if to press his invitation, so she quickly replied, "Yes, Mr. Armstrong and I are going to lunch."

The air was fraught with tension. The two men glared at each other, and she knew she had almost been forgotten in their own private vendetta. Ducking out of Malcolm's grasp, she muttered, "Just let me get my mail," and darted to the reception desk. There were no messages for her, and she had not expected any, but she loitered over a travel brochure, listening, mystified, to the two men's conversation.

"So, Armstrong, you waste no time where this young *Anglaise* is concerned. And who can blame you? That delightful creamy complexion—"

"Cut it out." Malcolm's voice sliced through the air like a knife. "We know what you're after, and it's not a pair of green eyes. It's not like you to be so unsubtle, Desmarets, but you homed in on Miss Simpson like a vulture—"

"Or a journalist scenting copy," Patrice interrupted, but Malcolm waved an angry hand.

"You can take in an innocent girl with that front, but not me. Nor most of the people in this town who know you. That story's as transparent as your guilt."

"If you have accusations to make, Monsieur Armstrong, I suggest you make them before a court of law, with witnesses and evidence.''

''Don't worry, this time I will. I could knock you down in this lobby, but that's too easy—the punishment the Afghan courts will mete out to you will be a great deal more effective than anything my two fists could provide. You've gone too far this time. You got one girl—one child with nothing to protect her but her innocence—and that made little enough difference to you. But by God, Desmarets, you'll not get this one. I would have killed you before if I thought it could have helped Theresa, but by then it was too late. But remember, if you come near Camilla again I'll tear you apart. I owe that to Theresa.''

Camilla, looking at Malcolm's face, was deeply frightened. He was red with anger, and he clenched his fists as if grasping for something that would restrain him. They had to be separated before something horrible happened. Coming swiftly over to them as they stood ominously facing each other, she twisted herself between them and took Malcolm's arm.

''Come on, we'll miss that lunch reservation, *darling*.''

The endearment, urgently spoken, seemed to shake him from his furious trance, and he looked almost gratefully down at her. ''Yes,'' he repeated, ''we must go.'' Without another word or glance at Patrice Desmarets, he went with her out of the hotel and down the steps to the Land Rover.

''Thank you,'' was all he said as they got in. She wanted to ask him who Theresa was, but somehow the tight set of his face stopped her.

Ali Shah was still waiting in the car, and he requested that he be dropped at the university. As they pulled out, Camilla noticed what in her haste she had missed before but Malcolm obviously hadn't: Patrice's familiar sleek automobile. Comfortable it might be, but Camilla decided she preferred the rattletrap Land Rover.

A short time later, Camilla had a good view of the large steel-and-glass buildings, high brightly painted murals and long expanses of garden and avenues that together made up Kabul University. She was impressed.

"Sometimes I give lectures here in the summer," offered Malcolm in a good-natured tone of voice. Somehow Camilla knew that he had sensed her change of attitude toward Patrice and he had the grace not to discuss it.

"Yes, I know," blurted out Camilla, and then, in case she gave him the impression that she was rather too interested in the things he did, she added, "You mentioned it to me at the Afghan Room." Her eyes swept over the green lawns and well-kept beds of brilliant flowers. "Oh, how lovely," she sighed. "Couldn't we get out and walk around? Those gardens are too inviting to pass up."

"Somehow I never imagined you being interested in gardens," said Malcolm, and his tone implied that he really wanted to know more about her.

"Oh, I am," she assured him. "When I was young we had enormous gardens at home, and in my apartment I keep lots of window boxes and indoor plants—though of course it isn't the same." As she smiled her eyes met the blue depths of Malcolm's for one long moment and her heart fluttered wildly at the strange lights she saw reflected there.

They all got out and wandered amiably around the university grounds. "You know," chatted Camilla, "universities always remind me of my father. He used to teach in one. I like the air of activity and importance universities have—like those students over there, arguing under that tree. It brings back...well, childhood memories."

Malcolm smiled at that but refrained from intruding on her memories. Instead he asked, "What did your father teach?"

"Medicine—well, actually he was a lecturer in pathology. We had a house just outside the university grounds, several centuries old, covered in ivy. Very traditional English."

"Your father was a doctor?"

"Oh, yes, and my mother, too. He was a part-time consultant and she had a general practice."

"So that must be why Meghan chose to be a nurse."

"You seem to know a bit about me," said Camilla, thinking of all the occasions when he had seemed to read her mind so easily. "Yet I know next to nothing about you."

"Not much to know," he replied. "I told you, I teach at the school, lecture at the university and do research."

"But where did you go to university?" She was curious.

"Cambridge, actually. I studied history."

"And got honors, I should think."

"Actually, you're right," he replied, his voice both

amused and intrigued. "But why should you think so?"

"You know you're clever, and it shows. Not that I mind," she added hastily, watching his lips twitch, but he only laughed, not unkindly. "Have you ever written anything besides history books?"

"Yes, as a matter of fact, I have." He looked intently at her. "Funny you should ask. I wrote a novel—*A Jug of Wine*, it was called. You look surprised."

Camilla's eyes had lit up. "You. . . but you're not Jacob Manling?"

"Yes." His eyes danced. "It was a pen name—a sort of literary affectation, I suppose. But how do you know the name?"

"Meghan raved about that book—she took it with her when she went away. She always said one of her three wishes was to meet the author. How funny. . . ."

"What?"

"That I should, and not her."

"Haven't you read it? If you have that probably makes two."

"Yes," she admitted. "You're quite a storyteller, but a very intellectual one. I did enjoy the book, although my tastes usually run to romantic fiction and mysteries. If Meghan were here, what discussions you'd have—she's an intellectual, too, reads masses. You'd really like her."

"Oh, I'm not complaining about the present company," he retorted lightly. "You're not too bad when you keep your temper. At least you've got spunk, Camilla. Misdirected at times, but spunk nevertheless."

A roundabout sort of a compliment, she thought. Still, it was the first, and probably the last and only she would ever get from him. She decided to smile lightly and reply, "And you know, when you're in this mood you're almost nice."

Surprisingly, he only laughed at this. "I've been called many things in my life, but never 'nice.'" His eyes probed her face for a brief disquieting moment. The depth of his gaze sent the now familiar spinal shivers racing, the quick pulse of desire telling her quivering nerves that "nice" was far too neutral a word for his magnificent blues and golds. Then he broke away and strode rapidly toward a bench in the shade of the spreading branches of a tree.

"I think we should sit down," he told her. His mood had again swiftly altered, from easy conversation to seriousness. She sat and studied his tanned face and his eyes, which seemed clouded with worry. He remained standing.

He ran his hands through his tangled mat of curls—a movement she had come to know as a nervous gesture. "I don't know why I've delayed telling you this," he began mysteriously. "It can't be any worse than the things you've already gone through, and it certainly can't be worse than keeping you in the dark—"

"No, it can't," she interrupted, but one blue flash silenced her. She looked down at her hands.

"It's just difficult to know where to begin." He seemed at a loss. Then he sat down determinedly. "To tell you bluntly what I think, more people are interested in finding your sister than simply you, me, the Hagans and Ali Shah."

"Such as?"

"Patrice Desmarets." He saw her mouth open to speak and raised a hand for silence. "Before you attack me for making such an obvious statement, let me guess what you were going to say: 'Of course he's interested; he's been helping me, and has been a great deal more help than you.'" Camilla blushed at that reminder. "What I mean is, Desmarets is involved for his own personal reasons."

"Oh, but I didn't—" Camilla began to exclaim, but then broke off, her hand raised to her lips, recalling in vivid detail the evening at The Golden Calf when she had been attacked, and the powerful, if irrational, fear of Patrice that had assailed her then—and which had never quite left her. She recalled, too, the meeting of the two men in the lobby of her hotel that very afternoon, openly hostile; Patrice's veiled menace, Malcolm's blunt threats, and the hatred that flashed between them. Malcolm, however, misinterpreted her long silence.

"I think you might have the courtesy to give a little more credence to what I say. I *am* trying to help you."

"I do know. I never—"

"Oh, let's not go into that again. I suspected it right from the beginning, when he seemed to show an inexplicable interest in you—"

In all fairness, Camilla could not help but blurt out, "No more inexplicable to me, at that time, than your interest and Johnny's."

"Judge mine as you like. Johnny is in the custom of helping every person he comes across who needs help. That's his nature. I also know something of

Desmarets's nature, and he is not in the habit of helping anyone unless it furthers his own ends—often inscrutable ends, but in this case I think not.''

"But...but what could I possibly help him to
achieve?''

Instead of answering, Malcolm reached down and
took one of her twisting nervous hands in his own.
He stroked its back with his other hand, while his
thumb lightly caressed her palm in smooth circular
movements. Camilla had always loved this gentle
caress, even as a child, and now his actions soothed
her even as, quite against her will, her limbs relaxed
and she leaned magnetically toward him. His voice
filled her with pleasure, adding to the sensation on
her hand. "Camilla—'' his voice was low, sensuous
"—tell me. Today, in the hotel—''

"Yes?''

"I knew the moment you saw Patrice—you're
afraid of him, aren't you?''

"Yes....''

"You're right to be afraid, Camilla. I was worried—but this time he went too far too fast. Don't
say anything—I know you think I'm overreacting.
But I think at last you're ready to believe me when I
tell you about him. The truth is, Desmarets is involved in the drug trade. Heroin and hashish.''

Camilla did not need him to link up the strands of
the story. The heroin found in the seat of Tom's car
was proof enough. She had not led a totally sheltered
life—she knew about the great drug-trafficking business of the Middle East. The French connection, the
opium trail and all that....

"Tom was a carrier.'' She said it dumbly, yet she

was not stunned. It was horrific that anyone close to her should be involved in something so criminal—and more, that he should expose Meghan to such danger and take her with him into such risks, with her in total ignorance. And yet Camilla could not deny that she had always, in the back of her mind, considered Tom capable of something as unsavory.

"There's no denying that evidence," agreed Malcolm. "At least we've come that far."

A sudden horrible thought gripped Camilla. It couldn't be true, but she had to know what Malcolm thought.

"Meghan—my sister—do you think she knew?"

"Do you think her capable of it?"

"Unless I've never really known her all my life, I'd say it was the last thing she could ever do. She always said drugs were mind-destroying."

"If she had known—and agreed—I think they might both still be alive. My guess is that probably she left him when she found out—after all, they weren't happily married, as you said. It wouldn't have been much of a wrench."

"No, that's true. I'm not sure if I would even *want* to find her if she had known and *hadn't* left him." She considered for a minute. "Do you still think she's with the Kuchis?"

"The possible answers to the question of what happened to her still stand: murdered, died, kidnapped or traveling with the Kuchis. I favor the latter, because of the lack of either a body or a ransom note."

That, for Camilla, was encouraging. She placed a great deal of weight on what he said. "I believe you.

And there is the gold watch Patrice found in the bazaar—that's further evidence.''

"Yes, I've been wondering about that," said Malcolm. She thought his voice sounded doubtful. "When he showed it to you, did you say you thought your sister was with the nomads before or after he mentioned he had found it in the Kuchi bazaar?''

Camilla thought hard for a moment. "After... I'm sure it was after. I said something like, 'So she *is* with the nomads.' ''

"What did he do?''

"Nothing—no, wait, he repeated to himself, 'nomads,' and asked if I knew which tribe. I said no.''

Malcolm sat thinking for some time, his long body bent, chin in hand. Camilla watched him, afraid to interrupt his thoughts. At last she could bear the suspense no longer.

"What do you think?''

"I'm afraid," he replied slowly, "that Desmarets has lied to you again. I think he didn't get that watch from the Kuchi bazaar at all, but had it all the time—maybe from Tom. He said he knew him, didn't he?'' She nodded. "He might have used the watch to help pay for the heroin, who knows?''

"But then why would he say the Kuchi bazaar? He didn't know what we thought.''

"That's true, but it probably just backs up my thesis: he may have a suspicion she is with them. We don't know how much he knows, but I'm afraid he knows almost everything we know. I think he was trying to pick your brains, under the guise of helping you.''

"I've been such a fool!" cried Camilla. "But why do you think he wants Meghan? How could she help him?"

"She must know the truth about the whole setup, and Patrice wants to make sure she never tells what she knows. Obviously *he* doesn't think she's dead."

"That's encouraging," said Camilla grimly. "But he can't know much more than we do. We both have a hunch she's with the nomads, but nobody's sure." She sighed and her shoulders hunched. "I've been such a fool," she repeated unhappily. "I still find it difficult to believe. Patrice seemed so nice at first."

"The nice guys are not always the good guys," remarked Malcolm bitterly. "Think about it. Every incident with him was arranged. The attack by the mullah, the threatening note, the brawl in the restaurant. Strange how he was present at every single one. And today—somebody tipped the police off that we'd been to the car and had some lovely white powder to show for our efforts."

"But how could he have known? We told nobody. . . ." Her voice trailed away.

"What is it?"

"Yesterday—at the car—I saw a sort of glass flashing in the distance. I thought it was just mica, but it could have been field glasses." A cry broke from her lips. "He's following me! Having my every movement watched!"

"He's afraid you'll reach the truth," agreed Malcolm. "At first I think he just wanted to scare you off, but once he suspects you're onto the truth—"

"Don't say it!" Camilla muffled a scream in her hands. With her head bent almost to her knees, she crouched on the bench, a pitiable figure as for the first time she had an inkling of the true extent of the danger she, and Meghan, faced. She had always thought that fear was an irrational emotion, but this fear that now set her body shaking was both real and uncontrollable. It was too frightening for tears, but her breath came in short painful gasps as she shook, and she felt cold despite the heat.

Malcolm moved up beside her and took her carefully in his arms. She felt the power of his long leg stretched against hers, and his arm pressed around her shoulders as if to urge the fear out of her. His warmth relaxed her clenched muscles and dissipated the coldness that gripped her. His other hand he gently placed above her breast, near her heart, which was pounding like a trapped bird against her ribs. Strangely, his touch, which before had been enough to send her pulse to soaring beats, this time stilled it as if by command.

His lips brushed against her ear and he whispered, "Camilla, don't worry. I won't let him hurt you. This time I'll be careful. This time I'll win." To set a seal to his promise, he pressed a kiss against the throbbing vein in her temple and let it rest there until the pulsing calmed. Then he stroked her hair with long sweeps of his hand, soothing her.

Camilla wanted nothing more than to melt into his embrace, to let him go on whispering that he would look after her, while she soaked in his courage and strength and found peace in his arms. But the kindness of his gesture was quickly becoming unbearable to her. Her feelings for him made her too vulnerable in his arms. Willfully, she drew away from him, pulling herself upright, and she managed to say, in a still shaky voice, "It's all right now. I'm...I'm not afraid."

At the sound of her voice he slowly drew his hands away and let them fall unoccupied at his side. Again she faltered, for he was still agonizingly close to her. "Perhaps we're being too hasty. It's all circumstantial evidence."

To her horror he went very white and hit the back of the bench with a hard clenched fist, exclaiming in a low impassioned voice, "Dammit, don't ever say that! It's always circumstantial evidence!"

She was too awestruck to say anything, for this sudden outburst was the most emotional she had ever seen from him.

He managed, after a moment, to calm down enough to go on. "I know we're not being too hasty. I *know* him. Camilla, you have no idea what he has done. My sister, my brilliant, lovely, laughing fourteen-year-old sister—he killed her. He killed my sweet little sister, Theresa. Oh, not directly, no—you see, he's a pusher, but only in a very select way, and he can pick them a mile off, the adventurous, rich, rather spoiled but innocent teenagers with pocket money to burn.... That was perhaps my fault, but I loved her. And I was abroad; I didn't know until she was.... I came home in answer to an urgent telegram and there in place of my little blond-haired sister, always singing to herself and dancing—there in place of Theresa was a gaunt-faced addict. She died, not much later, of pneumonia, but it was Desmarets who killed her. And we all knew—I, her friends, her teachers; but what could we do? It was all circumstantial evidence.

Nothing could be pinned on him. Too many friends in high places, a few bribes here and there. My God, Camilla, what sort of evidence do you have to produce to convict a man who'll sell heroin to fourteen-year-olds if they've got the money? I could have killed him then, but instead I left the country. Theresa meant nothing to him but profit.

"Circumstantial evidence!" These words seemed to sum up all the bitterness he harbored against the Frenchman. "And, Camilla, this happened quite a few years ago—and that man is still here, still carrying on as he always has. If it ever happened again...."

Those five words leaped in sharp relief into Camilla's brain: "If it ever happened again...." She remembered the young Spanish girl Nina, haggard eyed, her face already shadowed and lined as if her beauty had been spoiled before it had ever blossomed. Nina, looking hungrily at her, believing her to be Patrice's friend. A trembling desperate fifteen-year-old girl. Patrice had done that, had done it to Malcolm's sister, would do it again....

"I'm not afraid." Camilla was overwhelmed and humbled by Malcolm's grief. She felt her own sympathy was too small for it. Better to face the challenge he offered her with courage. "I'm not afraid of what might happen to me. But we must get to Meghan before he does."

"You understand that this man is totally ruthless? That he doesn't hesitate to kill?"

"I'm not afraid. I'm only sorry I was so foolish, but nothing can put right what I've done. I'll know better now. I'm willing to go on if you are."

"I—of course I am. Meghan's the one person with the evidence we need to convict Desmarets, quite apart from the fact that I'll do everything I can to prevent anyone else from ever becoming his victim. Camilla, my motives may be different from yours, but the end result is that I want to find your sister as much as you do. By helping each other we can help ourselves. We must work as a team."

"All right." She held out her hand for them to shake on the agreement. He reached out and took it, firmly grasping it and once again flooding her with his strength. Camilla looked squarely into his eyes, and he returned the gaze, his eyes burning sapphire with those strange haunting lights again. She tried desperately to halt her blush—by a sheer effort of will. It didn't work.

His gaze held hers for one long breathless moment. "Perhaps you do know how to be brave at the right time," he finally murmured in a low husky voice that did not quite match his words. Camilla lowered her gaze.

"Come on," he said, breaking the spell, then walked abruptly away from her. She ran to catch up with his long strides, and for a while they walked together in silence. Then he spoke again.

"I. . . back at the hotel—I hope you didn't mind the endearment."

"Oh." She knew he was referring to his calling her "darling." He had probably noted her startled reaction. How had he interpreted it, though? "No. If you're wondering whether I misconstrued it. . . it's a sort of code, isn't it? I mean, it's a very. . . strong word. It meant urgent."

"Yes. I see you understood." They reached the car, and he opened the door for her.

"Are you taking me back to the hotel?" she asked, slightly nervous of meeting Patrice when she returned.

"If that's where you want to have lunch. But I never thought their food was too good. I know a place in the old city—the Marco Polo."

Camilla was for a moment confused. "But I...I thought that invitation was part of the code."

"I admit I made it up on the spur of the moment, but it's lunchtime now, and we've both got to eat. Let me ask you again: would you like to come to lunch with me?" His manner was aloof once more. They were back on safe ground.

"Well, all right," replied Camilla as casually as she could, but somehow she knew that time spent with Malcolm Armstrong would never be casual.

CHAPTER NINE

THE EARLY EVENING found Camilla sipping tea in the cool of the Hagans' big living room as she chatted to Janet. Elsa's golden head rested against her knee—the puppy had been allowed the privilege of entering the house—and Camilla stroked her long ears. Janet sat across from her, knitting a baby's frock. The soft click-click of her needles was peaceful, and the two women conversed quietly.

At first their visit had been slightly strained, more on Camilla's part than Janet's. Camilla still remembered the frightful scene she had made in the Afghan Room and was prepared to be embarrassed, but Janet seemed to have totally dismissed it, and Camilla soon forgot her unease in the pleasure of Janet's company. They talked for quite a while about the baby.

"Do you want it to be a boy or a girl?" asked Camilla.

Janet smiled. "That's the first question anyone asks. I try not to wish for one or the other, in case I'm disappointed. I guess I'd really prefer a boy, but it doesn't really matter. They say that no matter how much you've wished for one or the other, when you finally have the baby it's always just what you wanted, and you'd never change it for one of the other sex."

"I think it will be a boy," said Camilla, twisting Elsa's long fur around her fingers. "You're just the sort of people to suit a boy. I can imagine what he'll look like: tall, strong, lots of red hair and muscles—and very good-looking, of course."

"Of course!" laughed the prospective mother. She was silent for a bit and then began tentatively, "Speaking of tall and strong males—how are you getting on with Malcolm now?"

"Oh!" Camilla felt herself reddening. Janet leaned over and tapped her comfortingly on the knee.

"Come on now!" she said cheerfully. "No need to get embarrassed. We weren't in the least upset—I know how het up you were that night, and if you ask me, Malcolm seemed to be baiting you a bit."

"No, no." Pride struggled with the truth, and truth won. "It was really my fault. I'm never ashamed to admit I made a mistake. In fact I was extremely rude to him and deserved what I got."

Janet's expression was curious. "You tell me if it's none of my business, but I've always wondered what he said to you after you marched out—in a very dignified manner, I might add."

"To paraphrase, he told me not to be such a silly little girl." But her hands trembled at the recollection of the contretemps in the elevator.

"That was fresh!" Janet put on a startled expression, and Camilla had to laugh.

"Oh, Janet, you show how trivial all these little things are. But it seemed important to me at the time. I was furious. Now...."

"Yes? Oh, I know I'm prying, but do go on."

Camilla shrugged. "I was wrong." How could she

put into words what she felt without seeming silly or sentimental or giving the impression that what she felt for him was somehow...? All she could say was that the two days spent in his presence had been the most exhilarating, and the most nerve-racking, of her stay in Afghanistan. Her dates with Patrice had always produced a nerve-numbed, even drugged sensation in her mind and a dragged-out feeling in her body. It appeared to her now that she had been almost—she tried to find a word—hypnotized. How otherwise could she have been so blind to what she now saw so blatantly—his true character? But Malcolm...he made her feel so alive. She didn't know how, or profess to understand it, but she missed him already.

"I used to think," she began slowly, "that he was just an incredibly selfish man who cared only about himself and his own reputation. But now I think it's really the other way around. The people I have met here are the most unselfish I have ever known—I mean you, Johnny and Malcolm, and even Ali Shah."

"That's what comes from living in a small community," replied Janet. "Everyone's problems become your problems, and everyone helps each other."

"I know that's it. You know, I used to feel aggrieved against him, but now I feel so...grateful." It wasn't quite the right word for the havoc of emotions he created in her, but it would have to do. "Do you know, he has just spent the past two days out near Ghazni with me, both him and Ali Shah. They took me to look at the remains of Tom's car."

Janet nodded. "So I heard. But I don't understand why that makes you feel guilty. He said he would help. You don't expect him to go back on his word?"

"No!" That Camilla had certainly never considered he could be guilty of. She hesitated before going on, but she needed to talk to someone about her association with the utterly stimulating man she was finding Malcolm to be. "Today we drove Ali Shah to the university, then we walked in the gardens and he...he told me about his sister."

"Oh, yes. I heard about that—but not from Malcolm. That was a long time ago—before we arrived."

"I realized that I'd made a complete fool of myself in Malcolm's eyes. But of course I'd had no warning of what Patrice was like—and that man's an accomplished actor. It makes me shiver to think how much I was taken in."

Camilla drew in a sharp breath. It was going to cost her a bit in pride to say what she was now going to say, but she still had to say it. "What I also realized was that I'd completely misjudged Malcolm. I learned so many things today—he's really an incredible personality, isn't he, with so many facets."

"Oh, yes," agreed Janet enthusiastically. "He certainly is."

"I found out that not only does he teach research and lecture, but he has written a novel that I happened to have read and truly enjoyed. And now at least I understand why he's going out of his way to help me. Before, you know, I wondered, why is this brilliant man, this stranger, wasting his time on me and my problems, and I couldn't work it out. I didn't think he believed my sister was alive. I thought he viewed it merely as a puzzle to be solved—and I hated him for it. But do you know, Janet, when he wants to he can be so...so kind and considerate and understanding; but you'd never think it when you first meet him."

"Camilla," Janet cried in mock astonishment, "can this be the same girl we talked to on Friday? I do detect a note of humility...."

"Yes, well, I ought to be humble," she replied, taking Janet's teasing words seriously. "It was entirely my fault that we got off on the wrong foot."

"I don't know about that," smiled Janet. "Malcolm can be pretty harsh when correcting what he sees as stubbornness."

"Well, I was stubborn." Camilla was, for the moment, just as harsh on herself. "In fact I was a little idiot. I acted out of sheer reaction if that makes any sense. Whatever he told me to do, I had to do the opposite. I'm not surprised he doesn't like me now, but at least our working together doesn't depend on mutual affection. What was it he said? Something like, 'By helping each other we can help ourselves.'"

"Camilla, now you are being silly. What on earth makes you think he dislikes you?"

How could someone explain such a feeling? Every time they appeared to be growing closer, he seemed to fight the feeling. He must not want to become attached to her for his own reasons, although sometimes, she had to admit, his determined aloofness toward her was weakened by his purely physical desires. But she couldn't tell Janet that!

"You always know when someone doesn't like you," Camilla finally replied, aware of how inadequate the words were. "I just sense it. Anyway, he never acts as if he enjoys what he's doing with me."

"I can't think why he should dislike you. I can't think why anyone would."

"I can," Camilla replied. "I was unforgivably rude to him the first time I met him." She paused and gave a sigh deeper than she realized. "I don't think he's the sort of man who forgives and forgets easily. Not like you and Johnny."

"I must tell you, Camilla, that when Johnny and I first asked him to help you, he wouldn't agree right away. He wanted to meet you first. It was only after that meeting in the Afghan Room, which you think was such a fiasco, that he agreed to help you. You must have made an impression."

"Yes, some impression." Camilla would have been surprised if she could have heard the bitterness in her own voice. "Maybe he thought I would be an interesting challenge. Or that he had to save me from myself. Not to mention Monsieur Patrice Desmarets. I could kick myself for that first evening!" she exclaimed. "We got off on totally the wrong foot, and I don't think now that he'll ever have the right impression of me."

Janet's eyes had begun to widen, but she said evenly, "Is that so important? After all, your working together doesn't depend on mutual affection, as you said."

Camilla was aware of the hinting in her friend's voice, but she answered as casually as possible, "Who can help but respect a man like him and want to be respected in return? With his wit, intelligence, honesty, courage, kindness—"

"You make it sound like a list of boy-scout qualities!" laughed Janet.

"Well, that's all quite aside from his looks. You must admit, Janet, that they're quite devastating. That hair—I've never seen the like of it on a man. And those eyes—"

"Yes," cut in Janet. "I believe those looks of his have attracted more than one woman."

Camilla should not have been surprised, but somehow Janet's innocent statement gave her a sudden pang. Of course his looks would bring women flocking to him, and she imagined that with his considerable magnetism he had broken more than his fair share of hearts. And probably did not much care, either.

"Well, he *is* attractive," repeated Camilla. She saw his face again in her mind's eye and ran her thoughts over him. "In fact, the most attractive man I've ever met. Of course," she added swiftly, for Janet's benefit, "I'm being objective. As far as I'm concerned what's important are the qualities that will enable him to find my sister."

"Yes, of course; I quite see that," replied Janet, and Camilla did not altogether like her teasing tone. Janet rose and picked up the cups and empty plate of biscuits. "Look, you've eaten the lot!"

"Oh, dear," laughed Camilla, "I'm afraid that was Elsa. I should have watched her. I was too wrapped up in the conversation."

"That's quite understandable. I'll just wash these up."

"I'll help." Camilla found the familiar routine of

domesticity helped to calm her after the upsetting talk about Malcolm with all its undercurrents. She tried to act cool on the subject for the rest of her visit, but found herself unable to steer the conversation completely away from him. "How long has Malcolm lived in Afghanistan?" or, "How old do you think he is—over thirty, I should imagine," or, "He's incredibly fit—Malcolm, of course—he must be an amateur athlete," or, "Where is the school, you know, where Malcolm works?"

This preoccupation did not escape Janet's notice, Camilla knew, for with a twinkle in her eye the American woman was often deliberately obtuse, avoiding direct answers in order to tease her and then deliberately leading the conversation back to Malcolm, and smiling as she observed Camilla's quickening interest. But strangely enough, Camilla did not mind, for in Janet she knew she had found a true friend and confidante.

Soon, however, Camilla decided she must leave, since Janet was beginning to look rather tired and, although polite, was obviously hoping for a chance to lie down. She gave Elsa one last pat, sent her love to Johnny and set off to walk back to the hotel with Janet's detailed directions fresh in her memory. It was a fair distance, but the evening was lovely and Camilla craved the exercise.

"I hope you and our mutual friend get on better," were Janet's words as Camilla had kissed her goodbye.

She had been rewarded with the fervent answer, "I hope so, too."

CAMILLA WAS PLEASED that her route home involved a shortcut through the university grounds. The sunsets of Afghan summers were long and brilliantly clear, due to the altitude and thin atmosphere. She was tempted to linger but did not want to be caught in the dark on the streets, so her feet took the rhythm of her thoughts, which were racing. One way or another Malcolm had dominated them all day, and she had time now to reflect on the scene that had passed here earlier. The revelations had been extraordinary, and as she had said to Janet, she realized that not only did she not know Malcolm's character at all, but she had to rethink her whole attitude toward him.

No, she mused, it wasn't just her attitude. What she didn't quite understand was her feelings about him. It wasn't merely a question of physical attraction anymore, which goodness knows she found difficult enough to handle without further complications. All had worsened when she realized she no longer thought of him as arrogant, selfish, egoistic, hateful. . . . Those had been the qualities she had used to fight that attraction. So how could she fight it now—for fight it she *must*. Her thoughts zigzagged back and forth. She knew she must respect him, admire him, for he deserved it. . . oh, God! How was she going to limit that respect, that admiration, that deep sense of. . . caring she was starting to feel?

She put a hand to her forehead as she walked, her neck bowed. What a trip this had turned out to be! She'd had a lot of dangers to face here, but never something like this. Was she really mature enough to cope? Could she really keep her distance and her cool and manage to hide these new disturbing feelings?

"Miss Simpson." The familiar musical voice made her raise her head, and she was pleased to see the friendly face of Ali Shah. "Is it not late for you to be out walking alone?"

"Look, Ali Shah, it's still quite bright." She indicated the sky, draped to the west with fiery colors. "I'm sure I'll get back before it completely sets."

"It is not right that you should walk unescorted. I am surprised Malcolm permits it."

"He has no say in the matter!" answered Camilla hotly. "Anyway, I haven't come from him. I've been visiting Janet Hagan."

"Ah, yes, the doctor's wife. I hope she will bear many sons," he said, smiling.

She felt the urge to tease him. "Why's that? What's wrong with daughters?"

"Women always want daughters," replied the Afghan. "But a man needs sons. They carry on his name, and they bring their wives into the household to help with the work. A daughter costs money to rear and her dowry is expensive; she carries it all away to another man's family."

"You don't really believe that, surely?"

"In my country it is still that way. Come now; I shall walk you home." She knew it was merely an offer, not a command, but she was reluctant to offend Ali Shah's ideas of propriety, and accepted.

"How was the lecture?" she inquired politely.

"Oh, not terribly interesting. But I feel I must attend them all. I would not like to lose a vital piece of information on account of laziness. Our final examinations are very rigorous."

"When do you take them?"

"In the autumn." He did not seem perturbed at the thought.

"And then? Do you plan a career?"

"I had thought it might be pleasant to continue assisting Malcolm in his research, but my family insist that I seek a government post, and a man in my position has responsibilities to fulfill."

She was about to ask what sort of responsibilities they might be when a car drew up in a flurry of dust beside them, and they realized it was the Land Rover, with Malcolm driving.

"How delightful to see you two young things with your heads together, deep in conversation." The words seemed genuine enough, but Camilla winced at the sarcasm in his tone that made a mockery of them. "Could I disturb you long enough to offer a lift?"

"My home is out of your way," pointed out Ali Shah. "But Miss Simpson is returning to her hotel. She was walking back, and I did not think she should do so unescorted."

"How fortunate you should bump into each other by accident, then," he remarked with a mirthless smile. "But I do agree with you, Ali Shah, that Camilla needs protection. Or is it her protectors who need the protection? What do you think?"

"As I do not understand your meaning," replied the Afghan, with more irritation than Camilla had ever heard him use before, "I think nothing."

"Well, perhaps you're fortunate." He leaned an elbow on the door and raked Camilla with his glance, saying in a voice like a taunting caress, "I've always found Camilla most thought-provoking."

She could not restrain herself. "And I simply find

you provoking!'' She was angry with herself as soon as she had said it. The progress they had made in their relations with each other in the past two days now seemed to collapse in the face of his unexplained scorn.

"I think," he said in a low sensual voice, "that 'provocative' is the word you would use, Camilla."

A pale blush stained Camilla's cheeks. She raised one hand to her face to hide it, as if she had been struck. He could not have guessed, surely, the weakness she felt where he was concerned? Had all her struggles to conceal it failed? And how could he now flaunt it in front of her?

"After all," Malcolm went on, "I don't doubt men have used it on you before." It was cruel, but in the realization that he meant her, and not himself, there was relief.

He turned his attention to Ali Shah. "Get in," he said abruptly. "I'll give you a lift home. It's not much out of my way. And since we can't have Camilla roaming the streets unchaperoned, we'll drop her off at the hotel."

"No, thank you," Camilla replied proudly. "It's a lovely evening. I set out to walk back and I intend to do so, and you shan't stop me."

She expected protest, but he merely shrugged. "Suit yourself." He started up the car. "By the way, dinner tomorrow. I'll be round at eight."

She was too astonished to do anything but let her mouth drop in the most undignified way, as he drove off in a cloud of dust. She shook the settling dust from her hair and had nothing now to do but walk home in the slowly gathering dusk.

FOR THE NEXT COUPLE OF WEEKS the search for Camilla's sister came to a standstill. Malcolm was coming to the end of a course of lectures at the university, and his time was taken up in writing, revising, testing and marking. He explained, and she understood, that he was not prepared to give less than the whole of his attention to any one thing. The days for her passed happily enough, out in the bazaars or sightseeing in the town, and she realized that her time was fuller than she would have expected, considering that so much of it was leisurely. She phoned the embassy people regularly, but they had nothing further to report on the case.

When she was not busy, she was daydreaming, dreaming of things that too often, she realized guiltily, had nothing to do with her sister. Emotionally she felt that she had at last reached a sort of equilibrium. She had admitted, and accepted, which had been the hardest part of all, the fact that she found Malcolm unnervingly attractive both outwardly and inwardly, and that herein had lain much of the roots of her antagonism toward him. But having recognized the draw he had for her, she felt able to combat it. She knew that at least for her, a mere visitor in this country, his homeland, there was no other way. So she had resolved to behave toward him with an attitude designed to encourage mutual respect and friendship—a stance that was never completely lost, though quite often it faltered.

She had to admit to herself that despite the delay in continuing the search for her lost sister she could not feel that they were wasting time. Malcolm made sure that most of his spare moments were spent with her.

Perhaps it was to keep her occupied, away from Patrice—she did not yet feel that Malcolm trusted her completely—or else to keep her from striking up new, equally unsuitable acquaintances. She did not want to delve too far into his motives—or into her own. She was only prepared to say that the evenings they spent together were the most pleasant hours of very pleasant days.

Almost every night they went out to dinner together, and quite often they were joined by Ali Shah or the Hagans. Every time they took her to a different restaurant: Camilla was overwhelmed by the variety of decor, cuisine and location. One evening they even drove out to a little village in the foothills of the mountains, called Istalif, famous for the making of pottery in brilliant colors: indigo blue, grass green, poppy red. Delighted, Camilla bought several jars and bowls.

They dined there at the hotel—the only restaurant in the village. Throughout dinner Camilla listened avidly to Malcolm's tales of the region, all the while hoping to put right the disastrous beginning to their relationship. Down the valley where Istalif was located lived the descendants of those troops of Alexander the Great who had marched victoriously across the Hindu Kush to India. Alexander had conquered empires by twenty-one, and in Afghanistan he had met his bride, the beautiful fiery princess Roxana.

All this Camilla learned with fascination, and for her the evenings would have been unadulterated enjoyment but for one thing: she could not convince herself that Malcolm was enjoying himself as much as she. It was all very well to resolve that they treat each other with mutual friendly respect, but she could sense that he still looked on her as a duty, a debt paid to Johnny—despite what Janet had said. Camilla wanted to believe her too much to be able to. It seemed to her that the way he lingered over the historical stories he recited to her was evidence that he was longing to be back at his own work. So she was shy, knowing herself to be a burden, and felt even worse because she knew she was boring him. She felt guilty and became snappish with him when she did not mean to be, angry at her own failure; she picked arguments with him and was remorseful later. Often she cut their evenings short with some lame excuse, torn between an urge to be with him and a desire no longer to feel herself a burden. She was moody with the Hagans, remembering what she had said or failed to say the night before. They, however, seemed to understand, as they always did.

All I want is for him to like me, Camilla wailed to herself. Was that so much to ask?

One afternoon she returned from a hot day tramping the streets in the carpet bazaar to find a telephone message tucked into her letter box at the hotel. It was a short note from Malcolm: "Have to spend the evening with a student, so won't be able to make it to dinner. Keep tomorrow free."

"That's him all over," she muttered to herself as she wandered to the elevator. "No whys or wherefores, just, 'you will do this,' and, 'you will do that.' The long and short of it is, he's stood me up."

She tried to smile at the idea, but she could not prevent her emotions from vacillating between relief and profound disappointment. She knew it was unrealistic to look on his free time as her prerogative, and just because he had spent eleven successive evenings in her company did not mean he had to offer any excuse for not doing the same with the twelfth. But all these excuses could not explain to her the mysterious sinking feeling in her stomach. She couldn't quite make out her own emotions on the subject. Why, she wondered furiously, should she mind so much that she was deprived for one evening of the company of a man who made her feel so very, very vulnerable? After turning the key to her room, she flung the note on the bed.

She tossed her hair and pulled a brush through it till it stood out in sleek coppery fullness. Why should she let her whole evening be put out because Mr. High-and-mighty Armstrong couldn't make it for dinner one night out of twelve, she demanded of herself sharply. She would take herself out. So she slipped on that cool dress that made her feel pretty, she put the book she'd been reading into her handbag and decided to dine at the little hideaway restaurant that Malcolm had taken her to the previous Wednesday—the Marco Polo.

An hour later the taxi deposited her on a little side street. Her hair was piled on her head, her cheeks were lightly rouged and she wore a little black liner on her eyes. She knew she looked good in the simple gray shift she wore, and it was rewarding somehow to look good for nobody but herself. The door to the restaurant was difficult to find, a little wooden gate in the plaster wall, but she remembered where it was and pushed it open.

Inside was a courtyard, surrounded on three sides

by a building, and there were tables both inside and outside. Lanterns were suspended from wires that ran from wall to wall, and insects danced in their glow.

The restaurant was crowded, for although it was small and difficult to find, it was popular among the foreign community. Camilla was lucky when the waiter steered her to a table for two in the courtyard, the last empty table in the place. She liked the bustle and the hubbub around her, and tried not to sense too strongly that something, someone, was missing. Applying herself to the menu opened before her, she tried to decide between the kebab and the roast chicken with pine nuts. The waiter approached. She looked up to give him her order.

Her eye was caught by a familiar movement in a far corner of the courtyard. She would know that form anywhere—that hair, the turn of that jaw. Malcolm stood, a bottle in one hand, silhouetted in lantern light, and across from him sat a beautiful young woman, her profile classic, her eyes dark and definitely Afghan. They were laughing together.

A sudden chill gripped Camilla. They could not have seen her—indeed it seemed unlikely they saw anything; they appeared oblivious to everything but themselves. The cork popped and some of the liquid gushed out while Malcolm's companion clapped her hands, her face glowing with delight. Each second she watched them, Camilla felt a knife slowly turn in her heart.

"*Memsahib,*" coughed the waiter. But she was riveted to the scene.

Malcolm was pouring the wine, which reflected

rainbows in the lantern light, into two clear glasses, and they clinked them together. The girl took a sip, then, smiling, tossed it over her shoulder and threw her arms about his neck, planting kisses on his cheek, his face. Then his arms slid around her....

"Memsahib?"

Camilla pushed her chair roughly from the table, half-blind with tears. "Nothing, nothing," she choked, and ran, dodging the seated diners, hands outstretched. She rushed to the gate and wrenched it open, weeping in the dusty empty street.

Tired, hungry, she was still sobbing when she trailed back at last to her room. And yet, she thought as she stretched on her bed, what right had she? He had never given her any cause to think he might care for her. Somehow it didn't matter who the girl was, or why they were there, or what very special event they were celebrating. Camilla only knew that at that moment she would have surrendered everything for the right to do what the beautiful Afghan girl had done: to throw her arms about his neck spontaneously, to kiss him—face, neck, cheeks, lips, eyes—without fear of rebuff.

She remembered the times he had been close to her, embraced her, kissed her.... That time in the elevator and again in Ghazni, when his fiery mouth had imprinted its heat on her and aroused in her an equally fervent flame. That other time, so different, in the gardens of the university, when he had kissed her forehead and her eyes, long, lingering, so gently, like a blessing, sending a wave of bliss running through her body. And all those other times—in the hotel lobby, in the street, anywhere, anytime that he had touched her flesh or ruffled her skin with his warm breath. Her responsive tingling had always told her just how attractive she found him. During every one of those moments all other thoughts had been driven from her mind—she could barely remember thinking at all, only floating, floating in paradise.

Now it was all gone. Ever since they had returned from Ghazni there had been more than a dining table between them, and not once in all the evenings she had been with him could she remember their touching once, even by accident; not even when he held out her coat for her to slip on did his fingers lightly brush her bare shoulders. On one or two occasions she had thought she'd caught a warm disturbing glimmer in his eyes as he looked across at her, but it was gone so quickly later she wasn't sure if she'd imagined it. In the end she'd decided it was only a case of wishful thinking on her part.

And now she knew that all that special closeness she yearned for was reserved for this other girl, who could throw her arms about him in a restaurant without fear, with love. What else could Camilla have expected? That Malcolm was a monk? The very timbre of his voice, which never failed to send shudders down her spine, assured her that that was the last thing he could ever be. She had hoped for friendship; she had striven for respect.

Why, Camilla, why are you crying for things you know you cannot have, she admonished herself, clutching the pillow to her heaving breast. She knew that it could not be any different, but she sobbed herself to sleep, still wishing that somehow it might be so.

CHAPTER TEN

As ALWAYS, the next morning Camilla was her rational self again. The clear hot light of day gave a very different perspective to everything, and she thought she would be able to face the prospect of a day in Malcolm's company with some measure of self-control. She dressed in a simple white frock, gathered at the waist by a wide belt and flowing in soft pleats to midway down her calf. Her arms were carefully covered. She pulled her hair back tightly into a ponytail that bobbed against the nape of her neck, and the severe style revealed the finely sculptured bone structure of her face. She did not feel the need for makeup; her deep golden tan enhanced by the white dress was enough.

Although she was not quite prepared for the leap her heart took when Malcolm drew up in front of the hotel in old rattling Sally, she pulled herself together quickly and hurried down the steps to the waiting car. Sliding into the seat beside him, she greeted him with forced cheerfulness.

"Lovely morning, isn't it?"

He did not answer, but raked her face with his eyes. "You look tired. Did you sleep all right?"

"Yes, of course," she answered. Then, looking

down at the space between her feet, she could not help asking, "Have a good time last night?"

"Mmm, I suppose so," replied Malcolm, not really concentrating on her words as he maneuvered a difficult turn beside a careering bus. "One of my students won a scholarship to university—confirmation came yesterday, so we had a bit of a celebration."

"That's nice," Camilla muttered between clenched teeth. Why did he feel the need to lie to her? Did he sense that she might care? She would have to be very careful, for she could not bear the humiliation if he discovered her true feelings.

"In fact," he continued, "I was thinking of asking you along, but since you don't know each other, I decided to keep the party simple and not run the risk of a strained atmosphere. You'll meet soon enough, I'm sure."

And what could be more simple than a little tête-à-tête, a glass of bubbly, thought Camilla bitterly. Malcolm took his attention from the traffic long enough to steal another quick glance at her, and noticed her clenched jaw.

"Are you in some kind of pain?" he asked conversationally. "You don't look too well."

"I'm fine. I feel just great," she replied, her voice rising above the rattle of the muffler. "Why don't you just stop nagging me?"

"Now, now, temper." He wagged a finger at her. "You redheads must simply learn not to give in to temptation."

"My hair is not red; it's auburn!" she shouted, and with a sharp movement turned her face away from him, uncertain whether she was going to burst into rage or tears.

They drove on for some time in silence, Malcolm concentrating on the traffic, which seemed abnormally heavy. Camilla listened to the sound of her own breathing—loud and labored, it seemed to her—drowning the noise of the road. She hoped Malcolm wouldn't notice how agitated she was.

Finally he reopened the conversation.

"How was your evening? Hope I didn't leave you at a loose end?"

"My evening was great, just dandy. Do you think that I have nothing else to do but hang around waiting to go to dinner with you? I had a nice quiet evening at the hotel. I...I had dinner with one of the gentlemen there—quite a respite, really, from the last fortnight's schedule."

He angrily jammed his foot on the accelerator and overtook a painted truck, loaded on top with shouting waving tribesmen. She stared fiercely in front of her, as he, with equal vehemence, glared through the windshield at the endless stream of white lines down the center of the road.

Camilla could have kicked herself. She had woken up with such good resolutions, and now, when she had a whole day together with him in front of her, she had ruined it already with her temper. She did not see how she could back down, but she knew that it was her turn now to break the silence. For some time they weaved in and out of the traffic system of Kabul, and finally she brought herself to speak.

"Where...where are we going today?" was her tentative peace offering.

"The Jeshn grounds," he growled.

"And what have they got there?" She could sense that her new false brightness was as irritating to him as her temper had been.

"Buzkashi." His words were clipped, brief.

"And what—"

"Here we are," he interrupted her, wheeling Sally into a place full of cars parked hither and thither without regard to ordered rows, but there were even more camels, bicycles and little gray donkeys. The car shuddered to a halt in a cloud of dust, and Malcolm swung his long legs out of the seat in one fluid movement, rose to his full height and strode off toward a collection of cement buildings. Camilla scrambled out of the car after him, pausing for a minute to shade her eyes against the sun and look over what he called the Jeshn grounds.

A vast field sprawled there, level, yellow, as large as three football fields, even bigger perhaps, for it was difficult to assess that sort of size. The area was flat and almost empty except for a pole pitched in the ground near to her end, close to what she could only think of as the goal line. A glimmer at the far end caught her eye, and she realized there was another pole parallel to the first one, but very, very far away. The huge field was surrounded by milling crowds of Afghans in their turbans and robes, Afghans in Western suits, tourists in shorts and summer smocks, women in their mysterious veils. There were people clinging to the roofs of vans, people lying on the tops of the cement buildings, people seated in the cement stands, and still more crowded into the rickety make-shift seats that had been erected especially for whatever athletic event she was apparently going to witness. There were people of all ages and dress everywhere, a bright and colorful mob, laughing, shouting, talking, gesticulating, creating a cheerful holiday din; but above all, there were horses.

She looked in Malcolm's direction, where the largest collection of horses stood, and realized that he had disappeared. She hurried after him, knowing how easy it would be to lose him for the rest of the day in this surging crowd. What had he been wearing?

It was strange, but she never noticed his clothes anymore. Once she had been continually startled at the difference between his English suits and his Afghan clothes, but now they seemed to make no difference to the essential man. Yes, he had been dressed in native fashion today, a powder blue that only emphasized his masculinity, the cloth hanging from him yet clinging in the right places as if it knew it could not hide the muscular power of his body. Then she remembered that he had also been wearing a pair of highly polished leather riding boots, English boots, glossy black and cuffed at the top with red. What was going on?

She found him with Ali Shah, and the young Afghan was dressed in the same clothes, although he wore shoes rather than boots on his feet. They were rubbing down a pair of splendid horses, perfectly formed and as lithe as panthers, with eyes like black pools. Ali Shah's horse was a bay with a black mane reaching to his chest, which he tossed impetuously. Malcolm's horse was larger and, she judged, the more handsome of the two, a long-limbed gray with an arching neck and fire in his wide eyes. He stamped his hoof as if in welcome at Camilla's approach.

She had always been slightly afraid of horses, but she knew that she could not allow herself to be anything but brave when under Malcolm's eye, so she walked up and laid her palm on the neck of the gray stallion. It was as soft as satin, but beneath the quivering skin she could feel the whipcord muscles rolling.

"How beautiful he is," she sighed, and rubbed her cheek against his coat, unable to resist the sensuous softness. "What do you call him?"

Malcolm, heaving a heavy wooden saddle from the ground, grunted, "Ajdahaar." He swung the weight onto his horse's back, and for a moment the animal staggered. Beneath the saddle was already secured a horse blanket woven from heavy Afghan carpet, beautifully patterned in red and gold. Malcolm pulled the girth tighter and, pushing a lock of hair from his eyes, looked up from his work to explain, "That means Dragon."

"And mine is called Malakh," offered Ali Shah, stroking the small velvety ear of his horse. "That means Grasshopper."

"Grasshopper?" Camilla laughed. "He doesn't look like one."

"You should have seen him when he was a colt, then," Malcolm said, grinning at her, seemingly having recovered from his bad temper. "Skinniest little foal I ever saw. Legs like toothpicks. They're from the same herd," he added, placing one hand on the neck of each animal. "So they're on the same team. I would have bought Dragon from Ali Shah's father, but since I played for the team he insisted on giving him to me.''

"Team? What team? What's going on?" Camilla looked from one to the other. "And what is this *buz—buzkashi?*"

"The Afghan national sport, which you are going to be privileged to watch. A bit like polo, only as wild as a tiger where polo is as tame as a cat. Here, Ali Shah." Malcolm handed him Ajdahaar's reins. "Hold him for a moment while I explain to Camilla."

He took her arm, and she had no choice but to follow where he led. He took her over to the edge of the field and, raising both hands, indicated its vastness.

"The game," he began, "is relatively simple. Ten seconds to learn, they say, and a lifetime to master. You see the chalk circle in the center of the field?"

"Barely, in this glare."

"That surrounds a shallow ditch where they drop the beheaded calf. The object is to seize the calf, carry it around the marked pole and then the other—"

"Wait, wait," Camilla gulped, looking rather green. "Did you say beheaded calf?"

"Yes, well, sometimes they use a goat, but today it's a calf—"

"You mean a real dead calf?"

"Come now, it would hardly be alive once its head was cut off, would it?"

"How revolting!"

He folded his arms and smiled at her. "Of all the things you will see in this country, it is *buzkashi* that you must know if you are going to understand the Afghan. The name means 'goat drag,' and that is what it is, in essence. You drag the dead goat, or in this case calf, around the two parallel poles and then drop it back in the chalk circle. Those are all the rules there are.''

"Well, it doesn't sound particularly exciting to me. It must be over in a few minutes.''

Instead of answering her immediately, Malcolm took a step back, tangled his hands in his hair, then looked into the sky. "Picture the scene!" He swept his gaze around to her and she was transfixed by blueness before he stared out beyond her again. "Twenty, thirty horses galloping in a dusty melee on that field. A man sweeps by, his thick braided whip caught between his teeth, the body of the calf tucked under his leg and half slung over his saddle. The other *buzkashi* players, called *chapandazi*, swerve and turn after him, thundering along. The men slash their whips at each other—it was only recently that knives and broken bottles were banned—there are cries of pain and delight. Another *chapandaz* rams the first alongside. The carcass falls; he snatches it, drops it; sweat flecks the horses. A man in a green turban canters up, swinging down low over the edge of his saddle, one foot out of the stirrup till he is galloping horizontal with the earth, his head level with his stallion's belly. With a swift grab he wrenches the calf out of the dust and flings it across his horse's back. Up and down, back and forth they race.''

Camilla caught the excitement in his voice and felt her wrists and temples throb with her rising pulse. "There are no holds barred in *buzkashi*," Malcolm continued. "It can last for two, three hours—an afternoon, until the calf is little more than a tattered piece of leather, still preciously battled over. Men and horses are often injured, not infrequently killed, in the struggle. Often this vast field is not big enough to hold the contest, and they burst through the stands, sometimes injuring the spectators. It's a violent game and an art. It sends the adrenaline rushing through your veins. Some say it's the soul of Afghanistan.''

He took a deep breath, and she tore her gaze away from the field where, in her mind's eye, she too had been breathlessly galloping with the rugged warriors. She watched him, head thrown back, overpoweringly handsome as he radiated a primitive masculine strength.

"That's *buzkashi*," he concluded.

"Malcolm," said Ali Shah, who had come up to them, leading the horses. "I've just seen Nurjan up in one of the makeshift stands. She's with some of the family. I haven't seen her since the news came. Do you mind?" He handed the reins to his friend.

"No, go on; she deserves congratulations. But then maybe I do, too—and don't forget she owes a great deal of it to you." Ali Shah just smiled and disappeared into the crowd.

Camilla still heard the hooves pounding in her head, still felt the thrill of the chase, so she hardly paid mind to the men's exchange.

"So that's the game you and Ali Shah will play?" she asked Malcolm. "I think I understand."

"What?" He turned unseeing eyes toward her. "Sorry, we were talking about *buzkashi*, weren't we?" He looked away. "The game will be starting shortly. You can stand on the sidelines or you could sit over there." He indicated the wooden seats. "If you can find an empty place."

"After what you've told me, I'd prefer to stand where I know I can make a quick getaway if they do burst out of bounds."

He hardly seemed to hear her, but was watching the stands where he had pointed. Camilla saw Ali Shah emerge from the crowd, walk up the rickety steps, make his way toward someone and greet her with a friendly kiss.

There was no mistaking that profile. It might be daylight instead of shadowy dusk, but the image was etched painfully on Camilla's memory. The girl was even more darkly beautiful in the full brightness of the sun. All magic was suddenly gone from the day. Camilla felt desperately chill.

"That girl. . ." she began, and realized Malcolm was looking over at her, too.

"I'd take you over to introduce you, but our groom hasn't shown up yet and I can't leave the horses alone. I would like to have a quick word with her before we start playing, though. Do you think you could hold onto them for a couple of minutes? They're spirited, but they're well trained and they'll stand quiet."

Camilla held out a lifeless hand to take the leather reins. "Yes, of course I'll hold them," she replied woodenly. "You won't be long, will you?"

"Only a couple of minutes. I think they're nearly ready to start." She looked out on the field where he pointed and saw that some of the horsemen were already mounted and gathering. Malcolm stepped away, but she knew there was something she had to ask him. She reached out as he was going and lightly touched his sleeve. He turned a questioning look at her.

"What...what did you mean when you said she owed a great deal of the congratulations to Ali Shah?"

"Oh, only that he got us together. It was his idea, really."

Then she dropped her hand and let him go, so he hurried through the crowd and was soon lost to sight. She had no desire to look up to stands where Nurjan sat; where, in a moment, Malcolm would emerge to embrace her. Camilla leaned forward and buried her face in the rippling white mane of Malcolm's stallion, breathing in the pungent scent of horse and dust and heat, trying to gulp back her tears.

She had never imagined jealousy could be as painful as this. It made her reel with unhappiness, until she flung one arm around the silky neck for support. How could she have allowed her emotions to go even as far as this? It would ruin everything. It would destroy her working arrangement with Malcolm, wreck her chances of finding her sister; it would— But she didn't care any longer. All that mattered was that she was the most miserable person in the world and would willingly at that moment fling herself under the sharp hooves of any galloping horse.

Come on, girl, her better half admonished her sharply. *Pull herself together. What you've got is a crush on the man. It's hardly surprising. He's handsome—the handsomest man you've ever seen. And he has a way with words. Don't let that fool you.*

You've had crushes before. You got over them. The most important thing at the moment is Meghan.

In her despair Camilla could no longer totally agree with her conscience. True, she'd had crushes—and something she had once, mistakenly, thought was love with Jeff. But never had she felt this bitter, intense, paralyzing emotion that she knew by instinct was jealousy. She shut her eyes harder and they burned with unshed teardrops.

"I will not let myself be jealous. I will not let myself fall for him. I will not let myself be jealous...." She repeated it over and over again, mumbling into the horse's mane. The repetition calmed her, but she still had her face pressed against the dappled coat of the limpid-eyed animal when Malcolm returned with Ali Shah.

"Don't fall asleep," Malcolm greeted her. "The excitement's just about to start." She looked up at him as he swung his long frame easily into the saddle, his back and thighs molding to the movement of the horse until it seemed to her that he and his stallion were one. Even in her misery Camilla was moved by the splendid partnership they made.

"Your eyes are red," said Malcolm, leaning over in his saddle toward her. "Not allergic to horses, are you?"

She only managed to avoid screaming, "No."

"Good." He touched his heels to his horse's flanks and they moved off in an easy canter, his body rising and falling in perfect rhythm with Dragon's steps. Camilla's face shone with pride and unshed tears as she watched them, beautiful man and beautiful horse. If only things had been different....

He was circling back now, coming straight for her, and she was so startled by the swiftness of his approach that she had no time to blink or move. Imitating what she later recognized as an old *chapandaz* trick, he leaned in the saddle, just as he had described to her, and with exact aim and timing wrapped his arm around her waist. She was swept up in a flurry of hooves, dust and flying mane, and they were already yards from where she had stood. Flung on her back, across the wooden saddle, her legs poised in the air, she instinctively clung to his neck to prevent her from tumbling to the earth. Her skirt swirled about her knees in the wind their speed created. His tanned face was tantalizingly close to her own, and he let go of the reins so that with his free hand he could reach up and take from between his teeth the brass-inlaid whip he carried.

The horse ran unbridled, his head tossed in the air, nostrils flaring. Malcolm reached down with his whip hand to push from her face her streaming hair, loosened from its bonds in the whirlwind. He bent her chin up and she, in reply, raised her head willingly the rest of the way to his parted lips. They kissed once, feverishly, their mouths burning as hot as the sand beneath Dragon's hooves. Camilla felt as if she were flying, for they seemed barely to skim the earth. Lost in the frenzied crush of his embrace, all she could do was twine her fingers in his tangled locks.

Suddenly Malcolm brought the stallion to a skidding halt, then tossed her lightly to the ground, feet first, so that she landed gently, still feeling the sensation of racing through the air. She raised one hand to her breast and tried to catch her breath. About her the dust swirled in golden clouds.

The horse pranced in tight circles, pawing the ground and snorting, his wild eyes rolling. The man mounted upon him, equally wild, raised his thong-tipped whip to his eyebrow and saluted her smartly, crying, "A kiss for luck!" Then he was away, locked in a crowd with about thirty other rearing trampling horses and shouting flailing men. The crowd surged to its feet and cheered deafeningly. The game had begun.

Camilla was glad that the thrilling ebb and flow of *buzkashi* gave her no time to concentrate on the turmoil of her own emotions, and she turned all her rapt attention to the game. The referee dropped the calf in the chalk circle; there was a wild scuffle and then one of the *chapandazi* won possession of the carcass. He flung it over the horse and was away, the rest of the field thundering after him, weaving and dodging in time like a school of fish. A rearing horse blocked the rider's path; he swerved, hesitated, and then a second horseman in a disheveled green turban came up on his left side and seized one of the legs of the calf. They galloped parallel to each other, tugging and pulling while their horses snapped at each other and members of their two teams belabored each other with whips.

It was violent, exhilarating and very cruel. But the Afghans did not seem to have any qualms about it. They had all, no doubt, been raised with such a sport, so thought nothing of it. Camilla knew, however, that once she was away from the field she would not be able wholeheartedly to approve of the violence of the day's proceedings, and shuddered especially for the injuries done to the horses. The men, she felt, were responsible for themselves. But aside from these moral considerations, the game itself was everything Malcolm had promised it would be, and now she was swept away with enthusiasm as in any sport, cheering with the crowd: "*Namani! Begeer!* Grab it! Get him!"

She shouted with the rest of them, but her exhortations were especially directed to one particular tall *chapandaz*, flashing in blue, his hair whipped by the wind and burnished in the sunlight.

"Malcolm! Malcolm!" she cheered, her body swaying in sympathy with his own, weaving and leaping there on the Jeshn field. Now the calf had spun again to the dust, lost from the grip of both men as their horses shied.

"*Wardar, wardar!*" The crowd lunged to its feet. "Pick it up!" Malcolm was already circling it, the whip in one hand beating off his rivals, while with the other he swung the carcass into the air and then tucked it securely under his leg. He spurred Dragon toward the pole, a quarter of a mile away, with Ali Shah racing by his side, keeping off the encroaching members of the opposing team. For a moment they seemed like eagles to outfly the rest. Camilla had a clear picture of him breaking away from the mob of the players, of the cloud of dust that enveloped them, the hooves of his stallion blurred in motion, he with his head down, leaning into the wind, galloping into the distance with the rest of the world at his heels. It was a supreme thrill. Camilla's body vibrated.

He circled the pole and ran into the tightly packed

herd of horsemen and horses that followed him. For
a moment she lost sight of him, and sand stirred up
by the milling horses veiled the scene. A horse reared,
and she saw it was Dragon, his gray flanks damp with
sweat. Malcolm thrust down with the butt of his
whip, and his horse kicked to create an opening, but
he was surrounded. He tried to toss the carcass to Ali
Shah, but another *chapandaz* intercepted the throw,
and in a moment the field was after him, Ali Shah
racing with them on his reddish brown horse.

Malcolm, however, had reined his stallion in and
was walking him slowly to the sidelines. Camilla ran
up to him, wondering what could have caused him to
retire so suddenly.

"What happened?" she asked when he reached
her. "You were doing so well."

"I think Dragon's strained a muscle—I could feel
him limping slightly. Hold him, will you, please?"

She took the reins and watched him run a sensitive
hand down the horse's back leg. "There, you see?"
he said as the animal flinched. "It's quite minor, and
he's dying to get in there and keep on running with
the rest. But I couldn't risk a permanent injury to
him. Come on."

She walked with him to the cement buildings,
keeping the horse between them. "Are you winning?" she asked presently.

"I think so, but the calf keeps changing hands. No
one's scored yet."

They reached the stable and Malcolm lifted the
heavy saddle from his animal's back, drew off the
thick dusty blanket and rubbed a handful of straw
over Dragon's glistening sides, which were still pant-

ing with the exertion. "Ah," remarked Malcolm, looking up as they were approached by a very fresh-faced boy with a halter in his hand. "Here's our groom." He exchanged some words with him and, patting the horse on his muscled rump, let the groom lead him away. Malcolm watched the horse's gait with a critical eye.

"He'll be all right. Nothing a bit of rest won't cure. But I'm glad I took him out of the game when I did."

An exuberant roar arose from the crowd, and both turned their heads toward it.

"Come!" he exclaimed, striding away. "Something's happened. Let's get back." She had to hasten her footsteps to keep up with him.

The crowd was clapping and cheering, grown men embracing each other. One of Ali Shah's team had scored a point, managing to circle the other pole with the calf and hold onto it until he dropped it in the chalk ring. Ali Shah and his teammates cantered around the circle, hands raised, swirling their whips and laughing in triumph.

"Have we won?" Camilla asked hopefully.

"We've scored a point," Malcolm corrected her. "Sometimes that ends it all, but today's game will go on."

Once again the referee started them off; there was the same mad dash and then the wild horses burst away from the herd as one *chapandaz*, the calf under his leg, raced for the pole with the rest in hot pursuit. The adrenaline surged through Camilla's body. She had never known such excitement as this—she paused at the thought, remembering who stood next to her, realizing that the feelings he aroused in her were very similar, and knowing the intensity of the sensation was doubled when he was near. What had he meant by that hot vicious kiss on horseback? It was dangerous but exciting, too. He was also aroused now, she could sense, but his spirit was with the horsemen on the Jeshn field. Whenever one of his teammates seized the carcass, or whenever it was wrenched from his grasp, Malcolm gripped her arm, transmitting his tension to her, and she relished the fierce grasp. As always, in those moments she forgot everything but him, the danger and the thrill.

"You were so right!" she gasped.

"What?"

"*Buzkashi*. I love it. It's so exciting."

He breathed deeply in the charged atmosphere. "No doubt about it, it's the symbol of Afghanistan. Warriors of courage. Listen...."

She tried to listen to what his ears were catching and could just hear, below the din of the sport and the trampling hooves, the old man near them who sang under his breath in a fluting Afghan melody. He swayed to the tune, which matched the rhythm of the hoofbeats.

"'Better come home stained with blood than safe and sound as a coward,'" Malcolm translated for her.

"I understand," replied Camilla, repeating the words to herself, identifying not with the violence but with the fearless drive of the players, the desire to meet the challenge of the game and ultimately win. Sometime, somehow, she would show Malcolm that she, too, had soaked up some of the spirit of Afghanistan; that she, too, could risk herself; that she was not a coward.

"Oh, no!" His exclamation froze her blood, and she jerked her eyes upward.

The horses were out of control. The *chapandaz* with the calf was using both hands to fight off his rivals, and his mount, in the dust and struggle, was running blind and guideless. They were heading straight for the rickety stands, the men too wrapped up in the game to see where they were headed and almost unable now, even if they had seen, to rein back their fiery horses in time.

"Run, run!" came the shouts from the threatened seats. Such an event was never totally unexpected in *buzkashi*, and most of the male spectators were already on their feet, immediately leaping to safety. The wooden structure swayed with their haste. But the wrapped veiled women were more hampered by their long latticed garments, and the air was filled with their cries.

"Nurjan!" gasped Malcolm, and was running to the danger area before Camilla could cry out. Etched in her memory was the image of his stricken face. She knew she ought to run after him, try to help, but her legs would not move.

The *chapandazi* now seemed to realize they were running headlong into disaster, but would they react in time to avert it? They began to pull on their horses' reins. The field was a screeching confusion: the calf was dropped, horses reared and kicked, men were thrown and lay about them clutching their whips, and spectators ran hither and thither. The momentum of the gallop still carried the remaining players toward the bounds of the field, but their speed began to slacken, and many on the outside of the combat were able to turn sharply and canter to the right or left. The majority of the two teams were still locked together, however, and at the moment of apparent impact Camilla screamed, clapping her hands over her ears and shutting her eyes.

A split second later she opened them, grasping for the first time the fact that Malcolm, in running to save Nurjan, had put himself in danger. This thought at last freed her frozen limbs. She gasped and ran. What if he had injured himself—broken a leg, his back, perhaps been killed? What if he had lost his life trying to rescue that girl? Fear, bitter jealousy and terror throbbed in Camilla's mind, and she imagined a thousand dreadful things, each one worse than the one before, and each made more painful by the thought that it was all for the sake of the smiling lovely Afghan beauty she had seen him embracing.

"I can't bear it, I can't bear it!" she cried.

The billowing clouds of dust were slowly settling, and the scene they revealed was one of anticlimax. The stands were vacant but still in place, although shaking. Many people were sitting on the ground, but none appeared injured. The crowd of spectators was still gesticulating and shouting, but strangely most were also laughing. Several riders had dismounted and were checking their horses for injuries as Malcolm had done. One *chapandaz*, his turban unwound about his shoulders, was spread-eagled on the ground, shaking his fist at his galloping riderless horse, which was fast disappearing across the now empty field.

"A close call," said a voice above her. She looked up and saw Ali Shah still on his bay steed, wiping his forehead with the back of his hand, but with his brown face beaming merrily. "Nothing like a bit of excitement to spice up the game."

"Is that what you call it?" she replied weakly. She looked around her again and agreed that none of the participants appeared the worse for wear. In fact, to judge from the tone of their voices and the expression on their faces, they had rather enjoyed their brush with death. Again she felt as far as ever from understanding the Afghan personality.

"Where is—Malcolm?" she asked Ali Shah shakily.

"With Nurjan," he replied, as she had known the answer would be. Slowly she turned to see Malcolm and the Afghan girl seated on the ground, laughing and relaxed. Camilla hesitated to approach them, reluctant to break in on the charming happy pair they evidently formed. But Ali Shah was riding over, so she followed. Malcolm leaped to his feet as they drew near, patted the bay's neck and smiled impishly at her.

"No injuries. A lucky escape for everyone," he remarked. "But look at this girl here." He turned on Nurjan a look so full of admiration that it stung Camilla. He went on, "I think she enjoyed every minute of it. Look at that grin."

"I'm a quick mover," admitted the girl in faultless lilting English. "I knew I could get away. A little taste of danger is always thrilling, don't you think?"

Under no circumstances would Camilla have admitted at that moment that she had been very far from thrilled. She did not want to concede that the Afghan girl might be made of sterner stuff than herself. Malcolm, however, had no such qualms.

"All I can say is, you had me frightened for a moment. I thought you were going to run right into the stands," he said to Ali Shah.

"You should know the skill of your fellow *chapandazi* better than that," his friend admonished him. "Anyway, when Amanullah captures his horse I think the game will go on. Do you want to ride Malakh for a while? Or stay with Nurjan?"

"Go on?" Camilla interjected in a startled tone. "You mean you're going to go on playing—after that?"

"Of course—" Nurjan began, but Malcolm raised a hand to stop her. He had noticed Camilla's extreme pallor and the way her hands shook, although he did not guess the real cause.

"I think our guest's had enough excitement for one day," he stated firmly, then tardily introduced the two women. "I won't stay any longer, Ali Shah. Can you arrange for Dragon to be taken care of—he's pulled a muscle in the off hind. I'll take Camilla back now."

Camilla experienced an overwhelming surge of gratitude for this act of consideration. As Malcolm shook hands with Ali Shah and Nurjan, as he smiled down into her dark, exotically handsome face, she realized something that surprised and pleased her. The joy and relief of finding him safe and sound had far outweighed the jealousy experienced every time she saw him with the girl.

NONE OF THE DAYS THAT FOLLOWED matched the excitement and anguish of the game of *buzkashi*. Indeed, after that day Camilla rarely saw Malcolm, and for that she was glad. She could live with the hurt she felt when she thought of him, but when she saw him it became almost unbearable. The faithful Ali Shah scouted the bazaars every day for news; he questioned every truck driver who arrived from the north, in the hope that one might have met a tribe of Kuchis with a foreign woman. They agreed among themselves that, while it was likely the police might have information that could be useful to them, it was better not to get involved with the law, especially after the near brush with the heroin. Camilla never knew what Malcolm had done with the drug, and she didn't want to know. That way, if they asked her she would not be able to tell them a thing.

They questioned the townspeople of outlying villages, too, and those who lived near the Kuchi grounds in Kabul. They were rewarded with little information: the townspeople were by nature suspicious of both the nomads and the foreigners and wanted little to do with either. Camilla could get nowhere with them. They were only moderately cooperative even with Malcolm and his expert Persian. They really opened up only with Ali Shah, who was proving invaluable. Camilla couldn't decide whether the people questioned actually knew nothing or whether they just wouldn't tell, but the investigation never uncovered anything worthwhile. Malcolm was afraid of seeming too obvious and attracting attention, so they didn't press their questions when the townsfolk became obtuse.

Their first break seemed to come when they got word that a tribe of Kuchis had arrived in Kabul. Malcolm's servant brought the news and they immediately drove out to the campsite, a few miles out of the city on some old military maneuver grounds. Camilla had taken the precaution of covering her auburn hair with a silk scarf, for Afghans of both sexes found its exotic color strangely magnetic, so that they were compelled to stroke it. The Kuchis seemed to approve of this modesty, for they were very welcoming, and for once Malcolm and Camilla had the pleasant experience of being less suspected than Ali Shah.

Malcolm and the Afghan went to have tea with the chief of the tribe, but Camilla was spirited away with the women. They were very handsome people, she decided; and she was surprised at the freedom the women enjoyed compared to those she had met elsewhere. They wore no veils, but were dressed in frocks of the same style as the one she had bought on Chicken Street, in startling colors—black, blue and red. Their necks were draped in heavy jewelry, their noses pierced as well as their ears, often with coins hanging in them. And on their hands they wore multiple rings connected from finger to finger with thin chains of silver, while their arms were covered with thick jewel-studded bracelets, solid from wrist to elbow. They were tall with strong fierce faces, dark and exotic.

Camilla was both intrigued and frightened by the Kuchis; unlike Meghan, she felt no strong attraction to them. These people were elemental, too close to the earth. Camilla knew now she was not one to pass up readily the good things in life. She was English, educated, accustomed to all the modern conveniences of Western life, and to live with these people she would have to forget all those things.

They all sat down inside a dark tent; tea was produced in a small tin pot, and she wondered how she was going to make conversation.

"I am looking for my sister. She is a nurse. *Parastaar*—my sister is a nurse."

As soon as the magic word *parastaar* was spoken Camilla was subjected to an endless parade of what she supposed were minor ills. She felt overwhelmed.

"I want to see my friend," she said firmly in the best Persian she could muster. One woman strode off and returned shortly with Ali Shah.

"Ali Shah, please explain to them that I haven't got any medicines with me."

"Why should they think you have?"

"Well," she admitted, feeling foolish, "one of the few words I know in Persian is *parastaar*. I tried to say my sister was a nurse, but I can't make them understand. I guess they think I meant me."

The Afghan laughed, showing perfect white teeth. "That was your number-one mistake."

"I couldn't think of anything else to say," she replied, "but don't tell Malcolm."

Quickly Ali Shah explained to the gathering of women that the red-haired *farangi* had not brought her black bag with her because she was not a nurse. They were disappointed and appeared to lose interest.

"And I thought we were getting on so well," said Camilla dispiritedly.

"Never mind," answered the young man, "we've

got to go now. We've found out everything they know, and that is not much." He took her arm then and led her out of the tent. Malcolm was sitting in the car and watched them come over.

"They do know something," he told her when she had got into the Land Rover. "They admitted they had heard a rumor that one tribe farther up north had a light-haired foreigner with them. They couldn't say which tribe, or where, or even if the foreigner was a man or a woman. But I can't tell whether that is really all they know or just all they want us to know. If a tribe really has your sister, they'd be pretty unwilling to lose anyone with medical knowledge. So they couldn't say either because they didn't know or they aren't allowed to—either way we're little better off."

"But it *must* be her! Who else could it be? All we have to do is search every single tribe—"

"Oh, no; I don't think you realize how impossible that is or you wouldn't have said it. This country is vast, most of it wilderness: we couldn't track down every tribe, nor search them if we did find them. We don't have the time or the money. Now I see your lower lip getting stubborn, Camilla. Don't think you'll run off and search every tribe by yourself. We'll wait until we get some more definite information before we set out on a hunt like that."

As if he were running it, and not she! But the mental protest was a reflex. She had no real desire to argue with him. She wished to show him she was capable of reasoning as well as arguing, of cooperation as well as dissent, and she held her tongue. Still, he did not seem impressed.

"No need to sulk, Camilla," he said coldly when he found she said nothing.

"I'm not sulking," she replied tartly.

"No need to snap, either. You must forgive me if I'm wrong, but you do have a tendency to sulk, you know. First impressions always last."

That was what she was afraid of.

IT WAS ANOTHER WEEK before the next lead turned up, and Camilla, to her great satisfaction, discovered it herself.

Janet was in the habit of frequenting the used-clothes bazaar behind the main street of the old city, and she often took Camilla with her. The English girl found it a fascinating, and sometimes amusing, place, like miles and miles of one enormous jumble sale, shady and cool beneath canvas awnings. There one could wander from shop to shop and find the most amazing bargains: a Gucci scarf, scarcely worn blue jeans, a silk evening dress, shoes and shirts in perfect condition, hanging on rails next to worn-out sweaters and tattered skirts. If one was willing to hunt one could make up quite a sizable wardrobe. The business of importing clothes from America and Europe was one of Afghanistan's most profitable industries, and Camilla was thankful for it. It was better than any flea market she had ever been to, and more exotic.

One day, finding she had a free afternoon on her hands, Camilla went for a stroll in the used-clothes bazaar. She had intended to buy several roomy white men's shirts in case they did any more work in the desert, but she found herself so tempted that before half an hour was out she had purchased a long billowing skirt in red velvet and, for a laugh, a Russian soldier's cap for only twenty-five afghanis. She still had not acquired the shirts she'd set out for, and set herself more firmly to the task.

She did not hurry along, for the place was so pleasant and the atmosphere so relaxed it seemed a shame to rush. Within the long dark covered alleys a soft breeze blew, hawkers advertised their wares in musical Persian and women in *chadaris* floated along, stirring up the dust where they passed so that golden motes of dust turned over lazily in midair, caught by the fingers of sunlight that crept through tears or gaps in the canvas.

Camilla paused at a corner of this maze of people, cloth, wood and earth to fully take in such a picture. Her heart gave a funny twirl; she felt like laughing and crying at the same time. She was reminded of that old feeling of strangeness and otherworldliness she had had when she first arrived; frightening then, it amused her now.

"Afghanistan grows on you," Johnny had told her the day she arrived, but she had not believed him then, because the foreign place had seemed something outside herself. She believed him now, though; the country had worked its magic on her, become a part of her. The dust, the heat, the sun, the men and women were in her blood as Johnny had said they would be. She no longer turned her head to watch a flock of fat-tailed sheep go waddling down the street, or to gape at the sight of a camel train. The melodious flow of Persian was more appealing to her ears than the continual chatter of English, and she could set her watch by the Noon Gun and the call of the muezzin, rather than the Greenwich mean-time signal. It was England that seemed strange now.

And even more surprising, the familiarity of Afghanistan was more wonderful to her than its original strangeness had been. For no reason she could think of, Malcolm came to her mind. He loved this place, too; that gave them something in common, for in loving the country she could perhaps understand him a little better. *And maybe he will like me a little more,* she wished fervently.

As she turned the corner, something caught her eye—she had a strong feeling of something personal, familiar, near to her. She turned back to the shop. It was the most extraordinary feeling—what had she glimpsed? A well-known combination of colors, a familiar line?

"Yes, *memsahib*?" asked the shopkeeper putting down a handful of clothes he had been about to move to another rack. Camilla realized she must have been acting strangely.

"Just looking," she replied, and started working her way through the racks of clothes.

A little shop boy with wide dark eyes wandered in from the back room and watched her curiously. She smiled at him and was warmed by the answering sparkle in his eyes. But she found nothing, and she felt a bit foolish, especially with the shopkeeper's bright eyes fixed upon her. She thought she would go. As she walked away from the man, in a bid to keep her business, he called out, "You not see what you like?"

"No, nothing I want today, thank you." Camilla

went to turn away, but his insistent voice called her back again.

"Perhaps you like pretty frock like this?" He searched through the discarded pile and brought out a dress.

Camilla's whole body quivered with excitement. That was what had caught her eye as she wandered by, but she hadn't been able to find it because he had scooped it up. But why that one? It was an uncanny coincidence. How could she be sure that it was the one she thought it was?

"It is a very beautiful dress," she agreed, holding out her hands. "Let me see it, please."

In fact, she thought as she fingered it, familiarity sinking in, it was not a very beautiful dress. She had never thought so. It was certainly not her style at all—the colors were all wrong for her hair and the line was too severe. But for Meghan, who had made it, it was perfect: she was wandlike, with an aureole of fair hair that Camilla had always envied, and the dress and the girl together had combined to give an air of simple sophistication.

Camilla wanted to take the dress and run, sit down, touch it, turn it over, contemplate it and what it meant. Immediately she put aside those longings, however. She must question, must get to the root of the mystery of this dress, or Malcolm would never forgive her. She grasped it firmly and began as matter-of-factly as she could, "It certainly is a very attractive dress. Where did you get it?"

The man shrugged. "Most of our clothes come from America."

She could feel the evasion and gritted her teeth; but

she could hardly accuse this man of being a liar in his own shop. Afghans, Ali Shah had told her, took such things very personally. She wanted this man on her side. More... tact was needed. Yes, she must appeal to his pride, not insult it. She thought quickly.

"It is such a good dress that I don't believe it could have come from America," she said tentatively. "I think it was made here in Kabul. Is that true?"

"Yes, *memsahib*," he agreed. The customer was always right. He was obviously going to be difficult to plumb. She tried again.

"If that is so, you must tell me the shop so that I can go and buy another dress." She was surprised at her own cleverness. She must be learning.

The man gulped; he saw himself both being caught out in a lie and losing a sale.

"Very expensive shop," he assured her. "Better to buy here."

"Ah, yes, but I am willing to pay for a dress that no one has worn."

"There is no shop."

"But you have just told me there is one," she pointed out sweetly. "A very expensive one."

His pride struggled with his greed; she could see the battle written on his face and wondered which would win. Greed did.

"I was thinking of other shop. This I buy from Kuchis." He looked gratified as her face lit up with excitement.

"That makes it extremely valuable," she said, almost trembling with the effort of hiding her emotion. "How long have you had it?"

Probably seeing that telling the truth seemed, for

once, to bring him profit, he answered what appeared to Camilla to be honestly. "Almost a week."

Camilla could have kissed him. "Six hundred afghanis," he ventured. But to his apparent surprise she didn't make a single attempt to bargain, merely paid the six hundred afghanis very cheerfully, shook his hand warmly and danced off, the dress over one arm, exuding joy. In a moment of recklessness, she turned back and gave the sweet boy a few coins. His beaming face was enough to assure her that she had made an instant friend.

After she had walked long enough to work off the first excitement, Camilla stopped, standing in a pool of light, and held the dress at arm's length. She could not believe her luck; in fact she did not believe it was luck. The incident reinforced a sneaking suspicion she had always had in favor of fate and predestination. Surely she was meant to find Meghan! At this moment she believed she was fated to success, and it was a wonderful feeling.

Then she felt a coolness on her back, as though a shadow had fallen across it, and turned quickly. She saw nothing out of the ordinary: men, women and dogs passing in the dust. Her eyes focused. She could see the clothes displayed outside a nearby corner shop swinging back and forth as though moved by a strong breeze, or recently brushed; the shadow was gone.

CHAPTER ELEVEN

CAMILLA'S INSTINCT commanded her to run in the opposite direction. But by an effort of will she did not. Instead she hurried forward, seeking around the corner for some explanation, and she saw a tall thick man forcing his way through the crowded alley. The people seemed willing to move to let him pass; in a few seconds he was out of sight. Perhaps he was a pickpocket. Camilla felt for her purse; but yes, all the money was still there. Probably he was late for some appointment, she told herself, trying to shrug as nonchalantly as the shopkeeper. She tried to forget the foreboding chill across her back; after all, the place was full of shifting shadows.

Finally emerging from the twisting bazaar streets, she raised one hand to shelter her eyes from the sun and, carrying all her purchases across the other arm, with some difficulty hailed a cab. She had to tell someone about her discovery—she was bursting with the news.

Malcolm. But she didn't know how exactly to reach him and she didn't have Ali Shah's number, either.

"Karte Char," she directed the driver. She would see Janet. She hoped she was in.

The black-and-white rattling cab drew up beside the now familiar high cement wall. Camilla was greeted by the barking wagging Elsa, even bigger now, and then Janet's smiling freckled face.

"Camilla, great to see you! Everything's in a bit of a mess—in fact a lot of a mess. I wasn't expecting visitors. But come on in; I'm in need of a break."

"I've got the most exciting news to tell you!" exclaimed Camilla, kissing her warmly on the cheek.

"Yes, I can tell you have. Are you and Malcolm engaged?"

Funny, thought Camilla, how unfunny she found that. She felt herself coloring and could not think of an answer as she followed Janet into the living room. *You must not be so sensitive,* she told herself.

"Hope you don't mind sitting in the aftermath of a hurricane," said Janet, still chuckling, more at Camilla's reaction to her question than at the joke itself. "I always like to do my spring-cleaning in the middle of the summer."

Camilla looked with concern at Janet's rounded figure. "Do you think it's good for you? I mean, in this heat. . . ."

"Oh, a little exercise never hurt anybody. And I get so bored when Johnny's away and I'm not working. Besides, Abdulah could never do the job properly. And I could invent a thousand other reasons, but mostly I just like spring-cleaning at all times of the year. It's so thorough! But come on," she said eagerly, slapping her knees, "news first!"

"I found this in the used-clothes bazaar," said Camilla a trifle breathlessly, holding up the dress, the precious dress.

"I *thought* you'd been shopping. Used-clothes

bazaar, eh? You're becoming a real addict. Don't mind my saying so, but pink—it doesn't suit you."

Camilla had to laugh. "No, it doesn't! This dress belonged to my sister."

Janet sat for a moment, her eyes wide, taking it in. Then she leaped up and, flinging her arms around the English girl, embraced her enthusiastically. "Oh, Camilla!" was all she could say.

They sat for a minute, Camilla nearly crying with happiness. Then Janet asked quietly, "So what does it mean?"

Camilla explained the whole episode to her, proud of the skill with which she had dealt with the shopkeeper.

"Well, you're becoming quite the detective," said Janet, smiling.

"An effective detective!" added Camilla, and they both laughed at that.

"I see Malcolm's taught you a lot," went on Janet, smiling, observing Camilla's reaction. She was rewarded with a shine in the eyes, an inclination of the body and a slight reddening of the cheeks.

"Malcolm!" exclaimed Camilla. "I wanted to tell him, but I don't have his number."

"Shall I get it for you?" offered Janet, a mischievous gleam in her eyes.

"Oh, yes, please. I was hoping...."

"Yes?"

"That you'd have it," finished Camilla lamely. That wasn't what she'd been hoping, but it was as good an answer as any. She didn't know exactly what she really was hoping.

Janet went off into the hall to fetch the telephone

book, and was not surprised to find Camilla followed her in a minute.

"Could you—I mean, would you mind. . . phoning Malcolm for me?" she asked Janet.

"Whatever for?" replied Janet innocently.

"I. . . I don't mean—I mean," she stumbled, looking at the floor. "I just feel foolish—so excited. He wouldn't get foolish or excited. He'd take it calmly. Maybe it isn't even important—I mean, maybe. . . ."

"Don't be so silly," Janet chided her. "I can't understand your reluctance." Although the knowing glint in her eye revealed that she could understand it perfectly well. "It's really important—well, I think it is—perhaps the most important single discovery you've made so far. Go on! Here's the number. You ring." Janet handed her the telephone directory and went out.

Camilla took up the receiver, listening to the scratchy dial tone. What if it wasn't especially significant or was even irrelevant, or what if she'd done something wrong—how could she be so proud over something so small? She couldn't bear it if she were wrong again and he were right.

"I don't hear that dial turning!" called Janet from the kitchen. There was another moment of silence and then, slowly, the whirr of the dial, the pause while the line was connected and rang at the distant location until someone came to answer it.

"Hello, is M—Mr. Armstrong there? No? Who is this?. . . Are you his cook?. . . Please, could you speak up. . . oh, thank you. . . . Where is he?. . . The school?. . . No, I don't want the number. . . . No, thank you. . . . When will he be back?. . . No, I'll ring again.... Miss Simpson, Camilla.... Yes, good-bye.''

"He's at the school, Janet," she told her as she came into the kitchen.

"Yes, I heard."

"Why would he be there now? I thought it was closed for the summer."

"He's tutoring one of his pupils. Brilliant kid."

"Do you think I should ring the school?"

"I wouldn't bother," replied Janet, shaking her head. "He wouldn't answer. Never lets himself be interrupted at his work."

"Never mind." Camilla was half relieved, half disappointed. "I can call him later. What nationality is this pupil? American?"

"No—Afghan." They went back into the living room and had coffee, chatting about this and that, but always coming back to two subjects: Malcolm and the search.

"It seems you're pretty close to the end of your search, then," Janet remarked as they talked. "Once you find Meghan I guess you'll be off back to England. We'll really miss you, you know...."

This remark was food for thought later to Camilla as she paced up and down her room in the hotel, wondering if she ought to phone Malcolm again. She paused by her window, looking out onto the busy street scene, drinking it in. Back to England. Once she would have said "back home," but it was not home any longer. Had it ever been home? Not for her, not as an adult. It had been home for Camilla the child, when her parents were alive, but then it had been a different place: the place of family, of jobs, of obedience, of the now forgotten Jeff. With those things gone, what was it to her now? Her independence, her pride, her freedom—these were born with her coming to Afghanistan. And Malcolm was here, dear Malcolm. There was so much here that she loved: the sky, the earth, mountains, deserts, forests, camels, the people, the clarity of the light—everything that she loved was here.

And what about Meghan? Camilla had never really considered what she might want; she had always assumed her sister was eagerly waiting to be found and taken back to England. But what was England to her? The same lost childhood as Camilla's, the nursing career so soon broken, a dead marriage with a dead husband, the round of housekeeping and polite socializing. Could she go back after a life of wandering? Would she want to go back?

And if Meghan would not go back, would she, Camilla, go back alone to an empty flat and a loveless future? Nothing could ever be the same since meeting Malcolm! How could she go back?

Her hand was shaking. She was holding the paper with Malcolm's number on it. It fluttered to the floor. She bent to pick it up.

There was a loud explosion, a crash, and Camilla heard a whistling streak by her ear as she swiftly flung herself flat on the floor and the bullet sped on to bury itself in the opposite wall. She clung to the carpet, her fingers and toes knotted, the frantic pounding of her heart making her head pulse with the beat and her ear tingle. She waited for a second shot—lifetimes, it seemed, but only seconds—then there was a shouting and uproar in the street, the bark of a rifle, not at her, but far away, car doors slamming and the rev of engines.

Slowly she stood up, not trembling, not white; strange, but she did not feel frightened as she walked to the curtains and drew them back, keeping herself hidden. The glass of the window was cracked and shattered in a pattern like a spider's web, but through it she could make out a chocolate-colored streamlined car lounging by the curb. It was waiting and watching, and she watched it. Across the distance she recognized him, the shape of his head, his manner of moving as she observed the gathering crowd. Then, with a tap on the driver's broad shoulder, the car began to move off, slow and suave, looking too classy to be involved in such a sordid occurrence. But Camilla knew better.

After it was all over, she was amazed at her presence of mind and agreed with Janet that she must be learning from Malcolm, for in this event her sangfroid equaled his own in the police search. She considered her position coolly and quickly.

The police would be there soon. She must be away before they came, for it was impossible to think she would escape in-depth questioning, having so recently been suspected of carrying drugs. If she could get out of the hotel, she could get a taxi and go to Malcolm. He would know what to do. There was no time to phone.

Hastily she formed a plan in her mind and printing it there went into action with firm steps. She picked up the dress, slipped it into a bag, grabbed her purse, walked out of the door and locked it, then went to the elevator, got in and descended to the ground floor.

Emerging, she found the lobby full of people. This was good, for she could slip unnoticed through the crowd. She walked through with unbroken strides, and seeing an American there whom she recognized slightly she called out, "What's going on?"

He waved and hurried over. "Miss Simpson! So you are all right."

She swallowed hard. Now she would have to act. She felt a betraying tremor behind her knees and ordered it to stop immediately.

"All right? Of course I'm all right; why shouldn't I be? What's going on?"

He looked at her oddly. "Didn't you hear? The man shot straight at your window—we thought you were dead."

"Dead—shot?" She forced what she hoped was a very realistic laugh. "Well, I assure you I'm not. You must be mistaken. I didn't hear a thing except this uproar. The rest of the people here don't seem very worried—no one came up to see if I *was* dead." She inserted a tone of humor. "It must have been another room."

"They were afraid to go up in case they found a body."

"Brave men!" Her laugh was incongruous in that nervous exclaiming crowd. "Anyway, who would want to shoot me?" She sauntered off again, deliberately keeping her pace slow, appearing uninterested so as not to call attention to herself, her hands clenched so that they would not shake. She gained the door, the only person fighting to get out among countless others fighting to get in. At last she was free of the crowd, and beating back a desire to run and hide, to protect herself against the gunman who might even now be getting her in sight from atop some roof, she kept her pace to an easy stroll on the hot pavement.

With a jolt she saw two policemen coming toward her, hurrying, their eyes fixed on her. She was surprised at the great calm that filled her, the relaxed inner voice telling her exactly what to do.

Easy, easy; if you break now you've had it. Walk, slow down, smile at them, that's it. They looked at you; do you think. . . ? No, they're going on, they've passed you—round this corner, good girl. . . .

The pavement seemed a hundred miles long, and her own speed less than that of a snail. It was the hardest thing she had ever done, and her heart kept beating steadily—*stay calm, calm,* she ordered herself. Was it only two minutes ago that the bullet had whistled by her head? No, it felt like two years. She had forgotten it.

Out of the corner of her eye she saw a taxi approach, and turning, she waved it down. Easily she bargained with the driver and with an almost forceful eagerness beat him down to the lowest price she had ever paid. She slid into the back seat. "To the school."

"Which school, *khanum*?"

She thought a minute. "American school."

"Ah, Darulaman."

The taxi pulled away from the pavement, and as they drove off she felt a sudden need to look back. She could have laughed; the same two policemen rounded the same corner she had just passed, and as they scanned the long street for her their faces fell.

She had pulled a magic trick, like the bikini-clad lady in the magician's box. She had disappeared.

The drive to the school was long but pleasant, for she forced all thought of the latest incident from her mind. She had never been along this street before. Each side was lined with plane trees and poplars, and it ran, straight as an arrow, toward the Summer Palace, a pale cream edifice like a doll's house in the distance, against a dark blue backdrop of mountains. She appreciated the beauty of the evening, the slanting sun and the fresh foliage.

But, it was all so strange, for she felt as if she were acting onstage or in some film with the scenery projected on a screen behind her. That bullet—what bullet? What gun? Patrice—who was he?

Almost too soon the cab stopped. When she got out she had red circles on the insides of her knees where they had been pressed together. Untwisting her fingers, she paid the cabman and he drove off.

The place looked less like a school than some sort of camp-cum-farm. To her left was one wing of the building, wood that was painted yellow with a tin roof, big glass windows and green curtains. To the right stood the other wing, with a porch in front of the door. The stretch of earth between them, for they were not joined, was dipped and worn practically bare between the two doors. Farther away was a primitive set of playground equipment, wooden monkey bars—unless it was scaffolding—and an old worn tire suspended on a frayed rope. The playing fields were wide, occupied by a herd of grazing Karakul sheep. The place seemed deserted.

She had put the events of the past half hour so

firmly out of her mind—in an act of mental self-preservation—that she almost forgot why she had come. She felt dazed, lost, moving with weights tied to her feet, as when one runs in a dream. It was like the pictures she had seen when young on the notice boards in her school, bearing captions like: Children's Mission in the Congo—Please Give Generously. She was reminded of missionaries—Albert Schweitzer and Dr. Livingstone.

So this was where Malcolm worked, where he gave generously of his talents. That genius was spending his working life in this shack; this peeling building was the center of his labors. Did he love the yellow school as he loved the golden country? It was really a hideous place, yet she wanted to know every part of it.

Dreamily she wandered around to the left. The first thing she saw was a high cement wall, painted light blue and also peeling, resembling a raised swimming pool. On top of it she could see rows of plants—cabbages, as far as she could make out. Some garden! She walked on behind the left wing of the school, past a large tangle of chicken wire. Through the windows she could see wall posters of scenic places with bright letters in red, white and blue: U.S.A. Maybe all American schools were like this. A goat was lying on the grass, ruminating peacefully, and chickens ran around and around behind the wire of their cage. There was a monkey that threw itself screaming against its bars, and some rabbits. Perhaps it was a zoo.

She could not reconcile this place with her image of him. He was big and golden, and the school was small and scruffy. He was outstanding—this place so modest. He deserved better; he could have it if he wanted, and she wanted to know why he didn't.

"Excuse me—are you looking for someone?"

Camilla jumped and turned, shaking, eyes widening like a frightened rabbit's.

"Miss Simpson!"

"Nurjan!"

Of course Camilla should have expected to find her here. In the evening light she looked lovelier than ever, with her sloe eyes, thick lashes, long heavy black hair and straight white teeth. Away from the excitement and danger of the *buzkashi*, her beauty was suffused with a gentle calm. Her dark eyes filled with sympathy as she laid a slender brown hand on Camilla's trembling arm.

"I am sorry that I startled you. I can see you are not well. Can I help you?"

Camilla could not prevent herself from shrinking away at the girl's touch. She could not accept her sympathy.

"Your face is white. You have had some sort of shock," Nurjan continued, her concern evident.

Pointless now to think of seeing Malcolm—not with this girl here. Camilla could not bear even to think of them together. Suddenly she felt herself reeling and her eyes swam before her; she turned away from Nurjan, stepping back and almost falling.

The Afghan girl put out an arm to catch her but then drew it back, saying instead in a gentle voice, "How silly of me; you have come to see Malcolm, haven't you?" The sound of his name on her lips made Camilla's heart hammer. "Can you come with me? I know where he is." She did not take Camilla's arm but walked in front of her, leading the way into the building. Camilla felt that she had no choice but to follow.

The interior walls were gray and lined with wooden lockers that were a dirty yellow. Graffiti, election slogans and brightly painted signs spattered the walls. Nurjan took Camilla to a door—also a washed-out yellow—and opening it said, "You can sit here. It's the staff room."

Camilla was still on her feet only by sheer effort of will. She managed to say, in a tight small voice, "I want to see Malcolm."

"You must sit down. You are shaking so much you can hardly stand."

"Please," pleaded Camilla, "let me see him."

Nurjan now took her arm firmly, ignoring Camilla's feeble efforts to break free, and forced her with a gentle shove onto the sofa. Camilla sat obediently, her hands clasped together. "I will bring Malcolm to you here," she said, and shut the door behind her.

Camilla looked desperately around the room. It was furnished with a variety of broken tables, springless armchairs and cracked mugs. The ceiling was painted with an exotic fresco of clouds and treetops, as if one were lying on the ground, looking up. Camilla fixed her eyes on it. Why was she here? Why had she come? Other questions crowded her mind, so confused that she heard none of them properly.

Then the door opened.

He filled the doorway and the light streamed behind him, lighting his gold hair and shadowing his eyes to a dark blue.

"Camilla! Camilla, why are you here? What's happened? Nurjan said she found you wandering about outside—Camilla? Camilla!"

For he was there at last and she, no longer needing to be strong, had begun to cry, deep racking sobs wrenched up from the depths of her breast, dry tears full of terror, as she rocked back and forth with her hands clasped about her knees and her head thrust back.

He was beside her in one movement, his arms wrapped around her so that she was cradled in them, giving her the warmth and comfort she craved. She pressed her face against his shoulder, clinging and weeping. The violence of her sobbing shook both their bodies, and he stroked her hair and dropped slow kisses on her forehead and neck in an attempt to calm her. "Shh, Camilla, shh, my dear. It's all right. I'm here; look, it's all right...."

The knowledge that he was indeed there, holding her safe, broke loose all her controls, and her weeping increased now that she no longer had to hold back her terrified emotions. She clung to his rocklike strength. In between her tears she drew deep stuttering breaths that refueled her hysterical crying. In her anguish, her hands clawed against his back.

Malcolm took the only way he could to stop her. The shock of his cool lips pressed against her shaking ones stopped her trembling, and his kiss was so long and deep that she could no longer draw breath to cry. The kiss that had so often sent her out of her senses this time, by its sensation, broke through her hysteria and brought back her self-control. Feeling her tensed muscles relax, he planted a kiss on each tearstained cheek and drew back.

She pushed a drenched lock of hair out of her eyes and looked up at him with a grateful expression. Several times she tried to speak, but the attempt was too much, and he hushed her. Finally she said in a tear-choked voice, "They tried to kill me!"

"Tell me."

"They shot through my window at me; they would have hit me, but I bent down to pick up a paper. They would have shot me in the h-head!" and she began crying again, miserably.

She never knew how long he held her in his arms, but at last the tears dried, the fears calmed a little, and she realized she was safe and it was over. Suddenly she felt embarrassed and moved away a little.

"Feeling better?" She started at the kindness of his voice, which she had never heard before and never dreamed to have directed at her. Her heart fluttered.

"Y-yes. I'm sorry."

"Why?"

"Your shirt—it's soaked."

He laughed, not at her or about her, not cruelly or cuttingly, but gently and softly. "That's the least important thing I can think of."

They sat in silence for a minute.

"Can you tell me?"

"Yes...now," she said, and twisted something in her hands. She looked down and saw that it was his handkerchief, and clung to it because she did not want to give it back. He saw and didn't mind.

"Keep it. But tell me now."

Slowly she recounted the events in the hotel, pretending to herself it was some story she was telling, perhaps the plot of a show she had seen on television. He listened wordlessly, but his brow was furrowed.

When she had faded away into silence, he stood up, running his tanned hands through his golden mane, eyes flashing. He seemed, for once, to be lost for words.

"Patrice Desmarets," he said at last, pronouncing the name with hate. His voice was loud, angry, filling the room and supplanting the silence that had fallen in the aftermath of her crying and her story. "There is no excuse for that man. None whatsoever. I can't doubt that he was responsible—I know no one more likely to kill a woman in cold blood."

"Maybe," faltered Camilla, "he didn't mean to kill me; just frighten me off, like the other attempts."

"Camilla," said Malcolm, and his voice was cold and deadly, "never apologize to me for that man again."

She shrank from him, and he struck his fist against his thigh in fury. She couldn't see his face—was he angry with her again? Right now she would not be able to face his anger. She couldn't argue, or even cry anymore, just curl up and die if he said one word of criticism to her.

He pulled his shoulders straight and turned around. Drawing a breath like a deep sigh he said quietly, "I'll take you home."

"No, no!" She couldn't go back to the hotel. "The police. . . ."

"Not the hotel." He answered her unspoken fears. "You're never going back there again. We've got two things to worry about—the police and Patrice. So you're coming home with me. To stay."

She agreed mutely, happily. Proprieties and conventions were blanked from her mind. All she thought about was that she was going where she would be safe.

"Nurjan! Nurjan!" He called down the corridor. The dark slender girl appeared with an armload of books. "Do you want a lift home?"

She took in the picture of the tall man and the quiet tearstained girl, quivering within the encircling safety of his arm.

"No, thanks," answered the Afghan girl. "It's a lovely evening. I'll walk."

They said nothing as they drove to Malcolm's house. He made her lie down in the back of the Land Rover, on a pile of blankets, then he covered her with another. She was glad of it, because now, with the real shock setting in, she began to feel very cold and weak. It was a long drive but seemed no time at all; she was always conscious of his warm presence in the front of the car, smoothly controlling the motions, taking the curves in a gentle swing. She found it impossible to be afraid any longer. The drive, the arrival, the house were all a blur, with an impression of great spaces and the continual comforting masculine presence. Then they were in a wide hall, dark, hot, echoing. Camilla became aware of the sudden appearance of someone feminine.

"Olga," rang out his deep golden voice. "Miss Simpson is not well. Please take her to the spare bedroom."

The woman replied shortly in the affirmative with a strong Scandinavian accent. Camilla wanted to cry out as the encircling arm was removed and replaced around her shoulders by an impersonal blanket, but her subconscious for some reason restrained her. She was so tired. Stairs to climb, many stairs, this time with the support of a plump soft female hand and the soothing sound of a whispered foreign language. She found herself lying on a bed, her shoes slipped off, her head—blessed relief—cushioned on a downy pillow, and the warm blanket tucked up around her chin. Ancient habit, childhood custom, nudged her. *It isn't dark yet,* she thought briefly, but sleep enfolded her before she could speak the words.

Somewhere behind her nebulous dreams she sensed the entry of a being, tall, warm and alive, into her room, and she struggled to lift herself out of the deep shroud of sleep to raise her eyelids to find out who, what, why. This effort, fluttering like the wings of a butterfly in flight, lasted only a few seconds. The presence remained and by degrees she felt calmed by its nearness. Content, she slipped back into dreamless sleep as a tall steaming mug was placed on her bedside table.

LIGHT FALLING ACROSS HER FACE awoke her, and as her eyes became accustomed to its brilliance, she looked around for the customary fittings of her room at the hotel, the white chest of drawers, the two upholstered chairs, the painting of a donkey, the black telephone—all the sparse furnishings she had come to regard as a sort of home. The realization was slow, but suddenly it hit her that this was a strange room, a strange house. Her head began spinning, all the events of the previous day came flooding back to her, and she cried out, pressing her face into the luxurious pillow.

Instantly the door opened and a little towheaded woman, tanned and wrinkled as a dried apple, hurried over to her bed.

"Miss Simpson. So you wake at last."

The strong accent struck a chord in Camilla's confused remembrances. "You must be the one who put me to bed last night," she finally said, rubbing her tousled head. "Olga, isn't it?"

"Yes, miss," replied the woman, her face cracking with her smile. She was obviously pleased Camilla could remember her name.

"Are you Swedish?"

"No, Norwegian, but many people make that mistake. They think there is only Sweden in Scandinavia." While Camilla, in her rather numbed state, took that in, the woman swept on, "You must be very hungry, since you have had no supper. I will go and fix you such a delicious breakfast your mouth will water ever after when you remember it."

Don't leave me, Camilla wanted to cry out, but at the same moment her stomach told her she was ravenous. She calmed, realizing that here, for the moment, she was safe, and held her tongue. She was about to let the woman hurry off again when something struck her, and she called from the bed, "Were you waiting for me to wake up?"

"I was knitting outside the door." And away she went.

The knowledge that she was being watched over reassured Camilla, and she began to anticipate the breakfast. Olga intrigued her. She liked the old woman. But at the same time she wondered what such a person could be doing in Malcolm Armstrong's house.

She knew where she was, and the knowledge gave her an extraordinary knotty feeling somewhere in the region of her heart. His curtains, his windows, his carpets, his chairs, paintings, books, bed. She lay back against the pillow and, hands folded, contemplated the room.

The most striking, and to her unnerving, difference between this room and her one at the Kabul Hotel was its unabashed luxury. The hotel room was a Spartan prison compared to the abundant expensive comforts found in this place. The floor was two inches deep in fine wool carpet, shades of cream, camel and yellow, thick and caressing. She delayed getting up to anticipate the pleasure of walking barefoot on it. The walls were an earthy motherly brown and the ceiling ivory, complementing the emerald green silk curtains. The walls were hung with European prints, framed with great taste, and brilliant Chinese tapestries in peacock colors. A glass case on the far wall caught her eye; it housed a Chinese watercolor of two old men on a misty mountain, exquisite in its simplicity. There was an empty grate with wrought-iron fire accessories, and a marble mantelpiece, and another piece of Oriental workmanship, a dragon-embroidered fire screen. On the mantel was a jade leopard with eyes of obsidian and a gold ormolu clock, unwound. There were few pieces of furniture—a walnut cabinet, a dresser, a well-furnished writing desk with clean straight lines, and a plain poplar bed and side table of charpoy, stained to the same color as the walnut bed on which she now reclined. Combined with the refined and rich decor, the whole effect was restrainedly elegant.

For a long time now she had been trying to imagine what Malcolm's house might look like—and never had her mind conceived a picture like this. She could not reconcile this tasteful display of well-spent wealth with her image of the man with whom, easily or not, she had been working for more than a month. How did this room fit in with the rattletrap Land Rover, this house with the shabby yellow school? How did the colorful Norwegian Olga come to run the household of a man who often dressed in Afghan garb? It made her wonder again about her own position—an unimportant, unknown young girl—in his life. He was an intellectual, an author, a teacher; and now, it appeared, a man of considerable means. And him, what about him, with his wealth and his talents, hidden in Afghanistan, lecturing at a minor university and teaching at some little school. How much there was to know about this man! She thought she had done so—she blushed to think how facilely she had summed him up when she had first heard of him, from Johnny, on the plane. But she had not even scratched the surface—she didn't understand a thing about him, the man of contradictions that he was, moody, sometimes laughing and friendly, sometimes cold and morose. She felt the cold finger of despair on her heart at the realization that she would never understand him, ever. And he understood her so easily, every single thought, all her motivations.

These desperate cogitations were broken off by the return of Olga, bearing a tray of delicious-smelling, delicious-looking eatables that proved, upon experiment, to be even more delectable than Camilla had imagined. To her relief, Olga sat on the end of the bed, prepared for a cozy chat. Thus Camilla was saved from her own thoughts, which were swirling disturbingly about.

In fact, Olga's conversation required nothing of its listener but a ready ear. She chatted gaily on about the past evening; Camilla learned she had spent a troubled night, tossing, turning and moaning, and once even screaming. Although her cries did not seem to have prevented her sleeping, they had kept the other occupants of the house awake.

"And Mr. Armstrong himself was very worried. He brought you a hot drink in the middle of the night—there it is; you have not touched it!"

"You mean this?" said Camilla, lifting the mug on her table.

"Yes, but it is stone-cold now. Let me have it." Olga took the mug between her two little hands.

"I thought I dreamed it," murmured Camilla.

Sooner than she had expected the entire contents of the tray had been devoured. Camilla could not have sworn as to their identity, except for some uniquely cooked eggs and the fragrant coffee that rounded off the meal. To her surprise she learned that it was one o'clock.

"But why did you let me sleep so late?"

"It was impossible to wake you."

"Where is Mr. Armstrong?" Camilla's wishes were divided, she half hoped he was there, half hoped he was not.

"Gone to school. He waited for a long time, but he has much work. He will return tonight."

"Oh, dear. Well, I can't wait. Tell him to ring me at the hotel."

"Why?"

Camilla was so taken aback by this question that she lost seconds trying to decide what it could mean. Olga, quickly grasping her houseguest's intention, laughed in her wrinkled way and said, "I see you think you should go back to the hotel. But never mind; it is not safe. Mr. Armstrong says you are not to go; you are to remain here."

"But—but," she said, trying to find some answer to counter the woman's assurance. "My clothes are all at the hotel."

"Ali Shah has brought them," replied Olga, and darting around the corner returned with one of Camilla's monogrammed cases. She placed it beside her bed and, taking up the tray, walked out with an air of definitely having settled the matter.

Camilla smiled to herself. Only the gentle-mannered inobtrusive Ali Shah could have so casually spirited her belongings out from the hotel, which must have been swarming with suspicious police. She decided she might as well stay, at least until Malcolm returned, and then after explanations he could drive her back to the hotel—or help her find another. She certainly could not stay here, even with Olga in the house.

Opening the case, she took out the white cotton shorts that lay on top and searched for a primrose yellow sleeveless top. Since she was going to spend the day inside the safety of high cement walls, she could dress as freely as she liked. Slipping on sandals, she left the room, deciding to find her way to the garden she had glimpsed from her window.

The stairs seemed endless. She did not want to run into Olga, for that lady had a very authoritative air about her, and Camilla thought that if the housekeeper decided she should rest in bed, that was exactly where she would spend this beautiful day. And that would be too much of a waste. She opened door after door, at first tentatively and then, emboldened by failure, more firmly, deciding it was worth risking being sent back to bed to get outside.

The house was immense, bigger than any she had yet seen belonging to foreigners in Kabul, and she wondered if the grounds would be of a corresponding size. That would accord with the disjointed spacious impression of it she'd had the previous night. At last, when she had almost given up hope, she found three little dark steps, went down them and, pushing at a door, suddenly found herself in glorious sunlight.

CHAPTER TWELVE

THE DOOR must be rarely used, Camilla decided, for the part of the garden in which she found herself was overgrown and plants clogged the pathway to the door. She pushed past a golden and mauve tangle of honeysuckle and chaste-tree and stood on the edge of a wild lawn.

In fact it bore more resemblance to some elfin forest glade than to the typical manicured lawn. Green was the basic color, in all shades and tones— pea, moss, emerald, gray green and bluish, the shadowed and dyed background to a tapestry. The grass was thick and luxuriant, rippling like an unripened field of corn. The expanse of ground it covered was irregular and in many places stony and yellowish, where there had once been rock gardens. Now there bloomed hollyhocks and the blushing amber eremurus, more brilliant than the lupin, yellow below and rising to a red color at its tip like a flaming candle. A confusion of roses tumbled over each other like drops of color from a child's paint-box—yellow, red, white and purple. Fragile opium poppies, pale pink or bloodred, waved their heads, and Star-of-Persia allium blossomed forth in scattered constellations. Other flowers she could not name dotted the garden in all hues of the rainbow, running wild, and behind them the trees—Judas trees, feathery tamarisks and heavily laden mulberries—formed a thick ring between the little plants and the walls, overgrown with trumpeting convolvulus.

Willows trailed by a little stream that ran through this immense rambling garden and Camilla went over and sat in the cool shade they provided. Here she could hear not the accustomed sound of traffic, but only the birds. Butterflies sailed from blossom to blossom, and bees droned somnolently through the scented air. On the distant grass two crested hoopoes walked up and down with their bobbing digging movements, uttering their drawn-out cry, "hoo poo," sad and melancholic. A chattering magpie was perched in the tamarisk.

Camilla could hardly take it all in. She felt like Alice in Wonderland, who fell through a dark tunnel and landed where everything was topsy-turvy. Was this wild blossoming garden also reflective of Malcolm's character, his appreciation of beauty? Then, to cap it all, there was a rustle behind the Judas trees, and a small donkey foal, a soft gray with enormous ears and eyes, came trotting to her and nuzzled her in welcome.

Surely, Camilla mused, some fairy godmother had taken her for Cinderella—or was it Sleeping Beauty, since it had happened overnight—and waving her wand had transported her in her sleep from the reality of the world into an enchanted playground, from noise to peace, from fear to rest. She held her breath, waiting for the clock to strike twelve.

After a while, when she had drunk in the beauty of

the garden, she got up to explore a little, the donkey keeping faithfully by her side. She jumped over the stream, where the flicking tails of goldfish sent shimmering gleams up through the water, and pushing back another trail of honeysuckle she found an overgrown flagged path. She followed this and not far along came to a little wooden gazebo, fitted with screens and furnished with a table and two chairs. She sat down thoughtfully.

Did Malcolm often use this place? It seemed unlikely, since it was so untended, but he had been very busy lately. It would be a charming place to sit and take afternoon tea, especially in the spring when the Judas trees and the mulberries would be in blossom. It needed a lot of work, but patience and talent could restore it to what had clearly once been its former glory. Perhaps he read here, or worked, putting a typewriter on the table. She ran her hand over the wood. Or perhaps he entertained here. Who? Johnny and Janet? Ali Shah? Nurjan?

The inexplicable pang she felt at this thought was cut short by the sound of Olga's northern accent through the trees.

"Miss Simpson!" She ran up, panting a little. "Why did you not tell me you were going into the garden? I had to run all this way to tell you you have a phone call."

Camilla felt contrite. "I really am very sorry." Then her heart leaped a little. "Who is it?"

"Mr. Hagan, and he seemed worried."

"Oh, Johnny!" Camilla started to run off. "Is he still on the phone?"

"Yes, go quickly!"

Camilla tore back to the house, her long legs like a gazelle's, through the rippling grass. Only when she was at the door did she remember that she had no idea where the telephone was, but she felt too foolish to turn back and ask instructions. So she went on in and fortunately found one after only a few minutes of hunting.

"Johnny, hello! Sorry I kept you waiting."

"It's okay, kid. Send you the bill for Christmas." The sound of Johnny's light good-humored voice brought her back into contact with the real world she had so suddenly been whisked away from. "I hear you're in the lion's den. Don't you know all the tracks lead in and none out?"

"Johnny, it's so good to hear your voice again!"

"It's only been two days. Boy, do you have a short memory!"

"Two days!" Camilla was wistful. "It seems like two years. Another life."

"Well, it would have been if Allah—or some of your famous female intuition—had not divinely ordained that you should bend down at that precise moment." He paused, wondering at the silence at the other end of the line. "Sorry. Maybe I shouldn't joke about it."

"No, it's all right," she replied slowly. "I don't want to remember, but if I have to it's better that I laugh. How did you know?"

"Malcolm phoned me."

"He did?" Her voice was questioning, anxious, surprised and delighted all at once. "When?"

"Last night, kiddo; don't you remember?"

"No, nothing."

"You must have been out cold, but your brain was working overtime. I was really scared you might have a fit. Malcolm called me over. Don't you remember talking to me?"

"No, I really don't remember anything—except when Malcolm came in with a drink."

"Yes, I gave him that for you—to make you sleep properly. Did you take it?"

"No, he didn't wake me. Just left it on the table."

"Feeble old fool."

Camilla bridled a bit at the thought of anyone calling Malcolm feeble. Then she had another idea. "Could I come over and see you?" She was surprised by his immediate refusal.

"Don't go anywhere, Camilla. The hotel is crawling with policemen. You don't want to fall into their hands. The embassy's a little interested, too. And you never know when that sniper will take another potshot." Camilla shuddered. "Know why he did it?"

"No," she lied. "No, I don't know. If anyone asks you, say there was no reason." She tried to make a joke out of it. "I might be Kabul's most wanted woman. Can you come over—or Janet?"

"I don't think so—sorry." Her disappointment was obvious in the silence that ensued. "I can't take time off and Janet's not feeling too well," Johnny explained. "I want her to relax. Anyway, we might be followed. You know, yesterday when you were first missing they thought you were with us—cops and everybody."

"Why wouldn't they think I was with—I mean, here? Malcolm's been quite obviously assisting me."

"I don't know...." Camilla was suspicious of his noncommittal answer, but he instantly changed the subject. "You know, there was a rumor you'd run off with the Kuchis, too."

She was suddenly tired. Fond as she was of him, she wanted no more chatter. Her head throbbed.

"Thank you for calling, Johnny. I suppose you have to get back to your work."

"Is this a dismissal?"

"My head hurts."

"Never mind; I left some more of those tablets in the kitchen, marked 'Camilla's tablets.' Should be easy to find."

"Yes, thanks, Johnny. My love to Janet."

She dropped the receiver onto its cradle, her head whirling. Olga was suddenly at her elbow.

"You do not look so well."

"Yes, I think I'll lie down. If anybody calls, say I'm not here, please." She trailed back to her room and lay down on the bed, which the sun through the windowpanes had warmed in patches. She tried not to think. Since she did not want to be put to sleep artificially, she would not take the pills, but her head ached badly.

Nevertheless she awoke, startled, from a doze she had fallen into, hearing a masculine voice downstairs. Malcolm, she exulted to herself, and still only half-awake she flung her long bare legs over the edge of the bed, surprised to find the floor rise up to meet them. Despite her unsteadiness she jumped up and hurried to the door, toward the sound of his voice.

Thank God he's here, she thought as she sped along the passage. *Now maybe he can explain exactly*

*what's going on and arrange for me to check into an-
other hotel. I'm sure he'll understand that I can't
possibly stay here....* Clinging to the banister she
went down one flight of stairs, along a print-lined
corridor, up and down another flight...and her
hopes died away. She recognized the musical accents
of the voice, but it was not the one she had expected
and longed to hear. Still, she was up now. She might
as well see him, and perhaps he would help her, either
to get her to Malcolm or to find her another hotel.

Finally she was on a landing, looking down on a
black-and-white diamond-patterned marble floor.
Ali Shah stood there, hat in hand, arguing with Olga,
his tall slender form towering over the elderly
woman's frail frame like a greyhound challenging a
pug. Camilla put a hand over her mouth to stifle a
giggle at this comparison her mind had conjured up,
but Ali Shah with his sharp hearing caught her muffled laugh and, standing upright, greeted her.

"Salaam aleikom." His eyes took in her attire, but
not even by a flicker of an eyelid did he betray his
thoughts. "I hope you are well?"

"Yes. And you?" she returned, coming down the
stairs.

"Miss Larssen has been telling me you are asleep
and not to be disturbed," he said.

"Well, so I was, but I'm awake now," she replied,
smiling, giving him her hand to kiss, since she knew
by experience that the Afghan was a stickler for all
European traditions. "The best way to wake a person
up is to argue loudly about whether you ought to do
it."

Olga gave a loud harrumph and bundled away.

"She is a dear," said Ali Shah. "She is so cute." He often made Camilla laugh by throwing together an English turn of phrase and an Americanism in the same sentence.

"I think she gets her own way too much," replied Camilla. "Though how she manages it with Malcolm around, I don't know." She looked in the direction the housekeeper had taken, to make sure that she was gone, and then moved closer to him.

"Listen, Ali Shah," she said, her low tones implying confidentiality, "she—Miss Larssen—won't let me leave the house. She has some silly idea that I won't be safe if I go to another hotel. She says Malcolm wants me to remain here. Of course that's ridiculous." What she couldn't tell him was how much turmoil it would cause her to be living under the same roof as the man she wanted desperately, but who was involved with another woman. Better to risk going elsewhere than to put her heart through such misery.

"Malcolm is at the school now," the Afghan told her uneasily. "I have brought your luggage from the hotel."

"Yes, I know; it was very kind of you, but really unnecessary." She smiled to show she wasn't trying to hurt his feelings. "But what I want you to do is take me to the school—to see Malcolm, so I can explain this whole mess to him. Or if you think he's too busy, I wonder if you could just run me back to the city. I don't feel quite strong enough to handle a taxi yet."

She noticed with some concern that instead of enthusiastically agreeing to her plan, Ali Shah twisted his hat in his hands with a worried expression and then motioned to a door. "Ali Shah..." she began again, but his voice cut her off.

"Will you come and sit down?" He was already leading the way and had opened the dark wooden double doors, so she could only hurry after him, annoyed at his evasions. "Ali Shah? Ali Shah!"

She stopped, because the room took her breath away. She had seen many beautiful things in Malcolm's house already, and many surprising things, but nothing like this room. The thick doors opened onto a spacious—almost sumptuous—lounge, and she stood on the threshold taking in the splendid sight. The walls were cream with long burgundy curtains, the furniture a dark brown exotic leather, well fortified with more inviting embroidered cushions. The inevitable luxurious fireplace and mantelpiece, twice as large here as in the bedroom, was spotless, a luminous marble and screened with filigree. A jungle of ivory animals prowled the window ledge, and poppies bloomed in a vase of Sèvres china. There was only one wall with a painting; the rest were lined from ceiling to wainscot with bookshelves, crammed with volumes of all sorts: paperback, hardcover, leather bound, slim novels and thick tomes. Each one looked well read, and some lay half out of their slots, or with bits of white paper protruding like flags from their tops. This was definitely Malcolm's room.

"Malcolm's very well-off, isn't he?" she murmured with a trace of awe. "This room—this house—I've never seen anything like it."

Ali Shah, however, did not seem offended by her bluntness. "Yes," he replied. "He is extremely rich, so rich that he does not have to work for his living."

This surprised her, yet his economic position was not what fascinated her the most—what did absorb her interest was how all that she had seen today helped to complete the picture of the Malcolm she knew: the devoted teacher, gifted scholar, hardworking lecturer, and the physical man, too, hard-riding, muscular, tanned. An outdoor man and yet a man of books. How much there was to know about him, this man who occupied her mind every single hour of her waking day...and much of the hours of the night, too. And how much she still had to learn.

Here, of course, was the right person to ask. She turned to Ali Shah. He was Malcolm's best friend. Surely he would be able to explain the enigma to her.

"How long has Malcolm lived in Afghanistan?" she asked as lightly as she could.

"He has always lived here; surely you know that? He was at university in England for eight, nine years, and of course he was sent to boarding school there...."

"You mean he was born here? I thought he was English."

"He is," began Ali Shah. Then he stopped abruptly and gave her a curious look. "Do you mean," he began again, "you know nothing of Malcolm's history? I would have thought he—"

"He's very reticent about himself," cut in Camilla. "I'm sure not even the Hagans know his background. As for me, I always assumed he was an English teacher, gifted but poor, who came out here to impart learning and to search for adventure. I certainly never imagined anything like this house—these ivories, the valuable paintings. I'm totally lost."

The Afghan paused, seeming to Camilla unsure of whether he ought to confide what Malcolm might perhaps prefer to keep secret. But Ali Shah had noted the eager, hungry, haunted look on Camilla's face, and he smiled almost to himself. "Malcolm's background is very interesting," he agreed. "Do sit down."

Camilla made herself comfortable in one of the leather chairs, tucking her legs under her. She was avid for Malcolm's story. No other mystery held half as much fascination for her—she had to know.

"To begin," said Ali Shah, "we must go back several generations, to the father of the father of the father." He counted the fathers on his fingers and shook his head. "I miscalculated. Four generations we should go back, to Malcolm's great-great-grandfather, who was a Lieutenant Armstrong, the Honorable Lieutenant Charles Armstrong—I understand this word 'honorable' denotes nobility in England. He was an officer with the British Army in India. You know that this army invaded Afghanistan in 1838, captured Kabul and reinstated the king we had deposed, Shah Shoja; but four years later we rebelled and in the winter we drove the British from our land. Almost all of the army was destroyed by the guns of our tribesmen and the ferocity of the winter weather in the high mountains."

Camilla did know all this, for Malcolm had taught it to her, but she listened avidly, eager to know what had happened to the Armstrong family. "Many of the officers had their wives and often also their children with them, and so did Lieutenant Charles,"

Ali Shah continued. "His wife was named Jemimah—you can see her there." He pointed at the mantelpiece.

Camilla rose and examined the prettily framed miniature; there, looking gravely at her from a faded portrait, were Malcolm's unruly golden hair and vivid blue eyes, softened in a feminine face.

"You can see her beauty was of a type to entrance an Afghan, and so she was fortunate. When her husband was killed she was captured by a chieftain, a Pathan prince, and he was good to her and to her infant son. This prince was an enlightened man, and when the treaty with Queen Victoria was signed, he insisted that his adopted son be sent to an English university and learn to be an Englishman."

"I see the looks have remained in the family," broke in Camilla, still musing over the picture. "Very striking looks, aren't they?"

"Yes. It is because Armstrong men always marry Englishwomen. Strange, this living in two worlds. They send their sons to England to be educated, and they marry Englishwomen, yet they always come back—come home, I should say—to Afghanistan. You see, I think their blood is English, but their heart is Afghan."

Camilla found these thoughts too stirring to be dwelled on. "Go on about the son, Malcolm's great-grandfather. What happened to him? Did he marry an Englishwoman and return to Afghanistan?"

"That's right. But first he went to India and made a fortune in gold and ivory and spices, which the family has retained to this day. Then he married a young English missionary he met while in Karachi, and returned here at the age of forty-five to build this house."

"I see," said Camilla, enraptured.

"He never left Kabul again, but in his old age he had a son—"

"Malcolm's grandfather," interrupted Camilla.

Ali Shah nodded. "Malcolm's grandfather went to English boarding school and university and became an eminent archaeologist. Then he married his assistant, a young woman who had charted castles in the Andes and dinosaurs in the Gobi Desert, and they returned to Kabul, to this house, where this Armstrong wrote all his books."

"So he was a writer, too?" mused Camilla.

"Their son also went to England for his schooling, and when the Second World War came he joined the air force and trained as a fighter pilot. Apparently, so Malcolm says, he flew more missions than almost any other pilot and near the end of the war was rewarded with the rank of colonel."

"A brave man," commented Camilla.

"His wife was brave, too," replied Ali Shah. "Malcolm's mother was a volunteer nurse in the war, and served for some time on the front. When they were married and returned to Kabul, Colonel Armstrong became an adviser to the Afghan army."

"Now Malcolm. He's next in the history. Go on, Ali Shah," urged Camilla, unable to disguise her eagerness.

The Afghan laughed. "Ah, but you know his story. The same education, the novel he wrote, the history he teaches. He does not need to work for a living, as you can see, but he loves teaching and

Afghanistan, and so he has returned here to work at the university.''

''I admire him for it,'' said Camilla. ''I admire his whole family. I never knew how interesting it was.'' The magic rapture on her face could not be hidden from Ali Shah. ''What fascinating characters! And it explains so much about him. From his great-great-grandmother Jemimah he got his looks, from his great-grandfather his wealth, from his grandfather his mind, and from his father his courage—maybe his arrogance, too.'' She smiled to herself for a moment, tenderly, lovingly, thinking of him and all the many aspects of his fascinating character.

Ali Shah coughed. She raised her glowing eyes to him and saw that he seemed to want to say something but was holding it back with difficulty. He seemed embarrassed yet urgent.

''What is it, Ali Shah?''

The Afghan shook his head, as if refusing to comment, then apparently thought better of it and said slowly, rather as a statement than a question, ''You love him very much, don't you?''

And the reply came to her clearly, sweetly, easily, without even having to think about it, three little words perfect in their simplicity. ''Yes, I do.''

''I had thought for a long time that it was so, but when I watched you today I was sure.''

That was all that Ali Shah would venture on the subject, and Camilla was grateful. She did not need him wishing her the best of luck when she knew, as she had known for a long time, that her love was hopeless. She did not need cheerful assumptions that all would work out well, or that she was just right for his best friend, or any of the nonsense someone less sensitive might have offered. Ali Shah could see as well as she could that her love was doomed, and so of all people she was glad he was the one she had finally confided in. She was glad, too, that it was this gentle conversation with him that was forcing her to come to terms with it, and not some violent altercation with Malcolm. Such a scene would have been unbearable, but there was something almost beautiful in acknowledging the fact of her love for an unattainable man in this quiet way.

It was the first time she had been able to face the truth, the first time she had admitted it, not only to Ali Shah but more importantly to herself. She was not at all astonished at how quickly and openly her answer to the Afghan's question had risen to her lips; she had known, subconsciously, for a long time, that if anyone ever asked the question she would not be able to make a denial. She loved Malcolm. The conscious realization that this was love, not infatuation, not a crush, was still too recent to admit of despair. For a few moments it was enough to know that she loved him.

Ali Shah's voice broke into her dream. "You know, Malcolm hasn't yet fulfilled the last part of the Armstrong tradition...."

Malcolm's strong face, deeply tanned, the square masculine jaw, the sensuous lips, hard and delicious, the eyes that were sometimes as bright as a clear day, sometimes cloudy and storm-filled, his frame of thick lion-colored hair, his beloved handsomeness—these were in her eyes as she turned to Ali Shah, and she saw not the Afghan but Malcolm. "What do you mean?" she asked with difficulty, for her thoughts were hardly on his words.

"I mean that he has still not brought back to this house an English bride."

An English bride! How wonderful it would be to be married to Malcolm! Mistress of this house, chatelaine of each of these lovely rooms, able to walk daily in the flower-filled fragrant garden, to support him in his work and to stand by him in good and bad times. . . . It was a dangerous dream and she knew that she must put it aside at once.

"I don't think there's much chance of that, do you? He's here to stay now—he'll find his bride in Afghanistan." Then, before Ali Shah could answer, she turned the conversation away from the topic of Malcolm's wife. "He's at the school today, didn't you say? Working, as usual."

"Yes," replied Ali Shah. "He generally spends his time there when he is not writing or lecturing. He tutors his pupils over the summer. I think he is tutoring Nurjan today."

Nurjan! And she had tried to steer the topic away from Malcolm's prospective wife!

"He does our family a great honor," went on Ali Shah quickly. "You did not know that Nurjan is my cousin?"

"No." Camilla's voice was so low that he could hardly hear it. "But I am not surprised. He is very fond of you. No doubt he got to know her through you?"

"Yes," replied the Afghan. He hesitated, then decided to confide in her. "Perhaps he did not tell you that Nurjan and I were engaged to be married?"

Camilla nearly choked with astonishment. This was a startling revelation she had not counted on—and she could hardly believe such a disloyalty to his best friend was in Malcolm's character. "What?" she gasped.

"But Nurjan changed her mind," he went on resignedly. "I admit it goes against the tradition of our country, but while Nurjan and I are Afghans, we are also aware that there is a modern world beyond our country, and we must—what is the phrase—move with the times. I was obliged to give up our engagement. When I heard what Nurjan's desires were, I was the one who fought for her rights in my family. I just wanted her to be happy, so I encouraged her."

"You *encouraged* her?" Camilla could hardly believe what she was hearing. "You're very noble, Ali Shah, but—but...." Her words trailed away. Could Ali Shah really be so thick-skinned? Or so fond of Malcolm that he could so easily surrender his fiancée to him? "But, Ali Shah, didn't you—I mean, don't you—love her?"

He smiled indulgently. "Marriages here are arranged on a very different principle from that in the West. Love is not taken into account. It is expected that will come after the wedding. You should understand Nurjan's motives—after all, you come from a country where women are already liberated."

For a moment his words eased Camilla a little. At least she need not think so badly of Malcolm now; but the jealousy she had felt at the mention of Nurjan's name was already eroding the brief elation that had lifted her when she had at last confessed her love for Malcolm. Then Ali Shah spoke again and shattered the last remnants of her calm.

"I, too, must confess," he said softly, "that I *am* fonder of my cousin than of any other woman I know." And she understood what a great sacrifice it had been for him to give her up, caring for her enough to let her wishes come first.

Camilla managed to swallow her hot tears. If only she could be so unselfish where Malcolm was concerned, but all she felt were her own pain and bitterness. She could not bear to talk any more on the subject. Another word would surely cause her to break down, and she could not do that before this noble restrained man. She lifted her hand in a desperate gesture, and he was silent.

Camilla turned her face into the warm leather of the armchair and breathed in its scent. She inhaled deeply, trying to still the turmoil inside her. It was no good. His name resounded in her ear with the echo of each of her heartbeats. Malcolm. Malcolm. Perhaps yesterday, this morning, he had sat in this very chair, reading one of those books. And now he was with Nurjan. Teaching her. Embracing her. Kissing Nurjan, caressing Nurjan, the way he had once kissed and embraced her. The picture was unbearable; a tear rolled down Camilla's face, then another, then another, till she was sobbing into the smooth leather.

"Please," she heard Ali Shah's pleading voice. "Please, do not cry, do not cry."

She pulled herself together. Her voice was shaking, but she tried to command her nerves. "Ali Shah, you must take me back to the center of town so I can find a new hotel at once. You know I can't stay here. It's impossible. It's—'' she tried to appeal to his sense of propriety "—it's improper. Please take me back.''

"No, I cannot.''

"Please, Ali Shah. I can't stay here any longer.''

"Why not? It is not improper. Olga is here; she will chaperon you. At any rate, you must stay here. I am sorry.''

"Why? Why must I stay here? Because Malcolm says so? Everyone just does what he says; everyone gives in to his wishes. I must find another hotel!''

"No,'' he insisted. "When Malcolm says a thing must be done, we do it because he is usually right. You cannot go back to the city because it is too dangerous. The police may pick you up. They are looking for you.''

"I know. Johnny told me.''

"And then there is the man who shot at you. He will try again. Here you will be safe.''

"Why should I be any safer here than anywhere else? In fact it seems to me, considering that Malcolm's been seen in my company quite often and it's general knowledge that we're well acquainted, that this would be one of the first places anybody who wanted to get me would look. You yourself, Ali Shah, could get into a lot of trouble if it were known you'd seen me.''

He seemed unperturbed. "My cousin, my mother's brother's son, is the second commander of the Kabul police force.''

"It seems everybody is related to you, Ali Shah.''

"There are police guards around this house right now. My cousin sent them here. Not, you understand, to look for you, but to protect my friend

Malcolm Armstrong from the man who attacked you, because it is known that you and Malcolm are associated. The possibility that you may be here has not escaped them. However, as long as my cousin is second commander of the Kabul police force you will be safe here, and nowhere else."

So that was what Johnny had been reluctant to tell her! Camilla leaped up from the chair and paced angrily to the window. She could see nothing through the glass but the high cement wall, but she could picture the gray uniformed officers pacing on the other side of it, carbines slung over one shoulder. She was trapped.

"Do not think of it anymore. *Inshallah,* we say. Leave it with Allah. I must go home in a minute." He walked over to her and held out his hand, which was clenched around something small. Camilla looked at it and then at him. The young man seemed suddenly overwhelmed with shyness, and all his excellent command of English forsook him. *"I az shumas."*

"Mine?" repeated Camilla. "What is it?"

"Tohfa ast." Then, regaining his tongue, he repeated in English. "A present for *memsahib.*"

"What? A present for me?" She was smiling again. "Oh, I couldn't, really; it's very kind, but—"

"In our country it is considered the act of an enemy to refuse a gift."

"You know I'm not your enemy, Ali Shah."

"It is the gift of a friend," he admonished her sternly, but with his eyes smiling. "From a good friend to a brave lady."

"Oh, really, I...." She could think of no reply, and blushed.

"When Malcolm told me what had happened to you, I was very upset, thinking how easily you might have been killed. But Allah knows you are brave, and I thought I must honor the courage of this woman—"

Camilla could not answer this speech. She was honored in return.

"—this woman who is also my friend."

Camilla was deeply moved by the tribute, although her conscience did remind her that as far as courage went, she was hardly worthy of it.

"So I went and bought this gift for her, and I hope she will accept it."

Camilla saw that there was no way she could refuse a gift so gallantly offered, so she said, "I will accept it with pleasure." Taking the little box in her hands, she opened it slowly, filled with anticipation of what might be in there. It was better than Christmas, because at Christmas she usually knew what present she was likely to get, but here she had no idea what he had chosen for her.

Out of a nest of cotton wool she drew a long silver chain in fine square links, and on the end—a little figure of a scorpion, worked in fine deep blue lapis lazuli etched in silver, with two twinkling ruby eyes. It was not in the least menacing, unlike the two she had encountered, but seemed charming, its tail curling gracefully at a jaunty angle. Somehow the silversmith had infused it with a wealth of character, and the jeweled eyes shone with a humor as deep as the Afghan's own. The gift was appropriate, and despite her despair she was cheered by the little creature.

"Thank you—thank you so much, Ali Shah. It couldn't be more perfect. It will be the best souvenir, the very best reminder of everyone here." In a sudden burst of pure affection for Afghanistan and all the people in it, especially the gentle man beside her, she leaned over and kissed the embarrassed Ali Shah lightly on the cheek.

Even as she did so she was aware of who had silently opened the door and was watching them, and she finished the kiss mechanically.

Ali Shah was aware of the presence, too, and pulled away from her, straightening. Although she knew who the intruder was, she turned slowly to see his face.

The door was closed behind him, and against its dark wood his fair hair glowed. His blue eyes were flaming and his lips had turned an odd white. Uncalled-for lines long forgotten from a once studied poet came to mind:

> "He entered, but he entered full of wrath...
> Regal his shape majestic, a vast shade
> In the midst of his own brightness...."

"Quoting Keats, Camilla, is no excuse." She was not aware that she had spoken the lines aloud, and she trembled at the anger in his voice. "Though I hardly think it was poetry you had on your mind. Unless, perhaps, some practical demonstration of Ovid's *Art of Love*?" The final word was wrung out bitterly.

"How dare you make such insinuations!" she cried, amazed at her own daring and instantly regretting it.

"I only remarked on the obvious," he drawled,

building Camilla's exasperation with him to a fever pitch. What was the use in arguing? He'd only think she was making excuses anyway. She turned on her heel to leave.

As she passed him on her way to the door, he glanced up and down at her figure, taking in her form in the shorts and light shirt with a sardonic stare. She opened the door with a wrench. He did not turn to see her go.

She was out and halfway up the stairs before she realized what she was doing. Was not this sudden departure a confession of guilt—what guilt she couldn't say now, but she and Ali Shah had both sprung apart hastily and looked fearful, as if somehow Malcolm's assumptions were justified. Removed from his presence, Camilla began having second thoughts. She wondered why she had let him push her aside so easily. How dared he assume so much from one innocent kiss of thanks? And what should it matter to him if it *was* more? From what Ali Shah had told her, his so-called best friend was guilty of far worse things than what he had caught her doing! Anger and jealousy rose together in her, giving her courage. Her temper flaring, she retraced her steps.

But long before she reached the library she could hear voices raised in argument, Malcolm's deeply modulated one and Ali Shah's accented tenor. The sound was heated but low, too low for her to hear what they were saying. She did not want to go in. She could guess what subject they were pulling apart so furiously, and felt still too weak to conduct a scene with both of them at once. It was impossible to tackle

Malcolm with Ali Shah there. She would nurse her anger and wait.

Dragging her heels, she wandered away, finding herself at last in a little second-story room overlooking the front garden and the path, where she could watch for Ali Shah's departure. He seemed a long time going, so she idly picked up a book and began to leaf through it. It was a beautifully illustrated leather-bound book of fairy tales, and she halted over each picture, drinking in the fine craftsmanship. Turning a page, she uncovered a watercolor of Sleeping Beauty, and the memory of the morning that the image conjured up nearly broke her resolution and threatened to stain the page with tears. It seemed so long ago that she had been in the enchanted garden, and here she was back at square one—the lion's den.

Camilla shut the book with a snap and looked out the window. She had been too absorbed in her dreams to hear Ali Shah leaving, but at some point he must have gone, because his little red sports car was no longer there. Now the lion must be bearded in his lair. She put the book down firmly and, gathering her courage, hurried along the corridor. Although she was eager to explain, she wondered if Ali Shah had already done so; wondered if Malcolm was even in the mood to accept explanations. She had a certain feeling that he was not. At last she was once again in front of the fateful heavy door—and feared she would always hate the room—and, hesitating for a moment, she gave a determined push and entered.

He was sitting at a table, open books piled before him, his back to her. This was intimidating, as his back presented a broad and unfriendly appearance.

She cleared her throat. "Malcolm?"

He did not turn around; keeping his back toward her he said, "Hasn't anyone told you I don't like to be disturbed when I'm working?" His voice held a strange uneasy note; anger, she thought.

"I'm very sorry, but I think it important that we discuss—that I explain this."

"You are in no position to tell me what is important and what is not."

She considered his attitude unfair. "I think it important that you not think badly of me."

His voice came back from a great distance, mocking, sardonic. "It's a bit late for that now, isn't it?"

She turned away and stumbled from the room, tears pricking her eyes. He was right: it was too late. She had lost whatever friendship or respect she had once gained in his eyes, and now she would never recover it. She had not asked for her love to be returned, but even the little respect she had struggled for was gone.

How much longer must I stay in this man's house, she cried to herself. *He doesn't want me here.* She lay on her bed, staring at the ceiling, which floated up and down before her eyes.

But why should I stay at all, she suddenly thought. *If Ali Shah refuses to drive me back, I'll just have to take a cab. I've got enough money. I don't have to be a prisoner here. I can go wherever I like.*

The decision seemed excellent. Quickly she threw a few clothes into the little case and ransacking the other found most of her toilet articles. The rest would have to stay, she decided; she couldn't carry it all without some difficulty, and it was best to be unhampered in a quick getaway. *He'll stop me if he can,* she said to herself, *because he thinks I'm incapable of looking after myself. He just wants to prove again how strong he is and how inept I am....* But even as she said this she knew it was unfair. It was the Camilla of the early days, of the preheroin episode, talking, the unawakened Camilla. But she clung to her thought nevertheless, for if she admitted he was again right she knew she would have to stay. And she couldn't stay.

Part of her wanted to, though. Remaining here was as impossible as everything else connected with him, and yet she did linger. She walked around her bedroom, appreciating the beautiful works of art, curling her toes in the woolly carpets, knowing that she would likely never live in such luxurious surroundings again. She touched the bright fire screen and leaned her flushed cheek against the cool marble mantelpiece. She stood by the window, lost in dreams, absorbing the wild loveliness of the unkempt wonderland garden.

Her reverie was disturbed by the light tripping steps of Olga. The woman stood just inside the door, the cheerful friendliness of the afternoon gone from her face and replaced by blank disapproval. She must have overheard their argument.

"Mr. Armstrong requests your presence at dinner," she announced briskly.

"Shall I dress for it?" asked Camilla flippantly, irritated by the criticism in her tone. But the woman had already gone.

Camilla debated for a minute whether to go or not. For a while she was tempted to defy his order, but she realized that to do so would be foolish and childish, and she was ravenously hungry. There would be no way she could escape now, while he waited for her to join him at dinner. It was not so much more to endure, after all—and with a pang she realized that it was her last opportunity of seeing him. When she left his house tonight, she would never return—she would have to cut herself off from him completely. There would be no going back; she would have to go on alone.

The thought was frightening and saddening. Camilla realized that for almost an entire day she had forgotten the reason why she had come to Afghanistan in the first place. In fact she had had nothing on her mind from the moment she awoke but Malcolm, his house, and her love for him. *Well,* she thought, holding her head high, *this is my last chance to set things right before I leave...forever.* She made her way slowly to the dining room.

Camilla expected to see elegance there, and little could have surprised her now in this house, but the grandeur of the dining room astonished her. As usual, the keynote was restraint. The floor was the same black-and-white diamond pattern, covered by one enormous warm red Afghan carpet. The walls were cream, the curtains red, the lighting dim from one great chandelier she could have sworn was jeweled, and the long table and chairs of polished wood appeared massively heavy. Malcolm sat at one end of the table, and the place at his right was set, the glass filled with wine. She went to it and sat down with all the grace that she could muster.

"Glad you could make it," he said coldly.

"I always eat at this time," she retorted, but felt little pride in having, so to speak, scored a point in their verbal warfare. She did not want their last evening to be spent like this, at odds with each other. But it seemed that was all the conversation there was going to be. Most of their evenings together had been quite talkative, but here they sat silently eating like strangers forced to share a table at a crowded restaurant. He was in one of his moods, and her stomach shrank at the thought that she was again the cause. No longer hungry, she pushed her plate away.

"Eat it," he ordered, pushing it back, and sensing the uncompromising tone in his voice she bowed her head to try again. The food curdled in her stomach; her own anger was quick-healing, but she was torn by the atmosphere in the room, the unspoken fury in him. It was all such a mistake; she could so easily explain, but he wouldn't listen. She determined she wouldn't be the first to break the silence though it probably hurt her more than it hurt him.

Dessert and coffee came and went, and he had said nothing but those seven words. She could hardly bear it and started twisting in her seat. Was this some sort of punishment?

At last he leaned back in his chair and said, "There is just one thing I have to say to you. Frenchmen are one thing, but seducing my friends in my own house is another...."

"Seducing!" She could not believe she was hearing such an accusation.

He glared at her with an ice-blue frosty stare and went on, "I cannot credit you with so little understanding of the Afghan character, for you've been here long enough, so any attempts to excuse yourself will be seen through. I can hardly think what else you had in mind, wearing such a—may I say provocative—outfit; luckily, it seems I walked into the cozy little scene in my living room just in time."

"He gave me a present!" she retorted. "I was thanking him for it. And I always wear shorts on hot days in England."

"You know it's not what he's used to," Malcolm pointed out coldly.

"I was wearing it when he arrived. I thought he was...." She stopped. Denial was useless—he was obviously not prepared to listen to reason. Her temper boiled again. How dared he assume a right to question her actions! She, who loved him, assumed no such right toward him—she fought any stirrings of such feelings. "It's none of your business anyway," she practically shouted. "If there was anything in it—which there wasn't—we're both adults. So why should you care?"

She had evidently touched a sore point, for he exclaimed, "Of course I care! He's my best friend—how do you think *I* feel?" Then he got a grip on his self-control again. "Anyway, I don't wish to discuss it further."

"Oh, no, you can't dismiss me like that," cried Camilla, red cheeked. Her temper had finally overpowered her. "We will discuss it further. We will trace your hypocrisy to its roots. How dare you— how can you stand there and criticize me for an innocent thank-you kiss when you have done things much, much worse? How can you stand there and call Ali Shah your best friend with a straight face?

How can you—you who cheated him in the worst way possible! You who stole his fiancée!''

Malcolm had taken out a cigar and with some pretense of self-possession had started to light it, but at these words he visibly shook and the match went out. "Who told you that?" he demanded roughly.

"Ali Shah himself," she said, laughing triumphantly. "Your best friend!"

"I don't believe it. You must have misinterpreted what he said."

"It was crystal clear! He loved her and wanted to marry her, and then you came along and she left him for you. He said, and these are his exact words, 'When I heard what Nurjan's desires were, I was the one who fought for her rights in my family. I just wanted her to be happy, so I encouraged her.' It seems to me his behavior has been a great deal more altruistic than yours—he even, can you believe it, told me he considered your being with her an honor. He is a better friend than you deserve."

"I think I can guess how your overactive imagination developed this whole ridiculous story. It's only too obvious how you feel about Ali Shah, and about me. So you set out to rewrite the story, casting him as the self-sacrificing hero and me as the villain." He struck the match once more, deliberately, and took a few good puffs on his cigar before he spoke again.

"Let me just set the record straight, my dear girl. It is true that Nurjan and Ali Shah were engaged. But Nurjan is a young, bright, gifted girl who excelled at school and wanted to continue her studies. Marriage would, of course, have put an end to any such dreams, but she had enough sense to confide in Ali

Shah. And he, as you rightly say, cared enough for her to back her up, rather than try to persuade her to forget her ambitions. I had just started lecturing at the university and he was in one of my classes, so he brought her along to me and I agreed to tutor her, if she could get her parents' consent. It was a hard fight, but the two of them stood by each other, and finally both families gave in, although they didn't like it then and still don't. Nevertheless, I tutored Nurjan for two years and she has recently rewarded me by winning a scholarship to university. I thought you knew this," he finished, his tone questioning.

At her blank look, he shrugged his shoulders and went on, "That's it in brief. Over the years my feelings have indeed changed toward Nurjan: I am now not only her tutor; I am also her friend and, I hope, her confidant." He stopped and in his tension snapped the fragile cigar between his strong fingers. He did not seem to be able to find the words to convey his feelings. Finally he added, "At least I hope I've set you straight on one point. I have no designs on Nurjan, matrimony-wise."

Camilla was facing him, her thoughts racing madly. Yes, she did see now that she had jumped to conclusions about what exactly Nurjan's desires had been. Originally they were concerned with her education, not Malcolm. But the rest of Malcolm's explanation had been too pat, almost as if he had carefully rehearsed it all. And Camilla could not deny the evidence of her eyes when she'd seen them together, kissing recklessly with the familiarity of lovers.

Whatever Malcolm's relationship with Nurjan was

now, it had definitely progressed from that of teacher-student, and Camilla would be incredibly naive to believe they were just "friends," as he'd tried to make her think. That would suit his purpose, she realized with a flash of insight: perhaps he and Nurjan were compelled to keep their intimacy a secret to spare Ali Shah's feelings. Camilla could only guess, but the matter was too supremely important for her to swallow wholeheartedly Malcolm's all-too-simple version of the story.

Then another thought struck her, and the situation became even clearer. "If you don't have marriage in mind with Nurjan, then your intentions are even less admirable than I thought," she could not help but hurl at him. At his angry look she went on, no longer caring what he thought of her, "Did you really expect me to believe your well-padded explanation when I know you're nothing but a liar—almost a convincing one, I might add—and a hypocrite?"

His eyes blazed fiercely. "I might ask the same question. Do you really expect me to believe your explanation when I know you're nothing but a cheap seductress?"

She recoiled as if he had struck her. Nothing he might accuse her of could be further from the truth—and yet if he could believe it, what chance had she of ever proving otherwise? Even when he had called her a thrill seeker, or foolhardy, he hadn't hurt her as much as this. She felt a hopelessness so black that all she wanted to do was to hurt him in return.

She whirled about, and the expression on her face had changed from anger to grim determination. Then her lips curved into a bittersweet smile and she raised her eyebrows as if in mock surrender. Inside her heart was beating furiously, the pulse so loud in her head that she could hardly hear what she was saying. Which was good, because later, in the dark, she would never be able to believe that she could have said such things to him.

"Yes," she purred, "yes, you're right. Can I help it if I enjoy making love?"

Malcolm drew away from her; she sounded so unlike herself. But this time she pursued him, putting a hand caressingly on his arm. Strangely, he did not move, only stared at her, his eyes hooded.

"I just can't help it—we're all subject to our physical desires, aren't we? But I admit it, Malcolm; it's quite useless for me to deny it anymore. Yes, I see that now. You know me for what I am." She brought her body close to his own, feeling the warmth that flooded between them. "I've had so many men, Malcolm. I know so much—but you're different. Like the way you hold me. The way you kiss me. You're so strong, so handsome."

Every word she uttered was true, and that made it that much more painful. For she was using all her feelings for him as if they were lies. She wanted to punish him as much as he had punished her.

"I want you, Malcolm," she whispered throatily in his ear. She used all the tricks he had once taught her—all the tricks she knew—running her tongue around the hollow of his throat and her fingertips down the sensitive nape of his neck, and was bitterly gratified to feel his quickening responses. "I want you now."

Her carefully controlled moan had roused him,

and he crushed her to him, sighing in reply, "I want you, too, Camilla. God, if only you knew how much I want you—but you will, you will." She no longer needed to work at his answering caresses; he needed no more encouragement.

His hands and mouth roved everywhere, her neck, back, thighs, sensitive breasts and hard nipples; her mouth eagerly raised itself to his lips, her hands reached for his hair, interlocking, twining. She had not expected it to be so easy, that he would be so quick to arouse. As she swayed in his muscular arms, carried away by the hypnotic bliss of his kisses, she felt for a moment how right and perfect it seemed. Suddenly she was no longer acting.

He was drawing her even closer, and with one hurrying hand he worked at the buttons on her blouse. She raised her hands to his, helping him, as eager as he to pull it away from her body to reveal the golden quivering skin beneath. The shirt fell to the floor, leaving her arms, back and breasts bare. Underneath her ribs her heart was pounding madly, and he pressed his hand to it, so that the warm pleasure of his touch erupted there and flowed all over her body.

"Beautiful, beautiful," he whispered in a voice like a song. "You're so perfect, Camilla."

The look he gave was one of naked admiration, and Camilla seized it and stored it in her memory like a trophy. His lips were pressed into the hollow of her throat, then his face was buried between her breasts, and she stroked the golden head, crooning, moaning.

"Yes, Malcolm, yes, I do want you so." While she spoke those words, she felt as if she had never wanted anything else in the world with such intensity.

The fierce pull of his hands on the waistband of her shorts brought her back to reality. Her eyes widened with terror as she looked down at him, on his knees, his tawny head level with her waist. Now she grasped the situation: she was no longer the seductress; she had become the seduced. She could not give in to him—oh, she wanted him desperately, but she could not make love now, in anger and a bitter thirst for revenge, when they had but a quarter of an hour ago been throwing insults and hateful accusations at each other. No, she loved him too much to settle for such a hollow victory, a semisatisfaction. She could not have his love, and she would not make do with just his body.

"No!" she cried vehemently, thrusting him from her. Before he could leap to his feet she had snatched her shirt and clasped it to her chest, and then ran from him, putting the length of the massive table between them.

"My God, Camilla, what do you mean, no?" His chest was heaving, and his eyes were still blurred with passion. He stumbled toward her, hand outstretched. "Come here. . . come here, Camilla. Let's finish what we've started."

"Keep away from me." Her voice was a tremble, pitched on the edge of hysteria.

"But, darling," he replied, and already the familiar hint of mockery was creeping back, "you started it. You invited me. Now what could have caused you to change your mind?" He came a step closer. "There's no need to be worried or shy. It was good, as far as it went—very good. You're everything I expected you to be. Surely you're going to let me see the rest of your act?"

How could she go on loving him when he taunted her like this? She didn't know; she only wanted to fling herself at his feet and implore his forgiveness and understanding, to confess everything to him. Instead she backed away from him, not trusting herself to keep control if he came too near, and to ward him off she answered, with a sarcasm to match his own, "Yes, it was a good act, wasn't it? I had you quite convinced there. I think you really believed that I wanted you—that I loved you."

She nearly sobbed at these cruel phrases, which were turning her deepest feelings into a weapon of punishment. In despair she echoed her own words. "We're all subject to our physical desires—aren't we, Malcolm? You just as much as all we less perfect mortals. I could hardly believe the speed at which you melted into my arms. And you profess to condemn *me*—to think *me* no better than a seductress. Where is your self-righteousness now?" She burst into hot tears and did not even try to hide them. "You thought I cared, didn't you? How easy you are to fool!"

Now it was his turn to recoil. Camilla at last had the satisfaction of seeing his own wounded face— surprised, betrayed. It was her revenge; yet, perversely, his pain hurt her more than all his insults and false accusations had ever done, more than her jealousy of Nurjan. It was worse than all these things to see him fall away from her, one arm raised in a defensive gesture. He grasped the back of one of the heavy chairs and leaned his full weight there for a moment, sagging. She stepped toward him now—held out her hand. She could not let it go on. "I'm sorry—I'm so sorry! Malcolm! I...I wanted to hurt you, the way you hurt me. It was wrong. I'm sorry.''

When he half turned to face her, she saw that a cold emotionless mask had slipped over his features. ''We've both been fools.'' He nodded to the piece of clothing she clutched. ''Get dressed. We won't speak of this again.''

She pulled her blouse on, and once it was buttoned she remained where she was, looking at him, wondering what she should do next, bursting to blurt out the true case of her love for him and afraid even to cough. His own gaze was inscrutable, but a sudden tremor ran across his brow, and he looked away.

''Please leave me now,'' he ordered brusquely.

Her words began to tumble over each other. ''Do you want me to go? I'll go—I'll go gladly, because I can't stay here.''

''Suit yourself. Go anywhere in the house.''

Was he being deliberately obtuse? ''I don't mean that. I want to go to another hotel.''

''You ought to have realized by now that that is impossible. The police will be keeping an eye on all check-ins, on the Hagans' house. Ali Shah and I were followed, and I was questioned twice, until Ali Shah's cousin—''

''The second commander of the police force.''

He went on as if he had not been interrupted. ''Ali Shah's cousin is blocking all attempts to get a search warrant and has set guards to protect me from that sniper. Tactfully, he hasn't inquired as to whether you are here. The Hagans have already been searched, and so, I might add, has your dear French friend. The gunman has not been caught, and there are others of equal skill in the city. Two of your hotel associates have been taken by the police for questioning. The embassy has been on my phone. Now you have, as you have made quite clear, reached the age of consent and are evidently old enough to make your own decisions. If you want to go, or if you think we aren't doing enough for you, you can leave now and I won't stop you.''

She considered for a moment, but there was no decision to make. Johnny, Ali Shah and Malcolm had each in his own way made it perfectly clear to her that she would be safe nowhere else but here. She could not have traveled a mile from his front gate before she was picked up. ''You know I can't go,'' she answered him at last, bitterly.

''Yes, I know, but it was about time you realized it, too. You will be safe here, Camilla, safe from everything. I promise you.'' He turned and lit another cigar.

She knew what he meant by safe. There would be no repeat performances of tonight's fiasco. And that was perhaps as much for his safety as for her own.

''Good night, then,'' she answered at last, quietly, and crept silently up the stairs to bed, chastened and full of miserable regrets. Her last attempt to gain some ascendancy over him had ended in dismal failure, and had even backfired on her. She stood lower than she ever had in his estimation, and now she was forced to live in his house, share his board. It should have been paradise, being under the same roof as the man she loved to distraction, anger and folly; but he in turn thought so little of her, beyond succumbing to an open sexual invitation, that he could hardly bring himself now to look at her.

Lying curled around her pillow, she imagined she was drowning, being washed away from the shore, with one wave sweeping her in and the next pulling her out, farther and farther each time. Criticism on criticism, idiocy on idiocy. Was there no end to her mistakes? She felt like a runner who continually stumbles and falls inches before the finishing tape. Every time she was in reach of the prize, of setting right his bad opinion of her, she was tripped up by her own quick temper, by her foolish love. And every fall made it less and less likely she would win the race, just as every wave pulled her farther and farther from the safety of land.

CHAPTER THIRTEEN

SHE SPENT THE NEXT TWO WEEKS locked inside the high cement walls of Malcolm Armstrong's house, and during that time discovered more about the man who was half her jailer, half her savior. In fact, she devoured information about him, and slowly won back Olga's trust by her obvious interest in every aspect of the "master's" life.

Much of what she came to know about him was gleaned by inference, Sherlock Holmes-type deductions; and she was careful not to draw any swift conclusions. A few things soon became evident. He had a great personal sense of duty; Olga, it came out, was his old nurse and had been elderly when he was born. Too ancient now to find another job, she was kept on as housekeeper in theory, though in fact most of the heavy work was done by other servants and the cook, so that the old woman's activities consisted mainly of getting in their way. This Camilla gathered herself, reading between the lines of Olga's chatter.

Malcolm also, despite Janet's opinion, had a soft spot for wounded or suffering creatures; a quality borne witness to by the presence of the young donkey, which, Camilla discovered, had been rescued from the knackers with a broken leg. Malcolm himself had set and laboriously tended the leg, which had healed leaving only a slight limp. The donkey's name was Ulysses, and he quickly attached himself to Camilla, following her around the garden like a faithful dog and braying mournfully when she went inside. She adopted a habit of feeding him herself by hand.

"You spoil that animal," Malcolm told her in one of their infrequent conversations. She was spoiling herself, too, with nothing to do all day but wander in the garden, continually making new discoveries of some little nook or rare hidden blossom. She also found another hobby to fill the leisurely hours: reading. Several mornings after she arrived she awoke to find a pile of books arranged on her floor by some considerate person—she didn't know whether it was Malcolm or Olga—and she read them all, finding in them a great pleasure, partly because they helped her escape from her tenuous situation. She read most of them in the little wooden gazebo; indeed, she spent most of her time in the garden. When she was in the house—too large and too grandiose for her—she felt like a prisoner and out of place, but walking in the garden she felt a privileged guest.

The owner of the house she saw only rarely during the day, and more often at dinner, which they took together nearly every evening. The rest of the time he was working—in his study or at the school or university. She was grateful for that, because the atmosphere between them was strained and unpleasant. They had not laughed together once since before that fateful evening.

She had developed a habit of ignoring ringing phones and doorbells, since she was not allowed to answer them. At first they rang continuously, even late into the night, until the expedient of leaving them off the hook was adopted. Later the heat of the pursuit dropped and they were left in peace.

She saw no one during those two weeks except Olga, the donkey Ulysses and, more rarely, Malcolm. So otherworldly was Camilla's present existence that only occasionally did it cross her mind to wonder why Nurjan never came to the house. Sometimes she decided it was due to the police surveillance. Other times she thought it was because Afghan girls were not allowed to visit bachelors unchaperoned—forgetting the hours Nurjan spent alone with Malcolm at the school. However, she had become so enclosed in the comfort of isolation that such external considerations could only touch but not disturb her. Strangely enough, she was absorbed in the luxury of solitude. She was determined to make the most of it, since she knew their search was postponed until the heat was off, so to speak.

It therefore came as a rude shock to her when Malcolm announced to her one night at dinner, "Tomorrow we're going to the used-clothes bazaar to see that shopkeeper who had Meghan's dress."

It had taken her several days to work up the courage to tell Malcolm about her discovery in the bazaar, and when she did finally tell him, she discovered her hesitancy to do so had been justified.

"From the Kuchis, the man said?" remarked Malcolm after hearing her out. "Which tribe?"

She had gulped, "I . . . I don't know."

"Can't remember?"

"No, I didn't ask."

He had drawn a deep breath of irritation. "Did you ask where the Kuchi had come from, what part of Afghanistan? Where the Kuchi got the dress? Why he was selling it? Did it come from a man or a woman? My God, Camilla, did you ask him anything?" The question had been rhetorical, and she had shaken her head dumbly, feeling tears welling.

"There's no need to go pitying yourself," he had said harshly. "We'll just have to go and talk to the man again." Then he had mentioned nothing more about it, and she herself was too ashamed to bring it up. She had failed once more.

He never spoke to her now with the laughing camaraderie of their trip to Ghazni, or with the tenderness of that evening at the school. He was always abrupt, with a coldness that cut her to the quick and a sardonic turn of phrase that was calculated to make her hate him. And yet she could not. It would have been easier to live in his house if she had, because she wouldn't have cared about the trouble she was causing him, nor would she have been hurt by his unfriendly manner. So she did not hate him, and she did care, and she was hurt.

Therefore it was with a mixture of delight and regret that she heard the police had lost interest in her case and they could safely go to the used-clothes bazaar. She was delighted, because she looked forward to getting out of the house and back in touch with the real world, and also because he was taking her, although she regretted the bother he had to go to and the annoyance that it caused. But he had decided the time had come for her to show her face around

Kabul once more. She awoke on the morning with butterflies in her stomach.

Wordlessly they got into the Land Rover. It was a beautiful day, sunny and cloudless as always; hot, too. Inside the walls of the estate all was silent, and little Ulysses trotted up to see them off. The gates were opened and they drove out. Immediately all the noises of the city assailed Camilla—the coarse roars of camels, dogs barking, the whirl of traffic, the cries of children, the call of the water seller, "Ao, ao," as though he were in pain. It was real and refreshing, like a draft of cool water to Camilla after a diet of heady wine.

Wordlessly they traveled across town. Camilla kept her eyes glued firmly to the window, looking at the scenery, but she remained always aware of the male presence beside her. Malcolm fixed his blue glare ahead of him. Driving like this for some twenty minutes, they came to the old city and the covered bazaars. It was a quick dash through sunlight from the shade of the car to the shade of the bazaars, and there he turned and spoke his first words since leaving the house. "Take me to the shop where you found your sister's dress."

She was afraid that she would not be able to find the place, but since she was even more afraid of appearing inept before Malcolm, she set off, trying desperately to remember where she had walked two weeks previously. She came to the shop where she had bought the skirt, then the Russian hat, turned right, left, right, left—what a maze! She began to fear she was hopelessly lost. Malcolm's unsmiling figure trudged along beside her, towering over her, and she dared not stop to get her bearings. Then she came to a corner she positively remembered, the one where she had watched the shadowy man hurrying out of sight in the crowds. The dress shop ought to be two down on the left; she was sure of it.

"I don't understand it," she said after they had walked up and down the alley twice and seen no sign of the booth she remembered. "If I had only seen it I might have thought my eyes were playing tricks on me, but I have my sister's dress to prove the place existed."

"Are you positive this is the place?" he asked grimly. "No offense, but you do seem to have a knack for forgetting important details."

Odd, she thought, that a remark she could once have shrugged off, or parried with another, now cut so deeply. She had no reply except, "Yes, I'm sure."

"Where exactly was it?"

"There." She pointed wearily. "I've told you."

"But there *is* a shop there."

"It's not the same one. The other sold dresses; this sells shoes."

"I'll go talk to him—he may have changed his stock. You," he added firmly, "stay here."

She had no intention of going anywhere else, but she followed him to the steps of the shop and stood there anxiously.

"Salaam aleikom," said Malcolm, holding out his hand. He and the shopkeeper went through the Afghan ritual of greeting and then got down to business. Malcolm began in English, but found that the shopkeeper spoke none, so he switched to Persian. Camilla listened, hands twisted, unable to guess the

course of the conversation. Then Malcolm turned back to her, and his face had fallen.

"All he can say is that he bought this stall a week and a half ago—dirt cheap, he says. Says he can't understand why the owner sold out. Perhaps that's really all he knows; anyway, he's not talking."

Tears seemed to come so easily to her now, thought Camilla, fighting back the urge to cry. This was her most miserable failure of all, and despite Malcolm's efforts there seemed no way to put it right. She had lost what might have been their only chance of finding Meghan. Running her hands bleakly through her hair, she was about to set out after Malcolm's disappearing form, which seemed indifferent as to whether she followed or stayed.

A hard tug at her elbow made her jump, and she was suddenly reminded of the day outside the Green Lantern when all this trouble had begun; when Patrice had forgotten his keys and she had been given the threatening note. Looking down she saw it was not the little urchin, but the shop boy who had served in the stall where she had bought her sister's dress, a handsome boy with the dark skin, coal-black eyes and flashing teeth she remembered.

"*Khanum*, you look for my master, yes?"

"Yes," she replied, surprised. "But why are you here? How did you recognize me?"

"I work for new master—I never forget pretty *khanum* who is so generous," he said, grinning.

"Where is your old master?" she asked eagerly. "Is he here?"

"No, he has gone to Herat." Camilla's hopes fell again.

"Why has he gone there?"

"Some rich men offered him plenty money," said the boy, rubbing his thumb and forefinger together.

"What rich men?" Camilla hardly needed to ask, because she had a strong intuition.

"*Farangi*, in a brown car, too much good!" The boy laughed.

"Do you remember the dress I bought?" The boy nodded. "I know it came from the Kuchis, but I must know which tribe. Do you know?" Her eyes desperately searched his face. She could see he was waiting, so she quickly drew out a twenty-afghani note from her purse and handed it to him.

He tucked it into the folds of his turban. "Thank you, *khanum*. I remember, yes. It was the tribe of Sher Muhammad near Bandi Amir. We buy lots from them. Many very...nice who sell." He pronounced the English syllables carefully.

To his surprise the pretty woman took his hand and shook it warmly, then, her hand shaking, drew out another twenty-afghani note from her purse and offered it to him.

"You are a good boy," she began, but even as she said it his whole expression changed, and leaving the money untouched in her hand, he broke away from her and ran. His eyes had been fixed on something behind her, and she whirled around to see a man disappearing around the same corner—a tall unmistakable man, the one who had stabbed her in the restaurant and followed her in this very bazaar two weeks earlier, she suddenly realized with numbing clarity. She felt a finger of fear twist her stomach, and her arms went halfway up to her head, as though she would wrap them around it for protection. Then she saw the futility of such an act: if they were going to get her, there was little she could do here, alone and vulnerable as she was, to defend herself.

Trembling, she hurried back through the maze, which was becoming faintly familiar, to the car, where Malcolm was waiting. He was smoking a cigarette with cool deliberation, and she knew him well enough now to recognize that smoking was with him a sign of intense irritation, but she was too frightened to feel guilty. As she swiftly climbed in he did not look at her.

"See anything you liked?" he inquired sarcastically.

"Take me home." The urgency of her tone pulled his gaze around to her, and his eyes snapped open. Camilla was not yet distraught enough to miss the effect—like the blaze of blue light in the morning when the curtains are first drawn back.

"Camilla! What's happened?" Even as he asked he had switched on the ignition and was reversing the car.

"One of Patrice's henchmen has been following me around. He disappeared when he realized I knew, but not before I got a good look at him."

"How do you know he's one of Patrice's men?"

"He's the same one who stabbed me in the restaurant."

Quickly she told him the rest of the news, and he took it in grimly, lips set in a thin line as he negotiated the rushing traffic, weaving in and out of the lanes.

"Do you think the boy's information was authentic?" he asked her.

"Why shouldn't it be?"

"Well, he could have been paid by Patrice to lure you out to Bandi Amir."

"I can't think why; he could kill me here just as well as there." She shivered at the prospect. "Anyway, the boy wouldn't have run off in terror at the sight of that man if he were in the pay of our friend. My guess now is that Patrice knows less about Meghan's whereabouts than we do, and is waiting for us to lead him to her."

"But why, Camilla?" Malcolm was studying her with frank admiration. But she was too engrossed in her recent discovery and her reasoning to treasure the switch in his attitude. Plenty of time for that later.

"Why, Camilla?" he repeated, and she had the feeling he was leading her toward unexplored territory.

Camilla was momentarily puzzled. "I thought he wanted to get me off the trail of his drug smuggling, to keep me from finding out the truth about him. But why would he want Meghan?" The answer came like a flash of lightning. "Because she must be the only one who knows the truth about Tom's death."

CAMILLA LAY TOSSING AND TURNING in her bed. The darkness of the room was overpowering, because she had drawn the curtains so tightly that not a glimmer of moonlight shone through. She was very hot but would not throw back the covers; she felt a need for protection, however slight. Uncomfortable and restless, she kept turning back to face the window, waiting for, anticipating, the sharp crash of broken glass and the whizz of a bullet. She could not get the picture out of her mind, nor the memory of moments of heart-pounding fear when she had lain on the floor of her hotel, not really knowing if she were alive or dead.

It was slightly reassuring that Malcolm had said he did not think they would try again. He believed she was perfectly safe—until she found her sister. Her sister! She felt a rush of joy at the prospect. But then she thought of small-eyed gunmen crouched against the wall, and curled farther under the covers.

Her sister! How far had she come to find a girl who might have changed, who might not want to return with her? And Camilla was not the same person who had stepped off that plane two months earlier. Her wide-eyed innocent self, full of big plans and pride so naive—where was she now? She twisted in her bed.

Her sister! She loved her sister, would do anything for her, but what had she herself got into? That plane had brought her to a country of brilliant colors and beautiful people; a country she loved—she could admit her love of it—but which had not loved her back. She had given up one home and could not make another. And the sordidness of what she had become involved in! Her cheeks blazed at the remembrance of assumptions so easily made back in London: two weeks at the most before she found her sister, who would immediately embrace her with joy and together they would fly home. She had never in her wildest dreams considered the nightmare it would become; her life and her sister's were at stake, trapped within a ring of murder, drugs, bribery and extortion...and who knew what else?

In one bound her heart had leaped onto a higher track—plunged, fluttered, dived, shouted and whispered, *Malcolm, Malcolm...*. She couldn't say now when it had happened exactly. She had been dishonest enough at first to tell herself it was no more than a physical attraction—which, honestly, no one can help. Then she'd had to confess that she did, well, like him a bit: that was why she missed him; he was nice, in a way, a friend. But now, in the dark or in the daylight, it always came back to her—the knowledge, lovely and anguishing, that she loved him.

It was for him that she worried, for him that she felt this great guilt, for she had involved him in this mess until his life, too, was at stake, and he had wasted his time, so pricelessly valuable where hers was so free, to help and aid her. And because she loved him she felt a keen pang in her heart when people asked her why she cared what he thought of her.

Her deep growing love explained a thousand other feelings—her depression, her desire to please him, her anguish at her blatant demonstrations of ineptness, her inability to keep him out of a conversation—and was the reason, too, perhaps, that she stayed on in this house. And her love for this country...what was it but an extension of her love for him? She loved what he loved; his people were her people; and in this place the skies were bluer because his eyes were there, the sun more vivid in the light of his golden curls, the clouds whiter, the grass greener, the water sweeter in his presence.

How can I go home, she wondered, anguished. And as soon as she thought that she realized she had made a mistake. He was her home. She would not leave him until he sent her away; she would follow him to the ends of the earth. She knew it would be better if she left tomorrow, but with all her pride gone she was too weak to do so. What she wanted to do was to run to him, throw her arms around him, kiss him uninhibitedly. Every vestige of her pride was stripped away, and all she wanted to do was to show him how much she loved him.

At the same time the recognition that this was the last thing she could do thrust itself in on her thoughts. She had never expected for one minute that he would ever love her; she anticipated only his sardonic laugh, and the more humble she became in her love, the more he would laugh at her. She could not have his love; what she had left of his respect—and that was little enough—she was determined to hang onto. When her love told her to stoop, she would stand tall, and when it told her to kiss his lips, she might shake his hand. She would salvage what she could from their relationship, and when at last she had to leave him, he would not remember her as a silly sentimental fool. Yes, he could never love her— she was in an honest mood and would harbor no false hopes—but he would not despise her.

Despite the hopeless, helpless truth of it, her heart leaped and surged with love—with complete faith in him and desire for him that went far beyond the purely physical. He was worth it, worth it all, and she only hoped a chance would come for her to save his life as he had so often saved hers. In the present circumstances it seemed not unlikely. Tomorrow he would find her a reformed woman; tomorrow, if it were not too late, she could begin to put right a relationship that had been on the wrong foot far too long. A difficult task, but anticipating it she fell asleep, embracing calm around her, now that she had owned the truth.

In her dreams her deeper unconscious set to work. Dressed in her shorts, she was being taken to the plane. She stirred and moaned as in her dream she tried to break away from the many hands that pulled her unwilling to the waiting craft. Someone had given an order; she did not know who. The plane was yellow and peeling. Together they threw her inside it, and she found herself in her hotel room. The floor—the floor was crawling with scorpions of every color, waving their stingers, gleaming, gleaming. Clouds swept by the window—

Then it happened. The crash of glass, the whining bullet. She fell to the floor, writhing among the scorpions, and cried out. Then she was standing, the bullet was coming and she falling. Over and over she stood and fell, with the bullets screaming in her ears and her head aching. She fell again and suddenly the floor was warm and strong, and was shaking her.

"Camilla! Camilla!"

The deep familiar voice told her it was only a dream. She came back to consciousness in the darkness of her room, but a comforting beam of moonlight shone through the curtains that had been parted. All terror fled away as she was held in his arms, and she clung to them desperately, just needing his strength. He seemed to understand, because he let her cling and said nothing. In the back of her mind was an awareness that they were sitting on the floor, sunk in the deep pile of the golden rugs with the bed-clothes tangled around her, but she hardly cared. She was luxuriating in the pleasure of being in his arms. She felt the butterfly touch of his lips on her hair and longed for them to rove. A flame of desire licked through her body, replacing the fever of the nightmare.

"Feeling better now?"

In answer Camilla raised her mouth, seeking his, and for a moment she was rewarded with a demanding kiss that promised, and offered, bliss. She drank deeply, parting her lips and uttering a languorous sigh. In these precious moments all thought was beyond her. She was filled with an awareness that this was what being alive was about; this feeling was the ultimate consummation, the reward of being flesh and blood.

He pulled away from her but held her tightly still, unwilling to let the moment pass. She looked up at him with open green eyes that reflected the depths of the sea.

"Camilla," he breathed haltingly, his voice as erotic a caress as the hand that stroked her slowly from the tingling roots of her hair to the warm hollow at the base of her spine. "We were both lying to each other the other night, weren't we? We told a part of the truth, but we tried to make it into a lie."

She absorbed the passion of his voice. She was tired of fighting, tired of waiting, sick with unfulfillment. This, she knew, was her moment. She held the outcome in the palm of her hand, the hand that tightened eagerly around his strong shoulder. Now she wanted to rise, take him by the hand, climb with him into the tangled sheets and let him teach her the nightly mysteries that enthralled the human race. The powerful needs—and restraints—of emotional love and its desire for promises and securities seemed to fade away to nothing, when the thrilling harmonious responses of their bodies throbbed in urgent demand for physical satisfaction. If they wanted each other, tonight, desperately, what did tomorrow matter?

She paused, closed her eyes, her senses humming—then she raised her lashes again to smile acquiescence into his hungry waiting gaze.

"My God, Camilla, don't look at me like that!" he exclaimed raggedly, and with a painful twist tore himself brutally from her arms. Her empty embrace was cold.

What had she done? Misinterpreted him? Had she delayed too long? Had she unwittingly somehow upset him, repulsed him? Disgusted him? She could not read the contorted expressions on his anguished face as she wrapped her lonely arms about herself in sudden misery.

"I'm sorry, Malcolm. What did I do?" She was determined to hold back her tears.

He took a deep breath. "Don't be. . .sorry, Camilla. It's not your fault. It was—it's just that—you're twenty-one, and I'm. . .I'm old enough to know better."

"Better?" Her voice trembled in confusion. "Better? What do you mean? What could be better than what we felt then?"

"A lot of things, and I. . . ." He raked his fingers through his tousled hair and looked away, as if unable to meet her earnest gaze. "I was wrong, and I...I apologize."

"Apologize!" She clasped her hands tightly together and swayed back and forth. "You weren't wrong, Malcolm; it was—"

"I know what it was," he interrupted brusquely. "And I won't have it from you. My God," he muttered fervently under his breath, "how can I expect you to trust me if I can't even trust myself?" He came near to her and knelt, but far enough away so that neither could touch the other except with some obvious calculated movement. Camilla saw this and shrank into herself. *He doesn't want to touch me,* her heart cried. *He doesn't want to come near me. Am I so repulsive to him?*

"Camilla," he began again, and she did not see what it cost him not to reach out to feel the bright disordered flame of her hair, "I have treated you badly. But please, try to understand. I think," he continued, but when she looked at him he stood up swiftly, jerkily, and finished in a strangled voice, "I think I should go."

The prospect of being left alone in that nightmare-haunted room was too much for her self-restraint. "Oh, Malcolm, Malcolm, please," she cried, half rising to her feet. "Don't go! Please, I'm so afraid— don't treat me like this. I...I didn't mean to do it. I was half-asleep and so afraid; you were like someone—something to cling to."

Looking down at her white-knuckled fists, she did not see the little light that went out in his cloudy eyes. However, he gave a grim cheerless smile, and moving to where she could see him he motioned her up.

"My poor Camilla," he said, though his tone was not as tender as his words. "Get back into bed. I know we've got to find some way to live together in this house. But if you're going to be plagued by nightmares, I'll move Olga into the room next to yours, so she can keep an eye on you. Or an ear, rather."

"Thank you," replied Camilla in a low voice. "You're very kind."

"It's not completely altruistic," he replied enigmatically. "Do you think you can sleep now?"

He had withdrawn from her again, eyes shaded to the color of a slate, cold and hard and impenetrable. What was the point, she asked herself desperately, in loving him so completely, when the only emotions she aroused in him in return were either an involuntary lust that disgusted him—she could see the anger in his face, hear it in the tone of his voice—or boredom and contempt? She knew the age difference he had mentioned was only an excuse. If he truly loved her it would not matter. He simply was fed up with her, she admitted despairingly, he was sick of her fears and no more than tolerant of her vulnerabilities.

She was a woman—loving him had made her one—and he was a man. But because they were simply a man and a woman thrown together through circumstance, the fierce passion that had sprung up between them did not have to have a deeper meaning—he would not let it. At most it became a weapon of revenge. Another realization, equally painful, came to her in a flash: because her femininity was the one thing about her that had ever affected him, it was that which he hated most about her, and so in essence despised her. Unable to bear the thought, she turned her face to the wall.

He evidently assumed she had fallen asleep, for his weight was lifted from the bed as he moved to go.

Don't keep him, a voice cried within her. *He doesn't want to stay; you have no right.* But the prospect of being left alone in that room full of terrors and dark shadows was too much for her. Even while her conscience was speaking, she turned involuntarily toward him and whispered, "Please don't leave me...."

His face was drawn with tiredness, his expression bleak. She thought he was going to walk out in disgust at her weakness. But he said, gently enough, "I'll stay, but you must sleep. You're as white as a sheet. I'll fix your blankets for you."

Such a sudden transformation from the coolly aloof man who had faced her was this man who carefully tucked in the sheets and blankets, who fluffed the pillow and pulled the coverlet up around her chin. She thought her heart was going to burst with the effort of holding herself back from flinging her arms around his neck and telling him how much he really meant to her. It might have been better to be left in the darkness than to have him hovering around her bedside, his face concerned as for some injured animal, his fiery eyes fixed upon her face. The stronger her feelings burned the stronger she had to be, and she turned away from him so that he might not see her slow tears in the moonlight. She feigned sleep—real sleep would not come that night, not while he sat there, watching by her bedside.

That was the real nightmare, the true-life one, that he should be so near and yet so far, so loved and so unloving. His arms had been around her to comfort her or punish her, but she would never feel them around her as a possessive enfolding of love returned. She lay curled like a child, feigning sleep, and at last she heard him get up roughly and go out.

SHE AWOKE EARLY. The sun, as usual, was a friendly hot glow, the sky clear, the doves cooing and the hoopoes crying outside her window. For a moment she could not remember why her heart was so deathly heavy, but it all came back to her, and she was angry with the day for being so happy when she was miserable. It only made her feel worse. She would have preferred rain, or at least overcast skies, so that something would be in sympathy with her.

Further sleep was impossible. She reckoned she had slept one or two hours at the most, but she would have to get up anyway. She felt not tired but drained. She pulled herself out of bed and dressed slowly, dreading the moment when she would have to go down and see Malcolm. Her heart beat faster at the thought.

She decided she would have it out with him today. Much as she longed to stay, her reason told her how impossible it was. She must convince him of that without giving away the truth. She didn't quite see how she could carry it off, because, as she knew from experience, he was very perceptive. Still, it had to be done. And the sooner the better.

She saw him sooner than she'd expected, for he was waiting for her outside her door. She was shocked to observe now changed he looked from the previous day—pale and drawn, with lines across his brow that she had not seen upon him before. His hair was unbrushed and wild, and a day's growth of beard roughened his cheeks. His eyes were haggard. *He looks as though he hasn't slept all night,* she thought.

But before she could say a thing to him he gave her a clipped order. "Get packed. Sturdy clothes, heavy boots. We're going to Bamian—I'll explain in the car."

He turned away swiftly and left her. Unquestioning, she went to do his bidding. Changing from the light cotton dress she had worn into a pair of tough denims and a cotton shirt, roomy and cool on her, she was ready in fifteen minutes. Case in hand, she hurried down to the garage.

He was waiting in the rattling Sally, her engine already going. Dressed in his Afghan trousers and shirt, a turban wrapped around his head, and his eyes, now sky blue and intense, transfixing her, he looked wild, almost frightening. He motioned to Camilla to open the gate, which she did, and drove out.

Camilla had no watch, but she could tell it was early. The sky was very clear, still retaining the pearly texture of dawn, while the city was, for Kabul, quiet, with only the occasional bray of a donkey, howl of a dog or cry of a cockerel. As she got into the Land Rover, the muezzin from the Hajji Jacob mosque began his fluting call to morning prayer. Five o'clock. After he ended his call, the city would spring to life.

They revved away down the empty streets, Malcolm's eyes fixed on the road ahead. Camilla did not dare ask him any questions when he was in this mood; she was content to sit beside him and go where he was going, for she knew he would explain in his own good time.

Soon they were out of the city and on the road to Istalif and Charikar. Malcolm's tense body relaxed, and he began to explain to her.

"Ali Shah called last night," he said. She was momentarily surprised, for she had not heard his name cross Malcolm's lips since that fateful evening; she was sure Malcolm had deeply offended him. "I thought the police had let up, but they had only been working on a new tactic. They are trying to get a warrant for my arrest." Before she could express the shock and fear that swamped her, he hurried on, "Also a warrant to search the house. Apparently I'm harboring a wanted person, and they're raking up interest in the heroin business...."

"What about Ali Shah's cousin?"

"He's doing the best he can to delay it, but someone with money is pushing it through."

She read his thoughts: *Patrice Desmarets*.

"So," he continued, "we're going to Bamian and then on to Bandi Amir to find your sister before the interested authorities put a stop to the search altogether. I wanted to wait for more information, but there's no time now."

Camilla's heart was filled with emotion—gratitude, admiration and love. Again her conscience pricked her—*you must not let him risk himself for you*—but she ignored it. She was selfish in love, and if she could not get him off the case when she disliked him, she would not even try now that she loved him.

Realistically, she knew she would not be able to do a thing without him, and if he was willing to stick with her, she could not say no.

"What did you do with the heroin?" she asked him.

"Burned it."

Several miles along the road he suddenly turned off toward a large building constructed out of mud, resembling some giant solid sand castle. The high wooden gates of the mud walls were open, and Malcolm drove in, pulling up outside a thick door set into the strong walls. Camilla looked at the square building. Little windows were dotted all up its sides, with brightly painted curtains hanging in them. The place seemed monumental—at least four stories high—and looked cool and secretive. She had a longing to wander inside it, where she was sure she would discover secret winding stairs, dark corridors, hidden doorways, veiled faces and strangely spiced food—all the mysteries of the East.

"What a fantastic place!" she exclaimed. "Like a Thousand and One Nights. What is it?"

He looked at her oddly. "Ali Shah's house. Haven't you ever been here?"

"No, I haven't. Is he coming with us?"

"Yes," replied Malcolm shortly, getting out of the car. "We might need him."

She was glad that he was joining them, and she hoped the two men had made up their differences. "Will we have time to stay?" She was longing to explore.

"No." He walked away. He knocked on the door and Ali Shah appeared, dressed in the same costume as his English companion. Camilla thought how wild and masculine they looked, and felt she would be safe as long as she was with them. Ali Shah carried a wrapped parcel in his hand, and when he got in next to her he took out a piece of steaming chewy *naan* and handed it to her.

"My sister has just baked it," he explained, and she bit into it hungrily. Malcolm also took a piece, and devouring it quickly and silently they drove on.

The first part of the road was familiar to her. They drove along the paved road that ran from Kabul to the Salang Pass—they were traveling up a valley into the foothills of the Hindu Kush. On either side of the road there was an expanse of flat plain divided into fields, which rose slowly into hills of tan and green. Some of these fields contained tall hive-shaped white silos or mud villages. Ahead of them the purple mountains rose. But after they passed the town of Charikar, Camilla no longer knew the territory, and it became more mountainous as they continued their ascent, with rocky hills and cliffs the color of slag on either side. They drove over a strong gray bridge that spanned a torrential river, and there was a collection of gray stone houses on the other side, and a network of irrigation. Even Camilla's untrained eye could see that it was an excellent engineering job.

"The Chinese built that," Ali Shah pointed out. "And the Russians recently built this road."

Another hour along the highway, and they had been climbing steadily, Malcolm turned to the left, after passing a cement factory. They were traveling now along a dirt road. It was like a descent into paradise, for the road ran high in the hills and looked down on a fertile valley, which was a startling green against the pale gray and tans of the hills, with a steely blue river meandering through it. They slowly moved down into this valley and continually crossed and recrossed the river on broad bridges. They passed through many little villages cradled in the curves of the river, and at one Malcolm stopped long enough for Ali Shah to buy some sticky sweet delicious mulberries.

They traveled on and soon were climbing again. The river became narrower and rushed more purposefully in the direction they had come from. They were following it upstream. The sward of green became narrower, too. The foothills and cliffs on either side were dramatic color—metallic purple, dark brown, streaky rust and shining gray—very rocky and bare of vegetation. The nearer fields were thick in wheat and rippling grass, with herds of cattle or flocks of sheep grazing on them. Poplars and willows lined the river.

Camilla had never been on such an enchanting drive, and she even forgot the necessity for it as her eyes tried to record every sight. The mountains came nearer and nearer, the cultivated land ever narrower, and in many places the cliffs hung over the road, with rock formations like turrets and battlements on medieval castles. All along the road were old crumbling towers, which Ali Shah told her had been guard posts or lookouts in the days when Afghanistan had an empire. Then they came upon the most startling outpost of all. Rising above the greenness, on an enormous dais of rusty earth and rock, stood the eroded shell of a once mighty castle, carved out of rock and still impressive in ruin.

"That is the Red Fort," Ali Shah informed her. "The last prince of it held out against the shah of Afghanistan but was betrayed by his own daughter. There is only one way to reach its walls up the sheer cliffs, and she gave the secret to her lover, who was in the army of the shah. They say her father had two snakes coming out of his neck, which every day had to be fed on a maiden or else they would eat his head off."

Camilla laughed but shuddered, too. "No one really believes that, do they?"

"I think in the West you have a superstition about walking under ladders?" Ali Shah countered.

"But nobody really believes it will bring bad luck!" protested Camilla.

"No, but I've yet to see a European walk under a ladder if he can possibly help it. The Red Fort is, like the superstition of ladders, so old that although people don't completely believe it anymore, they cannot quite rid themselves of a sneaking suspicion that it might be true."

"I see," said Camilla. "But it's still a very unpleasant myth."

"There are many things about life that are not pleasant," cut in Malcolm obscurely. She was surprised; those were the first words he had spoken for a long time.

At about noon, seven hours after setting off from Malcolm's place, they arrived in Bamian. Malcolm pointed out the road to the Kuchi camp, but decided they needed to rest up before proceeding. They drove along the same street to a hotel Malcolm recommended—called, rather appropriately, the Kuchi Hotel.

Camilla, used now to roughing it, was delighted with the accommodations.

All the rooms opened onto a central courtyard, with half of one side open for the entrance. The dining room was in the middle of the courtyard, underground, with a curved roof of felt covered by plastic and little windows cut into the ceiling. There were also several constructions like wigwams, which she learned were called yurts, made of bent poplar branches covered with felt and skins. Each had two beds and was surprisingly large inside.

"I'll have a yurt," said Camilla. Sleeping in one would be something to remember. Luckily, there were three yurts, so they each had one.

Descending into the depths of the restaurant for lunch, they dined on roast chicken and *naan*. There they discovered a delightful German couple who were staying at the hotel and spoke good English. Camilla and Ali Shah chatted to them about their country, but Malcolm remained aloof.

Camilla longed to know what was annoying him and had a sinking feeling that it was herself. It did not matter what she did or what she said: he despised her so much that the mere fact of her presence was enough to irritate him. She could not relax while he was so moody and unfriendly, so she racked her brains to think of some way of amusing him. Yet she found it difficult to talk to him, even to approach him. She could not understand her own feelings, for she wanted to be with him, but she was miserable near him. Even though she tried to put on a brave front inwardly her nerves were tense and her stomach gnawed—she could not concentrate on anything.

After lunch she proposed a walk into town. Malcolm said he would prefer to go to sleep but that Ali Shah would go. The Afghan nodded his assent. All the pleasure was spoiled for Camilla as they walked down the main street without the towering golden-haired man, and her thoughts continually wandered back to his little yurt.

As they drifted down the row of little shops, Camilla suddenly thought she would like to buy him a present. Once the idea was in her head, she had to carry it out. It was little enough in return for what he had given her, and little compared to what she could give, if only he would ask for it.

"What do you think he would like, Ali Shah?"

Ali Shah wasn't very interested in the purchasing of a present for Malcolm, but he gave her a few off-hand ideas. She finally bought him a large woolly sweater in a brown-and-cream pattern, and hoped it would be large enough for his rugged frame.

After that Ali Shah dragged her off to look at the ruins of the Buddhist monastery for which Bamian was famous. She had seen them from a distance, in the car: row upon row of caves, carved out of rock, black mysterious holes in the cliff face. These had been the monks' cells. Also there were two colossal statues in relief of upstanding Buddhas, sculpted from the living rock. From a distance they had been imposing enough, but close up they were awe-inspiring. The largest was almost two hundred feet tall, supreme in the shadow of the cliff in which it had been carved. As she stood below it Camilla was astounded by the quality of the workmanship, which conveyed delicate folds of drapery in the hard rock and imparted a divine sereneness to the Buddha's mouth. That was all that was left of his face, destroyed by the same Muslim invaders who had broken up the monastery more than a thousand years before.

"It is possible to climb up onto the top of the Buddha's head and look out over the whole of Bamian. Would you like that?"

Camilla agreed, so they paid the guide to take them up through the black labyrinth of steps and corridors. Every so often a patch of light would indicate a small window where they could look out and down a hundred feet or so of sheer cliff. At last they reached the Buddha, and Camilla gulped in fear.

A large doorway opened onto a cliff face that fell forty feet to the place where the Buddha's shoulders were joined to the rock. The head was joined to the rock of the cliff by an isthmus of stone a foot wide and perhaps seven or eight inches long. It was necessary to jump from the lip of the door to the flat top of the Buddha's head.

"Aren't there any guardrails?" asked Camilla, her palms sweating.

"Of course not," replied Ali Shah gaily. Their guide had already leaped and was sitting on his haunches, perched just above the area of the Buddha's brow. "It is very easy to jump."

"You jump first," prompted Camilla. He did. She took a deep breath and, holding his hand, leaped.

To her amazement she was on the other side. The view was breathtaking—miles and miles of it. Above her head, in the arch of the Buddha's niche, were the remains of holy paintings—feasts and dancing girls, which she thought rather odd subjects for monks.

Once having made the jump she did not want to leave, but stared and stared, striving to remember it all.

"Has Malcolm ever come here?"

Ali Shah seemed a bit disgruntled. "Yes, I have brought him here several times."

"I expect he found a lot to interest him historically—especially those paintings."

"They are very old," agreed Ali Shah.

"It's a shame he couldn't have come with us this afternoon; he knows so much about it."

"I know about it," said Ali Shah; rather sharply, she thought, for him. She supposed he and Malcolm were still not on very good terms.

CAMILLA WAS SURPRISED to find how fast the afternoon had gone, and she was starving when they trailed back into the hotel at dusk. At the height they were at the earth never retained its warmth, and the darkening skies were already bringing a colder temperature. She shivered.

"Have a good time?" Malcolm greeted them curtly when they came into the restaurant. He scarcely said another word through the rest of the meal, and Camilla was so miserable she could only pick at her food.

At last Malcolm made some excuse and got up to leave. She watched him go, her eyes pricking with tears. What had she done to make him hate her so much?

Why, why, why does this have to happen, she asked herself silently, furiously. *Why do I have to love him so much I can't eat or sleep? Why couldn't*

it have been someone more. . .more practical? But
she knew she would rather have the pain of loving
him than the pleasure of loving anyone else.

"Miss Simpson?" She turned and looked at Ali
Shah through a veil of tears. He sighed and looked
rather unhappy. "What is it between you and Malcolm?"

She looked away. "Wh—what do you mean?"

"You know. I have not seen you two for many
weeks. Before—" he paused, and she knew very well
what event he dated "before" from "—before, you
had started to get on so well together, and now. . . ."
Again he paused, seeking for words in a language
that was still too foreign for him to express what he
meant properly, and at the same time wanting not to
reveal, or ask, too much.

"He hates me." She supplied him his answer. But
to her surprise he shook his head.

"No, no. It is me he has not forgiven. You remember my talk with him at his place?"

How could she ever forget it? Sudden icy fear
gripped her. "Ali Shah, you didn't tell him? He
doesn't realize. . .?"

"No," the Afghan said, shaking his head. "He
doesn't know. He is never very perceptive in things
regarding himself." And then more quietly, "I wish
he *did* realize."

She gripped his arm. "You must never tell him,"
she whispered, and there was almost hysterical urgency in her voice. "Promise me!"

"Of course I promise." He took her hand and held
it. "I hope it may work out well, but I do not know.
He never trusts twice. Once. . . ." His voice faded

and he looked away from her. "I was once his best friend, and I was honored by it. But now...."

"Oh, Ali Shah," she sighed mournfully. "It's so unjust that he should treat you this way. What he has done to you...." Her voice in turn trailed away as they teetered on the edge of the topic of Ali Shah's lovely beloved cousin. "You are the best friend he could want. Why doesn't he *see*? Sometimes I wonder if he deserves a friend like you." Camilla went on, explaining earnestly to try to ease the rift between the men that she had indirectly caused. "I think he was far more angry at me than at you that day. It was me he blamed. He likes to protect people he cares about—I mean you—and I'm sure he still cares, or he wouldn't have brought you along. He's just acting stubborn, that's all," she said reassuringly. "You know," she added, to show he wasn't the only one who'd been hurt by Malcolm, "it's not for my sake that he's here. I'm a sort of useless appendage. It's for Theresa."

Ali Shah bolted upright to full attention. "He spoke about his sister to you? That's extraordinary! He never mentions her name. It's been years—"

"Since it happened, I know. He hasn't forgotten. Could you?"

"But, Camilla—"

She went on as if he had not spoken. "I've completely forfeited any claim to his attention. He's never thought much of me anyway, and I've made so many mistakes, it's easy to blame me for anything. And then...." She clenched her teeth, and her jaw and voice were tight, "And then, of course, there's Nurjan."

Ali Shah looked startled. "Nurjan? What has she got to do with it?"

Camilla was stunned by this sudden, completely uncharacteristic display of insensitivity. What had Nurjan, beautiful black-haired Nurjan, Malcolm's love, to do with it? The answer was, to her, so obvious that she could hardly find the words to speak it.

"Ali Shah, what can you mean? Of course Nurjan has everything to do with it!"

But he looked so perplexed that she realized she had made a grave mistake in mentioning his ex-fiancée. Much as he tried to hide his feelings, Ali Shah's love for the girl was written plainly across his face. Camilla could not cause him any more suffering, and if he preferred not to bring Malcolm's and Nurjan's affair out into the open, she would respect that. Or maybe he was not entirely enlightened about the exact nature of the relationship and preferred to be kept in the dark as a measure of self-protection. Camilla would not be the one to clue him in.

So she just smiled at him sadly, shook her head, then stood to leave. Her ability to stay and enjoy herself was now spoiled, anyway, by the ghostlike presence of Nurjan between them.

Ali Shah did not object. He just smiled back, regret in his eyes, and watched silently as she fled from the restaurant to the shelter of her yurt.

CHAPTER FOURTEEN

MORNING DAWNED CHILL AND CRISP, the air crystal clear. When Camilla rose, unwilling to lie in bed and dwell on her thoughts, long shadows stretched across the courtyard and ran up the western walls, and the sky was pale blue and sunless while the morning star lingered behind the purple hills to the east. The rest of the hotel was still asleep, and the town was as quiet as early-morning Kabul had been the day before. She reckoned it was before five o'clock, since the muezzin had not yet awakened the people, and she thought it would be pleasant to take a walk through the awakening streets. She could hear snores from the men's yurts, and guessed they would sleep awhile longer; Malcolm especially, since he had been exhausted after a previous sleepless night and a day of hard driving. So Camilla set out alone.

She turned left outside the gate and walked for a way down the street in the same direction she had gone yesterday, but twenty minutes walking brought her to the end of that street. She turned back and started up the other side of the street, and the muezzin began to call from his minaret. A cock crowed, she heard the clip-clopping of a laden donkey coming up the road behind her and a *"Salaam aleikom, khanum,"* from the driver. Shutters were thrown up, doors opened, the smell of *naan* baking wafted out, and the potato seller walked the street with his cry: "*Catchacatchaloo-aw!*"

Passing the gate to the Kuchi Hotel, Camilla kept on going. Another twenty minutes walking and she decided to turn around. Here the dirt road went around a bend and was lost to sight. She stood for a minute, drinking in the unpolluted beauty of the mountainous landscape, and then thought she must go back before they started to worry about her.

But as she stood to gaze for one more minute, two mounted men came galloping around the bend. One was on a loping camel, laden with harness of silver and wood and rich cloth, and the other was on a wiry gray horse. Jingling and thudding, they were nearly on top of her as she watched their passage, fascinated, when suddenly they pulled up and stared with equal fascination. Her nerves twinged, and she felt perhaps it had not been such a good idea to take an early-morning walk. She had a startlingly clear intuition that the men were Kuchis—she could tell from their dress, for Malcolm had shown her pictures—and she thought: *they have come to kidnap me as they kidnapped my sister!* But it was useless to run now, so she held her ground and stared back with what she hoped was sufficient courage to impress them.

They seemed pleased with what they saw, for they turned smiling to each other and spoke quickly in their strange tongue. Then one reached into the pocket of his coat. *It's a gun or a knife,* she thought desperately, and she would have run then, only she saw him pull out not a gleaming piece of metal but some white paper.

Urging his camel forward, the man leaned down and said in heavily accented English, "Miss Simpson?"

She cast her eyes wildly from one to the other, and could only nod. This seemed to be the sum total of his English, for he handed her the paper silently and she took it, her eyes never leaving their darkly handsome faces, which were surprisingly kind. They watched her in return for a minute, and then the man on the horse laughed, and they wheeled around and loped away.

Until then she had not been aware of the extent of her fright, but the relief that buckled her knees told her how nervous she had been. Then she looked at the paper in her hand and, sitting down rather suddenly, opened it.

My dearest Camilla:

I cannot begin to express what I feel! I can only talk to you. We are at Bandi Amir. Try to come today or tomorrow, since we will not be here much longer. Ahmad and Djalani bring this; they are good sorts. Hurry, please! I love you.

Meghan

Meghan! At last, after so many weeks, her sister at last! And it had been so easy in the end! So easy! She hadn't found Meghan, but Meghan had found her. She got up and ran back to the hotel as fast as she could on legs unsteady with joy.

Instinctively, she headed first for Malcolm's yurt. But he was not there. This threw her into confusion. Why was he not there when she needed him?

"Camilla!" She looked around, but it was not Malcolm, only Ali Shah entering the quarters. "We've been so worried!"

She could see it on his face, but no guilt could dampen her spirits now. "Ali Shah!" she cried. "It's happened! I've found her; I really have!"

"What! Your sister?" he cried out incredulously, catching her enthusiasm.

"Yes, or rather she found me! Look!" She held out the letter. He took it and read it quickly, then handed it back to her, his face shining with happiness for her.

"Those two Kuchis—Ahmad and Djalani—I met them at the west end of town when I went for a walk this morning." Any thought of disgrace for her impulsive disappearance from the hotel was out of both their minds. "If I hadn't gone out I might have missed them, and I might never have known."

"*Allah wh'akbar,*" said Ali Shah piously. "Allah is great," he repeated for her benefit. "It is by the will of Allah that you have found your sister."

"I must go and find Malcolm," she declared happily, smiling as she clutched the precious note in her trembling fingers. "We must set off right away— where is he?"

"He went to look for you," replied the Afghan, grinning as though it were highly amusing. "He was very worried, you know," and he added as a rider, "We both were."

"Which way did he go? I must find him quickly— he'll be so angry."

"Not when you tell him," pointed out Ali Shah.

"Oh, yes, he mustn't be! I'm so happy!" And in a burst of joy she flung her arms around the neck of the surprised Afghan and kissed him quickly on the cheek. "That's for being so sweet." Then she turned and ran out the open door of the yurt, slamming it behind her.

An arm, tanned and strong, reached out and grabbed her.

"Let go; you're hurting me!" she exclaimed, looking up into fiery blue eyes. She thought she had seen him angry but knew now that had been mild disapproval compared to this. Her heart was tearing through her chest in its frantic pounding.

"What is it? What's wrong?" She was frightened, and the voice that came from her was harsh, strangulated, unrecognizable.

"What's wrong?" His hollow laugh was unamused. "You think I don't know? I came in time to hear, 'Tell him.' So come on, tell me."

His grip on her shoulders was relentless, and his eyes burned into hers. She knew he had a quick and moody temper, but this anger was something more.

"What's the matter, Camilla? Cat got your tongue? You swing from me to Ali Shah and back again like a pendulum—or have you made up your mind now? Tell Malcolm, poor deluded Malcolm, why don't you? I may have been your patsy, but I'm neither blind nor deaf—"

"You are!" Camilla shouted, incensed at his unfair accusations. "You're blind and deaf and completely dumb. You think you know everything and you can't see—you can't even tell, can you? Or maybe you just don't care!'' It was bitterly, ironically ludicrous, and she broke into high hysterical laughter; it racked her like sobs, and she couldn't stop it.

A cold slap brought her to her senses. "Now is no time to be hysterical," he snapped.

"You two are such fools. You can't see what's plain to everybody else," said a calm voice from the doorway. "Let her go, Malcolm."

Malcolm threw her arm from him with such force that it slapped hard against her thigh.

"Go on, hurt me," cried Camilla, gasping hot racked breaths. "That's all you've ever done, hurt me. Why was I ever so stupid as to fall in love with you?"

She turned, running and stumbling, the ringing in her ears drowning all sound, drowning Malcolm's cries as he stood frozen to the spot. Blind with tears, she nearly fell over the Land Rover, and finding herself resting on the cold metal of the door handle she impulsively wrenched it open and flung herself into the driver's seat.

If Malcolm had not left the key in the ignition she would never have done what she did next. She had not planned to do it. But when she saw the keys swimming mistily before her, it seemed not only the most obvious, but the only thing to do—to turn the ignition on and career wildly out of the gate and off to the right, tires squealing, dust rising, leaving behind her the infuriating man she both loved and hated.

As she drove along the dirt track she had met the two Kuchis on, one thought kept hammering through her mind: why had she confessed her love for him, spat it out in anger and bitterness? Sick at heart, she realized she had burned all her bridges now. How could she ever go back and look him in the face?

Then she lifted her head proudly. What had she to be ashamed of? Loving someone was not a crime. Let him be ashamed for the way he'd treated her and for his own blindness.

But would he be ashamed? Wouldn't he think her more of a fool than ever—loving someone, who had no intention of loving her in return? It didn't matter anymore. She wouldn't let it.

It would be so much easier if she could just forget him. But she couldn't. There were too many memories of shared laughter, tenderness, companionable conversation, happy intimacy—and that ever-present burning desire. It was the good beautiful things that had sparked between them that had given him the power to hurt her as he did.

She could have beaten her head against the dashboard, but instead she gripped the steering wheel firmly in her hands and let the discipline of driving calm her. The most important relationship in her life seemed to have descended into madness; all that was left to her now was to find her sister.

The drive to the Kuchi camp outside Bandi Amir was longer than she had expected from Malcolm's clipped words yesterday, far longer. But she tried to relax and enjoy it as much as possible. She had driven quite a bit in England, so she quickly mastered the vehicle, amazed at how well it handled. And there was only one road, well marked if primitive, so she could not go wrong, but she met no other traffic. An aching loneliness swamped her. The road had taken her out of the comforting green valley into the wide gray-and-brown rolling barrenness of the steppes, ringed in the far distance by a hazy fringe of mountains. The vegetation was sparse, dull shrub and grayish coarse grass, and not a single tree broke the lines of the plains. She passed several nomad encampments, the small black tents tiny in the vast steppes. A horse ran wild in the open spaces and hawks circled the endless expanse of sky, but there was no life other than this. As she drove on, the incident at the yurts retreated into a nightmare, and the feeling slowly crept over her that she was the last being alive on earth.

For two hours she drove on in a silence broken only by the steady noise of the engine. Then she rounded a bend and between the folds of two pale sandy cliffs caught a glimpse of shining water, far down in a valley; water as blue as Malcolm's eyes, a sight that brought a sudden ache to her heart. Immediately the brilliance was lost again, and the Land Rover toiled up an especially tall hill.

The vista now spread out before her took her breath away. Afghanistan had held many surprises, but none more beautiful than this: Bandi Amir, the lakes of the king. The pools were like jewels—sapphires, emeralds, turquoises—gleaming in the folds of rough earth. Enchanted, she stopped and poised on the edge of a cliff that plunged some five hundred feet to the lakes below, letting the rushing wind fill her with the wild splendor of the place. One moment of indulgence was all she allowed herself, and then she moved on, down the track that overhung the sheer cliff face, rumbling to the bottom.

Once in the valley she discovered that the lakes had formed on a sort of platform, raised like giants' baths inside high sandy walls of rock and mineral, over which silver ribbons of water cascaded slowly in waterfalls. These trickled away into a stream that ran down through a graveyard and a village of mud huts, with flocks of sheep scattered about. She followed the road, but it became fainter; she passed a collection of flimsy wood structures built no doubt to satisfy the growing number of tourists: restaurants, snack bars and souvenir shops. The car climbed another hill, and she knew that soon she should be nearing her goal.

There, on the other side of the hill, nestled by the lakeside, was the familiar cluster of black tents, camels, goats and brilliantly clothed people. Camilla's heart beat fast with excitement and anticipation. Her hands were white and shaking. She stopped the car and walked down on foot to the Kuchi village.

Delicious breakfast smells, bread and coffee, reached her as she entered, reminding her that she had eaten nothing all morning. But all that was less important than the fact that her sister, once thought dead, was now only yards away. A child shouted when he saw her coming, and his mother, looking up, ran to a man standing by a tall handsome camel. He turned, and she recognized him as Ahmad or Djalani, one of the riders of that morning. She could hardly credit it as the same morning. Time had ceased to have any meaning.

She walked to him and held out her hand, giving the Afghan greeting, *"Salaam aleikom."* He returned it and by signs bade her to follow him. They walked through the camp, one of the largest and most impressive Camilla had ever seen. On every side prosperity shone through. Silently, she congratulated Meghan.

They approached a group of women, all dressed in flamboyant reds and blues with bright scarves covering their hair. Camilla would have gone on by, but then one of them stood up and throwing back her scarf revealed a wealth of blond hair streaming down her back in two thick plaits, and green eyes set in a tanned strong face.

"You did come," said the dear familiar voice, and Camilla, with a sob, embraced her like the long-lost sister she was.

"IT'S BEEN SO EASY," said Camilla to her sister. They sat in one of the black shadowed tents, drinking tea and eating barley boiled in stock. Meghan had cooked it for Camilla's breakfast. She sat easily, cross-legged and supple in her flowing dress; Camilla found her slacks more uncomfortable.

"Was it so easy to find me?" Meghan smiled at her over the cup.

After the first astonishment, the tears, the embraces and silent observations were over, the two were chattering like magpies, Meghan especially delighted to exercise her native tongue.

"No, not at all. . . ." A thousand reminiscences tangled in Camilla's brain. "I mean, since I got your note this morning, it all seemed to resolve itself so quickly. Like banging and banging on the front door for hours, only to find that the back door was open all the time."

"Did you not get the letter I sent a few weeks ago explaining everything?"

Camilla's eyes widened. "No—I've been here, in Kabul mainly, for ages it seems. Oh, Meghan! Why didn't you write sooner?"

"Did you come out on your own? I thought it was because of my letter." She studied Camilla's crestfallen face. "Oh, dear, I'm so sorry...I'd been meaning to write, but time just seemed to slip by. Everything was so new, so different...."

"It doesn't matter now," Camilla reassured her. "I'm just glad you're happy—and alive. Not that I ever believed you weren't, but everyone kept telling me—"

Meghan looked shocked. "Everyone? But who?"

Camilla set down her cup, and an intensely serious expression took hold of her face. "Patrice Desmarets, for one. How much do you know about him?"

"Oh, Camilla! How did you get mixed up with him?" Her sister's expression immediately became apprehensive. "How much do you know?" she countered.

"We know about the drug trafficking—we found a bag of heroin in the seat of your car. But—I have to know, Meghan, though I don't for one minute believe...." She twisted her hands together. "How much were you involved?"

"I was never involved," replied Meghan proudly. "I will tell you the whole story...." And she proceeded to explain.

"You realize Tom and I had been growing apart for some time—I think you always knew we were never suited. Growing apart! The rows we had! At first I think I was attracted by the glamour of his job more than anything else. Glamour, you know, is false, as I soon discovered. When we got to Singapore his real personality came out—lazy, greedy and dishonest. It was all I needed to turn me against the entire society that had produced a worm like him."

"I can see that," agreed her sister. "You were always the rebel of the family, always the one who fought the system."

"It wasn't so much fighting the system as being sure it wasn't right, without knowing a suitable alternative. I mean, the life we led in England—it wasn't right for *me*; I'm not talking about other people. And I was frustrated and unhappy because I thought there was no other way to live. But now...." The joy and fulfillment reflected in Meghan's face told Camilla everything she needed to know. "I'm so happy."

"I know you are," said Camilla softly, though her eyes for a moment filled with tears. They sat in silence, and then Camilla, blinking away her tears, reminded her sister, "You were telling me about Tom."

"By the time we left Singapore I was ready to leave Tom, and I would have done so if we'd come back to England together. But I decided to stick with him on the Asia trip, because I thought it might be my last real adventure before returning to the life I had given up when I married that...that snake. Also—" she looked down sadly "—I thought of it as a last chance, one last effort to prove that somewhere in this world there was a life in which I could be happy.

"Anyway, we set out, through all of Southeast

Asia and India and Pakistan, and all the time I was despairing because it seemed everywhere was spreading the bug of Westernization. Then we came to Afghanistan. You can tell the difference when you cross the border; it's—oh, I don't know...clean, refreshing, real. We arrived about the same time as a tribe of Kuchis, and when I was told about them I set out to visit them, just to see the way they lived. And that was it. I was hooked.''

"How could you be so sure?" wondered Camilla. "After just meeting them for a couple of hours?"

"I just knew," replied Meghan firmly, lifting her shoulders. It was an inadequate reply, but Camilla understood.

"Anyway, talking of that toad Desmarets," continued the elder sister, "I met him the day after we arrived and hated him on sight." Camilla shivered— the mention of Patrice's name was enough to start her looking over her shoulder for threatening men. Meghan went on, "He was very charming in an insincere way—just the sort of product I hate."

"I know," added Camilla.

"Well, to make a long story of rows and hate very short, we drove on to Ghazni after a few days, and there I noticed that my watch was missing. I was searching through the luggage for it and found a bag of that white stuff—heroin. I'd seen that stuff in action during my nursing days, so I suppose the shock of knowing my husband was involved in producing the end result—those casualties of society—was too much. I walked out to a field outside the city where this tribe was encamped, told them I was a nurse and asked if I could join them. I never saw Tom again.''

"You know he is dead, don't you?"

Not a single twinge crossed her sister's face. "Yes, I know." Again they were silent.

"But how do you know Patrice?" asked Meghan when she had considered for a bit.

"We are acquainted." Immediately Camilla saw that the flippant answer would not be enough, so she shifted into a more comfortable position and told her sister the entire story from the moment of landing in Kabul—the help the Hagans had given her, Patrice's charm and the friendliness he showed her at the beginning, the attack by the mullah, the persecution of letters, the stabbing in the restaurant, and—shuddering as she told it—the attempt on her life in the hotel room.

She poured out, too, the story of Malcolm. She felt reluctant to mention his name at first, but once it was spoken she could barely keep it out of every sentence she spoke. She delighted in spreading his perfections out before Meghan—his wild golden handsomeness, his bravery, his intellect.

"And do you know who he is? He's that very Jacob Manling you used to rave about—the author, you know."

Meghan agreed it was the most extraordinary of coincidences. And she observed how Camilla's eyes grew brighter when she mentioned his name, how a smile played about her lips when she thought of him, and a light blush colored her cheeks.

"He was angry at me this morning because I went for a walk alone," she finished, carefully understating the extent of his rage and again being filled with the remorse that her last encounter had left her with. "So I had to come alone."

She could not understand why Meghan's eyes brimmed over, but then her sister came over to her and embraced her, crying softly, "I think you are the brave one. You have thought of others the whole time. I have thought of no one but myself," murmured Meghan.

Camilla shook her head guiltily at this; she preferred not to mention the many days and nights when her thoughts had been occupied by Malcolm, her love for Malcolm and various other aspects of Malcolm. Then she took Meghan's hands and shook them firmly.

"You must never let Patrice get you," she admonished her. "He knows you know and he will kill you if he can."

"My people will protect me," replied Meghan confidently, and Camilla's heart sank to hear the way she referred to the nomads as her people. "It's you we must worry about; you could bring the law down on him with the evidence you have and put him away in one of those ghastly jails for a lifetime. He's already made one attempt on your life."

"I don't need reminding," said Camilla, her nerves tingling. "I'll be careful."

"What about Jeff?" her sister suddenly asked.

"Jeff? Who's Jeff?"

For the first time since their reunion Meghan laughed, her old hearty laugh. "My dear little sister, you can't hide a thing from me. How long have you been in love with this Malcolm?" Her laugh, so open and happy, was like a shard that pierced Camilla's heart.

"Forever," she admitted without a smile.

Meghan saw, and gently probed. "What about *him*?"

"Meghan, it...it's not that simple. There are so many components of love. Tenderness, understanding, admiration, sharing, protection, desire...." She stopped. "How many of them must you possess before you can say, 'I'm in love?' Please, let's not talk about it—it would take years." Quickly she turned away from the painful subject and asked, "There are a few things I want to clear up. How did Patrice get your watch?"

"I think Tom sold it to him to pay for part of the heroin."

"And how did the shopkeeper get your dress?"

"I sent Djalani to Kabul with it and some other things to raise some money to buy medicines. It was while he was there that he heard the rumor that *farangis* were looking for me, so I started some subtle investigations on my own—I suspected it might be Patrice and his men, for obvious reasons, and naturally I didn't want them to find me. Well, with Djalani's help—he's such a good soul, a true friend—I discovered that Patrice was indeed on my trail, but that an English girl had also been making inquiries at the embassy; which confused me, since I thought you would come directly to me at Bandi Amir. Anyway, I gave Djalani your description, but you'd apparently disappeared, according to the Kabul Hotel staff—"

"I was hiding out at Malcolm's place," Camilla interrupted. At Meghan's surprised look she added, a touch guiltily because of all that had passed there, "For safety reasons only—after the attempt on my life—"

"Camilla! If only I'd known that you were in such danger...." She shuddered. "But thank goodness you're here, safe, now. When you didn't show up at our camp, I thought that maybe you were sick. We were going to be moving soon, so I admit I was getting a little anxious that I would miss you. But then last night Djalani spotted you—your red hair, that is—"

"It's *not* red—it's auburn!" Camilla protested, smiling.

Meghan smiled back. "A thousand pardons—your *auburn* hair. He was at the Kuchi Hotel delivering some goats' milk. When he told me I was elated—I could hardly believe you were finally so near—but I'm sure Allah wanted us together again." Her eyes shone as she squeezed her sister's hands. "So I sent the note this morning. They were to give it only to you, as discreetly as possible in case Patrice was hovering around."

"They seemed to appear out of nowhere, like messengers from heaven, when I was on my walk." Camilla laughed then at the ludicrousness of Meghan's tracing her while she was busy in her own search. "And Tom—what happened to him?" she finally asked, her expression turning grave. Nothing could have prepared her for her sister's reply.

"My people killed him."

"Did—did you...?" Her words trailed away; she was shocked.

"No, I did not ask them. But when I told them

why I had left my husband, several of the young men, including Ahmad, rode away south and returned two days later. Then they told me what they had done, miles from the main road so it could be as private as possible. I wasn't sorry. He deserved it—he would have killed many more people with that poison he was carrying. It is my people's justice.''

"And what did they do with the heroin?''

"Scattered it in the wind.''

They talked on until three o'clock—Camilla had no watch but discovered that Meghan had learned to tell time by the position of the sun. Doing some quick figuring, Camilla decided that if she left now, she could be back at the hotel by six at the latest, leaving a good margin of time for any mishaps. Regretfully, she got up to leave.

"You're not going, are you?'' asked Meghan anxiously. "I had hoped you would stay the night.''

"Oh, I'd love to; you know that, Meghan,'' she said, hugging her. "But I have to go back. Malcolm and Ali Shah have no idea of where I am, and I took the car. But I'll come back tomorrow, and maybe... maybe Malcolm will come. I know you'd like to meet the author of *A Jug of Wine*.'' Inwardly she didn't know if she could handle being with Malcolm again, not after what she'd said, but he'd been so helpful in her search that he had to meet the object of that search. And besides, there was comfort in numbers. Camilla would simply avoid being alone with him.

"I would love to see your Malcolm,'' said Meghan wholeheartedly.

"He's not my Malcolm,'' replied Camilla bitterly,

and moved to the tent flap. But Meghan laid a restraining hand on her arm.

"What will you do now?" she asked in her gentle
voice. "Go home?"

"Home?" repeated Camilla, and half to herself,
"Where is that?" She thought and shook her head.
"I don't know." Her heart plunged at the realization
that she didn't really belong anywhere.

"You know." The two words were a profound
statement. Meghan saw that Camilla understood the
same forces that had driven her to her life with
Kuchis. *You can never go back, not after loving Mal-
com and this land*—that was the message in
Meghan's eyes as she kissed her sister, but Camilla
knew she had no choice but to return.

"All I want is for you to be happy. As happy as I
am," Meghan said softly.

They stepped into the afternoon sunlight, and as
they walked to the Land Rover, a young man, one of
the young men, Ahmad or Djalani, who had startled
Camilla that morning, came over to them. He wore a
wide grin on his face and carried a parcel in his hand,
which he handed, strangely shy now, to Camilla. She
opened it, and smiled as she saw two beautifully
worked heavy-banded gold earrings. Having learned
her lesson with Ali Shah, she murmured politely,
"Thank you, thank you very much," while her eyes
also spoke her gratitude.

"Ahmad and I are to be married next spring," said
Meghan to Camilla as she got into the Land Rover,
as calmly as if she had been announcing a trip to the
supermarket. Camilla's eyebrows shot up in surprise.

"Which one is he?"

"The one who gave you the earrings."

So that's why I received a gift, thought Camilla. Part of Meghan's openness had been imparted to her that day, so she queried with equanimity, "Do you love him?"

"Oh, yes, I do. He's so honest, so—well, I know it sounds silly, but wild and noble. The absolute opposite." Camilla knew to what she was referring.

"It's not silly, not when applied to these people. And does he love you?"

Meghan looked over at her betrothed, eyes filling with devotion. "I hope you won't misunderstand me when I say everyone does—I think it has more to do with my vocation than with my personality. But with him it is different."

"I know you are happy," said Camilla as she started up the engine. "You are also lucky." She pulled slowly away. "See you tomorrow! See you!" Dogs and children ran by the side of the Land Rover as she rolled up the hill, but picking up speed on the downgrade she left them behind, cruising past the wide still lakes, as translucent as opal now, their hues varying from pearl white to emerald green, and then she drove by a little mud-walled village—she was pulling out of the heart of Afghanistan, heading for the road that led to Bamian, to Kabul, and finally to the airplane back to England.

Meghan was lost to her for good now. She must put away any hope that her sister would ever return with her to England, so that together they could try to reestablish some shadow of a home. It was too late. Meghan had found her own home and Camilla would never be able—nor would she try—to take her from it. "All I want is for you to be happy. As happy as I am." There was no misinterpreting those words. Camilla must find her own happiness, her own life. Her sister had grown apart from her, gone her own way, and things could never be the same again.

But Meghan had always realized that the life the circumstances of her birth had forced upon her did not suit her; her long search had lasted almost from the day she had learned to speak, and it had taken her until now to find her goal. Camilla had just begun.

Was not Malcolm her goal? No, he was a part of the beginning for her; but, since she could never have him, her long search would consist of putting together a sort of life in which she could be happy without him. The prospect appalled her. She was filled with despair and for one moment was on the brink of turning the wheel over the cliff above those jeweled pools, but she swerved away. It was too easy, too cowardly.

Now that she had been reunited with her sister there was no excuse to stay on in this country—neither the hope of finding Meghan nor the hope of taking her back to England. What had begun with that cold letter of condolence from the embassy had ended here, on the high Asian plateau—and she had to force herself to go home and continue as if nothing had changed!

The return drive was too short for Camilla to organize all the confused thoughts in her head. The warmth of the sun's rays that slanted through the rear window of the Land Rover was soothing as she drove east. She hoped she would be back at the hotel before dark; Malcolm's face swam up before her, blocking her vision.

Please don't let him be too angry, she prayed silently. She was too full of emotion after meeting Meghan again to face another tense encounter.

Rounding a bend, she got a slight shock. She was accustomed to being the only traffic on the road, so the sight of the little sports car—unsuited to such terrain—broken down and blocking the road, seemed to her for a moment a trespass on her private property. However, it was only a thought, and as she passed the vehicle she slowed down, wondering if she could be of any assistance.

"Excuse me, can I help?" she shouted, leaning out of the window. But the driver was slumped over the wheel, she realized as an arrow of alarm pierced through her. She quickly parked her car, ran over and peered in.

To her horror, a tall brawny Afghan, whose face sent shivers down her spine, straightened and looked at her. Her persecutor, the stabber from the restaurant and the one who had followed her in the used-clothes bazaar. She was paralyzed with fear, helpless and unprotected as she was. Her heart racing, she knew now it was a trap.

Before she could force her limbs to move, he was out of the car. His arms reached out and pinioned both hers to her sides, with needless roughness and a great deal of pain. She twisted in his grip and heard behind her the familiar laugh she had subconsciously been waiting for.

"So, my fair English rose, fighting still?"

CHAPTER FIFTEEN

HE STOOD BEFORE HER, his slender elegant figure dressed impeccably in tan whipcords, a khaki shirt and a shading Panama. In one hand he held a slim cigarette. He was the epitome of coolness. He lifted his other hand, long, graceful, well manicured, and stroked it along her cheek. With her arms trapped, unable to retaliate, she could only jerk her head away.

"It was not always thus," murmured the Frenchman, his voice quite sad and pitying. But she knew now it was an act. "Ah, *ma chère*, I believe there was a time when you were rather fond of me."

"Never of you," she spat out. "Only of someone I thought was you."

"I have no time to indulge in metaphysics now, my dear," he replied, with a tone of impeccable politeness that she could not have credited from anyone else but him. She yearned to break his cool.

"Are you going to kill me?"

"Not kill, *ma choute*," he replied, waving his hand vaguely. "So vulgar. I prefer *'faire mourir'*—but *chacun à son goût*, eh?"

"Are you going to kill me now?"

"No, no, not for a while. I am taking you on a little trip." He made a motion to the heavy man holding her, who began to move her away. She would have to escape, and quickly—any chance was worth taking. So, catching him off his guard, she kicked upward with all her force where she was sure it would hurt most, and as he doubled up in pain she bolted from his grasp as quick as a hare. They could try to catch her, but she was running for her life.

The bullet whine in the air was the next sound she heard, and before she had time to think, her reflex of fear had flung her flat on the ground. She had lost her chance, for before she could get up and run again they were upon her, Patrice carrying a smoking pistol in one hand and a length of rope in the other, and the man hobbling behind him, intense malice in his expression.

"You should not do that to Khodim," Patrice told her with the air of a schoolmaster. "He doesn't like it."

She did not reply. He could do what he liked to her physically, for his was the superior strength, but there was one thing he could not do—get into her mind. Quickly and roughly the man tied her up and gagged her. Hands and feet bound, she was carried unceremoniously to Patrice's waiting brown car, which had been hidden over the hill. Another Afghan, smaller than her captor, stepped out of the long car. Patrice handed him some keys and he walked in the direction of the sports car. Camilla presumed he would drive it back so that it wasn't associated with her abandoned car in any way. Patrice was certainly clever: he had every angle covered.

The trunk was opened and she was rudely dumped inside. Fear of the dark, of enclosed places and suffocation, washed over her as they slammed the lid down, but then she realized she was comparatively safe in there. At least they were not touching her, and since, as Patrice had not yet killed her despite the ample opportunity for doing so, he must obviously want her alive, she felt she need not fear that she would be suffocated. Still, she was cramped and hot, and the raw rope bit and chafed. As she bumped and bounced along the dirt road, she felt a warm trickle at her wrist and thought of the scar she would have. Scar! She laughed bitterly. Maybe she wouldn't be in a position to see it.

The road became smoother, and she knew they were in Bamian. Frantically now she struggled to get out of the binding so that she could try to open the trunk and cry for help. She thought of the roadsides lined with people, perhaps turning to watch the car drive smoothly and elegantly along, people who wouldn't guess that a young woman was held prisoner in the hot small compartment. Her heartbeat was dangerously close to panic, and she tried to control it, knowing that panic would ruin any slim chance she might yet have for escape.

As they drove, it seemed many hours since her capture, and yet no time at all when she thought it might be her last afternoon drive if, despite all, she could not escape. If she must die, she wanted it over quickly. She did not want to be played with as a cat plays with a mouse, and yet she knew that with Patrice such an end was more than likely. He had no morals.

Suddenly the car pulled up with a screech of tires. She broke into a cold sweat. Was it now, in some lonely valley, that she would be pulled from the safety of the trunk and shot? But she would be questioned first—he wanted something, she could tell. She gritted her teeth. He would not get it.

Light flooded her eyes, blinding her, and before she could get her bearings a blindfold was slipped over her eyes and she was back in darkness. Not a word was spoken; it was spine-chillingly silent. Then she felt herself lifted by hard vicious hands out of the trunk and slung across a brawny shoulder.

They began to climb what she could tell was a hill, by the swing of her captor's steps. It was a winding path—she could sense that, too—and the exertion was a strain, for she felt him puff and pull. She hung like a deadweight, determined to make him as uncomfortable as possible.

There was a short walk over scree, and the pebbles crunched underfoot; then they entered what might be a cave or a tunnel, for she felt the disappearance of heat on her shoulders and hair, and was aware of a damp oppressive atmosphere. They were still climbing, and by the jerky movements she guessed they might be steps.

How long they climbed she did not know, for in her state time meant nothing. Then they came out into sunlight, and fresh air hit her coldly on the face. Her bearer made a funny leap, landing rather unevenly. She was thrown roughly to the ground, and he tugged off her bonds. She moved to take off her blindfold.

"Before you do that," drawled the cultivated voice, making her jump because it was so unexpected, "I must remind you that one move, one shout, one attempt to attract attention, and you are dead. Go on now; remove it."

Slowly she obeyed his order and blinked in the light, her pupils contracting. She took in the details— flat rock, high walls, a domed ceiling, colors—and her memory clicked. She whirled around.

The gun muzzle that was jammed in her side could not have frightened her more. She stilled, and let her predicament sink in. They were sitting on the head of the Buddha. She was trapped by a two-hundred-foot drop on three sides, and the foot-wide escape route was guarded by the heavy Afghan, pistol in hand.

"I warned you," said Patrice. "No sudden movements."

"You can't keep me up here forever," she told him, surprised at the forced evenness of her own voice. She could *not* break down. "The tourists will come again tomorrow. Maybe tonight."

"Not tonight." The long shadows stretched before he told her he was right; there would be no more tourists that evening. "And I do not plan to keep you here forever. Until tomorrow at dawn will be sufficient."

"If you think you can terrorize me into telling you where Meghan is, you're wrong. You can torture me. I'll never tell you."

"Torture is not my style," he replied suavely. "And I do not require that you talk. I know where your sister is."

"You're lying."

"Not at all. She is with the Kuchi tribe of Sher Muhammad on the northwest side of Bandi Amir."

"Why don't you kill me now, then?"

"I require a letter."

"What, a thank-you letter?"

He ignored this. "I have found it impossible to reach your sister because of the ring of protection the tribe has established around her. I need you to ask her to come to Bamian, where she can be confronted with some hope of success, when she is not surrounded by her warriors. Ask her to dinner if you like. She will know your writing."

"Why should I help you kill my sister when you're going to kill me anyway?"

"You do have a terribly coarse way of putting things. It is simple. If you help us in this, no one else shall be harmed. Otherwise I shall have to kill Malcolm Armstrong."

"Malcolm—no!" she cried, but her rush forward was prevented by the muzzle of his gun, while he clamped his other hand over her mouth. "It is a simple question of priorities."

"You could never do it," she hissed, breaking free. "You'd never be able to kill him."

"I could kill you now where you stand."

"But I'm not Malcolm."

"My patience is endless, *ma chère*. Your refusal will not mean that your sister will survive. One day I shall find my opportunity, and be sure I will take it. A short walk in the hills alone—a visit to the capital—and she does not return. And Armstrong, too; perhaps, a shot through his bedroom window, or cyanide on the figs in his garden. It is therefore a question of whose death you wish to cause."

She gulped and saw that she was cornered.

Damned if I do, damned if I don't, she thought grimly. "But what assurance do I have that you won't kill Malcolm anyway?"

"None at all," he replied coolly. "You are not in a position to ask for any."

She fell silent. It was impossible to argue with him; he had all the advantages, especially the most final: the gun. She turned away and looked across the dusky valley. Her last sunset, if he had his way. He made a motion to the Afghan, who disappeared, and she heard his hollow steps on the stone passageways. They were alone. Out of his pocket Patrice took a creamy sheet of paper and a fine gold pen. He put them down at her feet, then moved across the little foot-wide escape route and seated himself on the lip of the doorway.

"We are alone now." He spoke soothingly, silkily. "No one but I will ever know, if you write."

"I will know! Do you think my own life is worth more to me than my sister's?"

He reminded her softly, "I am not asking you to trade your life for another's, as I know from experience that is a poor method of bargaining. I am asking you to save Armstrong's life by helping me reach the person who will die sooner or later."

His arguments were persuasive. He was like a hypnotizing snake; she must not listen to him.

"We all die sooner or later." She turned away from him. He seemed to accept that the conversation had ended, because silence fell as the curtain of night drew over them.

She sat perched on the forehead of the colossus.

Why not jump, logic told her. *Jump now, and it*

will all be solved. What have you got to live for? Neither Meghan nor Malcolm needs you; you'd be well out of a dreadful mess. And think of Patrice's expression when he sees you've cheated him! But she knew that if her muscles made one move to throw her over that edge, her whole conscience would pull back and stop her. It was as impossible for her to kill herself as it would be for her to kill somebody else.

Hours passed. Patrice was silent. She turned and watched him as he sat leaning against the doorpost, the gun barrel glinting in the moonlight. Perhaps he was asleep. Hope sprang to her breast: she could tiptoe past him and run for it; her clothes were dark and he might not be able to see her or shoot. She started slowly toward him.

"I am awake, *ma chère.*"

Then she cried. It had seemed up till now like a story, some thriller seen on television that she could switch off when she chose. But dawn was creeping nearer—in several hours her body would lie shattered on the rocks below, Patrice gone. There was nothing she could do to alter it.

The reality of her death flooded in on her. The night was so dark. She wanted someone there to hold her, to stroke her hair and keep her warm and tell her it was all a nightmare. She wanted Malcolm, only Malcolm. Now, when it was too late, she thought of all the things she should have said, all the things she wanted him to know. There was one thing, one last thing she could do for him, and as she decided she saw it as a measure of how far this land had driven her and Meghan apart and forged for her new bonds. She would sign. She would write the letter. But not until she saw streaks of pink and orange score the horizon. When she saw the sun once more, when she heard the muezzin call, then she would write—and die.

Having given up hope, she wandered again to the edge of the Buddha, not, as before, scanning vainly for help, but just looking, wandering.

A flash of white caught her eye below, and hope tugged at her heart. She thought for a moment her eyes were playing tricks on her. Then the white moved—definitely a person; she was almost sure it was a man. She felt certain that he saw her, for an arm, tiny in the distance, waved faintly. She wasted no time wondering who could be strolling about the caves at this time of night; her mind had already bounded to the prospect of rescue. All her thoughts of the moment before, the calm and resigned despair, were gone—her head reeled, dizzy with hope. She begged silently, desperately, *don't let him cry out. Please don't let him call out.*

She was thankful that the dark concealed her face from her captor, but she knew it also wrapped her in a gloomy shadow through which her would-be rescuer could hardly see her. Her mind raced, straining—how could she attract his attention? How could she bring him up to her?

"What are you doing so near the edge, *ma petite?*"

She turned her head blindly, looking at Patrice but not seeing him, her fingers twisting as she tried to work out a plan.

"Come away. I would not want you to fall."

She walked mechanically back to the center of the Buddha head and sat cross-legged. Her palm outstretched on the rock touched something loose and hard. A stone. She had an idea.

"All this waiting for the sun. I'm bored," she said loudly, her voice echoing in the hollow dome. She prayed he would not detect any shade of hope, or deception, in her voice. "I wish it was all over."

"Waiting can be so tedious," he agreed, yawning politely. "If you would only pick up that pen. . . ."

For an answer she took the stone and threw it over the face of the Buddha. It clacked loudly in the black silence.

"What are you doing?"

"Just throwing stones." *Oh, please hear me, whoever you are down there,* she begged silently, lips pressed together, her hand tightening around another stone. She threw it. It resounded sharply. She threw another, and another, with what she hoped were firm meaningful throws.

"Stop it; it annoys me."

She did not trust herself to answer, and threw another.

"I fully expect you not to sign," he told her. "So seeing the sunrise is, as it were, an added bonus, I would stop if I were you."

She did not want to try him too far now, on the brink, perhaps, of rescue, so she quit. Rapidly she calculated that it might take the stranger fifteen minutes to reach the Buddha's head. She knew she had to keep Patrice distracted until the rescue arrived. What could she say to him?

"Patrice?" Her voice quavered.

"I thought you did not want to talk."

"I do. It's the last conversation I'll ever have. Please talk to me."

"What would you like me to say?"

"Were you ever married?" What an extraordinary question to ask, she admonished herself, and wondered why she had chosen it.

"How funny," he laughed. "Were *you* ever married?"

"I asked you first."

He clapped his hands softly. "Still she has spirit left in her. Good girl; I like that. If you did not know so much I would keep you with me. What do you think?"

"I think it would be better to be dead."

He laughed again. "No, *ma chère*, I meant about my being married."

"I think you were," Camilla answered quickly. "And I think you only turned nasty after she died."

"What makes you think she died?"

"Did you divorce her?"

"No—"

"Ah, there you are. You were married."

"No, you are wrong; I never was. But, *chère mademoiselle*, you must not judge me so harshly. I am not so very 'nasty' as you appear to think. And though perhaps I cannot match your English Malcolm, I was fond of you once, in my way."

"I cannot believe that."

"*Mon honneur.* You see, you are trying to put all the blame on me. But I am an innocent. I did try to get you to leave. You will remember, I tried to save you. But you were such a stubborn girl—I am very sorry it had to end like this."

"I suppose you're going to say that you don't really want to kill me."

He waved his left hand. "Kill, kill, kill. Always that word. Of course I do not. But a man of business cannot always do what he wants."

At that moment she heard the hollow echo of a disturbed pebble within the corridors of stone. She threw an agonized glance at Patrice to see if he, too, had heard, but he seemed sunk in his own contemplations.

"What I don't understand," she began, trying to recapture his attention, "is how you knew who I was and what I was setting out to do, even before I met you. It was you who arranged all those supposed accidents, wasn't it—the attack by the mullah, the stabbing in the restaurant, the letters, the shooting...."

"I have told you: they were to warn you off. But since you ask, I will tell you how it happened. You will never be able to tell anyone." He jumped across the escape route and sat down in front of it, his fingers wrapped around the gun that rested across his knees.

"I knew that the strange circumstances of Mrs. Cowley's disappearance would be likely to bring at least one member of her family out here to look for her. I also knew that such an investigation would lead to discoveries about my activities, and that Mrs. Cowley, if found, would have a great deal of what they call evidence against me. So I set to work." He smiled smugly. "In a country like this a generous man can find many friends willing to help him. I found out your sister's maiden name through the help of some acquaintances at the embassy, and I asked my friends at the airport to keep alert for any Cowleys or Simpsons entering from England. It was merely my good luck that you came, a very pretty but innocent girl. It was not difficult to follow your movements or to win your trust—but it was, I am sorry to say, very difficult to frighten you off. That is what has brought you to this pass. If only you had listened to me...." He sighed.

"Meghan's not interested in you—or your business," Camilla said angrily.

"I cannot take that risk," he replied almost sadly. "I do not need to justify myself to you—but perhaps it will make it easier for you. You have been interfering in what is none of your business. You condemn me out of hand, making no effort to understand. It is always the same. Those of us who make some attempt to bring people satisfaction are hounded and condemned until we are driven to defend ourselves in any way we can. I do not force what I sell on people; I could not sell it if they did not want to buy it. There is a market for it. Why? Because the world is such a terrible place. What I sell is a good thing. It helps people; people whose lives are unbearable through pain or loneliness, people who want some *plaisir*, some—what do you call it—amusement, fun out of life. And the world is a terrible place because it wants to stop these people from helping themselves. If the world would only leave us alone, instead of trying to 'save people from themselves,' as they put it, then we would all be happy. I want you to know," he added in a strangely pleading tone, "I did not kill Tom Cowley."

"I know. The Kuchis did. He deserved it."

"There you go again," he said, rubbing the barrel of his gun against his shirt. "Condemning something you know nothing about. A typical example of prejudice. That is why you have to die. Nobody understands. I do not want to hurt people, but they force me to defend—"

He broke off and leaped up, whirling around and firing into the darkness, so that the ricochet echoed across the dark valley. He missed, and a lean shape sprang out of the darkness at him, hurling him against the ground so that his pistol was sent flying out of his hand and skidding across the flat rock. The shape that pinned him down cried out, "Camilla, the gun!"

How well she knew that voice! And who else would she want to save her but his beloved self? Obeying instantly, she ran to the gun, but misjudged in her trembling haste, so that her foot gave it a blow and sent it hurtling over the edge to land with a distant ring of metal on the rocks beneath.

The action was too quick for her to feel remorse, and she saw that the combatants were too closely locked for her to have used the pistol anyway. She had no knowledge of such firearms. The two struggling men were fighting as they hung half over the side of the head. She saw Patrice's hand on Malcolm's throat, but Malcolm was on top, his knees digging into her captor's chest. She wanted to run to his aid, but her legs would not obey her frantic commands, keeping her rooted to the spot.

Even when struggling for his life, Malcolm spared a thought for her. "Get into the cave!" he shouted in a choked voice, and she found that her stubborn limbs were able to do his bidding. She collapsed in the dark interior of the cave. First she looked away, then she watched, then she looked away again. She could not bear to see the two men struggling on the edge of the precipice, and yet she could not wait in darkness for the outcome. Common sense told her she ought to run, but once again common sense was defeated by something greater—the knowledge that her life was so intricately bound up with Malcolm's that she could not go on living if he died. So she must wait, heart in throat, hands clenching when Patrice got on top of Malcolm, and relaxing when the situation was reversed. She waited to see whether the outcome would be life or death for Malcolm.

Suddenly she realized that the outlines of the combatants were becoming clearer; she could make out the golden tangle of Malcolm's hair, and Patrice's dark curls, now, for the first time since she'd known him, ruffled and disordered. Dawn streaked the sky above the towering mountains, and the clouds were a deep pearly gray. The scene was so beautiful she could not speak, and she realized that if she had to die, there was no better moment she could have chosen. Even the fiercely wrestling men seemed glorified by the beauty, so that their life-and-death struggle became almost a work of art.

It was over suddenly. They had rolled nearer and nearer to the brow of the great stone, and Patrice, with his last ounce of energy, held Malcolm's head and shoulders over the edge. Camilla saw his body relax and in one black moment thought, *my love is dead*. Then, with the determined power of self-preservation Malcolm darted up, twisting the Frenchman into the air. Patrice's slender manicured hands closed once on the empty air, and then he disappeared into the shadows below. There was silence.

Camilla ran to Malcolm. He stood up slowly, and her heart ached with love and prided to see him— tired and drawn and dirty, but alive. She would have looked over the edge despite herself, to see where Patrice had fallen, but Malcolm grabbed her arm and restrained her.

Suddenly remembering her thoughts when she had believed herself so near to death, when she realized how she might have vanished forever from his life without a single word to him of all that she felt, she no longer held back, or tried to, but buried her face in the wide strength of his chest and cried for joy, and relief, and love.

"It might have been you! It might have been you!" she murmured again and again.

They sank exhausted on the stone and sat there for a few minutes, closer than words in their touching. Then he lifted her face—pale, tearstained, dirty and quivering with emotion, and looked deep into her eyes, seeing there brimming pools of pure joy and verdant love.

"Yours is the dearest face in the world to me," he said in a voice she had never heard before, a voice that destroyed and rebuilt all her ideas of how gentle, tender and kind he could be. She felt the love in that voice, too.

"Camilla." Malcolm held her chin with trembling fingers and drank in the greenness of her eyes. "Yesterday morning, when we were fighting, before you ran away, you silly darling, you infuriating woman—

you said—I remember it perfectly, 'Why was I ever so stupid as to fall in love with you?'"

Camilla squirmed at the remembrance of that outburst, but he only held her blissfully tighter and went on, "When I realized Patrice had got you I was nearly destroyed by the thought of all the times I could have told you, but never did. I cursed myself for not running after you yesterday morning, and catching you, and forcing you to say it again and again and let me tell you that I loved you. We lost twenty-four hours of perfect happiness because I was such a fool! Oh, you were wrong, Camilla: it wasn't you who was stupid; it was I, stubborn and jealous and unperceptive. But please forgive me, my darling, because I love you, so much."

Her laughter was colored with an overflowing joy. "Malcolm, you have no idea how often and how long I've dreamed of hearing those very words from you." The adoration in his blue eyes was the loveliest thing she had ever seen. "I do love you, I do."

He buried his face in her hair, breathing in its warm scent. "I can hardly believe it. And to think I feared you loved Ali Shah!"

"Ali Shah!" Camilla clasped him closer to her. It was no time to dwell on past misunderstandings. "Oh, Malcolm, you couldn't have been more wrong. You're the only man I love."

"He was attracted to you, you know," Malcolm said quietly.

Camilla sighed, for she had sensed that, too. "I know but I was just a novelty to him. His feelings will blow away in no time. And I never encouraged him. I knew you were the right one for me."

He kissed her then, and when he did it was not a punishment, or a threat, or a mockery, or any of the many cruel and hurting things that kisses can be. It was a kiss of pure tenderness, lingering on throat and cheek and lips, a pledge of mutual love, while their hands moved almost with awe upon each other's body in the first proud exploration of possession. Again and again their hands met and clasped, promising never to be parted again.

When they pulled apart at last, she touched him lovingly on the lips with her finger and murmured softly, "That's a true kiss...the first true kiss you ever gave me. I hope it won't be the last." And he spent the next few minutes proving to her how unfounded her fears were.

They leaned, entwined together, against the rock and watched the slow gentle unfolding of the dawn. Somewhere on the hillside a bird began to sing.

"How long have you loved me?" he whispered to her, lips to her ear.

"Forever. It might as well be forever, when it's going to be forevermore." He seemed to find the answer satisfactory.

"I couldn't tell you the exact day I fell in love with you," his voice sang huskily in her ear, "but I can tell you the day I knew. That day when you came to the school and I found you there in the staff room, pale and trembling like a little fawn. It was then, when I walked in and saw you there; that was the exact moment when I knew you were dearer to me than my own life and that I would give myself to protect you from the slightest harm.

"But I didn't want to take unfair advantage of you

while you were staying in my home," he continued, "and you were so young and untouched, so I tried, unsuccessfully at times, not to lay a finger on you until I was certain you felt the same way. But I never felt that certainty and it drove me crazy, made me do and say things that were totally out of character, especially when I thought you were after Ali Shah."

"Oh, darling, darling, darling," was all Camilla needed to say in response. Then her eyes twinkled naughtily. "You didn't like me when we first met," she teased.

"You didn't like me, either, so we're even." They grinned at each other for a moment, remembering the antagonism of those early days, but it melted from their minds as they found each other's lips in a passionate embrace.

It was a long while later that they stirred to talk again.

"How did you find me?" Camilla asked at last. It wasn't a particularly important question—all that was of importance was here in her arms—but it intrigued her.

"I waited and waited for you to return," Malcolm said quietly. "I thought you were just cooling your anger somewhere. I admit I had been unfair. I never suspected you would head out alone to Bandi Amir. And if I went looking for you I was afraid you'd return and I'd miss you. But doing nothing almost drove me crazy."

He raked tanned fingers through his hair at the memory, then continued in a well-loved deep voice, "Five o'clock and no sign of you—you can imagine my panic. I nearly tore the hotel apart. At last the

Germans lent me their car and I started on to Bandi Amir—and found the Land Rover about five miles out. My first reaction was sheer despair that you weren't there; I don't know how anyone could imagine so many dreadful things in one second, but I did."

He paused to draw a deep breath. "Then I noticed that there was a mass of tracks around the Land Rover and that a vehicle had turned around and headed east, and I had noticed the same on the other side of the hill before spotting the Land Rover. Something was definitely going on." Camilla merely nodded. Later she would give him her side of the story; there was plenty of time for that.

"I got out and started looking for clues," he went on. "I saw the distinctly Kuchi earrings lying in your abandoned car, so I guessed that you had made it to Bandi Amir, had probably seen your sister at the Kuchi grounds near there and were heading back. Besides, your car was pointing in that direction."

He shook his tawny-colored head wearily. "That Desmarets was a most careless crook. He'd left some stubs from those fancy cigarettes lying around. So I set off back to Bamian, and soon discovered that a lot of people had seen that remarkable brown car of his heading this way. I found it myself, parked not far from here, in fact, but it was dark and I had no idea where he had taken you from there. So I combed these caves. It took me nearly all night. It was sheer luck that I saw you standing on the brow of the Buddha."

"Not luck—fate. You have saved my life three

times, probably more; I've lost count. My life is yours."

He took her hand, almost formally. "Let's get married."

"Married!" Never had she thought she'd hear those beautiful words uttered so lovingly from his lips. "Oh!" She started, grew cold and pulled away from him. How could she have forgotten something so drastically important? Perhaps the events of the night had dulled her brain.

He reached after her, but she shrank from his touch. "Camilla, what's wrong?" he cried frantically.

"Oh, Malcolm—you're so cruel to ask me when you know you're not completely free."

"Not free?" Confusion with a touch of impatience tinged his voice.

"What about Nurjan?"

"Nurjan!" He stood for a moment, and then he reached out and seized both her small hands with his tanned ones, swinging them back and forth. "You silly, silly, darling! I told you long ago, when you accused me of stealing Ali Shah's fiancée, what the true situation was. That I was merely tutoring her. That I was doing *him* a favor."

She twisted her toe in the dust. "That was how he put it. But I couldn't believe you. I'd seen you together at a restaurant once, you see. Laughing, kissing...."

Understanding dawned in Malcolm's sky-blue eyes. "Winning the scholarship meant a lot to Nurjan. I was happy for her. The kiss was...it wasn't like the ones you and I share; you must believe me. Besides, if any two people were more suited, it's Ali Shah and Nurjan. In their quiet way, they love each other. I think they will marry eventually, but not for many years. Nurjan's education must come first.''

Camilla saw how wrong she'd been about all of them, and more importantly, how little faith she'd had in Malcolm. Determinedly, she resolved to trust his word from now on. She had a lot to learn about love, but the foundation was solid now, and together they would build the rest—they had their entire lives.

''I do believe you, Malcolm,'' she told him fervently, her eyes promising him total faith.

In a single fluid movement they knelt, then entwined upon the ground. The flames that licked along her nerves made her crave his kisses, but even those could not quench the fire, only stroke it. She lay, heart pounding, every inch of her skin aquiver, her mouth locked to his. Sensually her fingers moved of their own free will across his expanse of muscled back. Malcolm's hands, his gentle inquisitive fingers, moved in turn, with reverential slowness, across each exquisite part of her anatomy, as if seeking to memorize the feel of every contour, the softness of each line.

''Your hair is so lovely,'' he murmured, letting the silky strands, shot with fiery gold in the dawn light, fall through his fingers like water. ''It has the sheen of satin on it. And your skin blooms like the soft petals of a flower.'' He lightly ran his fingertips in ripples down the bare skin of her arms until she cried out with desire.

''I know, my love, I know,'' his shaking voice

rasped in between the kisses he dropped on her throat.

He molded his body to hers until she felt they had almost become one. His face was so close to hers, pressed into her hair, that she could no longer see it, but as she looked up into the infinite blue reaches of the sky, she felt she was falling into his eyes. She wanted to be a part of him, for him to be a part of her. Then they could never be divided. Her body craved that complete satisfaction, a thundering demand that cried in her veins and her ears and in every aching of straining muscle.

"Now, Malcolm, now," she urged him with voice and hands that could not be controlled. She stroked his back and his thighs, where she knew she would have more persuasion.

His response was intense and immediate, and she exulted in her newly discovered power to excite and please him but he pulled away from her. She stifled a cry of anguish and watched him sit up.

"It's as hard for me as it is for you." So passionately was this spoken that Camilla understood it rather from his expression than from the words that trembled and faded. "You are a bewitching little angel—and I love you for that, Camilla. But I have waited so long that I can bear to wait a little longer—"

"I can't wait!" she moaned, crying out all the desire in her soul.

"Is three days really so long, when we have waited three months?" Seeing her look of amazement, he added, "I don't think we need much more time to arrange the wedding, do you? It can take place in my house; we'll want only a few guests; the Hagans, Ali Shah. It might take a day to arrange the license, but Olga can organize the reception, and as for the honeymoon—we can organize that afterward."

Caught completely off her guard but her heart filled to overflowing, she could think of only one inane question. "But... but what shall I wear?"

"I think you'll fit my mother's old wedding dress perfectly. I've still got it—she was about your size."

"Oh, Malcolm...Malcolm!" She flung her arms about his neck in a stranglehold of delirious rapture. "You really do mean it, don't you? You've thought of everything!"

"Planning our wedding," he confessed tenderly, "was one of the few fantasies I allowed myself when I used to think— Oh, Camilla, I'm the luckiest man who ever lived! I knew, even in my fantasies, that the wedding would have to be very quickly arranged, since I couldn't wait.... And I swore that it was only when I married you that I would really make you my wife. Then it wouldn't be just some rough-and-tumble thing on a mountainside. I'll be the best, most patient, most loving teacher you've ever had."

"And I the most eager pupil." She laughed and blushed delicately. "Hungry for knowledge."

The lonely call of the muezzin was echoing above the shadows of the valley. The red rising sun had heated to a shimmering white, dispersing the last misty tatters of cloud. Far down in the village people began to stir and move: dogs barking, donkeys braying, men shouting and greeting as Bamian awoke. A lizard stole across the rock near them.

Malcolm jumped up and hauled Camilla to her

feet, to the snug haven against his broad tanned frame. Their eyes shone as they looked at each other, and he said, "Speaking of hunger, let's go and have some breakfast, my lovely wife-to-be."

They took one last look at the panorama spread before them, from the tall ancient Buddha, then climbed down, hand in hand, knowing they would soar to even greater heights together.

SUPERROMANCE

Longer, exciting, sensuous and dramatic!

Fascinating love stories that will hold you in their magical spell till the last page is turned!

Now's your chance to discover the earlier books in this exciting series. Choose from the great selection on the following page!

Choose from this list of great
SUPERROMANCES!

SUPERROMANCE

Complete and mail this coupon today!

- -

Worldwide Reader Service

In the U.S.A.
1440 South Priest Drive
Tempe, AZ 85281

In Canada
649 Ontario Street
Stratford, Ontario N5A 6W2

Please send me the following SUPERROMANCES. I am enclosing my
check or money order for $2.50 for each copy ordered, plus 75¢ to
cover postage and handling.

☐ #1   ☐ #6   ☐ #11   ☐ #16
☐ #2   ☐ #7   ☐ #12   ☐ #17
☐ #3   ☐ #8   ☐ #13   ☐ #18
☐ #4   ☐ #9   ☐ #14   ☐ #19
☐ #5   ☐ #10   ☐ #15

Number of copies checked @ $2.50 each = $_____
N.Y. and Ariz. residents add appropriate sales tax $_____
Postage and handling $_____ .75
                                    TOTAL $_____

I enclose_____.
(Please send check or money order. We cannot be responsible for cash
sent through the mail.)
Prices subject to change without notice.

NAME_____
              (Please Print)
ADDRESS_____
CITY_____
STATE/PROV._____
ZIP/POSTAL CODE_____

Offer expires February 28, 1983   2075600000